Secrets
in
Summer

Center Point
Large Print

**This Large Print Book carries the
Seal of Approval of N.A.V.H.**

Secrets
in
Summer

Nancy Thayer

CENTER POINT LARGE PRINT
THORNDIKE, MAINE

This Center Point Large Print edition
is published in the year 2017 by arrangement with
Ballantine Books, an imprint of Random House,
a division of Penguin Random House LLC.

The text of this Large Print edition is unabridged.
In other aspects, this book may vary from the
original edition.
Printed in the United States of America
on permanent paper.
Set in 16-point Times New Roman type.

ISBN: 978-1-68324-427-1

Library of Congress Cataloging-in-Publication Data

Names: Thayer, Nancy, 1943– author.
Title: Secrets in Summer / Nancy Thayer.
Description: Center Point Large Print edition. | Thorndike, Maine :
Center Point Large Print, 2017.
Identifiers: LCCN 2017013433 | ISBN 9781683244271
   (hardcover : alk. paper)
Subjects: LCSH: Large type books. | BISAC: FICTION / Contemporary
Women. | FICTION / Sagas. | FICTION / Romance / Contemporary. |
GSAFD: Love stories.
Classification: LCC PS3570.H3475 S43 2017b | DDC 813/.54—dc23
LC record available at https://lccn.loc.gov/2017013433

To Tricia Patterson
with admiration
and heaps and heaps of love

Acknowledgments

I can't imagine living in a world without libraries and librarians. I wish I could thank by name every librarian I've ever met, from the kind women in Wichita, Kansas, where my mother took us to the library every Saturday long ago, to the Milwaukee librarian named Lorelei who drove a Corvette convertible.

I'm so grateful to the women who were and are the library directors of our splendid Nantucket Atheneum—Barbara Andrews, Charlotte Maison, and Molly Anderson, and all their assistants, and all the volunteers. I want especially to thank Leslie Malcolm, director of the Weezie Library for Children at the Nantucket Atheneum. If I've made mistakes or perhaps changed library policy, I've done it in the service of fiction, and I'll be so proud when this book is on the shelves of our island library. I want to thank Janice O'Mara, Lee Rand Burne, Christine Turrentine, Pam Kenny, Eileen McGrath, Maureen Beck, Ellie Coffin, Nancy Tyrer, Amy Jenness, Gillian Lewis, Pamela McGrady, Laura Freedman, Adelaide Richards, Christina Gessler, Ellen Young, Ben Murphy, and all the people who have sat at the circulation desk and helped me find a book or a DVD. It is true. If you want to know anything, ask a librarian.

I also want to thank all those who work with a Friends of the Library group. You make so many programs, events, and book purchases possible, plus I think (I know from experience!) you all have a lot of fun! My gratitude also goes to those who are on the board of trustees of the libraries all over this country. Not every country in the world has free public libraries. How fortunate we are.

And how fortunate too I am to be published by the fine team at Ballantine. I want to send enormous thanks to both of my editors, Linda Marrow and Shauna Summers, and to Elena Seplow-Jolley and Hanna Gibeau. Gina Centrello, Kim Hovey, Christine Mykityshin, Maggie Oberrender, and Paolo Pepe, a million times thank you!

Enormous thanks to my wonderful agent and friend Meg Ruley, and to the brilliant Christina Hogrebe and to all those at the Jane Rotrosen Agency.

Of course I send thanks to all our bookstores, especially to Laura Wasserman, Tim Ehrenberg, Wendy Hudson, Suzanne Bennett, Christina Macchiavelli, and the wonderful Mitchell's Book Corner. Thanks also to everyone at the marvelous Titcombs Bookshop in Sandwich, MA.

I couldn't write books without the support and great humor of my family and friends, and I include my fabulous Facebook friends in this group. So thank you, a million times thank you!

I couldn't write or do much of anything at all without my husband, Charley Walters, a man who also knows that books and libraries are essential for a happy life.

1

It was completely by accident that Darcy Cotterill spied on her ex-husband. She didn't *want* to see down into his backyard, or the yards of any of her neighbors, for that matter.

Really, it was the fault of the men who built these houses on Nantucket Island in the 1840s. Almost all the houses in the historic district, within walking distance to town, were built with an English basement, meaning the space was partly below ground but had large windows and its own door on the side of the house.

So, in order to walk in and out the front or back door of the main floor of the house, you had to climb a set of stairs at both the front and back doors.

That put the first floor, the main floor, ten feet above ground level, the perfect height for casually glancing into her neighbors' yards as Darcy went about her day.

And how was she to know her ex-husband and his new family would rent the house behind hers for the summer? She had no warning. One moment she was relaxing in her garden, and the next moment, *heart attack!*

Darcy owned this gorgeous house in the center of the town because her beloved, if slightly eccentric, grandmother had left it to her in her will. From the age of ten, Darcy had lived here with Penny, who was the only person in Darcy's dysfunctional family who stayed in one place long enough to take care of her. Darcy had adored Penny, and even now, every morning, she sent a prayer of gratitude to her grandmother.

Years ago, her grandmother had planted a hedge of spruce around the perimeter of the yard to form three tall thick walls with arched arbors on both sides of the house so friends could enter from the street. The backyard was private, and Darcy liked that. A narrow lane cut through on one side of her house, and she was glad the hedge concealed her yard. She had a public job, and she knew it wouldn't be appropriate if people passing down the narrow lane saw her as she was on this hot summer day, wearing only her briefest bikini.

And she wanted to keep this job forever. It was the job she had always dreamed of. She was a *librarian!* Specifically, she was the assistant director of the children's library of the Nantucket Atheneum. Her work was meaningful and pleasurable and involved lots of people. Still, she was glad when Sunday and Monday rolled around. These were her days off, her own special time to be alone to read and dream, especially in July and August when the island's population exploded from sixteen thousand vigorous year-rounders to sixty thousand summer people.

On Sundays, Darcy joined a group of friends—some married, some with children, some single—for a lazy day of swimming and boating and cooking out. Monday was her day to run necessary errands and work in the garden or, on a rainy day, lie in bed reading, with her cat, Muffler, beside her.

Because July 4th was next Monday, work schedules were scrambled, so Darcy had today off from work. She had time to relax. She lay on a thick cushioned lounger, surrounded by flowers and birdsong, a wrought iron table nearby for her phone and iced tea.

She tilted her head back so the rays could touch her neck. Her face was protected with sunblock, and she felt as pale as a parsnip. Too many days working. Although, she remembered with a satisfied grin, during the nights she'd spent in bed with Nash Forester, he had liked her skin just fine.

Next Sunday, when the gang met at Fat Ladies Beach, she'd wear something with more coverage, but she enjoyed the thought of Nash seeing her with new tan lines. And that was the kind of thought she hadn't had for a long while, if ever.

The sun beat down on her closed eyelids. Sweat began to bead up behind her neck, trickling down her shoulders. She remembered last Sunday with Nash, when she was in his arms and the waves rocked their bodies together while they floated in the blue Atlantic and—

Her thoughts were interrupted by the quiet growl of a car as it pulled into the driveway of the house behind her.

Of course. It was almost July. Her summer neighbors were coming—cue music from *Jaws*—to occupy the houses around her. Some were pleasant, some were loud hard-drinking partiers—as the joke went, "Summer people— some are not." Some said hello when they saw her on the sidewalk in front of her house. Most ignored her. For them, she existed outside their summer fantasy bubble. It was all good with her. She was glad people could live here for a summer month or two. She had when she was younger, and she'd thought it was paradise.

It still was, even as, on the other side of the hedges, car doors opened and slammed shut. Her new backyard neighbors spilled out into the sun, all talking at once.

"Oh, isn't it lovely here! And the house looks as pretty as the pictures!" *A woman, probably a wife and mother.*

"Mom. All the houses are gray." *An adolescent girl, her tone a mix of sarcasm and tenderness.*

"Come on, gang, grab a bag and let's see what this old place is like on the inside."

A man. Obviously the father. And something more, something *impossible*—it had been so long since Darcy had spoken with her ex-husband—surely it couldn't be Boyz. But this particular male voice made her eyes snap open and the hair stand up on the back of her neck.

It *couldn't* be Boyz. His family always went to Lake George for the summer. It was an unforgiveable *sin* not to go to Lake George for the summer.

"Willow, you can carry more than that. Take another bag of groceries." *The woman's voice. The mother's.*

The woman Boyz had left her for had a daughter named Willow.

Could it be Boyz?

"Here, Willow, take the keys and unlock the front door. I'll get the suitcases."

The man's voice had the same tone as Boyz's, and Darcy was certain she heard just the slightest fake European accent all the Szwedas had. Their family had been American for generations, but they liked to claim an exiled Polish count as a relative, to explain their aristocratic (Darcy thought *snotty*) attitude.

The family headed toward the back door. Everyone talked at once. The voices receded as the group entered the house, but any minute now they'd be checking out the second floor, choosing bedrooms—looking out the window at the view.

She knew she could see all the adjoining backyards from her windows, which meant they

13

could see her from *their* windows. She couldn't lie here like a strip of undercooked bacon, yet she recoiled from the thought of running into the house like a frightened heroine from a Gothic romance.

But Darcy knew she wouldn't be able to relax in the garden until she was certain that the man on the other side of the hedge was *not* Boyz Szweda. Even though it was *impossible* that it was Boyz, this was a pretty desperate case of seeing is believing.

She stood, picked up her book and her water bottle, and slowly, humming, she strolled through the garden to her house. Boyz wouldn't recognize her from the back, after all, especially since she'd grown out her once-chic asymmetrically cut hair so long it fell in dark waves below her shoulders. She didn't hurry. She even paused to check her Knock Out rosebush before climbing the steps to the back porch and stepping inside.

She shut the door gently, quietly. She put her gardening tools in their rack. She leaned against the door and drew in a few deep breaths.

This was ridiculous. This was so *not* her kind of behavior. She was no longer a divorced and lonely female sniveling herself to sleep at night. She held an important position in the town's library. She had friends—she had a boyfriend, a carpenter, big and handsome and very good with his hands.

She should have Nash over for dinner tonight! She could throw something on the grill and they could open some beer and eat outdoors. She could change out of her gardening clothes and slip into a pretty sundress. . . .

Really? Were these thoughts really coming from her own mind? Clearly, she wasn't plotting to seduce Nash. All she had to do was open the front door to seduce Nash. Obviously, she wanted to show off for Boyz who might not even be there.

Maddening. Here she was, an accomplished woman thinking like a love-scorned teenager.

The important thing was that Darcy was only *thinking* that way. Not acting that way. Yet.

She needed a distraction. She needed to get out of the house and away from this mood buzzing around her like a swarm of wasps.

So: Where was her cellphone? On the kitchen counter. Good. She hit Jordan's number. Darcy had known Jordan for only three years, but with some people a friendship fit perfectly and immediately, like the rare times when the first dress you tried on was instant magic. She had first met Jordan at the library—always a good omen. Darcy had taken her bag lunch out to the garden to eat on a bench by the crab apple trees, and she'd heard the unmistakable sound of retching. Expecting to find some inexperienced drunken teenager, she discovered a pretty

15

blond woman on her knees near the tulips.

"Are you okay?" Darcy asked. "How can I help you?"

Without looking up, the woman croaked, "My tote's over there. I've got some saltines in a plastic bag and a can of 7Up. If you could bring it to me . . ."

"Of course. And I'll get you some wet paper towels from the bathroom, so you can wipe your hands and face."

"Oh, thank you. But please don't tell the librarians that I barfed in their garden."

"We'll shovel some dirt over it. No one will know."

By the time Darcy returned with the paper towels, the other woman had managed to move to a bench, where she sat very slowly chewing a tiny corner of a saltine.

"Thanks," she said to Darcy. She carefully wiped her hands and face and a few strands of sticky hair. "I'm not drunk," she announced. "I'm pregnant."

"And I'm a librarian," Darcy told her.

"Oh, no!"

"Oh, yes."

"I'm so sorry I barfed in your garden."

"Better than if you'd barfed on the books," Darcy said wryly.

The other woman managed a weak chuckle.

They sat on the bench for an hour, talking. For

more than an hour, actually; Darcy went fifteen minutes over her lunch break, but she often came in early, so she figured she was allowed. She learned that Jordan was newly married to Lyle Morris, an island guy she'd known and adored all her life. They'd started kissing and making out when they were fourteen. They lost their virginity to each other when they were both sixteen, but it had been so quick and weird and they'd been so guilt ridden and afraid she'd gotten pregnant— she hadn't—that they never dated after that. After high school, Lyle went into the army. Jordan had worked at her parents' liquor store and tried going out with other guys, but it never worked. She missed Lyle. She started writing Lyle, cheerful, sex-free, letters. Four years later, when Lyle got out of the army, he walked into her parents' store on Main Street, picked Jordan up in his powerful arms, carried her to his car, and drove to his apartment out on Surfside Road.

"I know how to do it *right* this time," he'd told her.

And he did.

They'd married a few months later. They'd been married a year and they were going to have a baby.

Darcy gave Jordan a capsule summary of her life and promised a more detailed account when she wasn't working. That night, Jordan came to her house and drank milk while Darcy drank wine and told her about her fruitcake parents, her darling grandmother, her weird marriage, her divorce. By the end of the evening, they were both hoarse from talking fast and laughing hysterically. Their friendship grew strong and fast from that evening, and when Darcy joined Jordan and Lyle at the beach with their friends one Sunday, she slipped into the group as easily as a fish into water. She'd found her tribe.

Now Jordan answered her cell. "This is your neighborhood help line. I'm sorry, but you may not park your car in my driveway."

Jordan and her family lived in town, like Darcy did, and their big old house was surrounded by rental houses, just like Darcy's. Jordan's husband was a contractor, so he was responsible for some of the nouveau mansions built on the outskirts of town, with ocean views to die for, but Lyle and Jordan chose to live in town. They had a daughter, Kiks. They planned on having at least one more, and they wanted their children to be able to walk to the library, the pharmacy, the post office. They wanted to have that small-town feeling—and they did, until one by one the houses around them were sold off to people who used them as their third or fourth or fifth home or for rental income. Nice in-town houses could rent for a good five grand a week in the summer.

Most first timers to the island were shocked by how close the houses in town were built to one another. Some were only five feet apart. Probably the sensible builders of the nineteenth century intended these walls of houses along the main streets of the village to block the wind that howled over the water. Certainly the houses served this purpose. Maybe the forefathers and especially the foremothers, often alone while their husbands were out at sea, liked having neighbors nearby on this isolated island. The streets in town were narrow. Many were one-way. Few had garages; even fewer had driveways. Parking could be an issue—kind of like city parking—but no one expected problems here in paradise.

"What have you got?" Darcy asked, sitting down on the white bench in the back hall to take off her gardening clogs.

"Family with twin babies!" Jordan laughed. "Three months old. They'll scream even more than Kiks!" Kathryn—Kat—Kiks was Jordan's two-year-old daughter. She was a champion screamer.

As they talked, Darcy padded barefoot into the kitchen. She filled a glass with cool water and took a long drink. Nantucket had the purest, sweetest water in the world.

From her kitchen window, she could see right into her backyard, and over the hedges, some of the yard behind it.

"What about you?" Jordan asked.

"Boyz and his family are at this very moment

19

carrying their luggage into the house behind me."

Jordan went quiet. After a moment, she said in her best GPS bitch voice, "Recalibrating."

"I know. Never in my wildest nightmares did I imagine this. His wife, the luscious Autumn, is hauling in some grocery bags, and her daughter, Willow, who must be about fourteen now, is wearily schlepping in her duffel bag right behind Boyz, who's got three heavy suitcases."

"You're sure it's Boyz?"

"I was in the garden when they arrived. I heard their voices. And now I can see them from the kitchen window. Yes, dammit, I'm sure."

"I don't know what to say. This is beyond belief. Do you want to come over?"

"No, I'm fine. It's just so weird."

"Maybe you should invite Nash over for noisy time on a blanket in your backyard."

"Ha! My first thought, too!" Darcy left the kitchen and wandered through the dining room and into the living room and on into the room she called the library, which was what her grandmother Penny always called it, probably because its walls were lined with bookshelves and those shelves were packed with books.

"Is Nash coming over?"

"Not today. We were together all weekend. But, anyway, I don't need to impress Boyz! It's been three years since I last saw or even talked to him."

"But wait, Darcy, why would Boyz rent a house so near yours?"

"I can't imagine he knows I'm living in this house. He knew my grandmother lived on the island, but when I was married to him, Penny was in an assisted living center on the Cape. He met her, but he never came to the island with me. He never saw this house. We always had to go to Lake George in the summer. It was another one of the Family Traditions. I have no idea why he's here."

"You're bound to run into him this summer."

"I know. I can't believe it. But you know what? I hope I *do* meet him sometime so I can find out why he's here instead of at the family compound at Lake George."

"Do you really care?"

"*Care,* no. But I am curious. He was so all about his family—"

"Darcy, Kiks is howling. I'll call you later."

Darcy climbed the stairs to the second floor and entered the bathroom off her bedroom. It was one of the luxuries she had built in when she first inherited the house. Large, with a white tile floor and the original old claw-foot tub and a new shower and piles of thick white towels—it was her own private spa. She stripped off her clothes, turned the water on hot, and stepped into the shower.

Memories streamed down on her like rain.

2

Penelope Cotterill, Darcy's paternal grand-mother, hadn't exactly saved Darcy's life, but she had given her the best gift in the world—she'd made Darcy believe she was worthy of love, care, and respect. Darcy's parents didn't do so well at that.

Darcy's father, Eugene, had been a well-educated, slightly reserved normal guy, the son of New York banker Eustace Cotterill and his wife, Penelope. After graduating from Yale and starting work in the city, Eugene met Lala Benton and went right off the rails.

The party-loving Lala was a glamorous wild-haired bohemian, sexy and noisy and greedy and racy. Eugene was a man idly sailing on the calm waters of a sheltered harbor; Lala was a hurricane who swept him up into her tumultuous world. They met at a party and had sex that very night in one of the bedrooms—Eugene had never had sex at a party before and he felt like quite a playboy. After that, they spent all their time together, dancing or drinking or driving too fast. Lala made Eugene feel alive for the first time in his life, and he made Lala feel safe and anchored, which was what she thought she wanted.

They got married six weeks after they met by

a justice of the peace with two college friends for witnesses. Lala's parents were glad she was someone else's responsibility now, but Eugene's family, including Penny, refused to take this whirlwind marriage seriously. They didn't want to meet Lala; they didn't invite her to visit.

So it was easy for Lala to convince Eugene to leave the stuffy East Coast to live near Lala's family in the wilds of Chicago. Eugene worked for a bank there and Lala shopped a lot and they were both dumbfounded when Lala realized she was pregnant. Darcy was born to much celebration and joy—Darcy had an album full of photos proving that. For two turbulent years, they all lived together, playing at being a happy family. But Lala had an affair, and then another, and Eugene divorced her. Darcy was two, right at that toddling, shrieking, tyrannical untidy age when she seemed at times possessed by demons. Eugene was tired of drama by then. He paid child support for his daughter, but he went back to the East Coast and didn't think much about her. He sent a monthly check, but never remembered his daughter's birthday, never even came to see her.

In the early years of her life, Darcy and Lala lived with Lala's mother and her family in the Chicago suburb of Highland Park. Darcy's maternal grandparents and aunts were glad to take care of her when Lala had a date, which was often; but they were a noisy, easily bored, boisterous bunch. They fought dramatically, throwing pots, weeping hysterically, yelling and stomping and then sitting down together to watch *The Drew Carey Show*. It was like living in a tornado, only occasionally being able to rest in the eye of the storm.

As a child, Darcy slept in three different homes, and she seldom knew which one until she was dropped off at the front door. Her main home was with Lala and Lala's mother, Gwen, and overweight, grumbling father, Horace, who would not allow a cat in the house because of his allergies. Second, Darcy stayed with Lala's brother's ex-wife, Tracy, who also liked a good time and often went out to the movies or dancing or drinking with Lala while Darcy slept on a cot in the attic. Third, Darcy stayed with Lala's sister Topaz, who was young and single and the most fun of the unruly family because when she put on her makeup, she often made up Darcy's face, too. For Darcy to have someone's attention directed solely to her was a kind of blessing, and Topaz's light brisk dabs of eye shadow, blush, and lipstick were often the most affection she would receive for weeks. But Topaz worked as a bartender, and when Darcy was sent to her apartment for a few days, she spent most of her time alone. Topaz always gave her a bright purple air mattress to blow up for her bed, and instructed Darcy to put it on the far side of Topaz's bedroom, so that if

Topaz brought a "friend" home, they could use the couch in the living room. Topaz's theory was that her bed would block any noises she and her friend made in the living room. Topaz was wrong, but Darcy never complained. She was glad to have a place to sleep and cookies and Diet Coke for breakfast.

For the first ten years of her life, Darcy hadn't known at the end of the school day where she would go—to her grandmother's house or to Tracy's or Topaz's.

Darcy became a quiet and resourceful girl who understood she had no single, steady place to call home. So she created her own home within books. If she had a book with her, she could withdraw into that world like a snail into its shell. When she was with adults, she could be quiet, almost invisible, remembering a book. When she was placed in a new school, she could shield herself from whispers and stares with thoughts of a book.

Everyone bumbled along. Darcy was cared for, in a hit-or-miss, slapdash way. By the time she was ten, her maternal grandparents were beginning to have health issues, and it all became more difficult. Then Lala met an architect from Boston who wanted to spend more time with her. So Lala packed up her things—she never collected much except clothes—and took Darcy with her to Boston. The architect wasn't offering marriage. He found Darcy's needs for school and food and clothes an annoying intrusion on his fun with Lala, so Lala came up with a genius idea: Darcy could live with Penelope, Darcy's other grandmother, Lala's ex-husband's mother. After all, Nantucket was not far from Boston; it was in Massachusetts—it would be so easy for Darcy and Lala to see each other! Lala wrote a note to Penelope Cotterill, then phoned her, and then made the journey on the ferry to the island to introduce Darcy to her grandmother and the island.

"She's not easy, like us," Lala warned Darcy the day they boarded the ferry to cross the wide waters to the island. "She's a loner, kind of eccentric, aloof. She doesn't know how to have fun." Worried that what she'd said would cause Darcy to refuse to live there made Lala add in a slightly frantic tone, "But she's not *mean*. She's just—*quiet*."

Darcy grinned. *Quiet!*

Penelope Cotterill was seventy then, but was far from being a little old lady. She was tall and slender, with long silver hair she clasped to the back of her head with an amethyst hair clip. She had hazel eyes—like Darcy's, not green or blue like her mother's side of the family. Although she was quiet, she gave off an aura of tranquil unflappable contentment. Her clothes were expensive but simple. She wore long, slim dark skirts and long, loose cashmere sweaters for gardening; and when she visited the library or the local bookstores or attended the island's concerts and plays and lectures, she simply brushed off any specks of dirt, added her own grandmother's pearls to whatever she was wearing, and was ready.

Lala had met Penelope only three times, but she'd sized the older woman up quickly. And while Lala might have been unreliable, she was canny. For the visit to meet her grandmother, Lala made Darcy wear a black skirt and a white blouse. Darcy had looked like a pilgrim. A nervous pilgrim on the verge of vomiting. The ferry ride was rough. Darcy was suffering from nausea and nerves, and when she first saw her tall, elegant, meticulously dressed grandmother, it took all her courage to do what Lala had instructed, to hold out her hand.

Penelope bent forward to shake Darcy's small quivering hand—and in an instant, with that touch, Penelope fell in love. She dropped to her knees, put her hands on Darcy's shoulders, and pulled the girl to her. She hugged her hard.

"My dear," Penelope said. "Welcome. I do believe you have come home."

For the first time in her life, Darcy felt warm right down to the bottom of her soul.

After an obligatory hour of drinking tea and talking, Lala went back to Boston. After Lala left, Darcy's grandmother took her upstairs to the room that was to be her very own. It had a brass bed with an antique quilt and sheets smelling of lavender. It had a cherrywood desk placed beneath the window that looked over the wide backyard where hedges surrounded Penelope's garden. It had a large mahogany dresser and an amazing piece of furniture like a table with slender drawers and a stool with a needlepoint cushion and mirrors that could be folded in so that Darcy could see how she looked from both sides. Penelope called it a vanity.

The room had a bookcase.

It had books.

"I don't know what you've read," Penelope told Darcy. "Probably you've read all these books, but I thought I'd put them out just in case."

Darcy knelt before the bookcase and carefully pulled out each volume. *Little Women. Jane Eyre.* Nancy Drew. *The Secret Garden. The Adventures of Sherlock Holmes.* She could live in this room forever!

Penelope took Darcy out the back door to introduce Darcy to Penelope's own secret garden. She held her hand, urging Darcy to sniff the blossoms and touch the silky petals and learn the name of each flower. She took her around the small, picture-book town to introduce her to the librarians—for Penelope was a steadfast patron—and the shopkeepers. She drove Darcy to the grocery store and pushed a cart down the aisle, asking what Darcy liked for breakfast, lunch, and dinner. Darcy hardly knew what to say. She'd never been asked that before.

Little by little, Darcy grew to feel at home in her grandmother's house. When September came, she started school, and her life fell into a regular pattern. Every afternoon, she returned to the place she had left that morning. She really was at home.

Darcy's father never came to visit, and Darcy didn't miss him—how could she miss someone she'd seldom seen? Lala visited once a month, when the weather permitted an easy passage across Nantucket Sound. After she married her architect—without inviting Darcy to the service—she came less often.

It didn't matter. Darcy's grandmother invited her to call her Penny, and for her first Christmas on the island, Penny surprised Darcy with a kitten. Nickel, Darcy named her, an odd name for a cat, but a kind of homage to Penny.

For the first few years of her life on the island, Darcy spent a good deal of time with her grandmother. She helped Penny tend her garden. She joined her for long walks on the many beaches or in the extensive inland moors. She accompanied Penny to the library, the local bookstores, and the island's concerts.

When Darcy made friends at school, she was

allowed to bring them over to play in her room, as long as they played quietly, or even in the garden, as long as they stayed away from the flowers. Half of Darcy's friends had divorced parents with lives much more intrusive and hostile than Darcy's, which helped Darcy feel better.

Eventually, Darcy's father married a woman named Jean and moved to Florida. Lala divorced her architect and moved to Santa Fe. When Darcy first saw a picture of the birth of Venus she nodded her head in recognition. That was how she felt she'd arrived on this earth: alone, parentless, in the middle of the sea of life, with all the stability of a shell floating on a rocky sea. But just as there was a nurturing figure in the painting, her grandmother was there to receive her, to welcome her to the security of the island.

When Darcy was around sixteen, things changed. Darcy changed. Her hormones kicked in, her figure hour-glassed, and she wanted to flirt with boys. She wanted to kiss boys. She wanted . . . what most teenagers wanted.

While Darcy was getting faster, her grandmother was getting slower and a touch crabby and more of a disciplinarian. She gave Darcy a curfew. She took down the names of Darcy's friends—in case, she explained, something happened to her and she needed to get in touch with her immediately. Darcy knew she was only pretending to be worried that she might fall and hurt herself and the ambulance would come, and she'd be whisked to the hospital, where the nurse would ask for her next of kin, and she'd gasp out, "My granddaughter, Darcy, but I don't know where she is!" She thought Penny was truly anxious for herself. After all, she was seventy-six, edging toward old age. But she was also energetic and strong and she could still work like a longshoreman in her garden. The truth was, Darcy guessed, that Penny wanted to keep tabs on Darcy.

Secretly, Darcy was grateful for that. It made her feel safe to have Penny watching over her. Possibly it prevented Darcy from doing anything really stupid. She waited until she was older to do that.

When Darcy turned seventeen, she took a job in a boutique to make money for college. That was the year Penny's age began to catch up with her. Her left hip hurt her whenever she moved, and she refused to see a doctor, insisting it was only arthritis and taking aspirin for the pain. She still worked in her garden, but often Darcy would look out the window to see Penny holding her hip as she walked or sitting on a bench, bent double, rubbing her hands together as if to press away the ache. At last Darcy persuaded Penny to visit Dr. Ruby, who diagnosed Lyme disease, caused by the bite of a minuscule insect, the tick. If it had been caught early, antibiotics would have cured Penny, but her own stubbornness had brought her an enormous loss in quality of life. Penny took painkillers, but she was constantly fatigued and suffering pain in all her joints. She was seventy-seven, and Lyme disease aged her by decades.

Darcy did everything she could to help Penny. She bought all the groceries, cooked all the meals, and cleaned the house. She got stacks of DVDs from the library—Penny was often too tired to read—and once Darcy earned her driver's license, she took Penny for excursions around the island in Penny's valiant old Jeep.

Bravely, with a sick feeling in the pit of her stomach, Darcy offered to forgo college and stay home with Penny. Penny burst into laughter and promised she would disown Darcy if she dared to even think of such a thing. The next day, Darcy found Penny on the phone in the kitchen; and within twenty-four hours, Penny had hired a woman to come five days a week to clean house and cook Penny a decent hot meal. She also agreed to take the antidepressants her physician had prescribed. By the time Darcy left for college, Penny was much more active and cheerful. Maybe it was all an act, Darcy thought, but Penny had made her point.

College life at UMass/Boston suited Darcy perfectly—no surprise because she was surrounded by books and people who talked about what was in those books. She majored in English literature and by her junior year realized she wanted to attend Simmons for a master's degree in library science. Penny was thrilled. Darcy called her often and hurried back to check on her during long school holidays. She spent the holidays and summers with her, and Penny was slower, but in good spirits.

The time came when Penny could no longer hide or ignore her frustratingly merciless body. No assisted living facility existed on the island, except one that Penny called Death's Waiting Room. She had made herself fairly adept at the computer and found and compared the various assisted living facilities on the Cape. One weekend, Darcy accompanied her grandmother to the ferry across Nantucket Sound and drove her to Sea View Village, which amazingly had a view of the sea. To Darcy's surprise, Penny felt at home from the moment she saw it, or did an Oscar-winning act of pretending to. With relief, Penny settled in with others like her who were also withered, weakened, and dependent on the charming and capable doctors, nurses, and nurses' aides.

Darcy drove down to visit Penny almost every weekend. She often spent an hour or so trimming the older woman's nails and painting them an unusual color, like blue, or magenta with glitter, hoping the sparkle would brighten Penny's days.

Penny wasn't able to trim her nails herself. Her hands weren't steady or strong enough even to work a nail clipper. Those hands that had once dug ferociously into the soil to plant flowers; that patiently, relentlessly tugged weeds from her garden; those hands that had cooked healthy meals for Darcy and applauded when Darcy sang at a school concert—those hands had fallen limp and useless, spotted with brown age marks, trembling when she tried to lift a teacup to her lips.

In the last year of her life, everything had to be done for Penny. She could not bathe herself, dress herself, brush her own teeth. Arthritis was causing her increasing pain. She was weak. She wore adult diapers. The nurses at the home were kind and attentive, Darcy could see that, and was grateful. Darcy always stepped out of the room when a nurse came to change Penny's diaper and gently wash her body. Afterward, Darcy brought out one of Penny's photograph albums and went through it, pointing to a picture of Penny in her prime.

"Your wedding dress was gorgeous," Darcy would say. Or, "Check out this shot of you showing off the privet roots you'd dug up." Or, "Here is one of my favorite photos, you and me all glammed up in Boston, ready to go to the ballet."

Sometimes Penny would manage a lift of her

lips. Just as often, she'd remain blank faced, too tired even to enjoy her memories.

Still, Darcy drove down from Boston in Penny's old Jeep every weekend to visit her . . . although not quite so often after she met Boyz.

3

The winter Darcy met Boyz, she was taking her third semester at Simmons College. She had this "spring" semester and one more to go before she received her master's in library science. Where she would go from there, she hadn't decided, although she definitely wanted to stay in the Boston area. Her family was so scattered— her uninterested father in Florida with his second wife, Jean; her beloved grandmother Penny in a nursing home on the Cape; and her flaky mother, Lala, God only knew where. Darcy didn't have the kind of family that gave advice, so she was pretty much working out her life step by step, day by day, scanning the horizon and hoping that some kind of well-marked route would suddenly unfold itself before her.

In the evenings, she worked as a waitress at Bijoux, a posh restaurant in Boston. She shared an apartment near the Gardner Museum in Boston with another UMass friend, but Rachael didn't work because Rachael didn't have to worry about money. Darcy's father had agreed to pay the college tuition, but Darcy was responsible for everything else—rent, utilities, clothes, books— and she knew she could count on amazing tips at Bijoux, where she'd been working the past year.

So there Darcy was, in her chic uniform of tight black slacks and shirt, her short dark hair capping her head, her high heels already uncomfortable but looking amazing. She stood in the doorway of the kitchen, catching her breath after an already crazy-busy Saturday night. The maître d', Pierre—that was his real name—was showing a family to their table, a table in Darcy's zone, and Darcy absolutely gawked.

They looked like a gathering of angels. Five people who had to be father, mother, two sisters, and one brother, with gleaming silver-blond hair and lean, athletic bodies, who looked as if they had their wings folded beneath their fabulous simple but elegant clothing. She'd never seen anyone quite like them.

She put on her best smile when she greeted them, and it was a good thing she'd said the words so often they came automatically, because when she was closer to them, she was nearly dumbstruck by their gorgeousness. They all possessed the same pale blue eyes beneath arched blond eyebrows and they all seemed so *happy*.

They liked *her*, too. The father asked her advice, and took it, for the main courses and the wine, and they complimented her on her suggestions. She felt the son's eyes lingering on her, his appreciation of her almost steaming off him, and she knew if she let her eyes meet his, she would blush—and she did let her eyes meet his, and she did blush. They all wanted drinks first: the mother and the oldest daughter champagne cocktails, the younger daughter sparkling water, the father and son gin and tonics. The son's eyes remained on her as she walked away.

The rest of the evening passed in a hormone-thick blur. Darcy wasn't unaware of her own allure. She was tall, slender, and shapely, with dark hair and hazel eyes and a plump mouth. For Bijoux, she went heavy on the eyeliner, using kohl drawn a little up and out, giving her an exotic look. She didn't do this to attract men; she didn't especially want a man in her life. She was free, and she wanted to be free; she had plans. She wanted to work at the Boston Public Library; she hoped, by the time she was fifty, to be its president. If she'd ever had any kind of true home, it was a library.

The restaurant was clearing out, the bar still busy but several tables empty by eleven o'clock, when she returned to the table with the black leather folder holding the father's credit card.

"Thank you for visiting Bijoux," Darcy said sweetly. "I hope this is au revoir and not goodbye." Pierre's father, the owner of the restaurant, insisted his waitstaff say exactly those words and Darcy always obeyed, even though she wanted to roll her eyes as she said them.

The father cocked his head, peering up at her with a twinkle in his eye. "Well, Darcy, I know my son will be back. I can tell by the way he's been looking at you."

Darcy was too embarrassed to glance at the son. Of course she'd been flirted with before in the restaurant. She'd learned to flirt back carefully, playfully. But tonight, this table—especially the son, but not only the son—had captured her fancy and her admiration. The family had so much fun together, leaning toward each other to share a secret or a joke; and the father often whispered in his wife's ear, making her smile. They teased each other, she could tell, and they shared their food, passing their plates around, tasting, commenting, nodding in agreement. Certainly she'd made a point to be equally charming to all of her tables tonight, so that the Szwedas, especially their son, didn't know how bowled over she was by this family's allure.

So she blushed, tongue-tied, and hurried away from the table, hoping the family would believe she left so abruptly because other tables were waiting, and that was certainly true. She stepped into the kitchen, where the diners couldn't see her, and took a moment to breathe deeply and compose herself. When she returned to the dining room five minutes later, they were all gone.

She got back to her apartment around one thirty. As always, she was exhausted, but she summoned up the energy to open her laptop. Of course she had seen the name on the credit card, and a memorable name it was: *Makary Szweda*. She googled him and discovered he owned a real estate agency that seemed to handle upscale houses in the poshest Boston suburbs. The Szweda Real Estate Company had twelve agents. One of them was Boyzdar Szweda, the son. The older sister, Irena, was also an agent. Lena was a sophomore at Wellesley. Darcy found several photos of them on the Internet. The mother, always opulent at a charity function with her silver-blond hair and gleaming jewelry, was named Dita. The entire family was often captured together, lifting champagne glasses, toasting the success of a fundraising event.

She wondered how *Boyzdar* was pronounced.

That single event cast her into the most unsettled mood. The son, the handsome son, had smiled at her, really smiled. She had thought he was trying to connect, although that was a ridiculous idea: She was a waitress, he was almost a prince. But she couldn't get him off her mind the next day during her classes at Simmons. She felt unsettled and grouchy when it was time to leave for work.

That evening, her shift started at six o'clock. She took the T up to the Beacon Hill area where Bijoux was located, and slogged through dirty piles of slush. It was February, a gloomy month, a month Darcy had always relished, because it was so perfect for curling up inside beneath an afghan and reading. But today the weather held no delight. It was achingly cold, and the sky was as bleached as an old gray towel, the Christmas decorations that had brightened the winter were gone, and even Valentine's Day had passed, so shop windows were boring. It was a dreary time of year, depressing and colorless—

And there in front of the restaurant stood Boyz with an enormous bouquet of spring flowers! He had husky-dog pale blue eyes and he was smiling at her.

"These are for you," he said when she drew close. "To apologize for my father's comment." He wore a camel's hair overcoat with the collar turned up and a Russian-looking fur hat.

She was too stunned to speak.

"I hope you won't think I'm as discourteous as he was. I confess, however, he wasn't wrong, because I *was* staring at you all evening. So I brought you flowers for many reasons."

Darcy thought: *Oh, golly.* Her next thought was she wished she'd worn her good wool coat instead of her puffy down parka. She knew this was the beginning of something, so she made herself slow down and act like a grown-up instead of like the shrieking teenager doing cheers in her head.

"Oh, you didn't need to do that." She was so composed, the very picture of poise.

"Well," he said teasingly, "in that case, I guess I shouldn't give you the flowers."

"You absolutely *should* give me the flowers," Darcy said boldly. "And you must give me your address so I can write you a thank-you note." Was she saying these words? Was this who she was? It was!

"Ah, I see. Then I'll know *your* full name and address, so I'll be able to write you to ask you out to dinner."

The wind was howling down the street, crackling the cellophane around the poor flowers, and she was warm, heading toward sizzling.

"Or I could give you my cell number."

He smiled. "Or I could invite you to dinner right now."

"What a good idea!"

"Darcy, would you care to go out to dinner with me tomorrow night?"

"How do you know my name?"

"You introduced yourself to us last night. 'Hello. My name is Darcy, and I'll be your server tonight.' "

Darcy laughed, probably more than she should have, because behind the man with the flowers, on the other side of the window, the bartenders and two waiters were making lovey-dovey kissy faces at her.

"You have a very good memory," she said. "But I'm afraid *I* don't know *your* name." Of course, she did know his name but had no idea how to pronounce it.

"My name is Boyzdar Szweda," he said and he madc a slight bow. "But everyone calls me Boyz. My family is Polish, with a little Swedish thrown in."

"Boyz." Darcy tried the name. It was like saying *boys* but with a little zip at the end. "I'm delighted to meet you, and I look forward to dinner tomorrow night, but, I'm sorry, the idiots I work with are being ridiculous on the other side of the window." She was aware she didn't speak this way usually, so formally, and it was as if she were caught in a spell.

Boyz turned. The bartender and waiters stopped posing and waved. Boyz waved back.

"Your colleagues like to keep an eye on you," he said. "Shall we give them something to talk about?"

Before she could even imagine what he meant, Boyz put his arms around her, pulled her to him, tilted her back toward the pavement, and kissed her long and hard, managing to hold the flowers behind her back so they weren't crushed. Then, she'd swooned at such a romantic act. Later, she'd realized it was the first of many signs that Boyz was an actor and all the world his audience.

He drew her upright and steadied her as he pulled away from their kiss. With one gloved finger he stroked the side of her face. "My cell number is on the card tucked in the flowers. Call me when you can so we can lock in tomorrow night." He handed her the bouquet.

"Thank you," she said. "For the flowers. And for the kiss—I'll be the envy of all the staff."

Boyz walked away. Darcy floated into the restaurant with flowers in her arms. Immediately she was surrounded by catcalls and whistles and applause. Completely not her usual shy self, she performed an impromptu curtsy. Then she hurried back to the staff lounge to put the flowers in water and organize herself for the evening. Black shirt and pants, discreet black apron around her waist for her order pad, and energy sparkling all around her. She got enormous tips that evening.

She wore a red cashmere sweater to dinner the next night. Red always set off her dark hair and eyes, and besides, she *felt* red. Vibrant. Bold. She purposely did *not* wear anything too tight or cleavage exposing. Boyz picked her up at her apartment—she told him she'd come down, she didn't want to intrude on her roommate's evening, trying to make that sound mysteriously sophisticated. In fact, her roommate, Rachael, was slopping around in her stained pajamas, eating ice cream, and watching *Bridget Jones's Diary*—she'd just had a bad breakup. So Darcy waited just outside her apartment door.

Boyz drove a silver BMW convertible—*Of course he did,* she thought, as he stepped out to kiss her cheek and escort her around to the passenger side.

He took her to an Indian restaurant on Newbury Street. They were shown to a booth near the back, where it was quiet and dark except for the lights beaming from the exquisitely detailed copper and glass hanging lamps.

"This place reminds me of my favorite restaurant in London," Boyz told her. "I'm a huge fan of Indian food. I've never been to India. Have you?"

"I've hardly been anywhere," Darcy told him. She had had a serious talk with herself before the date, asking whether she was going to be frivolous and flippant about her family or be simply her lonely self. She had decided she couldn't carry off any kind of a happy-go-lucky act with this man, and she didn't want to.

"My parents are divorced," she continued. "My father lives in Florida. Sarasota. I've been down there exactly twice to see him. He doesn't come to see me or even his own mother. He won't leave Florida. And then I've got my mother, who is always traveling. She might be in the Southwest. She texts me now and then, but she hasn't invited me to join her. Oh, I did go to Washington, D.C., with my eighth-grade class one spring." God, she was sounding positively pathetic. "But my grandmother lives on Nantucket, and I've lived with her most of my life, and Nantucket is fabulous!"

Boyz nodded. "Nantucket." He seemed to roll

the thought around like tasting a new wine. "I've heard it's great. Our agency has a branch on the Vineyard, but I've never been to Nantucket. It's so far out in the ocean. Not very accessible." He brought his eyes back to her face. "So do you have any siblings?"

"No. I wish I did, but that didn't happen." Darcy tried to sound upbeat about this, but it was difficult.

Boyz put his hand on hers as it lay on the table. "You must be lonely."

Oh, dear, she was coming off absolutely pitiful. That was not how she wanted to seem—that wasn't how she *was*. "No, I'm not lonely. I have my grandmother, and I have some really close wonderful friends, and I have *books*."

"Books?" Boyz looked perplexed.

"Yes, books. I'm a reading addict. A bibliophile." She could see how he wasn't understanding. "I read constantly. Books cheer me up, teach me things, give me bits of wisdom, entertain me—" He still looked confused.

She should have known at that moment that no matter how gorgeous he was, he wasn't right for her. The waiter came with their orders. For a while, Darcy and Boyz focused on the hot and spicy food, the naan, the unusual flavors.

"I mean," she continued, "what do you read for pleasure? Thrillers? Grisham? Lee Child? Or maybe Henning Mankell? Camilla Läckberg?

46

They're Swedish writers with an international following."

"I'm afraid I must disappoint you. For pleasure, I read sales agreements and contracts. I'm immersed in our business, as is all our family. Our firm is quite important, top-shelf, and we want to keep it that way. Also, our family is quite—*active*. We have a house on Lake George, and we spend much of our summers there. In the winter, we stay there and ski at Gore Mountain. Sometimes if the winter is too long, we go to St. John in the Virgin Islands for swimming and scuba diving. Have you ever gone scuba diving?"

"No," Darcy responded simply, feeling slightly overwhelmed.

"Ah, you must go. It's a sensational experience!"

"Mmmm," she agreed, with a mouth full of chicken tikka and rice. It was an exciting thought, swimming in warm blue waters, gazing at wondrously colorful fish.

Deep inside, she had split into two halves: the Timid, Apprehensive Darcy who didn't know how to ski, was terrified of flying, and probably would go into a claustrophobic fit if she put on goggles and a tank and flippered down into the ocean, and the Brave Bold Darcy, who could do it all, and why not? She was young. She probably hadn't met all of herself yet.

That night Boyz didn't try to go to bed with

her, although he asked to take her to the ballet that Saturday. She usually worked weekends, but a waiter friend agreed to trade shifts with her, if she'd promise to tell him every detail of the evening.

She was excited about going to the ballet. It was *Swan Lake*. She knew the music and had seen clips of it on her PBS television station. She'd never seen it performed live. Boston Opera House was a stunning gold palace devoted to the arts, and Darcy was breathless when an usher showed them to the Szwedas' box. From there, she could see not only the stage but the gorgeously dressed audience. She wore a simple black dress with pearl earrings and knew she looked good, but it made her breathless to think she was part of this cultured crowd. At intermission, Boyz spoke about Tchaikovsky's life, his knowledge and enthusiasm practically making the man come alive before her eyes. Maybe it was the champagne they were drinking, or the rustle of silk and satin and the gleam of jewelry around her, but Darcy felt lifted into a rarified atmosphere, one she'd never visited before.

The next Saturday, he took her to a performance at Symphony Hall. Afterward, at dinner in the Top of the Hub, Darcy looked out over the sparkling city and shared insights about Shostakovich. *She* had read up on the composer earlier that day, but

Boyz spoke of him almost as if he were a relative. When their meal was over, Darcy leaned her chin in her hand and studied Boyz as he talked. True, he wasn't a *reader*. But he was a storyteller, one who knew much more about the complicated history of Eastern Europe and Russia than Darcy had ever known. Boyz mixed in anecdotes about his grandparents and great-grandparents with his stories about famous musicians and artists, and he spoke in such a way that Darcy could almost see the people shimmering before her eyes.

Later, after their marriage, she would hear these tales over and over again, and always word for word. Later, she'd realize that Boyz had his knowledge organized in categories, and he could call a subject up to fit the interests of the potential buyer of a multimillion-dollar home. *Golf?* Boyz could talk about Tiger Woods and Jack Nicklaus. *Baseball?* Boyz had season tickets to loge box 157; he'd be glad to share them. *Art?* He and his family were supporters of the Museum of Fine Arts. Boyz could arrange a private tour if they'd like. *Cars?* His knowledge ranged from the German Touring Masters to NASCAR.

That evening at the Top of the Hub, blissed out by the expensive wine and Boyz's conversation, Darcy fell in love with the man, or, more accurately, with her idea of the man. Later, she'd realize how flattering her wide-eyed attention was to Boyz. Later, she would understand that he was always in a silent competition with his father for title of *Most Fascinating, Cultured, Seductive,* and, of course, *King of Real Estate Sales*. But in the early days of their relationship, Darcy felt like Cinderella who had met her prince. It didn't occur to her that this had never been her favorite fairy tale.

For his part, Boyz enjoyed bathing in the glow of Darcy's innocent admiration. Darcy *looked* sophisticated; he was proud to have her at his side during important events. She had good conversation; she knew things from books. She was tender and undemanding in bed. She remembered how he liked his coffee, how he preferred his socks laid flat, not rolled. When he lost a sale, she put her arms around him and murmured sweet nothings. She was kind. She was nurturing. She was beautiful, and she was *his*.

After only a few weeks of dating, Boyz invited her to Sunday dinner at his parents' house. Darcy was nervous about that. She knew it was a significant occasion.

The Szwedas' house was a jaw-droppingly stupendous mansion in Belmont. Boyz's mother did not serve the dinner. They had a butler who served the food the cook had prepared. These were realms of wealth she'd never seen before, and she had lived much of her life on Nantucket, where a simple one-bedroom cottage might sell for a million dollars.

The sisters met her at the door. The oldest sibling, Irena, was restrained. The younger sister, Lena, bubbled with excitement.

"I'm so glad you're here!" she said, taking both of Darcy's hands. As she drew her into the living room, she continued, "Our family is so boring— all we talk about is real estate—and Boyz said you're a librarian and I'm a huge reader! I'm a sophomore at Wellesley and I *adore* literature. But chemistry is my favorite subject, isn't that weird?"

"Lena, let Darcy sit down," Dita, the mother, said, laughing.

"All right, I will, but first I have to tell Darcy a secret." Whispering in Darcy's ear, she said, "Boyz said he thinks you're the *one!*"

Darcy blushed and smiled and squeezed Lena's hand. She didn't dare look at Boyz.

Mr. Szweda rose from his chair by the fireplace and made a kind of half bow to her. "It's nice to see you again, Darcy."

"Thank you," she replied.

She sat near Boyz—but not touching!—on the sofa.

"Would you like a cocktail?" Mrs. Szweda asked.

Darcy paused.

"Say no!" Lena told her. "Unless you like drinking pints of straight gin."

Irena added kindly, "I'm drinking champagne."

"Oh, champagne, please," Darcy said, relieved.

The conversation at first was general chitchat about the weather, recent movies, and the Bijoux and other favorite restaurants in the area. At the dinner table, the Szwedas asked her about how she came to work at Bijoux. Darcy told them she was finishing a master's degree in library science at Simmons and needed to work to pay her rent.

"Ah, a master's degree in library science," Mrs. Szweda said, shooting her husband a cryptic look.

When she said Nantucket was her home—she didn't go into detail about her absent parents—both parents brightened.

"We've never been to Nantucket," Mr. Szweda said. "I hear it's trending now. Real estate is off-the-charts expensive."

"Dearest," Dita cooed, patting her husband's hand, "it's not always about the price of real estate." Turning to Darcy she continued: "We haven't gone there, because we're always up at our house at Lake George in the summer. People can be such creatures of habit, can't they?"

Chatty Lena chimed in, "Maybe Darcy would like to come up to Lake George this summer."

Dita gently ignored her daughter. "So you want to be a librarian, Darcy. When did you decide on this career track?"

"I love books, and I love people," Darcy answered simply. "I like bringing the two together."

"Ah." Dita clapped her hands lightly. "Now we have something in common. Makary and I, and really our entire family, love *houses* and people. We enjoy bringing houses and people together. That's why our real estate business is flourishing."

Elegant Irena spoke up. "A wall of books does give color and a sense of warmth to a room."

"Yes," Darcy agreed. "I suppose it does."

"You should go with Boyz sometime when he lists a house," Lena suggested. "He gets some of the most fabulous homes!"

Driving home, Darcy said wistfully, "Your family is so close, so devoted."

Boyz sighed. "That's true. Not always a good thing, you know."

"Really? Why?"

He made a flicking motion with his hand, as if dismissing the subject. "I often feel that everything I do has to please my father."

Darcy nodded. "I can understand that."

"But tonight isn't about my family," Boyz said. He parked in front of Darcy's apartment. Reaching over, he took Darcy's hand. "It's about you and me."

Darcy's feelings rocketed.

Boyz looked into her eyes. "Darcy, I knew the moment I saw you we would be good together." He cleared his throat, as if it were difficult to speak. "I don't mean to rush you or frighten you, but I think I'm in love with you. We haven't known each other long, and yet somehow I feel I know you, and you know me."

No man had ever spoken to Darcy that way before, with such candor, making himself vulnerable. This exotic, sophisticated man loved her? Believed she *knew him?* She flushed with pleasure. She felt glamorous and interesting and powerful. At last, she felt *wanted*.

They married that summer. It was an odd, lopsided wedding, with most of those in attendance members of the Szweda family. Darcy was grateful that Boyz's family didn't shriek in horror when they learned that neither of Darcy's parents would attend. Darcy did invite them. They were both busy. Of course they were. For the entire month of July. Her best friends from Simmons had already moved to different states, leaving her roommate, Rachael, and the waitstaff of Bijoux to be present on Darcy's side.

The sweet if slightly bizarre venue for the event was on the Cape, in the small chapel in the Sea View Community at the far end of the building. By then, Penny's aging body had been so afflicted by the Lyme disease that she was taking several medications for the pain, and still having trouble doing the simplest tasks. But her mind was as sharp as ever, and she'd insisted on ordering the flowers for the chapel and the reception—white Casablanca lilies in masses everywhere.

Darcy wore a plain white ballerina-length dress and the family pearls, Penny's wedding present. She wore a plain fingertip veil on her cap of brown hair. Everyone told her she looked like Audrey Hepburn. Two male friends from Bijoux escorted Penny, resplendent in turquoise chiffon and *her* grandmother's diamond earrings, to the front row. Chase, Darcy's favorite waiter, walked her down the aisle and gave her away. The retirement home minister performed the ceremony, with only the Szweda family and Boyz's best friend, Tucker, on the groom's side; a perfect and courteous balance to Darcy's small showing. After they said "I do" and kissed, Darcy noticed a crowd of Sea View residents peering in the door. All of them were smiling. When the newlyweds adjourned to the small party room, they invited the other people in for cake and champagne.

The newlyweds honeymooned in Paris—of course. They strolled hand in hand through the Luxembourg Gardens, sighed with amazement in the Louvre and the Musée d'Orsay, kissed at the top of the Eiffel Tower. They dined on a boat touring the Seine. They gasped at the Moulin Rouge. They toured Notre-Dame and shopped at Hermès and Le Bon Marché and Galeries Lafayette and brilliant boutiques tucked in along the Champs-Élysées. They ate and drank far too much and slept until noon every day. It was a dream honeymoon.

The honeymoon was the best part of the marriage.

Back in Boston, they lived in Boyz's apartment on Commonwealth Avenue for almost three years, always too busy even to consider moving to a house. After the honeymoon, Darcy didn't return to classes at Simmons, even though she would have finished her degree that semester.

"Don't go to class," Boyz had coaxed as they lay curled in bed in the morning. "Don't leave me all alone. You're my wife now, not some student."

She could finish her degree later, Darcy had thought, and surrendered to her husband's enticements.

He liked it when she did that.

Darcy did take a part-time job at the Boston Public Library to satisfy her book obsession. Boyz worked with his family, selling real estate. Most nights they ate takeout and collapsed in front of the television, but two or three nights a week they got dolled up and attended events where Boyz and his family could network. Charity events; galas for the ballet, the opera, the library, the hospital. Their lives were a whirlwind. Darcy was too busy to make any new friends or to see her old friends. She did visit her grandmother on the Cape every Sunday. Sometimes Boyz dutifully came with her; most often he did not.

At first, she liked the Szwedas' lifestyle: riding in BMWs, staying at the Four Seasons when they went to New York for theater, drinking Veuve Clicquot. After a year, odd and unsettling thoughts began to seep into her mind. Dita and her daughters were always so accommodating, so willing to please Makary and Boyz. Much of their day—and Darcy's day, too—was about shopping and grooming. Under Dita's knowing eye, Darcy lived on lettuce and salmon, took spin and weight-lifting classes, and kept plenty of Grey Goose vodka on hand for the times when Boyz lost a sale to another Realtor. She glittered at Boyz's side when he took prospective clients to dinner, smiling at the wives' chatter, even when she disagreed with their political views. She ignored Boyz when he flirted with the trophy wives and smiled when male clients with cigar breath put their hands on her knees. She never talked about being a librarian; that was a sure conversation stopper.

Not all the clients were unpleasant. Many of them were delightful and fascinating, and Darcy knew it was an honor to dine with the man who'd won the Nobel Prize or the woman who'd won a Pulitzer. When they spent a summer month on Lake George, she realized she was fortunate to reside in a handsome mansion, swimming, sailing, playing tennis . . . and often, because she faked difficult "female problems," remaining in her room, reading. She felt guilty because the cook had to bring her a tray—the family didn't want to see Darcy when she wasn't "up to it." But for her, a life without reading was flat and meaningless, no matter how fabulous the environment around her.

As the days passed, Darcy decided she had never before known such an active family. When they went to Lake George for a vacation, they didn't lie in a hammock in the shade. They went sailing or Jet Skiing or hiking or at the least swimming. If it rained, they didn't curl up with a good book. They played tennis on their Wii. They had friends over for drinks or dinner—the family called it "networking."

Darcy tried to connect with her husband's family. She tried to admire them and please them. To be like them. She did grow fond of Lena, the youngest of the family, and the most cowed by her outspoken father. Often, she thought she was closer to Lena than to Boyz.

The turning point came the day Lena graduated from college. After the ceremony, Makary Szweda hosted a champagne celebration and dinner for Lena and her classmates in a private room at the posh restaurant Blue Ginger. Darcy had learned that her in-laws liked her to schmooze and cultivate prospective clients, so she behaved with as much charm as possible, and was rewarded by a guarded smile from Boyz's father.

And then Lena clinked her spoon against her champagne flute. In her pale yellow party dress, she was radiant with happiness.

"Thank you all for coming!" she cried, opening her arms as if to gather them all against her. "And thank you, Father, for providing this celebration!" She paused, so everyone could clap for Mr. Szweda. Then she dropped the bomb. "And now I'm going to share some fabulous news— I've been admitted to the University of Chicago Medical School! I'm going to be a doctor!"

Everyone cheered and applauded . . . almost everyone.

Darcy took her husband's hand. "Boyz, isn't this wonderful? I had no idea Lena was"—she almost said *so smart,* but caught herself in time— "interested in med school."

Boyz shook off her hand. Smiling through his teeth, he hissed, "Foolish girl. She knows that's not the plan."

"What do you mean, 'the plan'?"

"You know very well what I mean by *the plan*. My father is building a dynasty. His children will inherit the business, and wc will pass it on to our children."

Darcy froze. She continued to smile, but behind her smile, her thoughts were racing. No, not racing. *Screaming.*

Dismal and embarrassed, she finally *got* it, why Boyz had chosen her—because she was pretty, yes, but mostly, because she was eager to please. She had no family bonds to compete with his. No need to divide or combine holidays, rules, obligations. Indeed, she'd been thrilled to become part of his family, a real true close-knit family who celebrated holidays together and vacationed together and were bound by a common desire: to be the best. At first, Darcy considered this kind of romantic, like a pioneer family harvesting potatoes and putting up jam to keep them all alive during the winter.

It was no longer a romantic dream, and Darcy knew that somehow she'd allowed herself to be drawn away from her first love—her first *passion*—books, reading, libraries. She vowed to herself that she would return to her first, real passion again. She was trying to be who she wasn't, some glitter bug who would impress the Szwedas. She wanted to return to her true self.

Boyz was eager for a child—a son—the next generation in the dynasty. When they were first married, Darcy continued taking birth control pills because she intended to attend Simmons in the fall and finish her master's degree. That didn't happen, but after a year, she still took the pill, although she didn't tell Boyz. She hardly admitted this to herself, she just popped a pill in her mouth after brushing her teeth and put the foil packet back in her Chanel makeup bag.

By their first anniversary, Irena was engaged to

the least famous nephew of a very famous New England political family. The organization of the wedding—for this would be a grand society affair—was splashed all over the newspapers and even made *Town and Country.* It took up almost a year of the Szwedas' lives. Boyz, spurred on to greater achievements in sales, spent more time working and less time in bed with Darcy, and for months at a time forgot he needed Darcy to get pregnant.

By their second anniversary, Darcy had second thoughts about the family she'd married into and about the person she was trying to become to please them. That fall, she returned to Simmons and finished her master's degree in library science. After that, she wanted to take a full-time job at a library.

"No," Boyz said when she told him her idea. "If you're bored, if you want to be part of something like you're always going on about, come work for the company. You're smart, you could get your real estate license—"

"Boyz, I don't *want* a real estate license. I'm a librarian. I want to work in a library."

"Fine." Boyz's jaw tightened as it always did when he was angry. "Be a librarian then, but when you get pregnant, you have to stop working."

"That's a deal," Darcy said.

When she was offered the full-time position

as children's librarian at the Arlington public library, she took it, even though it meant a long and often frustrating drive in heavy traffic every morning and night. It also meant she had to be at the library three nights a week until nine o'clock.

It also meant that one Thursday night, when a water pipe burst in the first-floor bathroom, they had to shut down the building immediately, so Darcy was free to go home early, and when she did—well, it was a cliché, really.

She unlocked the door of their apartment on Commonwealth Avenue.

She called out, "Hello! I'm home early! Have you eaten yet?"

Boyz wasn't in the living room. Or their bedroom. But Darcy heard rustling noises, so she opened the door to their tiny guest bedroom and found Boyz there, in bed with a stunningly endowed redhead.

Darcy, well mannered to a fault, said, "Oh, excuse me." She shut the door and went into the living room and looked out the window at the blazing lights of the city. She was aware of her emotions burning while her fingertips went numb. She felt so *alone*. She wished Penny were there to put her arms around Darcy and console her. Who could she talk to? Maybe Lena, but maybe not. Boyz was, after all, Lena's brother, and Lena adored him. Darcy realized that for the almost three years of their marriage, her closest friends had been Boyz and his sisters. And she had been guarded around even them, always wanting to please, never saying anything that would get back to Boyz and his parents.

She wrapped her own arms around herself and held on tight, letting the shock waves hit her. Astonishment. Pain. Rage. Sorrow. The knowledge that she wasn't enough for Boyz, she had never been enough, she'd never been *right* for him.

And he'd never been right for her.

Boyz came into the room, wearing a shirt held closed by one button. She heard him enter. She saw their reflections wavering in the window. He was tall and handsome and he had become for her a kind of jailer.

Now she was free.

She turned to face her husband, whose hands were held out to the side, ready for his explanation, which would be, she knew, that she left him alone too often.

"Boyz," she said bravely, "I want a divorce."

Boyz said, "So do I."

His words struck her like a slap across the face.

"Wow," Darcy said. "I didn't know you were so unhappy with our marriage."

Boyz sighed heavily. "Darcy, look. Do me a favor. Go into the kitchen and shut the door so I can allow Autumn to leave without running into you."

Darcy was stunned. "Autumn?"

"That's her name. Go on. Then you and I can talk."

Numbly, Darcy walked into the kitchen and shut the door.

Of course, she didn't shut it all the way. She kept it open just enough to be able to catch a glimpse of *Autumn*.

The other woman was older than Darcy, with wavy auburn hair and a fabulous figure displayed to advantage in a tight emerald-green dress. Exactly what an Autumn should look like.

Boyz whispered to Autumn before she went out the door. In response, she wrapped her arms around him and kissed him long and lovingly.

Darcy did an about-face in the kitchen, took out a water glass, and poured it full of wine.

Boyz called, "Come out now, Darcy. Sit down." He'd pulled on a pair of jeans and buttoned his shirt and left the door to the bedroom open. Darcy sat on the sofa. Boyz took a chair across from her.

"You know I care for you, Darcy," Boyz began. "I loved you when we married. I thought you were amazing—of course, you still are, but, let's face it, we haven't grown together in the past three years, we've grown apart."

She didn't respond. The protective detachment that had coated her only a few minutes ago was disappearing now, leaving her shaken and, oddly, ashamed, as if she had failed her husband; she hadn't met his standards. Her legs began to tremble.

"You know how important it is to me to expand my contacts. I'm in a competitive business. And you—a librarian!—have been no help at all in my work. Instead of joining the right clubs, you sit around doing *crossword puzzles!* You *read!* You hide from me in your books."

Darcy's entire body was trembling now as adrenaline hit. As the truth hit.

She nodded toward the bedroom. "So that was Autumn in there, helping you with your work?"

Boyz sucked in air as if he were going to roar. Instead, he paced away from her and then returned to sit on a nearby sofa. "I hate it when you're sarcastic. But, yes, actually, Autumn does help me with my work, because she makes me feel *adored.* Autumn would do anything for me, and she makes me feel like a king."

"Does she work?"

"She's a bit older than I am, and divorced. She's *sophisticated.* She knows how things work. She has a daughter, Willow, who is eleven years old. Autumn was well provided for in her divorce."

Oddly, that cheered Darcy—to know that a divorced woman could be loved.

"You were so eager to please when we first married," Boyz continued. "You were such fun."

"I was so malleable," Darcy whispered, more to herself than to Boyz.

"I thought you'd be an asset to the family business. But you insist on isolating yourself with your books, like, I don't know, like a little old lady. I'm not trying to insult you, Darcy, I still think you're beautiful, but you've grown more and more distant. Frankly, my entire family thinks so."

Darcy nodded her head. She couldn't disagree. Still, it *stung* to know all the other family members had been discussing her.

"If you could change, Darcy"—Boyz held out his hands toward her, as if offering her a gift— "or if you were pregnant, at least, and could give me an heir."

"What about me?" Darcy asked quietly. "What about what *I* want?"

"What else could you possibly want?" Boyz looked genuinely curious.

Darcy buried her face in her hands. She wanted to laugh hysterically; she wanted to sob. She'd thought she was getting a family when she married Boyz. She'd thought they would never divorce—she would *never* be like her mother. But would she ever have a family?

But she *did* have a family. She had Penny.

4

While the legalities of the divorce were grinding along, Darcy moved down to a small rented apartment on the Cape so she could visit her grandmother daily. By then, Penny's vision was so compromised by aging that she couldn't read or even watch television. She was seldom hungry, and when she ate, her digestive system caused her great discomfort. She was on various medications for the lingering consequences of Lyme disease, and the side effects of the medications were almost worse than the pain the disease caused.

Darcy brought fresh-picked flowers from a nearby farm stand to place in Penny's room so she could enjoy the familiar fragrances. She brought expensive delicacies—chocolates, figs, tomatoes fat and red and just picked that morning. Penny did her best to enjoy them, but by then the effort of eating offset the pleasure of the taste. Darcy spent hours reading to her grandmother—old British favorites such as Nancy Mitford's *Love in a Cold Climate*, or a biography of Virginia Woolf and her sister. Penny listened, nodding or chuckling at a certain passage, but she was always rubbing her hands, her arms, trying to ease the arthritic pain. When Darcy closed the book, rose and bent to kiss Penny goodbye for the day, she noticed the relief that swept over her grandmother—how glad Penny was that she no longer had to keep up some kind of pretense, that she could take more pain medication and sink into the oblivion that distanced her from her discomfort.

One day Darcy entered her grandmother's room to find Penny sitting in a chair, dressed and apparently having a good day.

"You look good," Darcy cried happily, kissing Penny's wrinkled pink cheek.

"I don't want to read today," Penny replied tersely. "Sit down."

Darcy obeyed, pulling a chair close to her grandmother. "Does the doctor—"

Penny cut her off. "Just listen."

Darcy nodded. "Jack Truman, on Nantucket, is my lawyer. He has my will. I'm leaving everything to you."

"Oh, Penny—"

"Don't interrupt. I hope you won't sell the house. I hope you will live in it. You know Nantucket has a fine library and I think you could be happy on the island."

"Yes, but—"

"I don't want any kind of memorial service. The people I liked are all dead now, and I don't want Eugene or Lala rushing up to cry crocodile tears and try to convince you to sell the house and split the proceeds with them. Do you understand?"

"I do."

"I want my body cremated. I want my ashes buried in the garden. It may or may not be legal. Lie if you have to, tell the authorities you tossed me into the ocean. I'd like to be next to the lilacs. If that doesn't freak you out too much, of course, to enjoy a garden with your crippled and cranky old grandmother haunting it."

"Penny, I—"

"If I had the power to arrange such things, I would have you live in the house all your life. I would have you marry a man who reads books and have several children who would play in the backyard, and I want you to know I will not be upset if you put up one of those hideous play sets for the children to climb on and slide on and whatever. I like to think I'll be able to hear their laughter."

Tears spilled down Darcy's face.

"You should sell my jewelry. No one wears such heavy pieces anymore, and the proceeds should help you pay taxes and so on. I know librarians don't make much money. The furniture is up to you. Some of it is unsightly, uncomfortable, or useless. Still, much of it is antique and could bring you a pretty penny."

Darcy reached over to put her hand on her grandmother's. "*You're* my pretty Penny."

That brought a smile to her grandmother's face. "You've always been such a clever child." Her body stiffened as she endured a wave of pain. "Go, now, Darcy. Please. Go."

"Penny." Darcy stifled her sobs, which she knew would irritate her grandmother. "I love you so mu—"

"Dear Lord, save me the melodrama. I know you love me. I've always known. Just as you've always known I love you. No more bedside banalities. Just go." Penny took a deep breath. "And ring for the nurse on your way out."

Three days later, Penny Cotterill, eighty-seven years old, died in her sleep.

Darcy obeyed her grandmother's wishes and embroidered on them, just a little, by not informing her father down in Florida about his mother's death until after Penny had been cremated and sprinkled in the garden by the lilacs. She was not surprised when her father's first question was "Has the will been read?"

All her life, Darcy had secretly yearned for a loving father, just as she had wished her mother had been more maternal. But she had learned how love comes in many forms, and often from unexpected directions. She had been blessed to have Penny in her life.

She moved into her grandmother's house on Nantucket. She kept the room she'd always been in, added a luxurious bathroom, and bought a few new appliances for the kitchen. She decided to take her time dealing with the rest of the house. Two weeks after Penny's passing, Darcy applied for a job at the Nantucket Atheneum. To her amazement, she was hired immediately, as the assistant children's librarian. It was March, summer would be upon them before they could blink, and they needed her, especially since she had housing on this crescent-shaped shoal of sand where rents were astronomical in the summer.

All this, she knew, was not *magic*. But she couldn't help believing in even the most rational corner of her mind, that somehow Penny was still somewhere at Darcy's side, nudging, warning, praising. Helping.

Loving.

That was three years ago. As Darcy settled into her new home, she felt lonely, so she went to the Safe Harbor animal shelter and adopted a homeless cat. Muffler was a skinny, skeptical, long-haired black male who'd been abandoned. When she brought him home, he hid under the sofa for two days before the odor of expensive cat food drew him out. Slowly, he grew to trust Darcy. Now he slept on her bed, sat on her lap when he wanted, and bossed her around. She was delighted with his company. Gradually Darcy accustomed herself to the seasons of the island. The library was insanely busy in the summer and quiet in the winter. She made friends with the other librarians; she made friends with other women her age.

So, on this ordinary weekday morning, Darcy woke to her alarm clock. She lay in bed for a while, enjoying the sun slanting through the window, thinking of the day ahead.

Then she remembered yesterday. Boyz. Boyz here, living on the other side of her hedge.

She went down to the kitchen for her morning cup of coffee. She felt like a cat with her hair standing on end because her kitchen looked out at the garden, and it was only natural, a habit, to look out her kitchen window. But now, on the other side of the garden hedge, lived her ex-husband and his family. She couldn't see Boyz's entire yard, but she could see much of it—the driveway, the side porch, a door. Lights in their windows.

She wanted to buy a powerful telescope, set it up, and aim it at their house.

Oh, dear.

Interesting, that she'd never thought about Boyz after they were divorced. She had made a mistake—and so had he. She had not liked the life Boyz lived, and his glamour dissipated for her when she was with him up close every day. After the divorce, she hadn't been inconsolable. She didn't yearn for him. Dream of him. Gaze at old photos of him. She hadn't even googled him, although she'd thought of doing so once or twice.

But now that he was here, next door, where she could hear him and see him, she was fascinated. Was he happy with Autumn? Did he allow clients to paw *her* while he got thoroughly drunk?

What was he doing on Nantucket, anyway? Had he broken away from his family?

Obviously, she would run into them one way or another. Nantucket was a small island, a small town. She couldn't hide from them and she refused to change her life because of their presence. She made a plan, short and simple: When she met Boyz or Autumn on the street, Darcy would smile, say hello, and briskly walk away. She was busy, she had her own life, she had no desire to linger and chat.

And that was all she would allow herself to think about him, because she really was busy. She took a quick shower and dressed, spooned up some yogurt with fresh blueberries, and drank her coffee, idly scrolling on her cell phone for news and weather. She picked up her book bag and laptop, and left for work.

It was a wonderful day. The air smelled sweet, slightly scented with salt and sea. The bushes and flowers gleamed as if they'd been recently polished. Fair Street was a charming old lane, narrow, one-way, with historic houses separated from the brick sidewalks by small, complicated, cleverly planned gardens.

It was such a pleasure to walk past these

houses. Some had clever door knockers or American flags flying above the doors. Some had window boxes spilling over with fresh-faced pansies. In one, next to a large blue and white vase, sat a Siamese cat, as still as a work of art, except for her turquoise eyes, which watched Darcy carefully as she passed.

As she turned on to Main Street, she saw shopkeepers arranging their window displays and preparing to open. It was breezy now, but the weather channels predicted a fine, clear, windless afternoon. Nantucket year-rounders were obsessed with the weather. June, July and August were the months when shopkeepers made the money that would support them through the winter. Cloudy, windy, and rainy days brought the most foot traffic into town because then people couldn't go to the beach. But too many cloudy, windy days made everyone cranky. The beautiful golden beaches, the gentle surf, the warm sun was why people came. The beaches were all open to the public, free, and most of them had lifeguards. This was not the case on most beaches along the East Coast.

On mornings like this, the library was busy, too. Readers rushed in to stock up for the week. The office of the director of the Children's Library where Beverly and Darcy worked was on the ground floor, in a small room tucked in next to the gallery. Later in the day, the gallery was the venue for story times, and Margery Trott taught wildly popular movement, dance, and yoga for children here as well. Darcy couldn't get to her office without going through the gallery, so a couple of extra hours of quiet were worth gold in the summer.

Darcy imagined every librarian in the world enjoyed the same smug tingle when he or she inserted the key into the lock of a door that opened a closed library. It was sort of like opening a new book you've been longing to read. That *anticipation*. Darcy would also admit to a momentary rush of pride and satisfaction. She'd been trusted with the keys to the doors of this grand, historic library. Okay, three other people had, too, and their custodian was often here before or after the library opened and closed, but still. *Still*. She felt like some mythic super-woman who possessed the secrets to opening the treasure chest.

It was silent inside. From where Darcy stood, she could go up the stairs to the children's library and cross the hall to the adult library, and she did that often. She sometimes even climbed the second flight of stairs to the Great Hall, just to be there, alone with all those books and computers and historic oil paintings and the secluded areas with fat comfy armchairs. A female figurehead from an old whaling ship stood in the corner of the small stage at the far end of the room.

Sometimes a librarian dressed the figurehead in a Christmas stocking cap or a wreath of flowers.

Today Darcy headed right down the stairs to her office. The library's basement, like many of the buildings in town, was half in, half above ground. It had its own entrance, and plenty of windows.

Light streamed in as Darcy woke her computer and scanned the various piles and folders on her desk. Summer was always crazy busy on the island, when their winter population of sixteen thousand exploded to sixty thousand. All the nonprofit organizations held at least one fabulous fundraising event—super-glam auctions for items donated by generous supporters held in four-star restaurants. Concerts by popular rock groups or classical musicians, depending on the taste of the benefactors. Nights of dining and dancing under the stars. Cocktail parties in the houses of the dazzlingly rich and famous. The island had just had its annual wine, book, and film festivals, each event with its own superstars to tempt the public to attend.

The library held several summer events. The most exciting was the dance festival, presenting ballet troupes from Boston. Amy Tyrer, head of programming for the library, handled the logistics, coordinating with Grace Pindell, the president of the library's board of trustees. Edith Simon, the library's director, had the responsibility for attending all these galas and festivities, and she did it with her trademark dignified charm. Beverly Maison, the children's library director, also did her charismatic meet and greet at the summer events.

Darcy held down the fort. She took care of a hundred daily minor matters, ordered books, coordinated story hours, and in a pinch manned the circulation desk or did a story hour.

Her job was *delicious*. It was a joy to do the behind-the-scenes slog that kept books available for children or to wander into the staff kitchen for coffee and a chat with the staff and volunteers. The town newspaper came out once a week, on Thursday morning, so it was fun to hear about who bought what house for how many millions, who filed for divorce or bankruptcy, who was in the court report. Two of the circ desk women were party girls, spending every night at bars and parties, returning with all kinds of fun gossip. As they said, if you want to know anything, ask a librarian.

At five o'clock, she said goodbye to everyone and headed home. The town was pleasantly busy but not frantically overcrowded as it became during rainy or windy days later in the summer. People were arriving for their summer rentals, settling in, preparing their home base for the next month or two. If any place on the island was busy, it was the Stop & Shop, where families were filling their carts high, so they would be stocked with food and beach chairs, sun block and tonic water, and could spend the next few sunny days at the beach.

Darcy walked up Main Street, leaving behind the small business district for one of the most beautiful avenues in the country. Wide enough for two buggies to pass each other on the cobblestones of the street, upper Main was graced by historic mansions. Brick or shingled, stately and aloof, these dignified houses had been built by the owners of the whaling ships that had made the town wealthy in the early half of the nineteenth century. The extremely wealthy lived in them now, for a week or so in the summer, before moving on to another of their houses in California or Switzerland. Still, their landscapers kept the flowers blooming all summer and into the fall.

She turned off onto Pine Street, narrow, one-way, and shaded by a canopy of trees. As she walked, she spotted a car parked in the driveway to the left of her house. Aha. More new summer neighbors.

An older woman leaned on a cane, inspecting the hydrangea planted in the small area between the sidewalk and the front of the house. As Darcy approached, she realized the woman was *quite* old—close to the age her grandmother was when she went into the nursing home. Already, Darcy liked her.

"Hello!" Darcy called out.

The old woman turned, a bit unsteadily. Darcy hoped she hadn't startled her. She walked up the drive a few feet, close enough for the older woman to see Darcy, not so near she was intruding.

"Hello," Darcy said again. "I'm Darcy Cotterill. I live right next door." She pointed to her house.

When the old woman smiled, something shone from her face, something generous and welcoming and gentle. Something so much like Penny's expression years ago.

"Hello, dear. I'm Mimi Rush." Slowly, she walked toward Darcy, wincing each time she moved her left leg. Before Darcy could move, Mimi waved a hand. "No, no, stay where you are. I've got to force these old pins to do their job."

She had deep brown eyes and that pure angelic white hair some people get. Her dress was a summer print of lilacs and she wore a lavender cardigan over it. She wore jewelry, too— amethyst earrings and a rather large brooch. A large watch on her wrist.

They shook hands. Mimi's was soft and plump.

"Tell me your name again?" she prompted.

"Darcy. Darcy Cotterill. I live here on the island year-round. I'm the assistant director of the children's library."

"Are you really? What a divine job. You lucky thing. Maybe one day you'll bring home some children's books for me to look at. I miss children's books so much—the illustrations, you know, and the humor. The presentation of the world in the most positive light."

"I know exactly what you mean."

Before Darcy could say more, Mimi continued, "As for me, I haven't *ever* lived here year-round as you say, but I've spent every summer on the island since I was a baby." She paused, dramatically, before adding, "Eighty-nine years."

"How wonderful."

"Oh, my dear, you have no idea. Nantucket means *summer* to me. I didn't think I'd be able to come to the island this summer—this past year has been rough on my ancient carcass. I've been living in a retirement home. Not assisted living. I can still take care of myself, bathe and cook and so on. But if I need someone immediately, a doctor or a nurse or simply a strong man to help me if I've fallen, all I have to do is press a button. Of course, they take care of the outside—shoveling snow, mowing the grass—and I have a housecleaning service and a food delivery service, so I'm not *really* dependent. But I don't have the same sort of help available here." She paused to catch her breath. Her eyes twinkled when she continued. "I am going to stop talking, I promise. I'm not one of those poor lonely creatures who babbles on endlessly when they've managed to trap someone. The point is, I had resigned myself to missing summer here, and then my marvelous grandson said he'd come here with me, and stay with me, for two entire months!" Mimi pounded her cane into the ground for emphasis. "How lucky is that?"

"I'm so glad for you."

More eye twinkles, and Mimi sort of playfully cocked her head to the side. "He's handsome, too. And single. Well, divorced."

Darcy laughed.

"Of course any grandmother would say that about her grandson, but wait till you meet him."

Darcy tried to derail her from the grandson topic. "Do you ever visit the library?"

"My dear young thing, I used that library before you were even born. I'm a compulsive reader, always have been. One of the benefits of getting older is that I forget what I've read, so I have a world of choices."

"We have a lot of programs going on, too. Lectures in the Great Hall—and I'm sure you know there's an elevator in the building now that goes from ground level in the garden up to the main floor and on up to the Great Hall."

"Oh, yes, I use that elevator and—" She broke off when the front door of her house opened and a man stepped out.

"Clive!" Mimi called. "Come meet our next-door neighbor."

Darcy's polite smile softened as the man approached. Clive Rush *was* handsome. Broad

shouldered, muscular, dark haired, brown eyed—
and unhurried. It was rare to meet a man her
age who wasn't in a hurry. Darcy made a silent
bet with herself: He was not a lawyer, business
executive, or Wall Street trader. And he was here
for two months with his grandmother? Nice,
Darcy supposed, but also kind of weird.

He held out his hand. "Clive Rush."

"Darcy Cotterill."

"She's a *children's librarian,*" Mimi piped up.
Turning to Darcy, she announced, "Clive is a
compulsive reader, too."

Darcy usually kept her distance from summer
people. Okay, "keeping her distance" was the
wrong phrase, because the houses, like all
Nantucket houses in town, were built close
together. But Darcy tried to be friendly, yet
reserved. It was a necessity for self-protection.
She had a life. Her schedule was full. She was
not, like the summer people, on vacation.

Still, if Clive asked Darcy to spend an evening
with Mimi so he could go out to a movie or a
party, Darcy wouldn't mind doing it. Mimi was
adorable, and Darcy would bet she knew a lot of
Nantucket history.

"Nice to meet you, Mimi, Clive." With one last
smile at Mimi, Darcy turned away.

Few Nantucket houses had lawns in the front.
Most houses bordered right on the sidewalk,
as Darcy's did, which was a wonderful thing,

because in just a few seconds, she walked up her front steps and entered her house.

She headed into the kitchen and poured herself a glass of the iced tea she kept in the refrigerator. The cold liquid was bracing, but Darcy wanted a *drink*. She preferred a glass of red wine while she cooked or when she was settled in front of the fire with a good book on a snowy winter night, but tonight, for some reason, Darcy wanted to drink with a friend.

She also wouldn't mind showing Mimi and her grandson that she wasn't some spinster librarian bowled over by Clive's good looks.

Muffler jumped off the kitchen counter and sauntered up to her, purring and waving his long soot-black tail.

"Yes," Darcy said to Muffler. "You're right. I may be a spinster librarian with a cat but I've got a gorgeous hunk of a lover."

She called Nash. "Come over for a drink?"

"I'm there."

Nash was a man of few words. Easygoing, a hiker, a traveler, a new guy in town, unattached and untethered to the usual duties and expenses of men his age. He said he'd come to Nantucket because the money was great and he liked construction work. Darcy suspected there was more to his story, but she didn't pry. Nantucket was a prime spot for people to invent themselves. He would tell her when he was ready.

Nash drove a red 2016 Super Duty Platinum Ford truck and would arrive straight from work, wearing jeans, a T-shirt, and work boots. When he roared onto her street, any neighbors who happened to look would know that a world-class hunk was in her life.

She'd met Nash earlier in the year, at a St. Patrick's Day party thrown by the group that Jordan and her contractor husband, Lyle, hung out with. When Darcy saw him, she got that swooning physical hit that had stopped her in her tracks the way her first sight of Boyz had. She hadn't felt that for a man since she'd met Boyz, and she wasn't sure whether that was a good sign or bad. That day had been rainy, so they couldn't cook out, and as often happened at these parties, the women hung with the women and the men with the men. Nash hadn't spoken to her that day, but he'd caught her eye and smiled.

Nash didn't approach her at any of the other casual get-togethers during that cold wet spring. Darcy hadn't spoken to him, either, which was strange. She would only have had to walk across the room with a platter of deviled eggs to start a conversation. It was the crowd, she realized, the gang. All good-natured, no malice among them, but they all, man and woman, noticed when a couple hooked up. That she was even thinking about this made her aware of her interest in the tall, sandy-haired man.

It had been a long time since she'd gone to bed with a man.

She'd never been one to make the overtures, but one exceptionally warm and bright Sunday afternoon in May at the group's first beach party of the year, she chugged some beer and swallowed her pride and crossed the sand to speak to him. He was leaning over the tailgate of his truck, reaching for beach chairs.

"Hey," she said.

"Hey," he answered.

And then they both were speechless, staring at each other, the physical attraction between them so powerful it was as if they'd stepped into a force field.

Nash cleared his throat and spoke. "I'm Nash Forester." Before she could speak, he said, "And you're Darcy Cotterill. You're thirty, divorced, and a librarian. Unattached at the moment, though only heaven knows why."

She blushed. "This group! They probably told you my IQ and weight."

"Actually, no. But if you're a librarian, you're plenty smart, and I can guess at a glance that you're light enough that I could pick you up and throw you over my shoulder without getting out of breath."

The very thought of this man even touching her flooded her cheeks with a deep blush. Fighting for a pittance of dignity, she cocked her head.

"And you're new to the island, working as a carpenter, good with tools, and I'm pretty sure if I invited you to dinner, you'd like my lasagna."

Well! she congratulated herself. *You just hit on a man.* It seemed like her hormones were up and running again.

Nash grinned. "I'm pretty sure if you served me a bowl of cereal, I'd be happy."

From behind them, Lyle bellowed, "Hot dogs are ready! Burgers! Get 'em while they're hot!"

"Hungry?" Darcy asked.

"Yeah." He had a crooked grin. "Before we plunge back into the crowd, let me ask if you're busy next Saturday night."

"No, I'm not busy." None of this "let me check my calendar" stuff. If she had something on her calendar, she'd cancel it.

"Good. Let me take you out to dinner."

"I'd like that."

Karl Ledbetter yelled, "Darcy! Nash! Stop flirting and get over here before all the food's gone!"

Darcy turned, keeping her face down, in case she was still glowing like a teenager on her first date. Beside her, Nash muttered, "Just like high school."

After that, they didn't have a chance to be alone. Eloise and Mac announced that they were expecting a baby and everyone cheered. When Darcy left, she searched the crowd. Nash was talking to a group of men, but he had his eye on her. She waved. He waved. She felt like a Disney heroine about to burst into song.

The next morning, as she walked to work, she called Jordan from her cellphone to tell her she had a date with Nash.

"Oh, man," Jordan moaned. "He is so hot. Listen, you stay home with Kiks and I'll go in your place."

Darcy laughed. "Yeah, Lyle would go for that."

"Lyle who?" Jordan joked.

All that day, as she worked in the library, her mind wandered back to that moment on the beach. To Nash's smile. His blue eyes. His deep voice.

The next afternoon, she carried some books that had been left on the children's librarian's desk across to the adult library.

At first, she thought she was hallucinating. Nash was standing in the new nonfiction section, pulling a book off the shelf.

Had he come here to see her? Darcy shook her head. Of course not—she was expecting way too much too soon.

Nash lifted his head and saw Darcy. He smiled that smile.

How could she not go over to say hello?

"Hey, Nash," she greeted him. "I didn't know you read."

"Yeah," he replied teasingly, "I learned how in

elementary school. It's just like riding a bicycle."

She laughed. "I meant I was surprised to see you in the library. During the day."

Nash nodded toward the windows. "We've got a thunderstorm and gale-force wind going on. No way to work on the roof today. I'm going back to work on the interior, but this is my lunch break, so I thought I'd stop in. Had to return some books anyway."

Some books? She couldn't hide her surprise. "You're a reader?"

"I am."

"Most of the guys in our group would rather have their fingernails pulled out than read a book."

Nash looked hard into Darcy's eyes. "I'm not most guys."

It took her a moment to compose herself. "What kind of books do you like?"

"All kinds. Nonfiction, fiction, thrillers. John le Carré is my all-time favorite. I like Henning Mankell, Kitty Pilgrim."

"I like them, too," Darcy agreed. "Well, I pretty much like everything that's ever been written. When do you have time to read?"

"In the evening. All evening. Okay, sometimes I watch the Red Sox. But most television bores me."

"Have you ever read John Buchan?"

Nash nodded. *"The Thirty-Nine Steps.* Yeah, I have read that book, but a long time ago."

"I have a DVD of the movie, the one directed by Alfred Hitchcock."

"That's a classic. Haven't seen it in years."

"Maybe we could watch it this Saturday. At my house. You could bring dinner—a pizza?"

"I'd like that," Nash said, his eyes warm, his voice low.

Darcy thought she'd melt right into the floor.

That night they didn't watch the movie. They didn't have the pizza Nash brought over until Darcy left their tangled sheets and brought the pizza up to eat in bed.

Nash was tall and lanky, with lots of sandy hair going in all directions—it did that naturally, unless he brushed it hard; he wasn't a man for gelling his hair up into spikes. His eyes were light blue, fringed with dark lashes, and he had the strong, well-muscled torso of a man who worked building houses.

Darcy wasn't sure how she felt about Nash really. He was mysterious. And she had come out of a long, cold, lonely Nantucket winter, so she'd been ready for a warm—sexually hot—relationship. She didn't know if she wanted it to be more than that. She didn't know what Nash wanted, either.

Today it was enough to know that Nash was coming over.

She changed out of her library lady clothes into a pair of shorts and a tank top. She put cheese, olives, nuts, and crackers on a tray to take out to the garden. And why not? She often sat in the garden with friends or alone when it was nice like it was today. She wasn't trying to put on a show for her ex-husband or her next-door neighbors. She was simply living her life.

In the garden, she set the tray on the patio table and poured herself a glass of red wine. She strolled around the garden, checking out the flowers. The peonies were past their prime but the hydrangea were opening. She didn't hear any voices from behind the hedges. It was only six o'clock on a warm summer day; her neighbors were probably still at the beach.

"Heigh-ho," Nash called as he walked beneath the arbor and into the backyard. He wore jeans and a clean T-shirt.

"Hey, Nash." Darcy watched him as he walked. It was very pleasant to watch him.

Nash kissed her lightly on the mouth—more friendly than amorous—and threw himself into a chair.

She sat across from him, handing him a glass of wine. "So how was your day?"

"Great. I was out near Surfside, working with Ramos's crew. Hammering nails, rock on the radio, fresh air, sunshine, nice work." He sipped his wine. "And you?"

"It was good. The summer families are trickling in. I spent a lot of time on the computer. Ordering books, answering emails. Tomorrow will be fun. I'll be doing a couple of story times."

"For little kids, right?"

"Yeah, those squirmy little rabbits. They're so adorable."

"My grandmother used to read Sherlock Holmes to me when I was around ten years old. I was all about sports. Thought I'd be a major league baseball player or maybe a star quarterback. Then I broke my big toe. It hurt like crazy, I couldn't go out for sports that spring, I had to wear an ugly boot, and worse, I broke my *big toe*. There's no glory in breaking a big toe."

"How did you break it?" Darcy asked, laughing. It was the first time he'd ever spoken in depth about his life. She wanted to ask him so much— *his grandmother?* She wanted to hear all about her. And Sherlock Holmes? Darcy adored those books.

"I kicked a rock." Nash shook his head at the memory. "It was on the beach, I thought it was just lying there, didn't see that it was like an iceberg, most of it down beneath the sand—"

A car pulled into the drive on the other side of the hedge. Doors slammed. Voices were carried by the breeze over the hedge to Darcy's she-was-ashamed-to-admit-it straining ears.

"I get the first shower." *The teenage girl. Willow.*

"I'll start the coals on the grill." *Boyz.* "I'll

rinse off in the outdoor shower and have a proper scrub down later."

"Willow, there are two bathrooms, you know." *The mother.*

"Yeah, but the water pressure changes and I can't get enough hot water if someone else uses the other shower." *Willow.*

"All right, go ahead. Honey, I'm going to pour myself a drink. Would you like one?" *The mother. The wife. Autumn.*

"A gin and tonic with lots of ice would hit the spot." *Boyz.*

"Darcy? Earth to Darcy."

She forced her attention to her own backyard. Nash was frowning.

"Sorry, Nash. Sorry." Her whole ridiculous little plan was backfiring. Boyz had no idea that his ex-wife was so near, talking with her lover. Instead, Darcy couldn't even concentrate on what Nash was saying because she couldn't *stop* eavesdropping on Boyz! She put her hand to her forehead. "I think I'm getting a headache. Too much going on."

"Should I go home and let you lie down?" Nash asked gently.

"No, no, I want to hear about you and Sherlock Holmes and the rock."

"*Sherlock Holmes and the Rock,*" Nash intoned in a radio announcer's voice.

"*Sherlock Holmes and the Case of the Broken*

Big Toe," Darcy shot back, proving she'd listened to at least some of what he'd said. "Why do people enjoy mysteries so much, Nash? The littlest children don't understand mysteries, but around seven or eight years old they can't get enough."

"For me, it never stopped." Nash held out his hands. "I'm a hopeless mystery addict. Especially in the summer, when I'm too beat to read anything intellectual."

"I'm that way, too!" Darcy exclaimed.

"Here's your drink, darling. When do you think the coals will be ready?"

"Thanks. Let's give them thirty minutes."

"It will take Willow that long to shower." Laughter.

They sounded so happy together. So complete. How had it happened that Darcy had been captivated by Boyz, and he by her, and they had married, and then everything absolutely went to shit? They had married too soon—she knew that was why, she'd thought about it endlessly, talked to friends, talked to a counselor—and she had gotten over it, she *was* over it, but what in the world did it mean that Fate had set him down right there, on the other side of the hedge of her own backyard?

Fate probably had nothing to do with it. It was only a mistake—people made mistakes all the time—but still, how could she trust her own instincts? Was she going to end up like her mother, going from man to man, genuinely infatuated at first, then losing that rush and needing another, like some kind of drug addict? Was that sort of thing genetic? But, no, she *wasn't* like that, she hadn't gone from man to man; after Boyz she had retreated into herself; it had been three years since Boyz left her for another woman, and she hadn't even kissed another man for the first two years. Finally, she'd slept with Nick Diaz. It was a cold winter, her friends urged her to *just do it,* and Nick was a really good guy. It had been very pleasant, too, going to bed with Nick, but they both knew it wasn't the beginning of a serious relationship. They never hooked up again, although when they saw each other at parties they were both friendly. After Nick, Darcy had a self-imposed drought before meeting Nash this spring. . . .

"Okay, so I'm going home." Nash stood up, yanking her back to the present.

How long had she been caught up in the chaos of her thoughts? Long enough to cause Nash to leave. "I'm so sorry, Nash, I'm not usually so hopeless, at least I hope I'm not—"

"Don't worry about it." Leaning over, he kissed her forehead.

She inhaled the good strong scent of Nash, soapy and sweaty and masculine and she wanted to take him by the hand and lead him up to her bedroom. Instead, she trailed behind him as he went under the arbor and around the side of the house to his truck. She didn't want him to leave, but she couldn't promise herself her mind wouldn't wander.

"I'm always like this at the beginning of the summer," she told him as he stepped up into the cab.

"Good to know." He smiled at her—a genuine, not-forced smile—and took off.

She dragged herself up the steps and into the house by the front door, not wanting to expose herself to any more backyard conversations. She shut the door and leaned against it, suddenly lethargic. She had to do something about this. She couldn't hide in her house, missing the joys of her backyard and garden. She wasn't a *weakling*. The crazy thing was that she hadn't missed Boyz *ever*, so why was she turning into such a nut job when she overheard him and his family? On the other hand, what the hell was Boyz even doing here? He should be at Lake George. Did this mean that the gorgeous Autumn had insisted on spending their vacation anywhere except with all the other Szwedas? Darcy could imagine that Autumn had distanced herself from Boyz's sisters and mother. Maybe that was exactly what Boyz needed.

She had to stop thinking about Boyz! She wanted to reach into her mind with invisible tweezers and yank out all knowledge of him. Or swallow a magic pill that would erase all thoughts of him—that would do the trick.

"Buck up!" Darcy told herself. In the low policeman's voice she used sometimes when reading stories to the children at the library, she added, "Miss, walk away from the door."

Behind her back, someone knocked on the door. Darcy let out a small shriek of surprise. Good, she thought. Nash was back.

But she opened the door to find a pretty and rather distraught woman standing there.

"Oh, thank heavens you're home!" She was wringing her hands. "I'm Susan Brueckner, we're renting next door for the summer"—she pointed to the house on her right—"and I forgot to buy milk. Otto said he wasn't coming but now he is and the boys can have their cereal raw—I don't mean *raw*—what do I mean? *Dry!* I mean dry! But Otto has to have milk in his coffee, and he always has a cup in the evening, and I'm wondering if I could borrow some milk? I'll pay it back tomorrow. The boys—they're nice boys, truly, Henry is ten, George is eight, and Alfred is six—are unsettled right now, we only just arrived, and I can't pack them all back into the car and I don't know where the grocery store is!"

Susan Brueckner was not the normal Nantucket visitor, but Darcy was instantly charmed. *Did people even ask a neighbor for anything these days?* Susan Brueckner expected the world to be helpful, and Darcy liked her for that. Susan was a pretty blue-eyed blonde, rather—wasn't the German word zaftig?—plump but comely.

When she paused for breath, Darcy held out her hand. "Hello, Susan, I'm Darcy Cotterill. I'd be delighted to give you some milk. Come in."

"This is so very kind of you. I'm not usually so disorganized. . . ." Susan followed Darcy down the hall and into the kitchen, her voice trailing off as she looked at the house, the thick Persian rugs, handsome furniture, and oil paintings that had been Penny's, Penny's pine table with pink and lavender snapdragons in a white vase centered neatly in the middle. Darcy's kitchen counters were shining clean, with delft blue and white ceramic canisters filled with flour, sugar, salt, and rice.

Darcy poured milk into a pitcher and handed it to Susan.

Susan said, "Please tell me you don't have children."

For a moment, Darcy was puzzled, but when Susan gestured around the room, Darcy understood. If Darcy had three boys, this was not how her kitchen would look.

"I don't have children."

"Oh." Susan put a hand to her chest. "I'm so glad. Oh, sorry, I don't mean to be rude, but my house has never looked so calm, so neat." Susan took the pitcher of milk and stared down into it. "It is a great disappointment to Otto. I wish I could change, but with three boys . . ." Susan bit her lip impatiently, holding back, Darcy imagined, a flood of words.

"I'm a children's librarian," Darcy said, "so I do understand the chaos children cause."

"Thank you! And for the milk, too. I'd better hurry back before our house is destroyed." At the front door, she paused. "I've never been to Nantucket before. We live in Boston—my husband's a lawyer—I didn't know everything would be so perfect here, so *beautified*. I wish we hadn't come here, my boys make so much *noise,* and all the women are thin and it's like *dust* wouldn't dare exist!"

Darcy couldn't help laughing. "I promise you, we've got plenty of dust. And plenty of normal women. Take your boys to the beach every day, let them swim in the ocean, and they'll be too exhausted to make noise in the evening."

Susan's face lit up. "Oh, what a kind thing to say. You're so nice. You must be a therapist."

"Um, no," Darcy gently reminded her. "I'm a children's librarian."

"Of course! Forgive me! I'm not a complete idiot, you know."

With that, Susan hurried back to her house, waving and calling thanks.

Darcy waved back, smiling, and closed the front door. She was immeasurably cheered. Someday maybe she would have a husband and children, but for now, she curled up on the sofa and picked up her current novel, and she felt even a little bit smug.

5

The next afternoon, not even five minutes after Darcy returned home from work, a tow-haired, straight-backed little boy appeared at her door with Darcy's pitcher in one hand and a gallon carton of milk in the other.

"My name is Henry Brueckner and my mother says thank you very much," the boy said.

His dignity was touching. "Thank you, Henry," Darcy told him, accepting the pitcher. "But this is much more than your mother borrowed. Let me pour some into my pitcher and you can take the rest home."

Henry looked worried by her words. He was a very formal child, one, undoubtedly, who as the oldest was often made responsible for doing the right thing. Darcy's offer confused and even dismayed him. How to decide? Should he hurry home and ask his mother or go ahead and accept her offer? After all, Darcy was an adult, so he should respect her decision.

"Come in for a moment," Darcy said.

Henry looked horrified. "My mother said I shouldn't bother you."

"Oh. Oh, I see. Well, stay right there." She hurried to the kitchen, poured some milk into her pitcher, and returned to the front door. "Now.

Tell your mother I took exactly what I loaned."

Henry's face brightened. What Darcy said made sense.

"And please tell her I'm very happy to meet such a polite and dependable young man."

Henry turned bright red. "Thank you," he said, and turned to hurry away.

"Henry," Darcy called. "We have a wonderful library here with lots of events for kids your age and story hours for your younger brothers."

He nodded and rushed off, clutching the carton of milk to his chest.

The next day was a rainy, windy, blustery day. After a couple of days on the beach with lots of sunshine, the summer people would be happy to use the library for a change of pace. If there were too many rainy days in a row, the adults and their children came in, restless and grumpy, as if the librarians had caused the weather.

Today so many children flocked in for story time that Darcy and Beverly knew from experience it would be impossible to keep order, so they quickly counted heads and split the children into two groups. Beverly took the older children down the stairs to the gallery. Darcy chose the area between two bookcases with the younger children.

"Today I'm going to read *The Mousehole Cat*," Darcy announced. She sat on a small wooden chair. The children sat on the floor and some of the parents did the same or perched on the child-size chairs at the perimeter of the group.

As everyone got settled, Darcy recognized Susan and her brood of blond boys. She winked and smiled to them. Susan smiled back. Darcy held the book high as she read; she had the words almost completely memorized. It was a charming story set in a harbor town in Cornwall that was not so different from Nantucket. After she finished the book, she asked the children questions—"Do you have a cat? Do you like stories about dogs? About boats?"—and directed them to books they could take home. It was such a pleasure to see children leaving the library, happily clutching books to their chests. She hoped Susan would come say hello, but by the time the crowd around Darcy had thinned, Susan and her boys were gone.

Over the next few days, the sun grew fatter and closer and more intense. After work in the afternoons, Darcy slipped into the restroom and changed into a bathing suit, pulled her sundress back on over it, and walked down to Jetties Beach for a cooling swim. She didn't go there as often as she should, like a New Yorker never visiting the Empire State Building. Darcy went to different beaches for different reasons. The south shore was good for surf and crashing storms. Darcy preferred the calm waters of the Sound at Steps Beach for swimming, but that was a much longer walk. If she had an afternoon off, she drove out to Quidnet and swam in the sweet waters of Sesachacha Pond or, her favorite, at the end of the harbor at Coskata, a small lonely beach past the Wauwinet Hotel, off a rutted dirt road that required a four-wheel-drive vehicle. Jetties Beach was usually too crowded, but today, by the time she got there, the crowds had thinned out as people left for dinner.

In the late afternoon, wearing a loose cotton dress over her wet bathing suit, her long hair hanging damp and cool down her back, Darcy walked from Jetties Beach over to the narrow cobblestoned lane she called Jelly Bean Road. She climbed the hill and ambled over to Main Street, circling past the crowded downtown area with its shops and crowds and never enough parking spots.

Her pulse quickened as she came to her street. So far she'd stayed away from her garden in the late afternoons, not wanting to be seen by Boyz, not wanting even to think about him. On the other hand, she didn't want to be a coward, fenced in by her own anxieties. She knew that if, for example, Boyz and his family were playing croquet in their yard, that did not mean she had to hide inside. Her garden was her connection with her grandmother, and more—it was her *place*. She *had* to weed and plant and trim. She wanted to have friends over for summer parties, when she strung the trees and bushes with miniature lights so the garden sparkled like a magic land. She had to be able to sit alone on her patio and read until darkness fell, and then let the book drop to her lap and her head fall back on the chaise so she could watch the sky slowly and tenderly transform the sun's gold into evening's silver as stars appeared. This was a special time for her, almost a sacred time, and she wouldn't allow herself to give it up.

At home, Darcy tossed her book bag on a chair and headed for the kitchen. This evening, she was determined to enjoy her backyard. She chose a Pinot Noir from her small wine rack and was uncorking it when she glanced out her kitchen window and saw, in the next yard, something out of place, peculiar, unsettling.

Had someone dumped a bundle of clothes in her neighbor's yard? But, no, there was movement—and all at once she realized that Mimi, that dear old grandmother, was lying on the ground, unable to rise.

Darcy set the wine down and raced out her front door, squeezed through the narrow passageway between houses, not caring if she broke a few petals off the blue hydrangea, and burst into the backyard.

"Mimi?" Darcy dropped to her knees beside the older woman, who lay facedown in the grass, her blue frock twisted all around her body.

Awkwardly, Mimi turned her head. "Oh, Darcy, dear. I'm so glad to see you. I was sitting in the lawn chair, and got too warm, and stood up to go inside, and *bam,* down I went like a villain on TV."

"Did you break anything? Do you hurt anywhere?"

"I might have twisted my right ankle. It hurts like the devil when I try to stand. I use a cane because of my wonky left ankle, so I do seem rather . . . grounded."

"Where's Clive?"

"Off buying groceries, doing errands. I promised him I wouldn't come outside on my own, but a day like this is irresistible. . . ."

"Let's see if we can turn you over and get you into a sitting position."

"I'd appreciate that."

They discussed the logistics of the maneuver— should Darcy push on Mimi's left side or her right? If Mimi could lift up a bit, Darcy could give her a gentle heave with one hand on her hip and one on her thigh. They counted to three and Darcy pushed. In vain. Mimi weighed a good one hundred eighty pounds, and many of those pounds were good healthy padding, perfect for protecting her when she fell but difficult to shift. Also, Darcy discovered that Mimi's upper arm strength was more or less nonexistent. All this meant that when Darcy shoved on Mimi's hip and leg, she managed to rotate the lower half of Mimi's body backward, but the upper half of her body stayed put and the lower half was finally, inexorably, pulled by gravity back down to the ground.

Mimi was trembling. She muttered something incomprehensible. For a chilling moment Darcy feared the older woman had had a stroke and lost her ability to speak. Darcy knelt close to Mimi's head and gently touched her neck. She didn't know what she was doing. All she could think of was what she saw on television cop shows: If someone was incapacitated, moving her head could cause injury to her neck.

"Did I hurt you?" Darcy asked.

Mimi spoke again, more slowly. "I have grass in my nose." She was laughing. Her whole body shook as she laughed.

Her laughter was contagious. "Shall I move your head sideways? Does your neck feel okay?"

"*Please* move my head sideways."

Carefully, unable to stop laughing, Darcy lifted Mimi's head and turned it sideways. A sprinkling of dirt and a few stray filaments of grass coated the older woman's nose and cheeks.

"Shall we try again?" Darcy asked.

"Yes. This time pretend I'm a rug, one of those heavy Persian rugs. Just unroll me."

They had both gotten giddy and breathless, giggling like children. Darcy positioned herself with her knees firmly on the ground, one hand on her shoulder, the other on her hip.

"On the count of three," Darcy said.

"Mimi!" Clive was suddenly there. "What happened? Are you okay?"

"I fell, darling, that's all," Mimi, still planted facedown in the grass, assured him. "Darcy's been trying to help me roll over, a Sisyphean task, it seems."

"You shouldn't be out here. You promised you'd stay in your chair in the living room."

"Dear boy, don't lecture me while my face is in the dirt. It's hard for me to concentrate."

"Sorry. Okay. Let me get you up."

"Can I help you?" Darcy asked.

He studied the situation. "No, thanks. I've got this." Straddling his grandmother's recumbent body, he wrapped his arms around her upper torso and gently lifted her, turned her, and brought her into a sitting position, her back against the lawn chair. Darcy held her breath, watching to see if there was anything she could do to help. And noticing, in spite of herself, Clive's body. He was of medium height but had large, wide bones; wide shoulders; large, long-fingered hands. He looked sturdy, strong, brawny; and he gently lifted his grandmother up and into her chair as if she weighed little more than a child.

When he got Mimi settled, he wasn't even winded.

Mimi was. While Mimi caught her breath, Darcy hurried to rearrange the flurried mess of Mimi's skirt and slip. She wore white sneakers with Peds.

"You have such pretty ankles," Darcy told her.

"I do, don't I! How nice of you to notice."

Clive looked at the two of them as if they were lunatics. "Pretty ankles? Mimi, your *pretty* ankles won't support you, and you know it." He glared at Darcy. "Did you bring her out here? Because obviously, she's not really ambulatory."

"Stop it, Clive," Mimi ordered. "I came out here myself, and I was ambulatory enough to get here. My cane is right there, just out of reach. I sat in the lawn chair in the sun for a while, and it was so pleasant, feeling the sun on my face, hearing the birds sing. Only when I decided to go back inside did my ankles give out on me, and down I went, all nicely cushioned by my blubber. Darcy saw me from her window and rushed over to help me." She grinned. "We were just getting started when you arrived."

The tension left Clive's shoulders. He smiled at Darcy. "Well, then, Darcy, thank you for helping her. I'm sorry if I was abrupt. She is such a bad patient, always getting into trouble when she should stay quiet—*as her doctor has told her many times.*"

Before Darcy could respond, Mimi chirped, "We're all here now and no harm done. Why don't you fix a nice cold pitcher of margaritas and the three of us can enjoy the evening?"

"Another time, Mimi," Clive said. "You've had a fall and you know you should rest. And I need to put away the groceries."

Darcy could see a small lump beginning to grow right where Mimi's cheek had hit the ground. She knew some things about the elderly, because of her own grandmother, and one of them was that their bodies were more fragile than younger bodies. Mimi was probably bruised elsewhere from her fall. She did need to rest.

"Thanks for the offer, Mimi," Darcy said. "I'd better get home."

"Thank you for helping me, dear. We must do it again sometime."

Darcy grinned. "We'll get you over to my garden some afternoon. I'll serve margaritas."

Darcy rose, made a humorous salute, said goodbye, and walked out of their yard. Mimi, she thought, was just plain adorable. Clive was gorgeous, but kind of severe. Still, she didn't know all that he knew about Mimi's condition.

Besides, Darcy thought as she stepped into her own house, it never had been her habit to get involved with her summer neighbors. This neighborhood was not like those on the mainland where neighbors called to each other from yard to yard and became familiar, family with family. Many of the people who had rented houses around

Darcy were astoundingly rich. They sent their kids here with nannies and a housekeeper and arrived on island themselves only to throw fabulous parties before taking their private jets back to New York.

In any case, today Darcy'd had more interaction with her summer neighbors than she usually had in months.

In the kitchen, the bottle of uncorked Pinot Noir awaited and she had messages on her cellphone. First she fed Muffler, who was twining gracefully around her ankles like a warm feather boa. Then she hit the play button.

Nash's low mellow voice: "Hey, Darcy, I'm still at the site. We're going to take advantage of the light and work until eight, so, as much as I'd like to, I'm not going to stop by for a drink tonight. I'll go home, hit the shower, eat a microwaved something, and go to bed. Hope you had a good day."

Jordan was next. "Darcy, a bunch of us are going out to Cisco this Sunday for an all-day picnic. Want to come and bring Nash? And a potluck something? Let me know. Kisses from Kiks and from me, too."

The rest were junk calls from telemarketers. Darcy erased them.

Outside, the sun was sinking, turning the sky into a Crayola box of colors. She was hungry, but she didn't feel like cooking, so she carried her wine and a bowl of mixed nuts out to her garden. It was still, no breeze ruffling the leaves, and no voices from any side of her hedges. She strolled around the perimeter, studying the flowers. Her Knock Out rosebush needed to be deadheaded, but she could do that tomorrow morning before she set off for the library. For now, she put the nuts and her wine on the patio table and sank onto her lounger and let her head fall back. It was quiet, the only sound the twittering of the birds high up in the trees. She allowed herself to relax, go limp, and breathe deeply. For a few moments she sort of blurred into the past. It was as if Penny were just out of sight at the other end of the garden, humming as she cut back the pansies and violets so new blooms would come. Darcy wanted to be a grandmother someday. If she could still be here, in this house, and she had her own granddaughter visiting . . . that would be heaven on earth.

She dozed a while and woke to find that darkness had fallen. Somehow a short nap outside was twice as refreshing as any sleep inside. Muffler had joined her and was curled in a silky fat ball of black fur on Darcy's legs. For a while, she gazed at the sky, spotting Venus and several constellations. From the three houses around her—Mimi's, Boyz's, and Susan's—golden lights beamed. Occasionally people would flicker past or voices would drift from the windows. Her stomach growled. She decided to make herself a scrambled egg sandwich.

"Come on, old friend," she said to her cat. "Let's go in."

Muffler stretched and yawned, making it clear that he'd go when he got good and ready. Darcy stroked his satiny head and moved her legs. He jumped lithely to his feet and they went into the house for the night.

6

Thursday evening after a light dinner, Darcy walked to St. Paul's Church, a handsome stone building only a few blocks from her home. The Women's Chorus of Nantucket was having its rehearsal there tonight. Usually the concerts were only twice a year, once at Christmas, once at Easter, but this year a notable and cherished woman "had gone aloft" and the women wanted to perform a tribute to her when the year-rounders and the summer people who knew her could attend. The Women's Chorus was not a professional group, but for amateurs they were pretty good. They were not performing for a month, but summer schedules were so wacky for everyone, they had to meet when everyone could.

Their indomitable leader, Beth O'Malley, had chosen songs that reflected the passion of Sylvia Marks, islander, wife, mother, grandmother, great-grandmother, and ardent birder. She led the Sunday morning bird walks for twenty-five years, wrote a book on the birds of Nantucket complete with her notes and photos, and inspired generations of young and old to appreciate the mysterious creatures that flew around the island. So the program consisted of songs about birds, especially songs that they knew Sylvia would enjoy. "Blackbird" by the Beatles, "Yellow Bird" by Chris Isaak, and "Rockin' Robin" by Bobby Day were in pretty good shape. Today they concentrated on an old dreamy favorite, "Skylark," written by Johnny Mercer and Hoagy Carmichael in 1941, and performed by singers from Ella Fitzgerald to k.d. lang. It sounded best when it was smooth, silky, languorous, and as a group, they hadn't achieved anything near smooth. Beth was wondering if this should be sung as a solo, and she was hinting that she wanted Darcy to be the soloist. Darcy hinted back: No way.

Rehearsal lasted about an hour and it was a tribute to how much they revered Sylvia that they all were willing to take an hour or two out of the gorgeous summer evening. The moment Beth said, "That's all for tonight, ladies, and thank you," at least half the group rocketed off, back to their families and friends. The rest filed out quickly. Beth cornered Darcy.

"You can do this solo, I know you can, Darcy. You're the only one who can."

"I'd faint from nervousness, Beth. I'm fine with the group."

"Will you at least think about it? Tape yourself singing, and you'll hear how good you are. Please."

Darcy shook her head. "All right, I'll think about it."

"Do it in the shower with your clothes on

without turning on the water. Bathrooms have good acoustics."

"Yes, well, that's weird."

"Come on, who will see you?" Beth shouldered her crocheted Mexican shoulder bag and slipped out the side door.

Darcy bent to tighten her sandal. When she rose, she saw Susan Brueckner hesitantly entering the church through the front doors. An aura of sadness enveloped her. Darcy was perplexed. Should she say a breezy hello and wave as she left? Or should she creep out the side door so Susan didn't know Darcy had seen her? Susan's eyes were downcast. Sometimes people needed to be in church privately, alone. Darcy opted for slithering out the side door, taking care to close it quietly.

These long summer evenings were so dreamy, perfumed with salt air and roses, the sky so high and luminous it made Darcy feel something close to joy. She strolled home, humming "Skylark," and as she passed, she overheard bits of conversation from open windows in the houses and from the yards. Laughter. Children playing. She didn't want to go inside, she wanted to linger in this pale blue-gray light forever. She entered her house, tossed her keys in their bowl on the front hall table, stopped in the kitchen for a fresh peach and a napkin, and drifted out into her backyard. She settled on her lounger and stretched like a cat. It was so peaceful, the air around her dusky, a streak of high sky still blue.

No sounds came from Mimi's yard. Something was making a rhythmic knocking noise in Susan's backyard.

"No, no, no," a man said gruffly. It had to be Otto, the father, talking to his sons. "Do not kick the ball against the house."

"But, Dad . . ." a boy whined.

"You will damage the house. Your mother took you to the beach today. You are tired. Play quietly."

Darcy took a bite of peach, chuckling to herself. Otto told his three little boys to *play quietly?* She bet herself that by the count of ten, the boys would be yelling and kicking the ball against the house again. After all, they were *boys.* Anyway, how could a ball hurt a house?

By the count of seven, she heard shrieking. The boys were chasing each other around the small yard—most houses in town had small backyards.

"Boys!" Otto yelled.

"Excuse me," a woman said in angelic tones. "Maybe your boys would like to play in our yard. We found a badminton set and a small round trampoline sort of thing in the shed. Our daughter is a teenager, so she doesn't use them, but your boys are welcome to come over."

Boyz and Autumn's yard extended in a kind of grassy dogleg a few feet behind Susan's yard.

Darcy closed her eyes; she could envision exactly where they were.

"That is very kind of you," Otto said. "Boys?"

The three boys sounded like a mob of barbarians crashing the gates as they ran, yelling, into Autumn's yard. Darcy ate her peach, happy in the knowledge that, because of her thick spruce hedges, no one could see her with peach juice running down her chin. She couldn't see them, either, but she couldn't help hearing them, and their sounds made her smile. The two older boys seemed to play a netless, rule-free game of badminton. The third son chose the trampoline, each jump accompanied by screams of delight.

"I'm Autumn Szweda."

"I am Otto Brueckner. I'm very pleased to meet you. My wife, Susan, has gone for a walk, and I confess I am not naturally inclined toward organizing children."

"I understand completely." Autumn's voice slid into a silky-smooth pitch. *Ah,* Darcy thought, *so even though he sounded like a stick, Otto must be attractive.* "My husband and I have only one child, and she can be so exhausting. I'm sure that's partly why my husband returns to the city so often." *Otto must be extremely attractive.*

"What does your husband do?"

"He's in real estate in Boston."

"Ah. I work in Boston, too."

"What do you do?"

"I'm a lawyer for the Mandel Corporation."

"That sounds much more exciting than Boyz's job."

It does? Which meant, Darcy thought, that Autumn was hinting that Otto was much more exciting than Boyz. Darcy wanted to peek through the thick needles of the hedge to see their expressions.

"Not exciting at all. Mostly reading contracts."

"Oh, but that means you can do some of your work on Nantucket, right?"

A laugh. "If I can ever get the peace and quiet to concentrate."

Darcy hadn't come out here intending to eavesdrop, but Autumn and Otto seemed to be standing right next to the hedge. She wondered where Boyz was. In Boston?

As if her question had wafted into Autumn's mind, Autumn said, "Boyz's in the city now. He'll take a week of vacation in August, but for July, he gets here only on the weekends."

"How old is your daughter?"

"Willow is fourteen. An extremely young and naïve fourteen and very unhappy with me because I limit the amount of screen time she gets."

"You are wise," Otto said warmly. "My sons do not have cellphones or computers yet. The electronics can become an addiction."

"True. It's hard, raising a child these days. Fortunately, Willow's addiction is books." Autumn waited a beat, then added with a self-deprecating laugh, "I'll admit, I get lonely here, especially in the evenings when Boyz is in Boston and Willow's shut away in her room reading." Her voice dripped with honey.

Hey! Was Autumn doing what Darcy thought she was doing? Was she coming on to him?

A wicked part of Darcy's psyche hoped so. That would scrve Boyz right! But then she thought of Susan Brueckner. She seemed to be having a hard enough time already.

"We should get together some night," Otto suggested, "for a nightcap. I could drop by—"

"Oh, *there* you are!" A woman's voice floated on the air. *Susan.* "I've been looking everywhere."

"The boys are playing in our neighbor's yard," Otto said. With the *thwap* of the badminton birdie and the squeals from the boys making it all seem so innocent, he continued: "Autumn, this is my wife, Susan."

The two women greeted each other, and Autumn invited the Brueckners up to her porch for a drink. But Alfred fell off the trampoline and hit his head and cried and the adults rushed to see if he was okay—he was—and Susan announced it was bath and story time. "Goodbye, goodbye," they called out.

Suddenly, Darcy was surrounded by silence. She could hear voices from the open windows, but no words. With the people gone, the birds cautiously flocked back to the feeder hanging from a low branch on her maple tree. She stayed very still so the birds didn't seem to know she was there. It was better in the early morning, when Darcy could see their colors, the blush of rose or lemon against the finches' chests. She simply sat and watched the darkness deepen. The flowers lost their colors, the grass grew dark. She liked seeing the glow of lights from other houses, beacons in the night. She wondered where Mimi was right now. Did she go to bed early, or was she one of the older people who couldn't sleep much? She wondered where Clive was now. Their kitchen light was on, and one light on the second floor. . . .

Good grief, she was becoming one of those weirdos living her life vicariously through her neighbors. *No,* Darcy argued with herself, *she was not! It wasn't her fault if people stood next to the hedge to talk!*

Gradually, her mind stilled, her breathing slowed, and she relaxed against the soft cushions of the lounge. The birds were quiet. Above her, the Big Dipper twinkled against the vast black sky. Something rustled in a bush—a bird? She hoped it wasn't a damn rabbit—they ate the leaves off her hostas. This was what refreshed

Darcy after a long day being with people, the complete quiet, the sense of living for a few minutes within a hushed but living world. Gradually her eyes adjusted to the darkness and her garden became different shades of gray. Some night she wanted to sleep out here. She was amused by the thought of catching her garden at three in the morning—would tiny velvet voles be skittering through the grass? She'd seen them once, when she rose early. It was often misty in the early mornings before the sun came up over the horizon. Darcy wasn't aware of thinking any kind of intelligent thoughts when she sat out here, but in a way it was her form of meditation.

And she felt less lonely.

She was thirty. She had lived on the island, in her grandmother's big house, for three years. Gradually, she'd developed a group of friends, and Jordan had become an intimate friend, her best friend. She'd gone out a few times with island guys and a few times with summer guys, but Nash was the first man to make her wake up and smell the coffee since her divorce from Boyz.

Boyz was charismatic and dramatic, and it had taken her a couple of years to realize he *needed* to be attractive to other people; it was part of his success in business, and more than that, it was a kind of drug for him. Giving people a look, a smile, a nod, and watching them be swept as if by magic into his web brought Boyz an almost addictive pleasure.

Nash had a different kind of energy and a different sort of charisma. He was a tall, silent man, genial, courteous, easygoing, but guarded. Nash was a challenge. When they made love, the sex was intimate, thrilling, intense, but when it was over and they lay side by side, Nash was silent. He held her hand, but he didn't speak. She *had* tried to talk. "That was amazing," she'd said, knowing that her words were a cliché even though they were true. All he'd said was, "Good." *Good?* It had seemed with Boyz that she'd been pulled *immediately* into the inner circle of his life, his thoughts, his family, his dreams. With Nash, she was still an outsider. Even when they were making love, part of him held back.

When they went out together, Nash was witty, gentlemanly, and amiable, and he gave her plenty of compliments, but something about him was *distant*. He told Darcy he had an unremarkable past, growing up in the 'burbs of Boston with a professor father and a quilt-maker mom. He spent Christmas with them. He cared for them, sure, but he'd left the nest. He had moved to Nantucket this winter, and he thought he'd like to stay here for the rest of his life, but on the other hand, Colorado and Vermont called to him, so next winter he might take off for a week or two to ski. Nash was four years older than Darcy. He never talked about having a family. He seemed content with his bachelor life in the apartment he rented over his friend Lois Cooper's garage.

Content. That was it. Nash was content with himself and his lot in life, and it puzzled Darcy. It challenged her—she wanted to break though his invisible wall. She wanted to make him *discontented*. She wanted to make him go wild for her, tell her he loved her, that she held his life in her hands, he needed her. . . .

Ridiculous. Nash didn't hold *her* life in *his* hands. She didn't *need* him. It was her bratty vanity wanting him to feel those things about her.

The clock on the South Church tower struck eleven times. Time for bed. Darcy gathered her peach pit and went into her house. She missed Nash. Some nights, especially when the spring gales howled over the ocean to batter against the houses, Darcy and Nash would sit together in the living room, her feet on his lap, both of them working on crossword puzzles.

"What's a five letter word for 'green energy'?" she would ask.

He'd answer immediately. *"Solar."*

"Ha! I thought it was something like spinach!" They would laugh together and go quiet again, absorbed in their puzzles but together.

Darcy wished he were here right now, not even for sex, but to sleep with, to curl up against, relaxing into the safety of his body, the sense of

123

belonging she had when his arm was around her, holding him against her, his breath warm on her neck.

Saturday, as Darcy strolled home from the library, she spotted a familiar figure on the brick sidewalk. Mimi crept along with her cane, head down—always wise no matter what age, because the Nantucket sidewalks were uneven, with bumps where tree roots shoved the bricks upward and sudden holes where entire bricks had come loose and disappeared.

"Hi, Mimi," Darcy called as she drew near.

"Darcy!" Mimi put a hand on a picket fence to steady herself. "How pretty you look!"

"As do you. I think we have the same taste in clothes." They were both wearing floral-printed summer dresses.

Mimi laughed. "But maybe not the same taste in shoes."

Darcy wore beaded sandals with a small heel. Mimi wore huge clunky rubbery support boats.

"Tell me, Darcy, how was your day? Is it overwhelming in town now? Do you get to read to the children or are you stuck with administrative duties?"

"Oh, gosh," Darcy said, remembering. "I was going to bring you some children's books. So, yes, I'll admit it is overwhelming in town. That's my excuse for being forgetful!" She laughed with

Mimi. "Look, would you like to come sit in my backyard and have a glass of lemonade with me?"

To her surprise, Mimi said, "Hm. I don't know." Her eyes twinkled. "Is lemonade all you've got to offer?"

It took Darcy a moment. *Oh.* "I've got wine, and I can make a mean margarita."

"Ah. Good. In that case, I'd very much like to sit in your backyard."

Darcy took her arm. Slowly they made their way beneath the rose-covered arbor into her garden and settled Mimi in a chair, cane in her hand.

"I'll be right back with some drinks."

From her kitchen window, Darcy observed Mimi surveying her garden, pleasure glowing on her face as she observed the flowers—larkspur, foxglove, phlox, all the old favorites. She also noticed that Boyz's car was not in the driveway and no people of any age or size were in the garden on the other side of the hedge. Good.

Carrying a pitcher of drinks and a bowl of nuts on a tray, she joined Mimi. She dropped down onto one of her cushioned chairs, kicked off her sandals, and luxuriated in the feel of grass against the soles of her feet.

"So tell me," Mimi said after taking a sip of her drink, "do you live in your huge house all alone? Why aren't you married?"

What? Where was the small talk? Darcy shot back, "Why aren't you?"

"Oh, don't you worry about me. I've had two husbands and a great number of pleasant dalliances."

"Oooh, *dalliance*. That's a great word."

"Certainly more appealing than 'friends with benefits.'"

Darcy choked on her margarita. "You are not the typical little old lady, are you?"

"Most of us aren't," she replied. "So you were going to tell me why you aren't married."

"I was married once. My husband left me for another woman. My grandmother willed me this house, which is why I live alone here. I spent much of my childhood here, so it's my home."

"And men?" Mimi prompted.

Darcy took a moment to consider her answer. Many older women, women in their eighties and up, liked to reminisce. Her grandmother certainly had. Penny had kept all discussion of her physical aches and pains to a minimum; she couldn't tolerate what she called "organ recitals." But she had enjoyed telling Darcy about certain people, certain times, and she'd told Darcy over and over again. In a way, Penny had relived those experiences, and Darcy never tired of hearing about them. Still, it was unsettling to have another grandmother ask these particular questions.

Mimi tilted her head, waiting for an answer.

"I have a—boyfriend, let's call him. Nash Forester."

"The one with the red pickup truck," Mimi said knowingly. When Darcy showed her surprise, she smiled. "I sit by the window and gaze out at the street. So sue me."

"Right. Nash is a carpenter. We've been dating for a couple of months. He's fun and he likes the same things I do. We kayak together, hike around the island, do some bird watching."

"He's awfully good-looking."

"What, you wear field glasses when you look out the window?" Darcy pretended indignation.

"I didn't need binoculars to see the build of the man."

They both laughed. Darcy sipped her margarita. Muffler strolled lazily over the lawn, waving his long luxuriant black tail.

"Meet Muffler," Darcy said. "When he purrs, you'll know why he got that name."

Muffler jumped into Mimi's lap and stared up at her, waiting for the proper adoration. Mimi complied, stroking his long, silky black fur and complimenting him. After a few minutes of this, he turned around and settled in her lap. Purring.

"We were talking about men," Mimi gently reminded Darcy.

Darcy took another sip of her drink and wondered if it was too strong. She didn't feel buzzed, like she did when she was out at the Box with friends, dancing and tossing back tequila slammers all evening. Instead, a calm flowed through her, as if she were in yoga class on a really good day.

"It sucked—" she began, catching herself for using that word.

Mimi grinned. "I use that word myself."

"Good. Thank you. Okay, well, it sucked, being dumped—divorced—when my husband had an affair with another woman. *Autumn*. His new wife's name is Autumn. She's beautiful and sensual—"

"You're beautiful," Mimi interrupted.

Darcy snorted. "Maybe, but I'm cerebral, not sensual. Boyz told me Autumn is all about pleasure, enjoying the moment, not living in books half the time. But anyway, it's done. It hurt, I was ashamed, I was lost, and then my darling grandmother Penny died shortly after the divorce. She had been my Rock of Gibraltar. I really did feel forlorn. Pathetic, I know. Anyway, Penny left me this house, and it seemed the only choice was to take what fate gave me. All that Eastern wisdom, let go, surrender, go with the flow . . ." Darcy's throat closed up.

"Have a nut." Mimi handed the bowl to her.

Darcy chose a cashew and chewed thoughtfully. "I don't need to cry anymore," she said thoughtfully. The cashew was salty. She took another sip of her drink. "I'm over that. I've made peace with my life. Look what I've been given—this wonderful house; this amazing garden; this glorious island; meaningful, absorbing work; some true-blue friends—how could I ask for more?" Before Mimi could say it, she added, "I don't need a husband. I don't even want a husband. I've gotten used to living alone, and it suits me. I'm not sure I could deal with a man messing up my life."

Mimi's face was tender when she said, "You're so young. Too young to go without love. I'm sure you can get all the sex you need, you're such a gorgeous girl. But sex combined with love is something of an entirely different magnitude. It would be a shame for you to miss that."

Darcy dropped her eyes, shifting uncomfortably on her chair.

Mimi laughed. "It's odd, isn't it, listening to an old crow like me talking about sex. No one wants to believe their parents ever had sex, and certainly not their grandparents."

"It *is* different, sharing these thoughts with . . . an older woman. I couldn't have talked with my grandmother like this, and we were very close. You're much more open than other women your age are. When I talk with my friends, usually when we're drinking—" Darcy held up her glass like a visual aid—"any sex talk is funny. We laugh like maniacs when we talk about sex. You're being rather . . . solemn. Anyway," Darcy continued, almost defensively, "sex is not what I mean when I say I don't need a man messing up my life."

Suddenly, a man walked through the rose-covered arbor into the yard. Darcy hoped he hadn't overheard their conversation.

It was Clive, all casual and relaxed, carrying a bag of groceries. "Sorry to bother you, but have you kidnapped my grandmother?"

Darcy took a few seconds to recover from the sheer sight of the man. He was so brawny, so *male*. "Yes," Darcy told him, her face serious. "She's my hostage, and I won't release her until she finishes her margarita."

"Clive!" Mimi called. "Come join us."

"Yes, please do. I'll get you a glass." Darcy stood too quickly and swayed, catching the table to steady herself.

Clive grinned. "How many margaritas have you had?"

Darcy smiled back, feeling a bit tipsy. "It's *her* fault," she said childishly.

Clive laughed. "It always is. Believe me, I know."

He bent over to kiss Mimi on her cheek. "You are incorrigible."

"Would you like one?" Darcy asked, holding up the pitcher.

"Thank you, no."

"Don't be such a stick," Mimi told him. "Sit down and join us for a while."

"Do you have any beer?" he asked.

"Absolutely."

Darcy hurried into the kitchen. First, she

drank a glass of water. Standing at the kitchen window, she quickly surveyed Boyz's yard—no car, no people. Whew. How hideous would it be if they'd overheard her conversation with Mimi? She filled her glass again and prepared a glass of water for Mimi. She put a triangle of Brie and some crackers on a board. She grabbed a Whale's Tale Pale Ale and went outside, opening the door with a bump of her hip. She went down the steps and across the grassy yard.

She set a glass of water next to Mimi and settled in her chair. She smiled at Clive. And knew her cheeks were flushed and hoped really hard that he thought it was the alcohol.

"Clive," Mimi prompted, "tell Darcy what you're doing this summer."

He rolled his eyes. "I apologize for my grandmother's bossiness. I won't sue you for kidnapping her, I'll pay you."

"You are a terrible grandchild," Mimi said. "Anyway, it's not like it's top secret code encryption you're working on up there in your aerie."

Aerie. Many people would call it an attic. Darcy had been through the house; she knew the layout. From his aerie, Clive could see down into his yard and hers and Boyz's, too.

Clive said, "I'm writing a book about the blues."

"As in music?"

"Right."

"Are you a musician?"

"A mediocre musician. But I'm a good musicologist."

"He has a PhD!" Mimi bragged.

"I take her with me everywhere," Clive said, rolling his eyes.

"Do you teach? Write?"

"Both. I teach the history of music and other topics at B.U. Music and the brain, our perception and reaction to music, the physics of sound, sacred music, the development of instruments—"

"And he's writing a book about the blues!" Mimi interjected.

"Mimi, we told her that already." Clive didn't scold her. His tone of voice was simply informational. But Darcy understood—Mimi wasn't tipsy, but she was sliding that way. To Darcy, Clive said, "I should tell you, because Mimi certainly won't, that she takes a number of medications to help with her blood pressure and arrhythmia. Alcohol interferes with their efficiency."

"Got it," Darcy said.

"My doctor says I'm allowed two drinks a day," Mimi reminded him.

An engine roared on the other side of the hedge. Car doors slammed and a family—Boyz's family—exploded into their yard.

"Get your towel and swimming suit!" Autumn called. "Toss it on the line."

Mimi raised her eyebrows at the noise. "I guess we can't talk about sex anymore. I wouldn't want to be overheard."

"Oh, no, Mimi, have you been talking about sex again?" Clive teased.

"Yes," Darcy said quickly. "We've been discussing the sex of flowers. Did you know that the *Arisaema triphyllum* can change sex over the years? It can be both male and female." She waved airily toward the garden, as if that particular plant was growing there, which it wasn't.

"Of course." Clive chugged his beer and set it on the table. "Time for you to go home, Mimi."

She didn't protest. He helped Mimi to her feet and kept an arm through hers as they slowly progressed over the lawn and beneath the arbor.

"We'll talk more another time," Mimi said. "And thank you for our chat and for the drinks."

They were all laughing as they went their separate ways. Darcy brought the things in from the garden, made a tomato sandwich for her dinner, fed Muffler, and settled in the living room with a book.

Muffler jumped lightly to the arm of the sofa. He stared at Darcy persistently. He didn't want more food, or he'd walk down her legs and over her torso until he reached her face. He was making some kind of point, though.

"I know," Darcy said, stroking his head. "It's nice, sometimes, to have other people around."

Muffler turned around three times and curled up in her lap.

7

Sunday, the library was closed. Darcy slipped into a bathing suit, a light cotton long-sleeved shirt for protection from the sun, and flip-flops. She was ready when Nash showed up in his red truck. They drove to Cisco beach and bounced along west until they found their usual list of suspects. Jordan and her husband, Lyle, were there with their toddler, Kiks. Lars and Angelica Stone and their toddler, Packer. The Driscolls with their newlywed hands all over each other. The Folgers, with a waddling pregnant Dee-Dee.

The guys surfed; the women tended the temporary nest, spreading blankets, putting up beach umbrellas so the children wouldn't get too much sun, setting out the food. It was kind of tribal. Nash and Darcy weren't the only unmarried couple. Missy and Paul had been seeing each other for three years, and Gage Wharton brought a different woman every week.

The day was clear, hot, and perfect for swimming. What wind there was came from the southwest in slight gusts, not enough to blow sand or even ruffle the blankets and towels they sat on. Darcy braced herself for the shock of cold, raced into the water, and swam fast and far, enjoying the stretch and strength of her muscles.

She flipped over and floated, soaking in the sun blazing down on her. All thoughts were washed away by the waves. What a wonderful life she led! She silently sent a prayer of gratitude to the heavens and to her grandmother.

Suddenly, something grabbed her and pulled her under. She wrestled around, surfaced, and gasped. And looked into Nash's blue eyes.

"Surprised?" he asked, looking pleased with himself.

Considering he did this at least once every time they went swimming, the truthful answer was no, Darcy was kind of expecting it. "You rat."

He pulled her close to him. They treaded water together, their bodies slippery, their legs touching as they scissored in and out. He kissed Darcy, who kissed him back, and they sank, broke apart, surfacing and gulping air.

Nash's sandy hair was plastered to his head.

"You look like a seal," Darcy teased.

"You look like a siren. One of those who lured Ulysses."

Darcy laughed and splashed water in his face. Nash had a habit of saying sweet things at unromantic times, never when they were in bed together. What did this mean? She would never understand men.

"I'm hungry," she said.

"Race you to the shore." Nash dove away from her for a head start.

They always had enormous quantities of food—cold curried chicken; egg salad; potato salad; pasta with olives, roasted red peppers, and eggplant; couscous; ham and cheese and pesto on focaccia; and always chips and salsa and guacamole. Most of the men drank beer; the women, iced tea. After lunch, the children fell asleep, so the moms left the kids with their dads and the women went for a long walk down the beach.

They ambled along, discussing the week's gossip, what they were going to wear to the next gala, why Gage didn't have a date today and who he would show up with next week. The beach was crowded with people reading in beach chairs, girls sunning on beach towels with their bikini ties undone, kids building sand castles or beachcombing.

Suddenly, Darcy's mind did a kind of jump.

She spotted Willow a few yards ahead. Boyz's stepdaughter, Willow. Darcy was sure. She had never met the girl, but she'd seen her several times from her windows. She looked like her mother, red haired, curvaceous, and virtuously—and unusually for her age group—clad in a one-piece bathing suit.

She was with a boy Darcy knew, Logan Smith, and Darcy literally stopped in her tracks. What the hell was she doing with Logan? Willow was fourteen; he was eighteen. He was an island kid, one of the bad boys—handsome and awesomely cool—but he was trouble.

Logan was leading Willow away from the water toward a shady hideaway between two high sand dunes. Darcy bent over, pretending to find an interesting shell, and watched the couple. Logan pressed Willow up against the dune, stroked her hair away from her face, and kissed her tenderly. Logan had been in the court report any number of times for misdemeanors—DUI, possession of pot, fighting, disturbing the peace—but he was an island boy, and the island wanted him to get through his awkward phase and become a good man. Now he had his hands on Willow's breasts, and he was pressing his hips against hers. *And he was eighteen and she was fourteen.*

It was none of Darcy's business, right?

Willow was not her child. Darcy knew nothing about her. Maybe Willow was already more sexually active than Darcy imagined. Still, she didn't like what she saw. And she had overheard Autumn tell Otto that Willow was naïve. . . .

So what were her options? Stomp through the sand with a stern librarian face and separate them? Forget about it? Forget about it, Darcy decided. What was that saying: *Not my circus, not my monkeys.*

Darcy sprinted to catch up with her group. While she'd dawdled, she missed the big news: Missy was pregnant. But she wasn't sure she wanted to marry Paul, even though they lived together. She'd seen too many divorces—her parents, her friends—she was afraid to marry. The women all chimed in with their opinions, and Darcy forgot Willow.

The sound of a crying child made them all turn.

"Kiks," Jordan said. "She often cries when she wakes up from a nap. I think she thinks we did something marvelously exciting while she slept, like eating her favorite mashed banana."

The women laughed and made their way back to the group. The sun slanted lower. Clouds were wandering across the sky, as they often seemed to do in the late afternoon, which was nice, because they caused more color as the sun set. The men had to work the next day—and some of the women, too. All around them the beach was emptying as people made their way across the sand to the parking lot. Nash and Darcy said their goodbyes and headed to Nash's truck.

"Want to stay over?" Darcy asked when they reached her house.

She was warm and lazy limbed, resting her head against the back of the seat.

"Better not. I need a shower and my clean clothes are at my place. Besides"—he glanced over at Darcy—"you know you want to watch *Outlander.*"

"No, it's over for the season." Darcy grinned wickedly. "But I can get *Grantchester* on my

Roku. You'd like it, it's a mystery with a vicar and a detective."

Nash shot Darcy a knowing look. "You mean that red-haired vicar who makes you drool."

"I don't drool!" Darcy protested. But she did, in her mind.

"Maybe tomorrow night," Nash said.

He helped her carry the cooler and beach towels into her house. In the front hall, Nash turned her toward him. "So see you this week?"

Their eyes met and suddenly even tomorrow was too far away. Darcy wrapped her arms around his neck and kissed him, pressing herself against him. He slid her shirt over her head and kissed her throat, her collarbone, the sweet spot between her breasts. His hands moved over her body. Sand made light clicking noises on the floor as they stripped off their bathing suits.

"Darcy." Nash knelt, pulling her down with him.

The rug in the front hall scarcely softened the hard floor, but Darcy was so caught up in her passion she didn't know, didn't care. Her need for him was intense, and her pleasure with him was overpowering. Afterward, Nash smoothed back her hair, all tangled and moist with sweat.

"Good grief," Darcy said breathlessly.

"Yeah, I know." Nash was smiling.

They lay together for a while facing each other, Darcy's head nestled against Nash's chest. His breath was deep and regular. She could hear his heartbeat. His arm was over her waist, his hand lying lightly in her back. She felt safe, content, and drowsy.

"You know we can't fall asleep like this," Nash murmured. "I have to work tomorrow."

Darcy stirred in his arms. "Don't go."

"Have to."

He pulled on his board shorts and T-shirt. They rose, kissed lightly, and Nash went out the door. Darcy showered and creamed her face and limbs with lotion. Her skin glowed from the sun, her mouth was tender from kissing.

In the T-shirt she wore to sleep in, she watched *Grantchester*.

James Norton was gorgeous, but he couldn't hold a candle to Nash. Darcy's thoughts veered over to Nash, who had the same kind of restrained, gentle manner the television vicar had.

The episode ended. She went through the house turning off lights and locking doors, finally climbing the stairs and entering her bedroom. She slipped between the cool sheets of her bed, stretching out with a sigh.

It would be nice to have Nash in bed with her now. Just to talk with about their days, their plans for this week, and then to drift off, feeling his warm male body next to hers. She rolled on her side, placing her hand on the spot where he had slept several times before, and fell asleep.

Mondays were Darcy's day for accomplishing all the chores she was too busy the rest of the week to do. Cleaning the house. Shopping for groceries—always a hellish task because their main grocery store, Stop & Shop, went from supplying sixteen thousand people in the winter to sixty thousand summer shoppers. Putting away the groceries and tidying the kitchen. Stripping her bed, putting on clean sheets, tossing sheets and towels in the washer. Vacuuming the sand she'd trekked in from the beach yesterday.

After all that, she sat down at her computer and answered emails from friends, cruised Facebook and Twitter and Instagram. She ironed some cotton shirts and a few gauzy scarves to wear during the week. She made a casserole that would last the week or serve Nash if he came for dinner. She talked to him on the phone—he couldn't come, it was a day of long light, perfect for finishing the widow's walk his crew was working on. He might not see her until the weekend. Darcy called Missy Linsley, the other single woman in their crowd. They walked to Cru, the restaurant at the end of Straight Wharf, for French pilgrim cocktails and roasted Nantucket oysters. They enjoyed an intimate gossip fest about their crowd that left them weak from laughter as they watched the sailors come in and the sun slant over the harbor.

The next day Darcy worked. Her desk was piled with seven thousand matters needing to be taken care of *right now.* She answered the phone seventeen times; she opened and organized the mail. At one, the director of the children's library closed the door to the office and they ate their abbreviated lunch of yogurt while they went over the schedule for the week. When Beverly rushed off to a meeting, Darcy stationed herself at the computer and began ordering the new books from a list they'd compiled.

At the end of the day, Darcy changed into her Speedo, pulled on her street clothes, and went out into the day, heading for Jetties Beach. It was after five, so it wouldn't be crowded. She needed a calm, cooling swim before heading home. The tide was in, so she didn't have to wade far before arriving at water deep enough for swimming. She did the breaststroke for a long time, loving the surge of her body, the way the water's swells washed her mind clean. When she tired, she flipped over and floated as the sun warmed her face. This was the perfect relaxation therapy. All thoughts dissipated into the salt air.

Back on shore, she dried herself as well as she could, pulled her clothes over her damp bathing suit, and took a moment to comb her hair. Not far from her, a boy and girl lay together on a blanket, kissing and whispering and giggling. She thought of Willow. She had to remember that was not her business.

She ambled home, smiling at the people she passed, swinging her book bag, humming a children's song. Inside, she poured a glass of wine and zapped leftovers from the picnic in the microwave, put it all on a tray, and carried it out to her garden. It was six thirty and the sun was still high in the sky. Birds sang from high in the trees. Over at the Brueckners', the three boys were playing in the sprinkler, screaming with glee.

Nash called. She curled up on her sofa and they talked about their day. It was so comforting to hear his voice, to make him laugh, to soften her own voice and flirt over the phone.

Gradually the island filled with people rushing to escape the heat of the mainland, walk the golden beaches, swim in the ocean, and shop in the marvelous boutiques. Darcy did two story times a day, answered emails, attended staff meetings, and cataloged the new books. Most books were cataloged on the mainland by CLAMS, aka the appropriately named Cape Libraries Automated Materials Sharing, and arrived on the island ready to shelve, but there were always exceptions, especially with self-published children's books. When a staff member had an emergency, Darcy took over the circulation desk upstairs, and she dutifully and happily attended the necessary posh gala fundraisers. It was good to wear a gorgeous dress and lots of bling and mingle with the beautiful people while waiters offered her champagne and scallops wrapped in bacon. She saw people she hadn't seen for nine months and caught up on their news—who was pregnant, who had broken a leg skiing, who had bought a villa in Tuscany.

Sunday, she and Nash met friends at the beach. That evening Darcy and Nash showered and glammed up for an art opening at the Artists Association of Nantucket. The place was packed, both downstairs and upstairs. The art was wonderful, landscapes and seascapes and abstracts and sculpture and jewelry, a sumptuous display of what the talented islanders had done over the winter. Small red dots indicating "sold" were everywhere.

Nash stopped to talk to a friend. Darcy slipped upstairs, wineglass in hand, to look at the new pieces; but as always, she met friends, and spent more time talking than looking at the art.

She was in the corner, studying a landscape, when a man behind her said hello.

She turned. It was Clive Rush. Handsome Clive Rush, in a navy blazer that set off his tan and made his fabulous smile flash.

Well, hello, sailor, Darcy thought in her best Mae West inner self. She was glad she was wearing her long turquoise skirt with its thigh-high split and her nearly sheer white sleeveless blouse. "Hi, Clive. Where's Mimi?"

He laughed, as if he had been confronted with this defense mechanism before. "She's downstairs, surrounded by admirers, and drinking far too much wine."

"At her age, I don't think there is such a thing as too much wine."

"I like this landscape," Clive said, gesturing toward a painting of a salt marsh with a small wooden bridge over water. "But I can't place it."

"It's Madaket Harbor, near the marina. On the western end of the island. Mr. Rogers had a house out there."

"Mr. Rogers? There's someone I haven't thought of for a long time. My mother made me watch him when I was a child. She thought it would calm me down."

"And did it?" She smiled, looking up at him. He certainly was pleasant to look at.

"I believe it did. Before I forget, next Tuesday night the Musical Arts Society is hosting a pianist who's performing an interesting mix of classical and contemporary. I'm going to take Mimi and we wonder if you'd like to go with us."

Darcy paused. There was that "*we* wonder," so would this be considered a date? Or could she tell Nash she was accompanying a darling older woman and her grandson? Should she even worry about what Nash thought? They hadn't talked about dating each other exclusively. "I'd like that very much."

"Good. I'll tell Mimi. She'll be thrilled."

"Why don't you both come for dinner before," Darcy offered on the spur of the moment. "I'll make something light so we can get to the concert on time."

"Great. How's six o'clock?"

"Perfect."

They smiled at each other, and the temperature in the room seemed to shoot up about a hundred degrees.

Clive said, "I'd better check on Mimi. It was nice bumping into you tonight."

"Me, too," Darcy said. *That makes no sense, but at least she spoke in English.* Fireworks were exploding in her mind, not to mention her body. *Probably Mimi told Clive to invite her. Or he wanted to have someone help maneuver his grandmother up the hill and into the Congregational church with all its steps.*

Or maybe he liked her. She wasn't making all that electricity by herself.

She walked on to gaze at a seascape for fifteen minutes, trying to sort out her thoughts, which weren't thoughts so much as feelings—lust, mostly. A large male hand slid around her waist, tugging her out of her daze.

"Oh!" Darcy cried, startled.

"You must like that seascape, you've been staring at it so long." Nash kept his hand on her waist as he checked out the upstairs for more friends.

"I do like it," Darcy said. "Do you?"

He took the time to study it. "Yeah, I do. It's a good depiction of the ocean during a nor'easter. I wouldn't mind having that in my house, looking at it every day."

"I know. It's complicated, with lots of movement."

"Well, don't like it too much," Nash told her. He pointed to the round red dot next to the painting that indicated it was sold.

"Ah, well . . ." Darcy pretended to pout.

Nash pulled her closer to him. "Don't worry. Whenever we get a good storm, I'll drive you out to the beach to watch. We'll take off our shoes and run in the waves."

"Well, there's proof you belong on the island. Everyone I know goes crazy when a storm hits."

"I go crazy when I look at you," Nash said.

Darcy gazed up at Nash for a few moments, speechless with pleasure at his words. Did he mean what he said? If he did, what did that tell her?

"Time for dinner?" Nash asked.

"It would be time for something else if we weren't in public," Darcy told him.

"Be good. We've got reservations."

Nash took her hand so he wouldn't lose her as they threaded their way through the crowd. He held her hand as they stepped outside, turned right, and walked to Fifty-Six Union, one of their favorite restaurants. His hand was big and warm and callused from carpentry work, and she liked that roughness against her own smooth skin. She shivered to recall the feel of those hands on her naked body.

Obviously, she was a nymphomaniac.

The restaurant was packed with gorgeous summer people relishing their newly tanned skin and sunburned noses, their sense of sensual freedom here on this island that had not one single traffic light, and no skyscrapers or polluted air or subways, expressways, or toll booths. The hostess led them to a small table against the wall. From here, Darcy and Nash could have a conversation—if they shouted—but they'd expected it would be like this and it was exhilarating after months of isolation. Darcy ordered her favorite appetizer: mussels from P.E.I., with hunks of thick bread to soak up the broth. She had salmon for an entrée. Nash had the swordfish, and they split their food in half and shared. They talked about the paintings they'd seen; the artists and their always attention-grabbing personal lives; the problem finding parking in town, which never seemed to be solved; the new blockbuster movie.

And all the time, under the table, Darcy stroked his leg with her foot.

When they left the restaurant, it was twilight, the long lazy twilight of summer.

"Let's walk down to the creeks," Nash suggested.

"Good idea."

They ambled along companionably down the street toward the harbor, where boats and yachts and dinghies bobbed gently in the evening breeze. They strolled past the Great Harbor Yacht Club and Sayle's fish market, and came to the beach at the harbor's end. You could wade here, where the water scrolled in to the salt marsh grasses, but it was too shallow for swimming. In the mornings, people practiced yoga on this beach. In the day, families kayaked into the inlets, spotting egrets and osprey and dozens of gulls. Now, at twilight, the beach was empty.

They sat side by side on the sand.

"It's still warm from the sun," Darcy said, scooping up a palmful of sand and letting it trickle through her fingers.

"Peaceful," Nash murmured.

It was just plain *nice,* Darcy thought, sitting here with Nash.

Nash said quietly, "In March, when it was cold and the crew didn't start work until eight or nine, I got up at six and came out here to walk. Or I went to Surfside. Sometimes the Jetties. I had the beach to myself. Okay, I shared it with the gulls and the herons and the cormorants." He paused before saying, "It fills me up somehow. Just plain being there."

His words took her breath away, not only because she did that, too, in winter, but because he had shared something private with her.

"Wow. You're a nature geek like me." Darcy gave him a sideways glance. He didn't balk at "geek," so she continued. "I do the same thing. Sometimes I drive out to the moors and walk on the dirt roads. No one else is around and you're right, it fills me up."

"What are the moors like in winter?" Nash asked. "I imagine it's bleak."

"True . . ." Darcy paused to collect her thoughts. "Everything's gray and brittle, except for the occasional cluster of pine trees. When the sky is cloudy, the entire world is gray. It's like walking on the moon. Usually the wind is up, whistling over the island. It makes the branches of the beach plum bushes rattle. I get kind of scared, or not *scared* exactly, but all shivery, not just from the cold. Then I spot a break in the brush, usually near one of the ponds, and, if I look closer, I'll see a track into the bushes and a flattened area where the deer shelter. I think of the deer, foraging for berries, then curling up together, their warmth filling their space. . . ."

"Will you take me there this winter? I've never walked on the moors."

"Yeah," Darcy said. "Yeah, sure, I'll take you there."

So he was assuming they'd still be together in the winter, she thought. She leaned against his sturdy, strong torso.

Nash put his arm around her shoulders and pulled her against him. Together they gazed out at the lights twinkling from homes in Monomoy, the lights blazing from the wide windows of the yacht club, the boats rocking in the dark blue water, the flash of light from the Brant Point Lighthouse. Except for the cry of the gulls, it was quiet. As the sky darkened, Nash's profile blended into the shadows, and then she could scarcely see him. It was the most natural thing in the world for her to turn her face up toward his, for his mouth to come down, warm and gentle, against hers.

"We should go," Darcy said after a while.

They held hands as they walked over the sand toward town. Along Washington Street, the harbor deepened and dozens of boats bobbed on buoys or rested in slips on the town pier. The silence of the creeks slipped away from them. Music and laughter floated over the water toward them and more and more lights lit up the street. Her house was only a few blocks from the artists' gallery, so they walked up Main Street toward

Darcy's, listening to the street musicians, gazing at the gorgeous shop windows, until they left the noise and the lights behind and turned onto her quiet lane. At the door, Nash pulled her against him and rested his forehead on hers.

"Want to come in?" Darcy asked.

"Better not. Early day tomorrow." He gave her a crooked grin. "I mean it this time. Stand back, woman."

Darcy laughed. "Call me?"

"Absolutely." He kissed her, watched her turn her key in the lock and step inside her house, then headed down her walk toward his truck.

Darcy shut the front door, walked through her house, and went down the steps to her garden. She wanted to replay this evening in her thoughts. Something had changed between her and Nash. Something had deepened. He was trusting her more . . . and she was trusting him more, too.

She settled in her lounger and looked up at the sky. The lights were mostly out at the Brueckners' house. No more music drifted from the Rushes'. It was completely dark, but not completely quiet. She let her thoughts drift down to the harbor and her conversation with Nash. He had been . . .

Something rustled in the bushes, and then, from the Szwedas' yard came sounds of . . . *sex?* Darcy froze. On the other side of the hedge, in the corner of the yard, a tall maple towered, its sturdy branches extending over both yards. Its wide trunk and roots would make a good hideaway, a resting place. Or a lovemaking nest. But would Boyz and Autumn really have sex outside in the yard? Boyz had never been that fond of nature.

"No, Logan, stop. I'm not ready."

Darcy's breath caught in her throat. It had to be Willow.

"Come on, baby. You're so beautiful." Logan's voice was like melted chocolate.

"I can't. I have to go in. This grass itches my back. And everyone's home."

"No one can see you, babe. Here, I'll put my shirt under you so your back won't itch. I'll take off my shirt, you take off yours. Nice trade, don't you think?"

They stopped talking. Darcy heard moaning. She was hot with embarrassment and angry and frustrated. Willow was fourteen! She wanted to stand on top of the picnic table and yell at Logan to leave the girl alone. If Logan got Willow to have sex, wouldn't that be considered statutory rape?

Anxiety gripped Darcy. Her mind worked overtime. She had to believe that Autumn and Boyz had discussed sex with their daughter. Still, should Darcy phone the Szwedas' house and tell them what was going on in their backyard? Would she be helping or interfering? Was she overreacting because Willow was Boyz's stepdaughter? No, she knew she would worry about anyone's adolescent girl.

"Logan, no! Stop! Something's jabbing my back."

"Here, baby, let me—"

"No. Not here. Not with my parents nearby."

More rustling noises. Their voices had changed. They sounded as if they were standing up.

"Let's go to my truck," Logan urged. "You can't leave me like this. You make me want you too much."

More kissing sounds, and then Willow said, "I've got to go in, Logan."

Darcy heard two doors slam—Willow going into the house, Logan getting into his truck. She relaxed and went into her own house. It took her a long time to fall asleep.

8

Monday morning, Darcy stocked up for the week ahead. At this time of year, her meals were mostly salads or slow cooker, though she tried to get fresh fish from Sayle's two or three times a week. She also needed the normal household items—toilet paper, laundry soap, milk, and of course kitty litter and canned food for Muffler.

Last year Stop & Shop had renovated their building, making it larger and more confusing. She found herself retracing her steps, trying to find olives, lemons, and a block of Parmesan cheese.

She was in the meat section—rump roast was on sale, and if she made a stew in her slow cooker, she'd have dinner prepared for most of the week—when she felt a presence, and heard Boyz say "Darcy?"

She turned to face him. "Boyz."

Her first reaction was that he had never changed, this man she had loved and married and divorced. He was still drop-dead handsome—tall, lean, with platinum hair. After a moment of gazing at him, as he was at her, she noticed changes. His hair was shorter than when she was married to him, sheared into some sort of edgy, bristly brush cut, and he was much thinner. He was pushing a grocery cart, so he looked casual and domestic, but he wore a peach polo shirt with the collar turned up and madras shorts—madras shorts, what a peacock he was.

He was bowlegged. Why had she never noticed that before? His legs were thin, like a crane's; his knees were knobby. In shorts, this usually elegant man looked ridiculous.

She had known that sometime this summer they were bound to meet, and she regretted that it was now, when she was wearing sandals and a not-too-racy high-necked sleeveless sundress. She never knew when she'd run into one of the library's benefactors and she always wanted to make an appropriate impression. That did not mean, however, a *sexy* impression, and for a moment, she was sorry about that. She would have liked Boyz to be stabbed with desire and regret.

Maybe he was. "You look great," Boyz said, after doing a rapid up and down eye scan of her body. "But what are you doing here?"

"I live here," Darcy told him. "My grandmother died and left me her house."

"I didn't know. I'm sorry."

"I'm the assistant children's librarian at the Atheneum."

"Well, hey, you always wanted to work in a library. I'm glad for you."

They stared at each other in silence then, simply looking, caught in a bubble of time. Darcy assumed Boyz was assessing her as she was assessing him. Wondering if that person was truly the person she'd embraced and cried and laughed and argued with.

Boyz seemed like a stranger. *Felt* like a stranger to Darcy. They had married too quickly, swept along by a tide of infatuation with themselves, with being young, passionate, impetuous. Their divorce had been oddly tranquil. Darcy had signed a prenup, and she hadn't wanted anything material. She had wished she could have kept Lena's friendship, but the moment Boyz told his family about their plans to divorce, the Szwedas, even Lena, had dropped her as if she'd never mattered to them at all.

Behind Darcy, a woman snapped impatiently, "Excuse me, but I need to get to the sirloin."

"Oh, sorry." Darcy moved her cart so that it was next to Boyz's. He might feel like a stranger to her, and he had been an unfaithful shit, but she knew she should tell him where she lived and what she could hear. "Actually, Boyz, it's very strange, but my grandmother's house is on Pine Street. Right behind the house you're in for the summer."

"You're kidding me."

"Not kidding," Darcy said. "I've lived here for three years."

"Really." Boyz broke into his great sparkling smile. "I wish I had known that. We're considering opening a branch of our office here, so I rented a house for two months. I want to check the place out, see if it's a good fit. You always talked about your grandmother's house. Maybe I can come over for a drink sometime. You can, um, give me the scoop on the housing market."

Darcy couldn't help it. She burst out laughing. "Same old Boyz. Sorry, but I don't think that's a good idea. I don't know much about real estate here, except that it's expensive. But, Boyz, I want to tell you about something totally off the subject of real estate."

"Oh, yeah?" Boyz leaned in closer to Darcy, fixing his blue gaze on her face.

Darcy took a step back. "I often sit on my patio next to the hedge between my yard and yours, and I can overhear what goes on in your yard."

Boyz shrugged. "So?"

An older gentleman coughed. "You gonna be there all day? You're blocking the aisle."

"Sorry." Once again, Darcy moved her cart. "Boyz, over in that corner, there's a kind of small café. Let's go there and talk a moment, okay?"

Boyz grinned. "I'll go 'talk' with you anywhere."

"Oh, get over yourself," Darcy chided. "It's not about you and me. It concerns Willow."

Without waiting to see if he would follow, Darcy aimed her cart down a long aisle toward the café. Once there, she turned.

Boyz shoved his cart to one side and approached Darcy, his face wary.

"What about Willow?"

"Boyz, I think you should know what I heard through the hedge this week. Willow has a boyfriend, a boy named Logan Smith, an island boy. He's eighteen years old and a troublemaker. He's handsome and he's charismatic, and I overheard him trying to get Willow to have sex with him the other night. In your backyard."

Boyz frowned. He pulled out a chair at one of the small white café tables. "Sit down with me a moment, Darcy."

She perched on the end of the chair.

He took a seat across from her. He still had the same *tell,* the sign that gave away a devious turn in his thoughts. He always patted the top of his chest, as if smoothing his tie, whether he wore a tie or not. "I hope you're not still angry with me."

"What? Because of your . . . the divorce? No. I'm all over that." Darcy smiled to prove it.

"Good. Because I wouldn't want to think you'd do something to get back at me. To hurt me, or Autumn."

Darcy laughed in surprise. "No. No, Boyz, I'm not fabricating what I told you about Willow for some twisted, jealous reason." She took a deep breath. She lowered her voice and changed course. "Boyz, I'm glad you and Autumn are happy. I have no anger, no resentment. I'm happy, too. My life is full."

He looked skeptical. "Okay, but frankly, Darcy, I don't know what to believe about what you think you overheard. I love Willow. I've legally adopted her. She is my own daughter. Autumn and I are caring, watchful parents. We know what's going on with her."

"But—"

"So if you want to spend some time with me, let's just do it. You don't have to make up excuses." He reached over to take her hand in his. "I always enjoyed being with you, Darcy."

How had this all gone so wrong so fast, Darcy wondered. She jerked her hand away from his and stood up. "Boyz, I didn't *invent* what I told you about Willow. And I won't 'make up excuses' to see you again. But you have to realize that I'm out in my garden a lot, weeding, watering, sitting with friends. I'm not going to hide in the house all summer."

Boyz rose, too. "Please don't," he urged. "Believe me, it would be—nice—for us to be back in touch with each other again."

"Oh, Boyz." There really were no right words, so Darcy shook her head and pushed her cart away, fast, right into the aisle that held diapers and Depends.

Darcy hurriedly chose and paid for her groceries, hoping she wouldn't see Boyz again. She didn't, thank heavens. Their exchange had rattled her. It had made her feel defensive—she hadn't been trying to flirt with him! Had he even *heard* what she'd said about Willow?

Safely settled in the everyday nest of her car, she picked up her cellphone and called Jordan.

"Can I come see you? Now? I just ran into Boyz in the grocery store."

"No, you did *not*."

"I did."

"Oh, good grief! Of course. Come over now."

Today when Darcy arrived at Jordan's house, her friend was in the backyard, watching her daughter, Kiks, sitting in a round blue baby swimming pool. It had only about three inches of water in it, but that was enough for Kiks to splash with her hands, shrieking with delight.

"She'll go down for a nap pretty soon," Jordan said. "But I can't wait. Tell me."

"I was in Stop & Shop." Darcy sat on the grass next to Jordan. "We simply bumped into each other, almost literally bumping carts. He wore madras Bermuda shorts, Jordan! And he has the silliest knobby knees, like a flamingo!"

Kiks giggled and clapped, as if she understood Darcy's words, and continued to slap her rubber ducky down under the water, shrieking when it bobbed up again.

"So you absolutely are over him, then," Jordan remarked.

"I'm so over him, the fact that I married him makes me doubt my sanity."

"You didn't experience even the tiniest rush of attraction?"

"God, no! I can't explain it. It was so bizarre, like staring at a fun house mirror, one of those wavery ones that makes you look all out of shape. But the ickiest thing was when I told him about his stepdaughter, Willow, and Logan Smith—he thought I was making it up!"

Kiks tossed her rubber ducky onto the grass. Darcy picked it up and put it back in the water. She did this probably fifty times while she described the entire conversation in detail to Jordan. By the time she finished, Kiks was getting fretful, rubbing her eyes and getting water in her nose in the process.

"Nap time for baby," Jordan said. She picked her daughter up, wrapped her in a towel, and headed for the house. "Come in. I'll rock her for five minutes, then put her down. You can make us some iced tea."

Performing the normal household ritual of boiling the water, pouring the water over Jordan's favorite Earl Grey leaves, setting the mugs on the kitchen table all calmed Darcy. Outside, the day was hot. Here, in the shady kitchen, it was cool, gravity still held the chairs

163

to the floor, and Jordan hadn't done the breakfast dishes. The world went on as normal. Darcy did the dishes while Jordan was with Kiks. She sprayed the counters with antibacterial cleanser and wiped them down. The room smelled pleasantly of lemon.

"Oh, you are a mother's dream," Jordan said, when she came in without her baby. "Thanks for doing the dishes."

"Consider it my payment for psychotherapy." Darcy dropped ice cubes into colorful outdoor glasses and poured the tea. They settled at the kitchen table. "If I hadn't been able to vent to you, I hate to think what I might have done. It makes me so angry that he completely dismissed what I said about Willow."

Jordan sipped her tea, cocked her head, and looked wise. "Are any of his family coming to visit? Are you still friends with any of them—the sisters, maybe?"

"I wish. I don't know. The first year, I missed Irena and Lena. I think I enjoyed being with them more than with Boyz. They were nice to me. His parents were always stuck-up. We're out of touch now, not even a Christmas card." Darcy stirred her tea. "Jordan, what should I do? About Willow, I mean."

"I think you have to let it go," Jordan said. "If Boyz doesn't believe you, what can you do? He told you they were good parents, he might pay closer attention to what Willow's doing, but you've got to stay out of it."

"She's a vulnerable young *girl*—"

"But not *your* young girl."

"Still . . . it makes me feel uneasy."

"Get over it. Forget it. Let's move on to the good stuff—like when's your date with Clive Rush?"

Darcy laughed. "It's not a *date,* Jordan. Or if it is, we've got our own version of a duenna. Mimi is coming with us." As she talked, her fears for Willow dissipated and her own life filled her thoughts. "It's tomorrow night. And I've planned my menu around Mimi. I hope the weather holds and we can eat in the backyard. I don't want to embarrass her by serving something she has to cut, like steak, because I'm not sure how strong her hands are. So I'm making a casserole of rice, shrimp, scallops, and bacon. I thought of linguini, but that might be tricky for Mimi, too. It's hard to wind those noodles onto a fork. . . . And no salad greens, especially arugula, because it's impossible to eat elegantly. Bartlett's tomatoes, sliced."

"Sounds delicious, Darcy. What's for dessert?"

"Cups of cold chocolate mousse. Gosh, I'd better stop talking and go home and start cooking. I work tomorrow, so I'll have to prepare the mousse today." She rose and took her car keys from her tote.

"Have you told Nash you've got a date?" Jordan asked.

"Jordan, it's *not* a date!" Darcy sank back down into her chair. "Sorry. Didn't mean to snap. No, I haven't told Nash, but do I need to? We're not exclusive—we haven't said the magic *L* word. I'm absolutely not going to have sex with Clive tomorrow night. Mimi will be with us all the time."

Jordan gave Darcy a long, challenging look.

"Okay, fine," Darcy capitulated. "I'll tell Nash tonight. But it's not a date."

Darcy didn't want to tell Nash face-to-face because she was afraid she'd blush or look guilty or seem as if she was trying to manipulate Nash into being jealous and forcing him to tell her he wanted them to date each other exclusively. She didn't want him to feel caged, and she didn't want to feel caged, either. Okay, what she had with Nash sexually was like nothing else she'd ever known, but she'd hardly had a lot of sexual partners, and anyway, sex wasn't *everything!*

She spent the day preparing for Tuesday night, then showered and washed her hair and finally, with a glass of wine in her hand, she hit Nash's number. It was dusk outside; he would be home.

"Hey," Nash answered. "I was getting ready to call you."

"How was your day?" Darcy asked.

"Unusual." Nash laughed. He was part of a crew working on the roof of a huge new house.

They'd finished putting up the scaffolding and got up on the roof to shingle, and Juan, a huge, strong guy from the Dominican Republic, who could carry twice the weight of any other man, discovered that he had acrophobia. He'd never been up so high before, and when he looked out at the view, he became paralyzed. He couldn't move up, down, or sideways. It had taken the better part of an hour for Nash and another man to get on either side of him, keep their hands on Juan's arm, and slowly back him down to the staging platform. It was funny, but it was also scary, because each of the guys helping Juan could use only one hand to keep purchase on the roof, and moving Juan was like tugging a grand piano. Then, when they finally got Juan down to the staging platform, he threw up. The crew had to deal with hosing it all down, and that was disgusting. When Juan's feet finally touched the ground, he fell over in a dead faint, coming one inch from a metal rod that could have slammed open his skull. They turned the hose on Juan to shock him out of his faint.

"Now," Nash said, when they stopped laughing, "tell me about your day."

Darcy took a sip of wine. A big sip. She and Nash had exchanged the briefest of romantic histories. He knew she'd been married and divorced. She knew he'd spent some time traveling around the country with a woman

167

named Buffy. Darcy had restrained herself from any remarks about vampires, and she was secretly glad to know Buffy was now traveling in Europe. She wanted to tell Nash about her accidental meeting with Boyz in the grocery store today, but that was all *so much.* Too much for a casual phone call. Nash probably hadn't even had dinner yet.

Besides, she needed to tell him about tomorrow night.

She decided to tell him the simple truth.

"I've spent the day shopping and cooking. I'm going to the chamber music concert tomorrow night with Mimi and her grandson Clive—they invited me to join them. So I told them to come over before the concert for a light meal." She described the menu to Nash, emphasizing the care she was taking to make the food easy for the older woman to deal with.

"That's nice of you," Nash said. "Don't make it too spicy. My grandmother enjoyed spicy foods, but as she got older, they gave her terrible hiccups."

"Hiccups!" Darcy laughed, and suddenly she was flooded with a wave of affection for this man. "Nash, do you like classical music?"

"Some of it. Beethoven, Tchaikovsky, Shostakovich. But chamber quartets make me kind of itchy."

She laughed again. "I know exactly what you

mean." Impulsively, she added, "Nash, I have so much to tell you."

"Good to know, but let's save it for another time, okay? I've got to shower and eat and lie down. I'm exhausted from hauling around a three-hundred-pound man."

After they said goodbye, Darcy took a glass of iced tea out to the backyard and stretched out on a lounger. Above her, the stars were just beginning to emerge as if the darkness were a curtain, pulling itself back to reveal their sparkle. Her conversation with Nash had been so easy. He hadn't even asked about Clive. Well, what, after all, could he have asked?

She gazed around the table, imagining where she'd put the plates and glasses, wondering whether to use candles or the tiny delicate lights she had strung in the hedges. They ran on batteries, and she didn't know how long they'd last. Candles, she decided. Besides, it would still be light out when her guests arrived.

9

The last piece of music the chamber quartet played was too fussy, Darcy decided. It made her feel fidgety—Nash had called it itchy.

Or maybe it was the realization that the concert was about to end, and she and Clive would help Mimi into the car and out of the car to the house on Pine Street, and then what would Darcy do? What should she do? Clive had driven his rented Subaru, and Darcy had sat in the backseat, of course, so that Mimi could have the front passenger seat. So that was the way they would drive home.

And then what? Should Darcy simply step out of the car, thank them for the concert, and walk across to her own house? She imagined how she would wave to them as she put the key in her front door.

Yes, that was exactly what she would do. This night was about Mimi.

Although . . . while they ate their dinner out on the patio, Clive had talked about the book he was writing about the blues. How the music was urgent, raw, visceral. Muddy Waters. Robert Johnson. Bessie Smith. How rock 'n' roll grew out of the blues, how the Rolling Stones were influenced by the blues, how the lyrics were often simple and true, howls of pain because of lust or infidelity or alcohol or poverty. When Clive spoke about his subject, he seemed more alive and capable of passion.

"I didn't know any of that," Darcy said at the end of their meal. "I'll have to listen to some blues sometime."

It was a casual comment—she was stacking their plates on a tray to carry inside—and she didn't mean to be asking for an invitation.

"Come over some evening," Clive said. "I'll give you a concert. I've got stacks of CDs."

"And that's an understatement." Mimi chuckled.

"Oh, well." Darcy hesitated. "Yes, that would be nice." She turned away, flustered.

And felt Clive's hand on her waist. "Here," he said. "Let me carry that tray in for you. I'll come back and help Mimi to the car."

During the chamber music concert, Clive and Darcy bookended Mimi as they sat on the hard wooden pews. The Congregational church was at the top of a short but steep hill, with steps rising from the street, but Mimi couldn't negotiate thosc, so Clive went to fetch the car and brought it up the drive next to the church. Darcy helped Mimi down the ramp and into the front seat. Darcy slid into the backseat, and they drove through the narrow winding streets home.

She stepped out of the car and helped Mimi

171

slowly lift her weakened legs and pry her bulk from the seat.

"Tonight was fun," Darcy said when they were home. "Thank you so much."

"Thank you for dinner, dear," Mimi said, patting Darcy's hand.

Clive said casually, "Come in for a nightcap, why don't you?"

"Oh." Darcy looked at her watch, which was only a stalling tactic while she decided what to do, because it was dark now, and she couldn't see the numbers on her watch. "I have to work tomorrow. . . ."

"Just one short drink," Clive said.

"Well, that would be lovely." *Lovely? She had to use the word* lovely?

Once inside, Mimi said, "Dears, this has been a delightful evening, but I need the comforts of my bed." She kissed Darcy on the cheek and thumped with her cane down the hall to her bedroom.

"Join me in the kitchen," Clive said. "Brandy? Wine?"

"A glass of ice water would hit the spot," Darcy told him. "The church is always so hot on these summer evenings. It doesn't have air-conditioning and their windows don't open very far."

This house had central air-conditioning, an unusual feature in an old home. The owners had taken care with their renovations, leaving the handsome wide board floors while updating the kitchen with slate counters and an island. Darcy slid onto one of the stools and leaned on the counter, watching Clive move around the kitchen, pouring ice water for her and a Scotch and water for himself.

"Let's go in the living room," he said. "It's more comfortable."

"Blue and white." Darcy laughed as they entered the room. "Whenever a designer gets hold of an old Nantucket house, they furnish everything in blue and white. Nautical, you know." She sank into an armchair, smoothing her skirt over her knees.

"I can't say I've really noticed." Clive took the end of the sofa across from her. "But the air-conditioning is a godsend. Mimi has trouble breathing when it's too humid."

"You're so good to your grandmother."

He shrugged. "I'm glad to do it. She's always been there for me. When I got divorced, my parents gave me all kinds of grief, especially about my girls, but Mimi was cool."

"Tell me about your girls."

Clive's face softened. "Alyssa and Zoe. Twins. Seven years old. They live with their mother in Boston. Helen—my ex-wife—teaches at BU, and so do I, so we have a relatively easy system of caring for the girls." He took a sip of his drink. "What about you? Do you have children?"

"No," Darcy said, and not wanting to sound pathetic, joked, "but I do have an ex. Boyz lives in Boston, too. He's part of a large real estate firm." She held up her glass of water. "If only life were so clear . . ."

"Ah, what would be the fun in that?" Clive leaned forward and put his hand on Darcy's knee.

Darcy met his eyes. Her breathing went jagged. "I suppose . . ." Her brain had melted. She couldn't put words together.

Clive slowly slid his hand up her thigh and onto her arm. Softly, he trailed his fingers down her bare arm to her hand. He scrolled his index finger in the palm of her hand, then clasped it firmly. "Come over here."

"I—"

Clive tugged her hand. He was smiling mischievously and his remoteness was gone. He was warm. He was focused on her. "Come on. I promise I'm not going to ravish you in the living room with my grandmother nearby."

Well, Darcy thought, *why not?* She was such a novice in romance. She probably took it all too seriously. Clive *was* gorgeous.

She moved onto the sofa next to him.

He put his hand on her cheek. "You're beautiful."

Darcy flushed from his touch and his words. Before she could retort *I bet you say that to all the girls,* Clive pulled her toward him and kissed her mouth. The kiss was lingering and intense. His warm breath was scented with whiskey, his lips nuzzled hers, his tongue slipped between her lips. He gently slid his hands down to cup her breasts. Her nipples hardened. She thought she just might ravish him in his grandmother's living room.

He pulled away. "I want you." His breath was ragged. He took her hand and put it on his khakis, right at the crotch, where his erection pushed at the material. "You see how much I want you?"

Darcy's mind was an explosion of sensations and thoughts. Desire rushed through her. But what about Nash? She didn't want to be unfaithful to him, but did she need to be faithful when they weren't committed to each other? Clive seemed so . . . *experienced.* Maybe she was a terrible person, wanting Nash and now wanting Clive.

"You look worried," Clive said softly.

"I do?"

"You're frowning." He lifted her hand away from his body but kept it clasped in his. "I've had many responses to my sexual advances, but a frown is a first."

She laughed, grateful for his wit, his charm. "I suppose . . ." She didn't know what she supposed. She supposed too many things to express.

"You work tomorrow," he reminded her. "We don't have time tonight, I know that. Still"—

that smile—"I couldn't help myself. I've been wanting to kiss you since I first saw you."

"Me, too," she said, then shook her head and rolled her eyes and laughed at her words, and the spell she was caught in was broken. She stood up. "I should go home."

"I'll walk you."

"You don't need to, it's just next door."

"If I walk you home, I can kiss you good night."

She shook her head. "Another kiss like that, and I won't sleep."

"Oh, I've got lots of different kisses," he told her.

She knew he was joking, being clever, and yet a danger alert, like a dog lifting its head at a noise she couldn't hear, resounded within her. He was joking, but he was also telling the truth. This man was a sexual expert. He had an entire armory of kisses.

But was that a bad thing?

They compromised. Clive walked her halfway home, and kissed her chastely on the cheek. Darcy waved at him from her front door, and stepped inside her house.

She leaned against the door. Her black cat strolled down the hall toward her. He planted himself in front of her and lifted his head and meowed.

"I don't know," Darcy told him. "I really don't know."

●●●

Thursday the library was open until eight p.m. When Bonny from the circulation desk asked if Darcy could do her evening shift, Darcy was glad to agree. She'd been too busy during the day to think about Clive or Nash, and she wanted to keep busy and let her thoughts churn away at the back of her mind. Maybe they'd offer her a decision on a platter: Sleep with *only* Nash? Sleep with Clive *and* Nash? Tell Nash about Clive? But what if Nash slept with another woman—and she knew plenty of women who wanted to sleep with him—would she be riddled with jealousy? She kind of thought she would.

The children's library was crazy busy all evening. Darcy didn't have a moment to think about herself, and it was with relief she locked up and hurried home. She poured herself a glass of red wine, kicked off her shoes, and went out to her garden. The grass beneath her bare feet was cool and oddly cheering. Sinking onto her lounger, she took a deep breath and looked up at the sky. It was dusk. The sky was slowly withdrawing the clear blue of day, allowing night to arrive. The light was on in Clive's window and music softly drifted into the air.

She knew she had messages on her cellphone, but she hadn't brought it out with her. She needed to be alone for a while. She wanted to relax and sort out her thoughts. Clive was a player, she was pretty sure about that. But Nash hadn't expressed any desire for a long-term relationship. If she told him about Clive, would Nash think she was pushing him for some kind of commitment?

"I thought your yard was strangely quiet."

Darcy almost jumped off her chair. The voice was so near her, she thought for a moment that someone was standing next to her.

"And thank God for that." It was a man, on the Brueckners' side of the hedge. So it was Otto.

"Where are your sons?" Now Darcy could place the voice: Autumn's.

"Susan's brother and his family are stopping in Boston on their way to London. Susan took the boys up to see their cousins. They'll be gone for three, maybe four, days."

"Oooh, interesting. You know, Boyz is in Boston, too. He won't be home until Saturday."

A moment of silence. Darcy could feel herself holding her breath.

"How do you like your rental?" Autumn asked. "Is it large enough for you and your family?"

"It is large enough." Otto replied. "And you, do you like your rental house?"

"Very much. I'd invite you over to see it, but I've given Willow this night to watch something on television."

"Would you like to see mine?"

"Very much."

"Perhaps I can offer you a glass of wine."

Their voices trailed away as they crossed the yard. Darcy held back the urge to stand on top of her patio table to peer over the hedge and call out, "I can hear you!" She didn't care if Autumn was unfaithful to Boyz, but she hated the idea of Otto cheating on Susan.

But what business was it of hers? Plus, why would she even suspect they were cheating? Maybe he was only going to show her the house and she was only going to tour it.

Darcy chuckled softly, remembering the summer a group of parents rented the house next door for five of their college-age sons. The boys went to the beach all day and partied all night. Darcy had never called the cops even as the summer deepened and the parties grew louder. She could have; a town regulation required all loud noise and music to stop at eleven o'clock. But she had kind of enjoyed the boys. Kind of envied their carefree lives, their maniacal laughter, their freedom to revel in the summer. Her only defensive action had been to walk around her garden in the morning, pick up the beer bottles and cans that had been tossed over the hedge, and rather gleefully throw them back in the boys' yard.

Why had she changed? Why did she care if Otto Brueckner slept with Autumn or if Willow had sex with Logan?

Well . . . Nash was a new element. Lust was

179

easy; lust felt good, it made her blood pound and her worries disappear behind a fog of desire. But love . . . she wasn't sure she had a handle on love yet, not even after having been married.

Darcy knew Lala and Lala's family had loved her when she was a baby and a little girl. She had photo albums; she had memories. But Lala wasn't about love, not really, she was about being pursued, being caught, being adored. She was like a seductress with an extremely short attention span. Lala wanted nothing as confining as marriage. She wanted to be gorgeous and naughty and desired. She reveled in the gifts men gave her, the trips she enjoyed with them, the flowers and phone calls and nights out. The seduction, the lure, the intrigue, the *catch*.

As a young girl, Darcy had been mesmerized by her fabulous mother. She had thrilled to the moment the door opened and Lala swept in, carrying with her a flotilla of fragrance that filled every corner of the room and lasted long after Lala had left.

"Darling child, Mama's beauty, I'll see you in the morning. Sweet dreams." Lala would kiss Darcy's forehead and drift away.

That bright, twinkling, precarious appearance, that *sparkle,* had been what Darcy thought was love. No wonder she had married the sparkling Boyz. He and his family were an entire chandelier of sparkle.

Penny had loved Darcy, too, in her own calm, reliable way. She had made Darcy feel safe and cared for.

So maybe that was what love was, part sparkle, part safety.

Autumn, Boyz's new wife, was definitely sparkle. Who knew what kind of unspoken agreement she had with her husband about fidelity? Certainly fidelity had not been included in Boyz's definition of marriage with Darcy. But she'd bet it was part of Susan Brueckner's understanding of marriage. Or maybe not. What did she know? Maybe Susan was meeting her boy toy in Boston while her sons played with their cousins.

Or maybe the Brueckner marriage was one of convenience. This was not the Jane Austen age, yet she knew people who had married for reasons other than *true love,* whatever that was. She'd never been a romantic fool. She'd dated in high school, but she'd known what the guys really wanted, and she'd remained a virgin. A skeptical virgin. In college she'd finally had sex, and for a year a guy named Sid Byrd with a Lenin-like mustache and beard had sworn everlasting adoration, but she'd grown tired of his seriousness, his dramatic fits of jealousy, his vague, ambitious dreams to save the world. He had been handsome, kind, intelligent, faithful, and good. But he hadn't been fun, and she knew she was shallow to think less of him for that, but she broke up with him and dated casually for the rest of her college life.

Darcy had often wondered why someone as extroverted and ambitious as Boyz would choose to marry someone as quiet and bookish as Darcy. There was the chemistry, of course, but Boyz had enough electricity for both of them, and Darcy was infatuated and grateful. Then, not long after their marriage, they went to Martha's Vineyard so Boyz could list a new house that a friend of his from college wanted to sell. Darcy had come along for the pleasure of being with him, seeing the Vineyard, enjoying lunch at the Black Dog. Boyz was elated about this new house. It was gorgeous, and it was expensive. His father was, naturally, the king of their real estate agency, with the right to skim the cream of the real estate market for his own, leaving the less-esteemed properties for his son and daughters. Over a lunch of calamari, Boyz excitedly confided to Darcy how he was going to make the Vineyard market his own.

"And when your grandmother dies, I'll be the one to handle the sale of her house. That will provide me a head start for a branch of Szwedas Real Estate on Nantucket."

Darcy felt as if her husband had punched her in the belly. "But I don't want to sell my grandmother's house!"

"You told me it's old and in need of renovation. Why would you want to keep it?"

"We could spend some of the summer there. Summers are—"

"We'll need a base for our agency there, not a decrepit old house."

"How can you say it's decrepit? You haven't even seen it—"

Boyz rolled over her words with his own. "You told me the house is in a residential area. We'll *have* to sell the house. With the proceeds of the sale, we could buy something in the business district." Finally Boyz noticed the pain and anger in Darcy's eyes. "I'm sorry, Darcy. I apologize. But please understand, the real estate boom in Nantucket makes it the perfect opportunity. I want to forge my own territory, my own kingdom, before my father or sisters do."

Yet in the three rushed years of their marriage, Boyz didn't get to Nantucket.

Only now did Darcy realize that it wasn't Boyz's overwhelmingly packed calendar or the family's tradition of going to Lake George. It as also that Darcy hadn't encouraged Boyz to visit the island, to see her grandmother's house and the island itself. For him, it would be only real estate, one more property to value in monetary terms and sell.

She wondered if in the past few days Boyz had strolled around the block from his rented house to survey Penny's house—Darcy's house now—to estimate how much he could have made on its sale. She'd bet he had.

A light went on in the Rushes' attic. A few moments later, Bessie Smith's raspy voice lilted out into the night as she sang simply, with shrewd humor, "A good man is hard to find."

Amen, sister, Darcy thought.

10

Star Trek Beyond was out, and the Dreamland Theater was packed. Darcy and Nash had found seats on the upper deck, and while the last stragglers hurried in, Darcy spotted the faces of friends and waved to them. Jordan was there with Lyle, and no child, which was probably the first time they'd left Kiks with a sitter. Beverly, Darcy's boss, was there with her husband, and Angelica and Lars, and Gage Wharton with a woman Darcy didn't recognize.

Susan Brueckner was there with her three sons. Otto wasn't. Neither was Autumn.

It was a weekday. Boyz was probably in Boston, working, leaving Autumn alone; and even though Darcy scolded herself, she searched the crowd for Willow. And there she was, on the other side of the aisle and the end of a row, cuddling with Logan. Darcy felt a twinge of worry about the teenager. And she realized this meant that Autumn had an empty house for a couple of hours if she wanted to entertain visitors. Like Otto.

Really, Darcy was ashamed of herself. She didn't run the world; she didn't have the right to interfere or even a way to interfere. If Otto and Autumn had an affair, fine. But if Logan was having sex with Willow . . . if she was, it still was none of Darcy's business. As the lights dimmed, she forced herself to concentrate on the show.

The movie was loud and explosive. She walked home, holding hands with Nash, delighting in the summer warmth, the whispering of leaves as a salty sea breeze stirred them. Many of the shops were still open, and lights were on in all the houses on Main Street. A line from Natalie Merchant's song, "These are days we'll remember" played through Darcy's mind as she felt the warmth of Nash's hand, his strong presence next to her, the wind teasing her hair, and smelled the sweet fragrance of all the flowers blooming in all the yards. If she could capture this particular moment and contain it in a jar, she could keep it until she was an old lady like Penny had been, and then she'd open the jar and all this would drift out, not just a mental memory but the sensations, the gentle night, her youth and strength welling powerfully inside her, her anticipation of being in bed with Nash. . . .

They entered her house. Darcy shut the door behind her. Nash put his hands around her waist and drew her against him, kissing the top of his head.

"Nash," she said, "could we talk? Just talk . . . don't get scared, this isn't about us—I'm not going to go all mushy and possessive on you. I'd like your advice on something."

"Sure." Nash released his embrace. "What's up?"

186

Darcy headed into the living room, clicking on table lamps here and there. "Want some coffee? Wine?"

"Not yet." Nash relaxed in one of the club chairs.

Darcy sat across from him on the sofa. "I didn't tell you before . . . in one way it's not that big a deal, at least not part of it, but part of it has really gotten under my skin. Um, okay." She changed positions, crossing and uncrossing her legs. "Remember I told you I was married before?"

"Yeah, to a guy with an unusual name."

"Right. Boyz Szweda. Well, he's rented the house behind mine for July and August."

"That's weird."

"He didn't know I live here," Darcy explained. "When I knew him, I lived in Boston and then on the Cape. He told me he is thinking of expanding his real estate company to Nantucket. But never mind him, it's his stepdaughter, Willow, I'm concerned about. She's fourteen. She's Autumn's daughter—Autumn's his wife now. Boyz has adopted her, and he says he loves her like his own . . . he told me that when I ran into him in the grocery store. I know I'm jumbling this up, but stay with me here."

"Right here," Nash assured her.

"Okay. When we were at the beach two Sundays ago, I spotted Willow with Logan Smith. He's a local boy and he's trouble. He's eighteen, and

187

she's fourteen, and he had her pressed up against a sand dune. . . ."

"Are you sure it was Willow?"

Darcy shook her head, irritated by the interruption, although it was a fair question. "Then, I *assumed* it was. I've never met Willow, but she has her mother's red hair, and I've seen the girl from my kitchen window several times. She was carrying groceries into the house with her mother, stuff like that. But the other night when I was sitting out on my patio, I heard them. Willow and Logan. He was trying to get her to have sex. She was protesting, but also kind of not. I didn't know what to do."

"What did you do?"

"Nothing. Willow stopped him and went into the house. I heard Logan get in his truck. I was relieved. I wasn't sure that it was my place to intrude. But on Monday I was in Stop and Shop, and I accidentally ran into Boyz. Literally. So we said hello and it was polite enough, but then I told him about Willow and Logan, and he brushed me off. He went all superior and told me he and Autumn are Willow's parents and they know how to take care of her. He accused me of making up a story so I could get his attention. He thought it was all about him. I don't know why I'm surprised."

Nash frowned. "You know having sex with an underage girl is statutory rape, right?"

"I do know that. I also know that lots of island girls that age are having sex. The community tries to warn them about diseases and pregnancy and of course the laws, but it's hard to be logical when you're a teenager." Darcy studied Nash's face. "You think I should have done something."

"I would have."

Darcy waited for him to say more. When he stayed quiet, she said, almost defensively, "I talked to Jordan about all this. She thinks I should leave it alone. It's true, I don't know anything about Willow, what she does when she's off island." Tears swelled in her eyes. "I hate this, Nash. I feel like I'm being judged."

Nash rose. His expression was so serious, she was afraid he was going to leave, just walk right out the door.

Instead, he came around the coffee table and sat down next to Darcy.

"Hey." He pulled her against him in a comforting hug. "I apologize if you think I'm judging you. I'm not. I think I'm probably more of a straight arrow than lots of people. Hell, I've never even driven the wrong way on any of all those exasperating one-way streets on this island."

Darcy smiled, glad she knew he was trying to make her smile. She closed her eyes and relaxed against him. "I was telling you all this because of Boyz, really. I mean, I know how bizarre it is that he and his family are living right behind my yard for two months. But when we divorced, neither of us was mad. I guess I'm trying to say we had a passionless divorce. I want you to know I have zero interest in the guy. If anything, I think he's more arrogant than he was when I met him."

"Okay, then. I have zero interest in the guy, too." Nash sank into the sofa cushions, wrapping his arms around Darcy, snuggling her against him.

"As for Willow . . . it helps to know your thinking. Boyz's family—his parents, his two sisters—are very close. The father and mother sort of rule the roost. They're sophisticated and snotty, but their basic values are sterling."

"That's good." Nash kissed the top of her head lightly.

Darcy sighed. "Life is hard to figure out."

Nash nodded. "Yeah, it's easy enough to know what to do from a distance, as a rule. But when it's personal, it gets confusing."

Darcy heard a note of sorrow in his voice. "Did something like this happen to you?"

Nash tensed up. "Nah. Just speaking in general."

There it was, Darcy thought, *the door to Nash opening an inch and quickly closing.*

She didn't press him. They sat together in silence. Darcy was exhausted from worrying about it all—what Nash would think about Boyz being on the island and so near. And she thought that in a way, they had almost had their first argument.

Nash pulled away. "I've got to go home and get some sleep. I almost fell asleep right now. Fresh air and construction work, a sure cure for insomnia."

Darcy walked him to the door and lightly kissed him goodbye. She had thought she was telling Nash about her and Boyz, yet in a way, she and Nash had learned something new about each other.

Darcy was out in her garden the next morning, weeding around the foxgloves and humming as she worked. She had to leave for the library, but she'd risen early, dressing and spinning through her morning chores as happily as Cinderella with birds on her wrists.

"Alfred, go back and get your flip-flops." Otto Brueckner's voice was pleasant but firm.

"But I don't need them on the beach," the boy protested.

"Maybe you'll need them if we go into a restaurant for an ice cream sundae," Otto said, his voice coaxing and kind.

Darcy sat back on her knees and shamelessly listened. She couldn't help overhearing the sounds of the doors slamming on the car, the giggles of the children, and Susan calling, "I've got the picnic basket and the towels. I think we're ready."

They were a happy family, Darcy decided, and the meetings between Otto and Autumn were simply her imagination embroidering events that had never taken place. Neighbors *did* talk to each other, after all. Look at her and Mimi. Look at her and Clive. Okay, maybe she and Clive were not the best example. Still, as she gathered her gardening tools and kicked the dirt off her clogs, she vowed she would stop making something out of nothing, spinning drama from normal life. Obviously she read too many books.

Maybe she was exaggerating what she had with Nash, too. If her marriage to Boyz had taught her anything, it was how easily she adorned reality with her dreams. From that first dramatic kiss in front of the restaurant, when Boyz had swept her down in his arms as if they were stars in a movie, Darcy had let her imagination run wild—and how could she not when Boyz and his family were so beautiful, so captivating? How fortunate she was to have a grandmother who'd left her a house on the island; how lucky she was to have a job at the library, doing work she loved. But life was full of ups and downs, twists and turns, shocks and sins and loss and disappointments. She knew that from experience.

She showered and dressed, twisting her long dark hair into a figure eight at the back of her head, securing it with a long, jewel-headed pin. She chose to wear a plain white shirt with a mandarin collar with her flowered skirt today, and succeeded, she thought, in looking professional, chaste, and even slightly severe.

Good. She was going to be in Perfect Darcy mode today, something she did occasionally. She would eat nothing, drink only kale and spinach smoothies, which she did when she'd been eating and drinking too much. In her Perfect Darcy mode, she moved more slowly; forced herself to take one deep breath before saying anything to anyone; and focused on the work she had to do, refusing to let her thoughts wander. As she walked to work, she reminded herself she was stepping on the same brick sidewalks and crossing the very same cobblestone streets as Maria Mitchell, who had discovered a comet by looking through a telescope on her house on this island. A Quaker, Maria Mitchell became the first librarian of the Nantucket Atheneum where Darcy now worked, and later she taught astronomy at Vassar. In 1842, Maria Mitchell stopped wearing clothes made of cotton in a protest against slavery. She was a woman of principle and dignity. Compared to her, Darcy was a lightweight, daydreaming about Nash when she should be concentrating on her work. Well, today she was going to concentrate. She would finish the filing. She would be infinitely patient with the children during story hour—no, she would be *enchanting*.

She went through her day exactly as planned.

In the afternoon, she weeded the collection, one of the most difficult jobs in the library. She had to find books that hadn't been checked out for months, or books that were torn or stained beyond hope, and put them aside for the book sale. A time-consuming job, it demanded that she concentrate, and she was surprised when five o'clock came and it was time for her to leave.

She didn't stop at any of the restaurants for one of their yummy carryouts. No, she was still in Perfect Darcy mode. She would prepare her own meal, using leftovers from her refrigerator. And while she ate, she would read the biography of Benjamin Franklin that had sat on her bedside table, ignored for weeks. No fast-plotted thrillers tonight, no entertaining family saga. History. Because she should.

When Nash phoned on his way home from work around eight-thirty, she told him she had been Perfect Darcy all day. His laugh boomed over the phone, making her laugh, too.

"Tell me what you do to be Perfect Darcy," he said.

"Okay, well, first of all, I try to remember to have good posture, to walk as if I'm holding a penny pinched between my shoulder blades. That makes me stand up straight, hold my tummy in, and keep my shoulders down."

"Sounds like it would make you stick out your breasts, too."

"You would think that"—Darcy laughed—"and you're right, although that's not the purpose. And when we hang up, I'm going to read a new biography of Ben Franklin."

"Very admirable, Darcy, but forgive me if I never attempt to have a Perfect Nash day." He was quiet for a moment before asking, "Are you atoning for anything?"

"No!" Darcy said, perhaps a beat too quickly, because maybe she kind of was. She shouldn't have kissed Clive, not when she was with Nash, but *was* she *with* Nash? *Exclusively?* She couldn't ask him about that now, when he was tired from a day's labor and had to get up early tomorrow.

Nash remained silent, as if he knew her response was a lie.

"All right, I suppose I am," Darcy admitted. "For some reason, I'm spending too much time worrying about my neighbors. Oh, I sound nuts, I know. Let's talk about it when we have more time."

"Good. I think I'm headed for my sofa and the Red Sox game. Maybe we can get together tomorrow when you're not so perfect."

Darcy laughed and headed for her own sofa. She'd changed into shorts and a T-shirt and flip-flops. Tonight, cozy and casual, she would spend with Ben Franklin, improving her mind. Usually she alternated reading a good novel with a good biography, but something about this summer made her yearn for books that made her laugh or cry, that allowed her to free the emotional chaos inside her. When she was engrossed in a book, some kind of barrier broke and all kinds of feelings and questions and needs spilled out. It was like this sometimes—not always, but sometimes—when she saw an especially adorable commercial for dog food.

"Why don't I have a dog?" she would wonder out loud, while her cat sat looking as if he'd roll his eyes if cats could roll their eyes. She'd weep and ask the empty room why didn't she have a brother or a sister, why were both her parents so absent from her life, why did Boyz choose Autumn who was six years older than Boyz— okay, Autumn had huge breasts, but that couldn't be the only reason—why was Darcy thirty years old with no children of her own and no husband and here she was, alone in this great big house and why was she so selfish and self-centered, she should become a nurse and take care of people with incurable diseases. . . .

Tonight, she slammed *Ben Franklin* shut. "You're not doing it for me tonight, Ben." She hadn't had wine with dinner, so she poured herself a glass and kicked off her flip-flops and walked out into her backyard. It was all out here, fresh air, the mingled scents of flowers, the laughter of people passing by on the lane, the lounger that held her in perfect comfort, and when she looked up, so many stars in the sky.

It was quiet. Not the slightest breeze stirred. No one spoke. The lights were out in all the houses around her. It was only about nine thirty. Where was everyone? And why did she even care? She rolled her own eyes at herself.

"My parents aren't home."

It was Willow speaking. The way the girl was cooing her words suggested she was talking to Logan.

"I like it out here. It's cozier. More hidden. When do your parents get home?"

"Not till late. They're out at a party on someone's yacht."

Okay, so much for relaxing under the stars. Darcy was going inside. Boyz didn't want her interfering with his stepdaughter, he said he and Autumn knew what was going on, and Darcy did not want to sit out here and listen to the sounds of teenage passion.

"Hey, baby, maybe we've got time for some extra fun."

"What do you mean?" Willow asked.

Silence, then, "Ever donc hcroin?"

Darcy froze.

Willow's voice got smaller, almost a whisper. "No, Logan. That's way too scary for me."

"Hey, don't I take care of you? When we had the vodka the other night, I didn't give you too much. You didn't throw up, did you? I know how to get a good high without causing any downside."

Willow's voice shook. "Couldn't we just smoke a joint again? Or we could get some vodka from the house."

"Baby, baby, don't be scared."

As Darcy listened, she couldn't help but interpret the silence, the murmurings. She could clearly read what Logan was up to. He was kissing Willow, cuddling her, making the girl feel safe and secure. Darcy had heard rumors about Logan dealing, but this was going past dealing.

"I promise you, baby, you'll feel euphoric. You know what that word means, right?"

A sharpness in Willow's voice. "Of course I do!"

"Well, this will be euphoria like you've never imagined. You'll get so high, and I'll be right here holding you, and after a while, you'll get relaxed, a little sleepy, it's called 'on the nod.'"

"Logan—"

"Okay, fine. I spent some money to get some really good, pure, sweet stuff for you, but I don't want to force you."

Thank God, Darcy thought, relaxing her shoulders.

"I'm sorry, Logan."

"No worries. I kind of thought you were too young for me, anyway."

The grass rustled. Logan was moving away from Willow.

"I'm not too young for you," Willow protested. "I love you, Logan."

"Well, I snort heroin and I kind of imagined us doing it together . . . and then doing it together."

"Are you going to snort some now?"

"Not now. I wasn't going to. I wanted to stay clear and watch you for your first time. See how you do. Look, see this packet? Look how small it is. I wouldn't use more than half of it. I'd make a line of it on my hand, and you'd snort it—you've seen people snort heroin, haven't you?"

"In movies."

"I wish you trusted me."

Another silence.

"All right," Willow conceded in a small voice. "I'll do it."

"My baby. You won't regret it. You know I love you, don't you, Willow?"

"Do you? Really? You've never said that before."

As Darcy listened to sounds of what was undoubtedly some major kissing, she stood up, hands clenched at her side, panicking. Willow's parents weren't home. She had her cell, she could call someone, she could call the police, but they couldn't get here soon enough to prevent Willow from snorting the heroin. Willow was not her child, she, Darcy, was not responsible for Willow, she'd been told by Boyz to butt out of Willow's life, but this, *this* . . .

"Okay now, see this nice straight line on my hand? Hold one nostril shut with your finger, put your nose down—"

"Don't do it, Willow! I'm coming over there!"

Darcy sprinted through her yard, beneath the arbor, around and down the narrow path near the Brueckners'. She burst into the Szwedas' backyard. Willow and Logan sat staring at her wide-eyed and openmouthed as if she'd landed from outer space. And she sort of felt like it, as adrenaline flooded her system. She was shaking, and she was red-hot mad.

"No, Willow, you are *not* snorting heroin." Darcy kicked Logan's hand, and the white powder flew into the grass.

"Hey!" Logan yelled. "Lady, that was a lot of money you just lost me."

"Good!" Darcy eased her voice down from bellow to loud. She wanted to sound threatening but in control. "I live on the other side of the hedge, and I've heard every stupid word you've just said. You're Logan Smith and I know your parents, and I've got a cellphone in my hand and if you don't get your sleazy, sneaky drug-dealer ass out of here *now,* I'm calling the police."

Logan looked at Willow. "Are you going to let this freak tell us what to do?"

Willow's teeth were chattering so hard she couldn't speak.

Darcy held up her cellphone and hit a button.

"Bitch," Logan said. He stood, tall and so thin Darcy thought she could push him over with one hand. He glanced down at Willow. "Coming with me?"

Darcy stepped between Willow and Logan. "No. She's not coming with you. She's not coming with you ever again, especially after I tell her about the girls you've knocked up."

Logan narrowed his eyes. "I'm gonna get—"

Darcy folded her arms over her chest. "Shut up, Logan. You would be extremely stupid to threaten me. Leave. Just leave."

"Nasty old snake-face bitch."

Darcy said nothing. She knew he would go more readily if she let him have the last word.

Logan turned and walked away, sauntering, so Willow knew he was no coward.

He disappeared from sight. A moment later, a truck door slammed and an engine roared and Logan laid some rubber. Then he was gone.

Darcy was trembling. She knew it was the adrenaline rush, but she wanted it to stop. She wanted to appear calm and sensible to Willow. She knew she'd frightened the girl. Hell, Darcy had frightened herself.

She squatted down in front of the girl. "Willow, my name is Darcy Cotterill. I live in the house on the other side of the hedge."

Willow was still shaking too hard to speak.

"I'm not some weird voyeur. You can trust me."

Darcy hesitated. "I know your stepfather, Boyz Szweda."

"Okay," Willow whispered, still clutching herself tightly and shivering.

Darcy sat down on the grass next to Willow. "This is a very cool spot," Darcy said. Soft grass beneath an ancient maple, with two of its roots veeing out, the trunk of the tree served as a backrest and concealed them from the view of anyone in the house, while the porch lamp provided enough light for Darcy to see Willow. "I'm a librarian," she said. That should reassure the girl. Everyone thought librarians were helpful and bossy. "Here, at the Nantucket Atheneum. I live here year-round. So I know all about Logan."

"Don't tell my parents. Please. They would totally kill me."

"I don't know, Willow. I've got to think about that. But let's go inside. I'll make hot chocolate and we can talk."

"Hot chocolate?" Willow drew back, suddenly looking like a normal teenager being offered something truly lame.

"Beats heroin every time." Darcy stood, held out her hand, and breathed a sigh of relief when the girl took it. She pulled Willow up. "If you don't want hot chocolate, we can just go in your house and talk for a while."

Willow hung her head, as if ashamed to admit it: "I like hot chocolate."

"Good. Let's go. We can go along this funny path between my hedges and my neighbors' house—there's a family there this summer with three little boys." She held Willow's hand as they walked. "You might have met them. The Brueckners. They borrowed some milk from me." *Babble, babble,* Darcy thought, but it was soothing her to talk and she hoped it was soothing Willow. "I have a cat. Do you like cats? His name is Muffler and he's extremely vain."

"I like cats."

They came out into the narrow street, turned, and went into Darcy's house.

"Come in the kitchen while I make the hot chocolate. If we're both in the kitchen, Muffler will get curious and make a guest appearance. Be prepared. He will expect praise for his awesomeness."

Willow smiled weakly. Darcy felt like she'd won the lottery.

"Sit down." Darcy went to her cupboards and took out the tin of Hershey's cocoa and the sugar bowl. She measured two cups of milk into a pan and began to mix the ingredients together.

Willow looked puzzled. "You're not making Swiss Miss?"

"What? No. No, I like making it from scratch. It takes more time, and I have to stand here and stir, but the taste is worth it. Ah, I've got a bag of mini marshmallows, too."

"How do you know my stepfather?"

Oh, boy. Darcy continued stirring, considering her answer. "I was married to him," she admitted. She hoped Willow knew her stepfather had been married before.

"Wait, what? Okay, I've heard about you." Willow relaxed in her chair. "Isn't it odd that you live next to us?"

"I've lived here for three years. It was my grandmother's house."

"Does your grandmother live here, too?"

"No, she died a few years ago. It's okay—she was in her eighties. She'd had a good life."

"My grandmother, my mom's mother, works in Vegas. We don't see her very often. My mother doesn't approve of her. My dad's mother—my real dad—well, I've never met her. I don't see my real dad much. I'm supposed to say my birth dad. He lives out west somewhere. . . ."

"That's kind of the way my parents are," Darcy told her. "They got divorced a long time ago. My father got a new wife and moved to Florida and never gets in touch with me—"

"Really?" Willow brightened at Darcy's words. "*My* birth dad doesn't either. I mean, he never sends me a Christmas present or even a birthday card."

Darcy carefully poured the hot chocolate into two mugs and added the mini marshmallows on top. She set one mug on the kitchen table in front of Willow and one mug across from the girl. She handed Willow a spoon and took one for herself.

"Careful," Darcy said. "It might be too hot."

"I like watching the marshmallows melt."

"I do, too."

Willow stirred her cocoa. "Swiss Miss has a packet of these really tiny marshmallows."

"Cool."

"Plus, it's quicker than making it your way."

While Willow bent over her mug, stirring the marshmallows, Darcy studied the girl. She had her mother's abundant red hair and green eyes. She had her mother's body type, too. Darcy could understand why a guy would be attracted to this fourteen-year-old even in her jeans shorts and a loose cotton T-shirt.

"I'll have to try Swiss Miss sometime," Darcy said.

"Yeah." Willow sipped her drink. "This is good, though."

Muffler swanned into the room, waving his glorious long-haired black tail.

"Oh, he's beautiful!" Willow cried.

"He certainly thinks so."

In one light leap, the cat jumped into Willow's lap.

"He likes me!"

"He'll like you more if you pet him."

For a while, only the sound of Muffler's loud purring filled the room. *What next?* Darcy thought. They say if you save someone's life, you're responsible for them forever, which Darcy always thought was kind of backward, because if you save someone's life, shouldn't *they* be responsible for *you,* in a sort of turnabout is fair play? Besides, she hadn't really saved the girl's life. Except maybe she had. Getting hooked on heroin was a slow and ugly death sentence. Willow had asked Darcy not to tell her parents, but Darcy thought she had to. The girl was young and impressionable and too pretty for her own good.

She deliberated about what to ask Willow. She didn't want to start a series of monosyllabic responses to boring adult questions. Besides, she wasn't a certified therapist and Willow had a lot to process. She didn't feel comfortable letting the girl return to an empty house, though.

"Want to watch TV? Until your parents get home? On Demand? Maybe *Pretty Little Liars?*"

"Cool! My parents won't be home till midnight."

"Want me to pop some popcorn?"

"No, I'm good." Willow stood up, holding Muffler in her arms.

Darcy led Willow into the living room. They settled at either end of the sofa. Darcy pushed the buttons on the remote control until they'd gotten to the show, then handed it to Willow.

Willow raised the volume slightly. When the

show began, she took a deep breath. Obviously being on a sofa, watching television, was a safe place for her.

Darcy had never watched the show. She was stunned at the perfect beauty of the actresses, and especially liked Alison, who was worried about her sanity. Her mind raced as the show went on: She wanted to be with Willow when her parents came home. She wanted to make the events of the evening clear. Somehow she had to get to the doing heroin without talking anymore about sex, since Boyz had made it clear it was none of her business. But heroin . . .

As if Willow had read Darcy's mind, she said, "Will you come with me when my parents get home?"

"If you want me to."

Willow chewed on her thumb, then spoke so lightly Darcy could hardly hear her. "Logan really is my boyfriend. And all the girls at home are doing it."

Darcy gasped. "All the girls at home are doing *heroin?*"

Willow laughed out loud. "No! I meant they're all having sex. Or kind of sex. They give their boyfriends BJs. That keeps everybody happy and no one gets pregnant."

Words fail me, Darcy thought, and couldn't speak. The girl at the other end of the sofa had a sprinkling of cinnamon freckles over nose and cheeks. *If Willow wore her hair in braids . . .* "I wonder if Anne of Green Gables ever gave BJs to Gilbert Blythe," she mused.

Willow burst out laughing so loudly that Muffler, insulted, jumped off her lap.

"Wait, what? That is a very bizarre thought!" Turning on the sofa, she studied Darcy. "You really were married to my stepfather?"

"I was."

"You were a waitress when he met you."

"Yes, that's right." Darcy smiled, remembering. "At Bijoux. I had so much fun working there. So many great friends."

"Why do you live on Nantucket?"

"My grandmother left me this house. I sort of grew up in it, and I've always loved it. Plus, I had finished my degree in library science, and there was a job at the children's library. Everything fell into place."

"My stepfather thinks he's going to open a real estate company here, on this island. He says Nantucket has *cachet*."

"Do you think you'll move here?"

"Gosh, I hope not!" Willow made a grimace and covered her mouth. "Sorry. I mean I know some people totally choose to live here, but, wow, there's no mall or Dairy Queen."

"I love Dairy Queen. When I go off island, I try to get to one for a Pecan Mudslide."

"I love Mudslides, too! They're my favorite!"

"Well, you know," Darcy said in a jokey voice, "pecans are very healthy."

"I try not to eat too much ice cream. Mom says I can't afford to get fat, that as I get older, any weight I put on will be hard to get off. But I don't know any kids my age here. So I get kind of bored. I'm not big on going to the beach, either, and the one time I went, Logan hit on me." She sighed. "You see how well *that* turned out."

Darcy said, "I think you're perfect, maybe even too thin. . . ." She let her voice trail off. She didn't want to contradict anything Autumn had told Willow. Still, she had an idea. . . . "Willow, do you like kids?"

"Duh. Who doesn't?"

"I guess I mean kids in crazy noisy hordes. We do a summer story time program at the library, and our enrollment is full, and I want to offer another story time, maybe even two. They last about an hour, and it's simply reading a book with cool pictures to a group of kids about two to five years old. You could choose which mornings you wanted to do it. The library would pay you, not much, but something."

"Wait, what? I can read stories to kids? Awesome sauce!" Willow almost bounced off the sofa. "That sounds like so much fun! Gosh, I haven't looked at picture books for years and *years*." Willow talked as if she were fifty years old. "I used to spend hours with picture books."

"You'd have to be capable of dealing with rambunctious kids," Darcy told her. "And of course, we'll need to get permission from your parents."

"Oh, they'll give me permission. The library with old ladies and little kids? They'll be thrilled." Willow squinted her eyes as her words replayed in her head. "I don't mean *you* are an *old lady*. I just . . ."

"It's fine, Willow. And look, I think your parents are home. Lights are on in some of the rooms now."

"Oh, groan." Willow's shoulders sagged. "They're going to be wicked pissed."

"Let's go get it over with," Darcy said.

11

As they walked down the lane to Willow's house, Darcy tried to push back her misgivings. Of course she'd done the right thing, stopping Willow from snorting heroin. But Boyz wouldn't like that Darcy had asked Willow to work in the library and he especially wouldn't like that he'd told Darcy he knew what was happening with Willow and tonight Darcy had proved him wrong.

At the steps to the porch, Willow came to an abrupt halt.

"They're going to kill me," she whispered.

"You can handle it," Darcy said. "They love you. Come on."

She started up the steps to the side door. Willow stood frozen. Darcy reached back and took her hand. She was surprised when, as they entered the house, Willow kept a tight hold on her hand, and there they were, in the gleaming space-age granite-countered kitchen, standing together like two girls facing their headmaster.

Boyz was at the refrigerator, taking out a bottle of carbonated water. "Autumn, want some water?" he called. He wore a navy blazer and a striped button-down shirt, open at the collar. Loafers without socks. Party clothes.

"God, no, I'll be up peeing all night as it is."
Autumn came to lean against the door from the
dining room. She'd kicked off her stiletto heels,
and still looked stunning in a tight pink strapless
sheath. Her abundant red hair was falling down
from its elegant chignon. Seeing Willow and
Darcy, she recoiled. "Willow! What the hell?"

Boyz turned, startled, then snorted. "Oh, Darcy,
honey, this is too much."

It was Willow who spoke first, in a shaky little
girl's voice, and she squeezed Darcy's hand so
tightly as she spoke, Darcy thought she'd have
bruises.

"Dad, Mom, listen. Something happened. I
have to tell you."

Autumn surged toward her daughter. "Are you
all right?"

"I'm fine. But I almost did heroin with Logan."
Willow rushed out the words in a breathless
squeak.

"Take a deep breath, Willow," Darcy whispered.
"You're hyperventilating."

"Darcy ran into the yard and stopped us."
Willow gave a half grin. "You should have seen
her—she was like a maniac, she totally scared
Logan!"

Autumn put her hands on her daughter's
shoulders and ran them up and down Willow's
arms, in the process accidentally—or not—
sweeping Darcy's hand away. "Are you okay?"

"I'm fine. I—"

"*Heroin?*" Boyz crossed the room in three steps and loomed over the women. "Are you telling me you did *heroin?*"

"Oh my god!" Autumn burst into tears.

"*Heroin,*" Boyz muttered. "Way out here on this isolated sandbar."

"Mom, I said I *didn't* do it. Darcy stopped me."

"What the hell was Darcy doing there?" Boyz demanded.

"I just *told* you. We were in the backyard— Logan and I—and he wanted me to snort some heroin, and Darcy, like, *exploded* into our yard and kicked his hand and the stuff flew into the grass and Darcy yelled at him and he left and Darcy took me to her house for hot chocolate."

Autumn stared at Darcy, who was almost painfully aware of how sloppy she looked in her T-shirt with its slogan—*The library, a great place to get checked out*—and shorts and flip-flops. Darcy couldn't remember when she'd last brushed her hair. She'd never met Autumn. The other woman had flawless skin and a killer figure, was taller than Darcy, even barefoot. Darcy felt she was being judged by a really sexy schoolteacher.

"I don't understand," Autumn said. "Who's Logan?"

Willow cringed, drawing her shoulders up as if she wanted to be a turtle hiding in her shell.

213

"Maybe we should sit down," Darcy suggested. Trying to inject some calm into the situation—Willow was trembling, Boyz's face was crimson—she gestured toward the kitchen chairs.

"Right," Boyz snapped. "Right, tell us what to do in our own house."

"I'll leave if you'd like, but you might want to hear what I have to say," Darcy replied, keeping her tone neutral.

Willow wrenched herself from her mother's hands and plunked down in a chair. She crossed her arms over her chest and hung her head.

Autumn pulled out a chair next to her daughter. Boyz sighed mightily and sat, and Darcy took a seat at the far end of the table.

"All right," Autumn said. "Let's begin at the beginning. Who is Logan?"

"My boyfriend," Willow muttered.

"Your *boyfriend?*" Autumn broke into a relieved laugh. "Honey, you're way too young to have a boyfriend."

"Oh, please," Willow rolled her eyes at her mother's naïveté.

Darcy spoke up. "Logan Smith is an island boy. As I told Boyz, I overheard him trying to . . . have sex with Willow. In the backyard. I was sitting in my backyard. I couldn't help overhearing."

Willow lifted her head. "See? I *am* old enough to have a boyfriend. Logan's really nice. And totally hot."

But Autumn was glaring at her husband. "*As Darcy told you?* When did Darcy tell you this piece of news? And where?"

Willow's head whipped toward Darcy. "Wait, what? You told my father?"

"Cool your jets, Autumn," Boyz said. "We ran into each other in the grocery store. Before that moment I had no idea she lived here, on the island or on the next street. It's the only time I've seen her since we've been here."

Darcy cut in. "I told Boyz that I knew Logan Smith. He's handsome and he's charismatic and he's a troublemaker. I've heard rumors that he's dealing heroin. Now I know."

Autumn stayed focused on her husband. "Why didn't you tell me, Boyz?"

He shifted uncomfortably in his chair. "I knew you'd be pissed that I'd seen Darcy."

Autumn scowled. "Well, I can't say I'm exactly thrilled."

"I wasn't, either, Autumn! For God's sake, I didn't want to see Darcy. I didn't *try* to see Darcy."

Autumn leaned belligerently over the table toward her husband. "And yet you saw her."

"In the Stop and Shop! By accident. No, now that I remember it, I think she accosted me."

Darcy bristled at the word *accosted* but didn't have a chance to object before Autumn stabbed her with an accusing glare.

"So you've been stalking my husband?"

Darcy couldn't help it. She broke into a laugh. "Please, this is getting ridiculous. I was shopping for groceries and we accidentally bumped into each other. I was worried about Willow—"

"She asked me to meet her at the café," Boyz said.

"So I could speak with him about Willow and Logan," Darcy added, wishing she didn't sound so defensive.

"What café?" Autumn demanded of her husband.

Darcy answered, "Not a real café. A quiet spot in the corner of the store where we could talk—"

"A *quiet* spot? And you didn't tell me?" Autumn snarled at her husband.

"Because I knew you'd be upset and I didn't want to upset you," Boyz explained.

"But I wanted to tell him about *Willow!*" Darcy nearly shouted. "Your daughter. Who is only fourteen. And maybe having sex with Logan. Who is eighteen."

"What our daughter does is none of your business," Boyz said.

Darcy kept her voice level. "It *is* my business—it's everyone's business—if I hear a boy trying to get her to snort heroin."

Autumn turned to her daughter. "Is this true? Was that boy making you snort heroin?"

"He wasn't *making* me . . ." Willow equivocated.

"Why would he do that?" Autumn demanded.

Willow looked down at her hands, but she was unable to hide the emotions playing over her face—guilt, sorrow, confusion.

Darcy intervened. "Because he's a dealer."

"Did you take—snort—any?" Autumn asked.

Willow mumbled, "I didn't use any. I was going to, but that's when Darcy stampeded into the yard. She was yelling like she was mental, and she kicked Logan's hand. He was really mad. She was going to call the police—she had her cellphone—but Logan left. He called her a nasty old bitch." Willow smiled. "A *snake-face* bitch."

Both Autumn and Boyz stared at Darcy, as if looking for the snake face.

She was relieved when Autumn relaxed. "Well, then, Darcy, thank you."

"Yes, thank you." Boyz stood up, as if to demonstrate that this conversation was over. "You don't have to worry about Willow. We'll make sure she doesn't see this boy Logan. You won't have to listen to Willow or have anything to do with her anymore."

Darcy knew she was being dismissed. She rose, and then Willow cried, "But, Dad, I'm going to help Darcy at the library. I'm going to help her read to the little kids."

Autumn gasped. "We brought you to this beautiful island, and you want to stay inside with a bunch of children and books?"

"It won't be all day," Darcy interjected. "And

not every day. I'll phone Willow with a tentative schedule. . . ."

"Give me your cell number," Autumn said to Darcy.

Darcy told her; Autumn punched the numbers in her cell. She moved to the door. "Bye, Willow."

"Oh! Well, bye, Darcy." Willow made an abrupt, unexpected move, pushing her chair away from the table, rising, and rushing over to hug Darcy. "Thank you. Thank you so much."

"You're welcome." Darcy looked at the girl's sweet face, seeing the freckles across her nose, the tilt of her pretty mouth, and a warmth moved through her and a sense of joy. Whoever collaborated to make this girl, Darcy was glad she was here on earth. And she felt, probably wrongly but still strongly, a sense of connection, almost a sense of guardianship.

She released herself from Willow's hug and went out the door before Boyz could say something that would turn the moment sour.

Darcy couldn't fall asleep that night. She tossed and turned so much that Muffler, who always slept next to her, finally jumped off the bed and stalked from the room, his tail twitching with indignation.

She woke to a day bright with sun and fresh air, as if her corner of the world had been washed clean overnight. As she walked to work, she called Jordan on her cell and told her about the drama.

"That girl has no idea how lucky she is," Jordan said. "What if you hadn't stopped Logan? I hate to think. Are you going to the police about this?"

"I'll call Sheriff Perlman on my lunch break and tell him about Logan."

Darcy turned onto Main Street and entered the core district of the town. Doors were opening, shopkeepers were sweeping the sidewalks and watering their flower boxes, a UPS truck was parked by a store, the farm trucks with their bounty of fresh vegetables waited at the corner of Main and Federal. Here and there, pairs of people sat on benches, drinking their coffee and gabbing. A woman with a Borzoi hurried into the Hub. A man in a suit—a rare sight here in the summer— came out with a cup of coffee and a newspaper.

"Jordan, I'm almost at the library. I'll call you later."

Once she set foot in the library, Darcy cranked into autopilot mode, doing three things at once, handling the good tasks—cataloging the new books, holding a story hour with twenty children—and the more unpleasant tasks— helping a child who had vomited all over himself because his babysitter had caved and bought him a huge candy bar for breakfast. She answered the phone, shelved books, sat at the circ desk when one of the assistants needed a coffee break, gulped down a yogurt for her lunch and an iced coffee at three o'clock, and called Art Perlman to tell him about Logan's possession of heroin. Art told her they'd been watching Logan for some time now and thanked her for the information.

In the middle of all this, Willow arrived. Darcy had spoken to Beverly about hiring Willow on an informal part-time basis; Beverly said she'd run it by the director of the library, but until then, to pay the girl fifteen dollars an hour and take it out of petty cash. While Darcy did one story hour, Willow sat at the back, watching, her eyes bright with excitement. Darcy had a chance to say only a few words to Willow before her work phone rang and Beverly, rushing out of the office on her way to an appointment, handed Darcy a pile of forms to deal with before the end of the day.

Walking home, she caught a call from Nash.

"How did we ever live before cellphones?" she asked.

Nash laughed. Darcy loved his laugh, a nice easy low rumble. "We probably moved more slowly and had better concentration. On the other hand, this nice piece of haddock Karl gave me wouldn't be as fresh when it was cooked."

"Want to bring it to my house?"

"No, I think I'd like to grill it here. I've got some new potatoes, too. You could bring over a few of those green things you insist on eating."

"Vegetables," Darcy said, knowing Nash liked

vegetables as much as she did, except for kale and spinach, which he said made him gag. "I'll bring a big salad. Do you have wine?"

"I do. White and red and, yes, I know white is supposed to be eaten with fish, but you've been on a tear recently about drinking red because it's got antioxidants, so I bought both kinds."

Darcy smiled. It was very nice to have someone remember what you liked to drink. "I'll be over as soon as I can get there."

She knew Nash lived in an apartment over a garage, but this would be the first time she'd been there. She was excited. She'd find out more about this man—was he a slob, was his place all giant-screen TV and video games, what did he keep in his fridge? Plus, his invitation seemed to indicate a deeper level of intimacy. He'd been in her house a lot, and in her bed a lot, but she'd never been in his. Would the sheets be clean?

Nash lived on Meadowview Drive, a long curling lane of homes with big yards and mature trees. She parked in the driveway behind his truck. The house itself had that closed-up look. She remembered he'd told her the owners were in France for the summer.

Nash came out to meet her. His blue eyes were warm and he smiled as he took the salad bowl from her arms. "The grill's back here."

Behind the garage, a lawn opened up, stretching to a bank of rose of Sharon bushes not yet in bloom. A small stone patio extended from the back of the garage, with a grill on one corner, a small table and four white plastic chairs in the middle, and a line of terra-cotta pots with cherry tomato plants growing in them.

"Pretty," Darcy said.

"You're pretty," Nash told her. He set the salad bowl on the table, took her in his arms, and kissed her for a long time.

She pulled away. "Tonight we are going to eat and talk before we do anything else."

"Well, that sounds ominous."

"It's not, really. It's just complicated. I need to tell you about some stuff, and I'd like your advice on something."

"Okay." Nash moved away. "Let's talk."

"Wouldn't you rather eat first?"

"No, let's talk. It will take only a minute to grill the fish and the potatoes are ready."

They sat across from each other at the round table.

Darcy took a deep breath. "All right. It's more about Willow. My ex-husband's fourteen-year-old stepdaughter."

She explained how she overheard Logan trying to convince Willow to try heroin last night. How she ran around to the other yard and kicked Logan's hand and sent him away. How she calmed Willow—and herself—with hot chocolate and television. How she explained it all to Boyz and Autumn when they came home.

"So," she finished. She looked at her beer bottle. It was still full, and she'd peeled off most of the label. Nash's expression was stormy. "I didn't *try* to eavesdrop on Willow. The hedge is so thick and on their side, a tree provides a nice nook to hide in from anyone in the house. . . ." Darcy couldn't get a read on Nash's thoughts. "Do you think I was wrong, to interfere?"

Nash reared back as if she'd hit him. "Do I think you were wrong to interfere? Good God, *no,* Darcy. You did the absolutely right thing. Except if it had been me, I would have called the cops and slugged that asshole hard enough to break his nose. That Willow is lucky—she doesn't know how lucky—that you were there, that you cared. Her parents sound like idiots."

The intensity of his response surprised her. "I know. I'm going to keep an eye on her. I've asked her to help me with story time at the library. I really like her, Nash. It's just kind of odd, I guess, wanting to spend time with my ex-husband's wife's daughter."

"She's a kid. Someone ought to keep an eye on her."

"Well, it's not like I'll be seeing her every day. Plus, I don't know how to say this—" Darcy hesitated, tearing the last bit of label off the beer bottle. "I mean, I don't want you to think I'm interested in Boyz. He—"

"I don't think that." Nash abruptly shoved back his chair, rose, and paced away from Darcy. His hands were clenched at his side.

She could see the tension in his shoulders. *Oh, no,* she thought. *He's going to tell me he's seeing someone else.* She waited.

"Look," Nash said suddenly, turning to face her. "I don't talk about this to *anyone*. And I don't want to dwell on it. You don't need to say anything. But I want to tell you. Not just because of Logan and the heroin."

Darcy didn't move a muscle. She had no idea what he was going to say, and the need to know burned like a fire in her heart.

Nash stared at the horizon as he spoke. "I had a brother. He died of an overdose of heroin. He was twenty-two."

"Oh, Nash. That's awful." She sat quietly for a moment. "What was his name?"

"Edgar. What a hell of a name. Grandfather's." Nash sat down in his chair, his eyes looking far away. "We used to call him 'Edsel' because of the car thing, you know, Nash and Edsel. Our family lived in western Mass. Dad taught at Amherst. Mom did the mom thing. We were a typical more or less happy family. I'd just joined a law firm and moved to Boston. I had an apartment near BU. Edsel hadn't finished college yet. He'd been using for three years but I didn't have a clue. I thought he was bored, because he was really smart. He was scary smart. He started and stopped going to college several times. When I found out, I thought if he came and lived with me, in Boston, you know, where no one knew what a fuckup he was, where there were lots of colleges, and I could keep an eye on him . . ." Nash set his elbows on the table and leaned his head in his hands. When he spoke again, his voice was low. "I was such an asshole. Going off in my fucking suit and tie, carrying my fucking briefcase. But he was cool about it. I told him to use my laptop to look for jobs. When I got home at night I'd fix dinner or bring takeout, and we'd eat and watch TV and make stupid jokes and drink beer."

Darcy leaned as far as she could over the table. She could barely hear Nash. It was as if he was talking to the ground.

"He told me he had a job, just grunt work at a removal firm. I believed him. He'd come home exhausted, he'd tell me about the guys he worked with. Man, Edsel was a major bullshit artist. About a week after he 'started work,' I came home and found him on the bathroom floor with a needle in his arm. I called an ambulance right away. They got there fast, but he was gone."

"Oh, Nash. I'm so sorry."

Darcy watched Nash, trying to read his face, his posture. What should she do? He seemed so alone, and he was so near she could almost touch him. She wanted to go to him, to embrace him.

But she knew his sorrow belonged to him, he held it close to him, it was huge and dreadful and the best she could do was respect his grief. She sat quietly, waiting.

Finally Nash looked up at Darcy. His expression was bleak. "So, yes, I believe you did the right thing with the girl." He rose, walking over to the grill. "The coals are almost ready."

"I'll get the salad." Darcy respected his need to change the subject. She tossed the salad, then set out the plates and utensils he'd brought to a side table.

Nash closed the grill. "Five minutes."

Darcy cocked her head. "One thing, Nash."

He looked at her warily.

"Law firm? *Briefcase?*"

Nash barked an abrupt laugh. "All true. I was going to save the world. Ha. I couldn't even save my brother." He slumped into his chair. "Yeah, I went to law school, passed the Massachusetts bar. Got a job with a firm in Boston that did ten percent of its work pro bono. But after Edsel . . . I didn't see the point. I wanted out of my head. I was driving myself nuts with words. So I joined a construction crew building houses on the Cape. Now *that* was work. That was clear. Lift boards, pound nails, at the end of the day you've got a wall. Keep doing that, you've got a house. Do it well, that house will last a long time." He nodded to himself. "Yeah."

"And you traveled."

"Yeah, I did. In the winter, we didn't have as much work. I traveled. This winter I came here, joined Ramos's crew—and stopped traveling."

"Do you think you'll stay on the island?"

Nash shrugged. "I might. It's nice enough here." He stood up. "Time to eat."

She could tell he was done with intimate talk, so she asked him how his day had gone, and he told her about a guy working on a house across the street who got his foot stuck in a tray of paint and the guys nearly fell off their ladders laughing. Darcy told him about the vomiting child in story hour, and that brought a smile to his face. By the time they'd finished eating, the tension had evaporated.

"Dessert's inside," Nash told her with a grin.

"Can't you bring it out?" Darcy teased.

"It's ice cream. In the freezer."

"Well, let's go in, then."

They carried their plates in and up the stairs to his apartment. It was a good-size space, spread over the two-car garage, living room with kitchen, bedroom, bath.

Nash's furniture was an unusual mixture of tag sale and Ethan Allen—his sofa, armchair, and king-size bed were handsome and new. He had, of course, a flat-screen TV and, surprisingly, a shelf of vinyl and a record player. Two window air conditioners cooled the rooms. His kitchen

227

table and chairs were used and scarred, but his laptop was on the kitchen counter, set to a page of recipes.

"Recipes?" Darcy asked.

Nash shrugged. "I like to cook. I watch *Chef's Table*."

"So do I! In the winter, when things calm down, let's have some cooking dates," Darcy suggested. Nash had his back to her—setting plates in the dishwasher—and when he didn't respond, anxiety pinched her. Was she too eagerly assuming they'd still be together in the winter?

She forced herself to study his shelf of books. She bent over to scan the titles—science fiction, nonfiction, thrillers.

"Nice."

"I think so." As he spoke, Nash put his hands on her hips and pressed himself against her.

Lust shot through her so fast her knees went weak. Straightening up, she turned in his arms and kissed him.

"Ice cream later," Nash said.

They couldn't let go of each other, couldn't stop kissing, touching, sliding hands up beneath shirts, so they half walked, half stumbled into the bedroom, falling on the bed. Nash was ready, she could tell through her clothes and his jeans, but he surprised her by pulling her arms above her head.

"Slow. Let's go slow."

She sank into the bed, eyes closed, and gave herself over to him as he slowly kissed her face, her neck, her shoulder, the inside of her elbow. Her fingers. He tugged her skirt and panties down and kissed her ankles, her knees, her thighs. She was going to explode with desire. She twisted on the bed as he ran his hands over her breasts and kissed her belly.

"Can't wait. *Please,*" she begged, even though somewhere deep inside she could tell this was a different kind of making love than she'd experienced with Nash so far.

That was it—it was not having sex, it was making love.

Then he was naked, and then he was inside her, and she held him to her, and there was an intimacy between them that hadn't been there before, a depth, a ferocity, a claiming. Nash was making her his.

Afterward, he smoothed back her hair, which had gotten tangled and moist with sweat.

"Good grief," Darcy said breathlessly.

"Yeah, I know." Nash was smiling.

They spooned close together and drowsed. Darcy woke to the sound of the shower. She walked, naked, to the bathroom and pulled back the shower curtain.

Nash's mouth curled slightly. "Don't even think about getting in here with me. I am done for tonight."

"You mean you want to check the Red Sox game," Darcy said, only half kidding.

When Nash stepped out of the shower, a towel around his waist, Darcy stepped in. After she dried off, she dressed and found Nash in the living room with two bowls of ice cream. Curled up on one end of the sofa, Darcy ate her ice cream and watched the television, knowing that this evening between them had changed things. She felt closer to him than ever before. She thought maybe he felt the same, and was too scared to talk about it.

She was scared, too. What she felt was huge. It could change their lives. The ice cream, the ball game were a resting place, a time-out. They both needed it.

At nine, she yawned and stretched. "I'm falling asleep here. Gotta go. Work tomorrow."

Nash walked her down the stairs and out to her car. She set the salad bowl in the backseat and opened the driver's door. Nash took her in his arms and kissed her forehead.

"Listen," he said. "You know what I told you tonight—that's private. I'd appreciate it if you don't tell anyone else."

"Of course, Nash."

"Not even Jordan."

"Not even Jordan," she assured him.

12

The Women's Chorus performed its tribute to Sylvia Marks on Wednesday evening. The church was packed and to her surprise, Darcy spotted Mimi and Clive in one row and Willow seated at the back. She'd told Nash not to come—he'd be bored, she told him. The music was sappy. The truth was, she didn't have a strong voice and was afraid of embarrassing herself in front of him.

But there, seated in the back row, was Nash. And his presence made her feel—*lifted up*. Something like a golden lantern lit up inside her, something about the sight of him made her feel warm and glowing.

The group had never sung better, Darcy thought, and she knew most of the audience, island people who had treasured Sylvia. She was only slightly nervous when she stepped forward to sing the solo. The lyrics by Johnny Mercer were haunting, and when she sang, she saw several women silently weeping.

When the concert was over and people headed for the reception, Nash gave her a thumbs-up sign and slipped away. So did most of the people with jobs and children. It was an older crowd who stayed to enjoy the homemade cookies and peach-flavored punch. They complimented Darcy and Beth O'Malley, their leader, and some gathered in clusters to retell stories about Sylvia and her devotion to birds.

The crowd was thinning out when Willow approached her.

"You were awesome," she said. "I didn't know you could sing."

"I didn't, either," Darcy joked. "And I have no plans to sing a solo ever again. I'm surprised I didn't drop dead from nervousness." Willow wore a skirt with a sleeveless white blouse embroidered with small flowers. "You look so pretty tonight, Willow."

The girl blushed. "I didn't know what to wear. We don't go to church much."

"Darling girl, you were marvelous!" Mimi swept up to Darcy and kissed her.

Clive, behind Mimi, added, "Yes, Darcy. Well done."

Clive had a way of looking at her that seemed warm and intimate, as if they shared a secret. Flustered, Darcy hurriedly put her arm around Willow, drawing her close.

"Clive, Mimi, I'd like you to meet Willow—"

"Willow Szweda." Willow completed the introduction with the poise of one who had said it often before. "My stepfather's family is Polish. When he adopted me, I took his name."

"I'll bet your parents call you Sweet Willow," Mimi said, smiling at the young girl.

Willow smiled. "No, actually, I don't think that's happened."

Darcy stepped in. "Willow is helping me at the library. She's doing a couple of story hours every week. We're so glad to have her. She's amazing with the children, and we've got so many children registered we can scarcely keep up with the demand."

"What fun to read children's books," Mimi said.

A twinge of guilt pinched Darcy. She'd promised to bring Mimi some children's books to look at and had forgotten to do it.

"I wonder," Mimi said to Willow, "would you consider reading to me? I don't mean children's books, I mean one of my old darlings like Dickens's *Great Expectations* or Mark Twain's *Huckleberry Finn*. I'd pay you, of course. It's just that my eyes get tired so easily at my age. That's why I like children's books, because the pictures are fascinating—plus I don't have to keep the plot straight in my head. I used to keep a list of characters on a page that I also used as a bookmark, but now I keep losing the paper, finding it a month later, and wondering if these are people I should invite over for tea."

Darcy and Willow laughed. Clive watched his grandmother with such open affection on his face it almost brought tears to Darcy's eyes. She wished her grandmother could have met Mimi.

Clive shifted his gaze, catching Darcy in the act of staring at him. She blushed. He grinned at her, amused.

Really, he was rather gorgeous in a professorish sort of way. His hair was longer than most men wore theirs, and his chocolate-dark eyes made him seem sweet.

"Would you like to stop by my house for a drink?" Darcy found herself asking.

"Oh, thank you, darling, but I've got to get my tired old bones in bed." Mimi took Clive's arm for support.

Quickly, Willow said, "I'd be glad to read to you, Mrs. Rush. Any time."

"Then we've got a plan." Mimi patted Willow's hand. "And please call me Mimi." Reaching into her purse, she brought out her cellphone. "What is your number?"

Darcy watched, entranced, as Mimi dealt with her cell with the ease of a pro. She exchanged a glance with Willow—amused, impressed.

"Darcy, aren't you coming?" Beth O'Malley hurried up to Darcy.

Well, this was embarrassing. She'd been so entranced by Mimi and Clive, she'd forgotten about the after-party at Beth's home.

"Of course," Darcy told her. "I'll be right there. I was just—" *I was just standing here gawking at Clive.*

"Don't worry about us," Mimi said. "Clive drove me here and we can take Willow home with us. She can cut through the backyard."

Darcy smiled.

Beth O'Malley tapped Darcy's shoulder. "Party, Darcy?"

"Yes, I'll come for a while," Darcy said. "I've got to get up early for work tomorrow."

She said goodbye to Mimi and the others and followed Beth out to the street.

"Everyone else has gone on ahead," Beth said. She'd worn a sleeveless black dress to conduct the group—it was hot in the church and there was no air-conditioning. "My dress is sticking to me everywhere. I was afraid someone would faint from the heat. But you look cool enough, Darcy. How do you think it went?" She gave herself a tiny slap. "Stop it, Beth, you're babbling."

Darcy laughed. "Nerves. You were cucumber calm during the concert and that's what matters. The concert was *perfect,* Beth. You packed the house and I saw lots of people crying."

"I hope Sylvia saw us from wherever she is now. Heaven, I hope."

"Yes, heaven," Darcy agreed. "She probably has her own special section, full of all the birds she's never seen before."

"And the ones she banded here," Beth added.

Beth's house was wall-to-wall people, not only

the chorus but some of their friends, especially those who knew Sylvia. Darcy made her way to the dining room table, covered with a crisp white cloth, the centerpiece a spectacular arrangement of native Nantucket grasses and flowers. As she took a glass of champagne, she found herself surrounded by friends, praising her and congratulating her for her solo. At first she was shy, and almost argued with the others, insisting her voice wasn't really good, it was too weak . . . but after a while, she simply said thank you, because wasn't it just possible that her voice was, if not trained, at least good enough? She knew it had gotten stronger, more flexible, while she was rehearsing. She knew she'd moved up a rung in her self-confidence because of her singing, this group, the music.

Jordan approached Darcy with a great wide smile. "Congratulations! You were wonderful, Darcy. And the entire concert was so moving."

"It was wonderful, wasn't it? A real tribute to Sylvia."

"It could be surpassed only if all of you had whistled like birds for an hour." Jordan laughed, then drew Darcy close. "Who was that gorgeous man you were talking to?"

"That was Clive Rush and his grandmother Mimi. I've told you about them. He's a musicologist, aka fascinating man next door."

"He was undressing you with his eyes."

"Don't be silly, Jordan. And, anyway, if he was, he probably looks at every woman that way."

"Are you going to sleep with him?"

"Jordan!"

"Hey. You know you'll get married again someday, if not to Nash, to someone, and then, honey, the drawbridge slams up and no one else ever enters your castle for the rest of your life."

Darcy narrowed her eyes. "Are you having an affair?"

"I wish. By the time Lyle gets home from work and I've got Kiks in bed, we're both too tired to even say the word *sex*."

"Lyle is a wonderful man," Darcy stoutly reminded her friend.

"And I'm a wonderful woman. And Kiks is the cutest kid in the world. I still miss romance."

"Read a novel," Darcy advised her. "Listen, I'm beat, and I've got to work tomorrow. I'm going to slip away."

"Fine, but you've got to promise to tell me if anything happens with you and that Clive guy. I'll want every detail."

Darcy laughed. "You are so weird."

She couldn't get close to Beth, who was surrounded by admirers, so she caught Beth's eye, blew her a kiss, waved goodbye, and hurried out the door.

Darcy hummed tunes from the concert as she walked home. Her humming made her think of bees and how they lived together in hives, and she laughed quietly, imagining that the Women's Chorus was a humming hive with Beth as their queen bee.

She'd never been part of any kind of a group before, except perhaps the waitstaff at Bijoux, and that was different. There they were working for money, for themselves. The women in the chorus came together to make beauty. What they had in common was the desire to sing, because singing was a gift and a pleasure. Pretty Kate Ferguson was a nurse. Ursula Parsons, who stood next to Darcy in the middle row, went around at night clipping back the limbs of any plants whose leaves or flowers dared to protrude even half an inch into her yard, often killing her neighbor's plants. Marylee MacKenzie kept a kennel of dogs and a stable of horses, and when she came to rehearsals, she reeked of manure and had bits of straw caught in her hair. Andrea Barnes had an eating disorder and draped layers of loose clothing over her skeletal body; she was pale and timid and jittery, but she had a gorgeous soprano voice. She'd been far too shy to sing the solo Darcy had sung tonight, and as Darcy hummed along down the street beneath the summer sky, she realized it was a huge achievement for her, to sing a solo. Tonight she had felt the support and goodwill of all those women, eccentric or not, around her as she sang.

A lamp glowed from her living room window.

Muffler raced up to her, mewing his displeasure at her absence.

"Hello, pretty boy." She picked him up and carried him to the kitchen, loving the warmth of him in her arms, his reverberating purr. "Let's get you some treats." She dropped a few catnip tidbits. She ran herself a glass of water and stared out her kitchen window at her garden. Lights were on in all the houses around her. Her blood was still buzzing from the concert, as if she'd ust drunk a pot of coffee.

Her phone rang. She picked it up before it had rung twice. "Hey, Nash."

"Hey, yourself, Adele."

Darcy laughed. "More like Lady Gaga," she joked.

"That concert was nice. You were spectacular."

His compliment took her breath away. "Hardly. And I was so nervous you could probably hear my knees knocking together."

"You didn't look nervous. You looked beautiful."

Darcy carried her water into the living room and curled up on the sofa. "Thank you. What did you think of the chorus?"

"They were fine, I guess. I can't really judge. Most of the concerts I've been to in my life have involved electric guitars and amplifiers and crowds jumping up and down and waving their phones in the air."

239

"You're not going to get much of that on the island. Except maybe for the Boys and Girls Club summer gala."

"That's okay. I prefer listening to music alone. Or with you."

Gosh, Darcy thought, *this conversation just gets better and better.*

"Did you ever sing? Play an instrument?" she asked.

"Ha. My mother made me take piano lessons when I was a kid. I hated it. Edsel, now, he played the drums. He was a natural drummer. In junior high he put together a band. You never saw such scrawny, zit-faced, jug-eared guys, but they sounded pretty good. They did a concert in May on the high school football field. I was cramming for finals, so I didn't go. I've seen the video. They were awful. Still, I wish like hell I'd gone. Wish I'd shown up for him."

Darcy asked carefully, not wanting to spook Nash now that he was opening up to her, "Was Edsel scrawny and zit faced?"

She'd said the right thing. Nash laughed.

"Nah, he was cool. He was one of those guys who just was effortlessly cool. Girls all swooned over him. Guys all wanted to be his best friend. He had this attitude like he couldn't be bothered to take anything seriously. Damn, he used to make my parents angry. They'd bitch him out over something he'd done, and he'd sit there very straight—*yes, sir, no, sir, yes, ma'am*—and you could tell from his eyes he was secretly laughing his ass off. Yeah, he was a handsome kid. Brilliant, too. Annoying as hell. When he lived with me in Boston, he pretty much trashed the place, left dirty laundry everywhere, dirty dishes, cigarettes stubbed out in coffee cups—oh, yeah, and used condoms on the floor near the sofa where he was sleeping. That was an especially charming touch."

"He wasn't in a band when he lived with you?"

"No. He'd gotten bored with that. Bored with school, bored with our quaint little town in the Berkshires. That's why he came to live with me in Boston. I don't know when he started using. I met some of the girls he brought home and they didn't look druggie. They were nice girls. . . ." Nash took a deep breath. "God, Darcy, I'm sorry. I wanted to talk about your concert. I didn't intend to drag you down like this."

"You didn't drag me down, Nash. I like hearing about your brother. I like knowing about your life."

"Well, okay, but it's private stuff. I don't know what got me going on Edsel."

"I won't mention him to anyone, Nash. Hey, I wanted to ask you, did you notice anyone in the chorus who seemed um, a bit off tune?"

"Not off tune, but that woman, what's her name, Ursula Parsons? She always sang the words about a millisecond before the rest of the chorus, like it was a contest and she was freakin' determined to win."

Darcy laughed. "Oh, fabulous, Nash, you've pegged it exactly."

They talked more about the chorus, spinning off in tangents to trade gossip about some of the women or their families. They talked for over an hour. Darcy slid down on the sofa. Muffler jumped up beside her hip and fell asleep. Darcy came down from her concert high and began to feel sleepy. She had to work to keep her eyes open. But she didn't want this conversation to end. When they finally said goodbye, she found herself smiling, even as she brushed her teeth, even as she curled up in bed.

The next day, in the professional space of her office, Darcy forced herself to do something she'd known she had to do. She had asked Willow for Autumn's phone number, because maybe it was all too unconventional, Darcy spending time with her ex-husband's stepdaughter. Willow was a child. Autumn was her mother. Darcy should make arrangements with Autumn, or at least bring her into the mix.

She called Autumn.

"Yes?" Autumn's voice was sweet and clear.

Darcy plunged right in. "Autumn, this is Darcy Cotterill. I'm calling about Willow, and

I apologize for not calling you sooner, but you know we've asked her to help with story time at the library. I hope that's okay with you. I know I should have checked with you first—"

Autumn interrupted with a silvery peal of laughter. "About helping with story time in the library? Are you kidding me? Honestly, Darcy, I should pay *you*. I'm delighted you're keeping Willow busy."

"She should be with kids her own age—"

"Forget that. The girl's too shy, plus look at the loser she met on the island. Already, bad instincts in the male department. Frankly, Darcy, Willow's had a tough time lately. She's trying to pull away from me and I totally get that. She's good at home, but here she can't seem to get a grip. You're just the role model she needs, and what could be better than keeping her occupied at a *library?*" Another burst of laughter came over the phone.

Fine, Darcy thought, let Autumn think librarians were chaste and boring. "Also, I don't know if Willow mentioned that our neighbor Mimi Rush has asked Willow to read to her in the evenings, and—"

"I know. Willow told me. I mean, what more could I ask? The library and an old lady?"

"Well, we might do something some evening. Go out for dinner or for a drive or something. I want you to know you're welcome to join us—"

"Oh, you're so sweet—you don't want me to feel left out. Listen, I think it's good for Willow to have her own group, even if it is old people. I don't think she'd enjoy having me butt in. Honestly, I think it's great how you're being nice to Willow."

"Okay, that's good."

"Great. Listen, I've got to go now. Thanks for calling."

The weird thing, Darcy thought as she said goodbye and ended the call, was how much Autumn reminded Darcy of her mother. That same good-natured carelessness. The same rushing speed through life, or at least through their phone call, because Autumn didn't have much time for discussions about her daughter.

The main thing was that Darcy had made contact with Autumn. She had, in an informal kind of way, gotten permission from Willow's mother to have Willow be at the library for part of the day. Autumn had made it crystal clear that *she* wanted nothing to do with Darcy and Mimi. A snarky thought snaked through her mind. She could have said, "I know you enjoy spending time with some of your neighbors, like Otto Brueckner." But she hadn't said that, and she was glad. It would have made Autumn think Darcy was even more boring than she already did.

13

And then the heat hit. Humidity rose, and the outdoors became a sauna. The library was air-conditioned, but Darcy's house wasn't. The summers she'd spent with Penny when she was younger had never been so hot they'd needed air-conditioning. Just a fan in the kitchen when they were cooking or baking. Darcy could close her eyes and remember the low, soothing hum of the fan as it oscillated left and right in unchanging rhythm.

Out in her garden in the evening, beneath the shade of the neighbor's old maple, it was tolerable, and by night it was even pleasant. But as much as she enjoyed her garden, she had to eat, dress, and sleep inside her house, so she broke down and bought two window air conditioners and phoned Nash to ask him to install them.

"I'll bribe you with drinks and dinner," she added.

"Hm. That might not be quite enough," he teased.

She played dumb. "Ah. Let me see. What else can I offer?"

"I'll show you when I get there," he said.

"I'll be ready."

She was smiling when they ended their

conversation. His easy bantering woke her brain. It absolutely woke her body.

Nash arrived straight from work. It was almost eight o'clock, and he was in his work clothes—jeans, T-shirt, work boots. His sandy hair had sawdust in it. His white T-shirt was dirty and stained in places, but the thin material showed off his muscular torso quite nicely.

"Well, hello, sailor," Darcy said as he came in the door. She threw her arms around his neck and raised her mouth to kiss him, but to her surprise, he drew back.

"Let me get a shower first, Darcy. I'm all sweaty."

"Just the way I like you," she purred, pressing against him. What was it about his odor that was so sexy? It drew her to him like a moth to a flame.

He put his hands on her shoulders and held her at arm's length. "First, air conditioners, next shower. Then we'll see what happens."

But installing the air conditioners nearly put her over the top. She held the door open while he carried the air conditioners in from the car, moving effortlessly. She followed him up the stairs to her room, unable to ignore the way his muscles bulged in his shoulders and arms, and the long lean line of his back.

He set the air conditioner on the floor. "Which window?"

She'd already studied the situation and decided.

The room had two windows facing the street and one facing the narrow lane between her house and the Brueckner's.

"There," she said, pointing to a front window. "Can I help?"

"No need." He raised the window and the screen, lifted the air conditioner into place, lowered the window, and screwed the plastic accordion flaps to the window frame.

"For a lawyer, you really know how to screw," she joked.

To her surprise, Nash's face shut down.

"We're not going there," he said.

"What?" For a moment, she couldn't imagine what he meant.

"I'm not a lawyer anymore."

"But you could be if you wanted to?" she queried.

"I don't want to. And I don't want to talk about it right now, okay?"

She was stung. A kind of shame flooded her, as if she'd been attempting an intimacy that didn't exist. She consoled herself, remembering how Jordan said she could never ask Lyle anything important until he'd had a drink and eaten dinner.

"Okay. Let's get the other one in," he said. He walked past her and headed down the stairs.

"Right. The other one goes in the living room window. I spend most of my time there. In the summer, I eat salads or takeout." Darcy knew she was babbling, but she wanted to get away from that uncomfortable moment between them.

Nash worked quickly. When the air conditioner was in place, he turned it on. It hummed and gurgled and warm air swept into the room and finally the cool air arrived.

"You're a lifesaver!" Darcy told Nash. "Want a beer?"

"What I'd really like is a shower."

"Disappointing as that is, go ahead, help yourself. I'll get dinner ready." She sighed with relief. The awkwardness between them had disappeared.

Nash headed back up the stairs. Darcy went into the kitchen and found Muffler sitting by his food bowl, glaring at her indignantly.

"Oh, sorry. Didn't I feed you yet?" Darcy filled his bowl with the gourmet moist food the cat liked, then set about getting the human dinner ready. She'd made a pan of mac and cheese with lobster the night before, and she heated it in the microwave while she sliced beefsteak tomatoes and sprinkled them with oregano. When she heard Nash coming down the stairs, she opened a beer and carried it to him, and burst out laughing. He was wearing her turquoise kimono, and it barely met at the front even with the cloth tie.

"Couldn't tolerate getting back into those clothes," Nash explained.

Darcy laughed. "It's a good look for you. Plus I can hardly wait to see what happens when you sit down."

They went into the living room, which was nicely cool and dry. Nash sat, and the robe parted, exposing pretty much all of him.

"I can't eat like this," he grumbled.

"Let me get you one of my sheet towels," Darcy said. "You can wrap it around your waist and keep your treasures secret."

"I'd appreciate that."

As she went into the laundry room and fished a clean towel from the drier, a thought occurred to her. Should Nash keep a set of fresh clothes here? He ate here several times a week, and the heat wave was not going to be over any time soon. But if she proposed it to him—did that seem like she was pushing for something more, something serious?

She brought him the towel and watched him wrap it around his torso.

"That's better," he said.

"Not for me," she joked, but he'd already turned the television on and the Red Sox were playing Cleveland. "I'll bring in dinner."

"Need some help?"

"No, it's easy." She filled two plates, put them on a tray with utensils and napkins and carried it in.

"Thanks," Nash said. "This looks great."

Before she could respond, he yelled, "Ramirez, get a grip!"

Darcy settled next to Nash on the sofa and focused on the game. She was an ardent Red Sox fan, and she adored the sportscaster Jerry Remy, who had the most contagious laugh. She sensed Nash relaxing as he ate and watched the game, and she decided that television had probably saved more than one relationship. It was like putting a child in time-out, or having a buffer guest at a dinner party. The tension eased. Nash had a second heaping helping of the mac and cheese. They watched the game to its end—the Red Sox won—and Darcy brought in bowls of ice cream for them both.

As the last of her ice cream melted in her mouth, Darcy wondered if Nash had gotten over his sulk.

"Do you want more ice cream?" she asked.

"No," Nash said. He put his bowl on the table and turned to her. "Now I want this."

He took her in his arms and kissed her. His towel fell off. She wriggled out of her clothes without ending the kiss. They slid down onto the couch together, and although the TV continued with the after-game show, they didn't even notice.

Often a Nantucket summer was blessed—or cursed—by a week of rain, fog, and wind. Darcy felt oddly guilty when this happened, because it ruined so many holiday plans, especially for those who had rented a house on the island for only a week. It didn't bother her—she liked the rain a lot, the fragrances it brought out from the garden, the soothing sound of it against her bedroom window, and the pleasure she took in offering story times to children who couldn't go to the beach.

By Thursday, she realized that the Brueckner boys had been to story time every day that week. At first, they sat politely, but when they showed up on Thursday, they'd obviously exceeded their ability to be still and listen. While Darcy perched at the front of the room on a chair that allowed her to show the book's pictures to all the children—and to see what all the children were doing—she noticed George pinching Alfred, and Alfred, the youngest and weakest, wriggling away from his brother, accidentally bumping into children next to him and causing them to snarl at the boy. Susan, settled on the floor at the back with the other mothers, was aware that her sons were misbehaving. She looked miserable. Outside, the rain sheeted down, pattering against the windows, turning the lawn into a soggy stretch of mud.

"Alfred," Darcy said. "Would you do me a favor?" She saw the alarm in Susan's eyes. "Would you come up here and turn the pages for me? It's really hard for me to hold the book and turn the pages."

Alfred's eyes widened. Braced for a scolding, he had to take a moment to understand her invitation. Then he jumped to his feet and almost ran to join Darcy. She continued to read, pausing to whisper to Alfred, "Please turn now." By the end of the book, Alfred was smug and his brothers approached him with something like admiration.

Afterward, the children and their mothers streamed out the door. Susan approached Darcy. "That was so nice. Thank you, Darcy. Alfred, you did such a good job!"

Susan looked terrible, Darcy thought. Her eyes were puffy and her posture spoke of a woman who was struggling simply to stand. As the room emptied out, the two older boys, Henry and George, started shoving each other and calling each other names.

"It's this rain," Susan said, seeming entirely defeated. "They aren't constitutionally built to be quiet."

"Take them to the beach anyway," Darcy suggested. "It's warm out, they'll get wet swimming. Or take them to the Life Saving Museum."

Susan nearly sank to her knees. "Oh, *thank you*. I was running out of ideas. . . ."

"Look," Darcy said, "The Dreamland's rerunning *Cinderella* tonight. I'm going with a couple of friends. In fact, it's Mimi, who lives to my right, and Willow, who lives behind me. It's supposed to be a gorgeous movie, with Cate Blanchett as the wicked stepmother. Come with us."

"Oh, thank you, but I couldn't leave the boys."

"Won't your husband be there?"

"Yes, but—" Susan bit her lip. "He's not very good at handling them all by himself."

"Have him bring the boys to the movie."

"But *Cinderella* is so girly—"

"It's got mice and horses and magic," Darcy reminded her.

"Well, I suppose I could bring them."

"No. Have your husband bring them. *You* absolutely *have* to come with us. We'll have a girls night out, maybe go for a drink afterward."

Susan stared, dumbfounded, as if such an activity had never reached even the outer limits of her mind before.

"Mommmm," the boys cried, shoving up against her. "We're bored!"

Susan's shoulders slumped. "All right, boys, let's go. I want to show you the Life Saving Museum."

"They have videos of shipwrecks there," Darcy told them.

"*Shipwrecks!* YAY!" The three boys danced around the room.

Darcy smiled at Susan. "You see, I have good suggestions, don't I?"

Susan nodded. "All right, I'll come with you."

"I'll knock on your door at six thirty."

Cinderella delighted everyone. Well, probably not Otto, who stormed through the crowds leaving the theater, his three sons trailing behind him like the tail of a kite until he reached his wife.

Because he was in public and Willow stood on one side of his wife and Mimi and Darcy on the other, he attempted a smile as he bellowed, "Okay, you saw your movie with your friends. You must come put these children to bed."

Before Susan could speak, Mimi said, "We're taking Susan with us for a little drink."

"We won't be long. You can put them to bed yourself, can't you?" Susan implored.

"I think your sons look more than ready for sleep," Darcy added, nodding toward Alfred, who was yawning.

"Your boys are so nice," Willow chirped. "If you'd like, I could babysit for them sometime, so maybe you and Mrs. Brueckner can go out together."

Otto was clearly flummoxed by the persuasive wall of women facing him.

He wavered, obviously desperate to come up with an argument they couldn't refute, and Darcy took advantage of his momentary silence.

"So, okay, great. Let's go, ladies. Bye, guys!"

Darcy took Susan's arm and pulled her away from Otto.

"All right, boys," Otto ordered. "Let's walk back to the house. Your mother will be home later."

"But, Dad," Alfred protested, "I'm tired. Do I have to walk?"

"It's only a matter of a few blocks. You're not a baby."

"But I'm *tired*," Alfred whined.

"Stop sniveling. If you three can walk home without complaining, I'll let you go to bed without brushing your teeth." Otto raised his voice as he put forth this proposal, probably in the hope that such rebellion against good parenting would cause Susan to change her mind and rush back to deal with the boys.

But Mimi had taken Susan's other arm, and as the crowd dispersed, the women hurried across the street and away from her husband and sons.

"Let's go to Town," Darcy suggested. "We can sit out on the patio."

She steered them a short distance from the theater, turning onto a narrow lane paved with Belgian blocks. "I know it's tricky walking," she told Mimi, "but we're almost there."

"I'm fine," Mimi insisted. "Willow's got me."

They broke into pairs, Darcy and Susan on one side, Mimi and Willow facing them. They were seated at a table, and for a moment, as if they were obeying some natural law, all the women settled in place, gazed up at the night sky, and breathed deeply of the fresh salt air. Nantucket's harbor was only two streets away.

Susan spoke first. "Thank you for inviting me. I'd forgotten how delightful *Cinderella* is."

"That was a charming movie, and very pretty," Mimi said. "But I have never been a fan of the basic story."

Darcy sensed a discussion heading down the tracks toward them, so she sided with Susan, wanting to encourage her. "Why not, Mimi? It's all so adorable—the mice, the fairy godmother, the rags-to-riches story."

"Because," Willow cut in, "it's basically about a woman being rescued by a prince because of her beauty."

"More than that," Mimi added, "because of her size. The size of her feet, anyway."

"I think it's about *magic,*" Susan insisted. "We all need a little magic in our lives in order to go on. We all need to believe that what happened to Cinderella could happen to us—not that we'll be rescued by a prince, but that we can change someday from undervalued housemaids to beautiful princesses—well, okay, not *real* princesses, there are no princesses in our country, but you know what I mean!"

A waitress arrived, and Mimi took charge. "Three glasses of champagne and an interesting sparkling water for our young friend." She turned her attention back to Susan. "Did you not see—oh, drat, what was the name of that movie with Julia Roberts and Richard Gere?"

"*Pretty Woman*," Willow said.

Susan was shocked. "*You* have seen *Pretty Woman*? How old are you?"

"I'm fourteen. So I've seen it on DVD. I'm young, but I'm not, like, clueless."

If you only knew, Darcy thought, thinking of Willow with Logan Smith.

"Still," Susan persisted, "that movie's older than you are!"

"But the topic is ageless," Mimi cut in. "The twist the movie gave it was what Julia Roberts says at the end, something like 'He rescued me—'"

"And I rescued him right back!" Willow spoke the words with Mimi.

Mimi and Willow smiled at each other.

"Besides," Willow continued, "the whole ugly stepfamily is so over. Half my friends are part of blended families, and it's all good. And look at me, Boyz is my stepfather, but he's totally cool."

"Still," Mimi continued, "the message of being chosen because of your beauty is another age-old message that I'm wishing we could make *so over,* too."

"That's never going to change," Susan said, pausing as their drinks arrived. "It's built into our

DNA. It's out of our control. Women will always go for the strong, handsome man, and men will always go for the most beautiful woman. It's Darwinian law, nature's way of making certain the strongest survive."

"Intelligence is part of the mix now," Mimi argued. "We aren't cavemen anymore. We've learned to make fire; we've invented the wheel; and during the past three decades, we've started to value the intelligent person, not just the pretty one."

Susan said. "But men still think with their . . ."

"Pricks." Willow whispered the word.

"I've got three sons," Susan wailed. "How can I raise them to be good men if I'm already defeated by nature?"

Darcy sipped her drink and relaxed, watching the other three women talk. Their table was illuminated by a candle, and small lights had been hung around the patio. The soft light blurred the edges, erased the wrinkles, provided an almost antique cast to their faces. Willow, her skin flawless, her auburn hair abundant, her eyes bright. Susan, with signs of weariness cast over her pretty face, her blond hair drooping as if it were also tired. Mimi, white-haired, plump, with sparkling eyes. They could represent the three ages of women, Darcy thought: youth, maturity, age. She wanted to snap a photo of them just like this, to remember in the future. It was an unlikely gathering, and special.

And what age would Darcy represent? she wondered. She was past youth, but she didn't feel completely mature. . . .

"You're awfully quiet," Mimi observed, turning her attention on Darcy.

"I'm still considering Willow's words about blended families. That has been a significant change in people's lives. So much divorce and remarriage—"

Mimi cut in. "Darling, perhaps you're correct about divorce, but there have always been blended families. For hundreds of years, women died giving birth or of some ghastly disease. They might have had two or three children, and someone had to take care of them, so the husband married again, and had more children with his new wife. Or a man was killed in some hideous war. The woman married again, partly for economic reasons. She needed a man to support her financially while she pounded the chaff from the wheat so she could bake bread."

"But with all our modern technology, things have changed, haven't they?" Susan asked, her forehead furrowed as she tried to reach a point.

"Absolutely," Willow stated. "Women don't need men anymore. We can support ourselves financially."

"Some of us can't," Susan argued, warming to

her topic. "Some of us have three children who need supervision and healthy food and love, and furthermore some of us—not you, obviously, Darcy, since you have a position as a librarian, and probably not you, Willow, because you are young and smart and free—but some of us can't work."

"Everyone can work," Mimi said.

"I can't!" Susan cried. "I can't think of one single thing I could do to make money."

The table fell quiet. They all realized Susan had brought them crashing in from the philosophical into the murky reality of daily life. Her daily life.

"What kind of work would you do if you could?" Willow asked.

Susan blinked, dumbfounded. She lifted her glass to her mouth and drank deeply, giving herself time to think.

Willow chattered away. "I mean, I've always wanted to be an astronaut, but I know that's not possible. I'm claustrophobic and not good with numbers. I babysit a lot now, and I'm a good babysitter, and it's about the only way someone my age can make money. Unless I were a tech geek and invented something in my garage. I know when I grow up my stepfather will want me to sell real estate, that's his business, and he makes tons of money, but I want to major in environmental biology. Maybe I'll focus on clean water. I know that involves math, but we've got such cool technology to help us now, I won't have to do fancy math."

Susan set her empty glass on the table with a definitive thump. "I would like to work in a yarn shop," she announced defiantly.

Darcy waved the waitress over. "Another round of drinks, please."

"Really? Why?" Mimi asked.

Susan ran her hands through her blond hair, changing the carefully tidy locks into a wild tangle. "I enjoy knitting. I always have. I made the sweetest sweaters for my boys when they were babies. You should see the yarns they have now, I mean you should *feel* them. They're not all itchy like yarns used to be. They're silky. And so many colors!"

"But why not have your own yarn shop?" Willow asked. "Why work for someone else?"

"I don't want the responsibility. I am so tired of being responsible, for my children, for my husband's meals, for balancing a household budget. It's exhausting! I want to work for someone who has to keep the records and place the orders. I'll unpack the yarns and work behind the counter, selling and helping women choose the right color and weight. If the shop isn't busy, I'll work on knitting something intricate and unusual that will inspire other knitters." As she spoke, Susan's face flushed, and her entire personality seemed to transform from shy and quiet to bold and beautiful.

Mimi laughed and patted Susan's hand. "It seems you've given this a lot of thought."

"Oh, well, I suppose, when I try to fall asleep at night . . ." Susan deflated a little.

"Three young boys are a lot to deal with," Darcy remarked. "I don't know if I could do it without going crazy."

"If your husband helped, you could," Mimi said, facing Darcy but floating the suggestion to Susan.

Susan shrugged and continued to shrink back into her old self. "Otto is far too busy to help with childcare. What he does is important. I'm fortunate that he agreed to come to the island with us. He couldn't do it, if it weren't for technology, the computer, the Internet." Blushing, she added in a whisper, "Plus, he makes an enormous salary. That's why we were able to come here."

"Well, then, you needn't worry about money," Mimi concluded. "You could work part-time, for the pleasure of it—"

"And I could babysit!" Willow chimed in. Quickly she turned to the others. "I would still help with story hours, too. And read to you in the afternoons, Mimi."

"Have you seen Flock yet?" Mimi asked. "The yarn store on Orange Street? You could walk there in five minutes."

"It's so late in the season," Susan countered. "I'm sure they have all the help they need."

"I wouldn't be so sure," Darcy said. "Lots of people will leave the island in August—kids going back to college and so on."

"You could at least stop in," Mimi said.

Susan's face glowed and she broke into the prettiest Mona Lisa smile.

"OMG," Willow whispered, leaning in. "That guy over there is totally checking you out!"

"Who?" Susan asked.

"Well, not me," Mimi joked. "And Darcy's back is to him."

"He's cute," Willow said. "Take a look."

"Oh, don't be ridiculous." Susan shook her head and laughed. Then she looked. Then her neck and face flooded with a highly becoming blush. Then she jerkily moved her head and sat as if paralyzed.

Darcy glanced quickly over her shoulder. "He is cute."

"Please," Susan said, her lips scarcely moving, "stop it. I'm married."

"But not dead," Mimi told her. "For heaven's sake, Susan, a little flirting is not going to turn you into a scarlet woman."

"If Otto knew . . ." Susan paused, worried.

"Personally," Darcy said, "I think it would do your husband a lot of good to remember how attractive you are." She knew she could say

263

more. She could tell Susan that she'd seen Otto "visit" Autumn at night and also the weekend that Susan and the boys were in Boston. But after all, maybe the visits were innocent. And this moment, while Susan was all flustered and blushing and happy, was not the time to bring Susan's high spirits crashing to the ground. Plus, Willow was there. She didn't need to hear Darcy's suspicions.

The waitress arrived with a fresh round of drinks. "These are from the gentleman at the far table. The man in the red rugby shirt."

"Thank you," Darcy said. "And give him our thanks." She turned to Susan, who was staring at her drink as if it materialized right out of the air. "Susan," she hissed, "you need to lift your glass, smile at Red Rugby Shirt, and mouth the words thank you."

Susan put a trembling hand on her glass and paused.

"Goodness, child," Mimi scolded, "haven't you ever flirted before in your life?"

Susan shot back, "Of course I have. But long ago, before I had three children."

"It's just like riding a bike," Darcy cooed encouragingly.

Susan lifted her glass, smiled at Red Rugby Shirt, and said softly, "Thank you."

Darcy had to force herself not to turn around and gawk, but she noticed that Susan's smile brightened even more as her eyes kept contact with the man's.

Finally, she looked away. "Now what do I do?"

"Drink your drink," Mimi said sensibly.

Willow slipped her phone from her small shoulder bag and surreptitiously snapped a shot of Susan. "Should I get one of Red Rugby Shirt?" she asked.

"No!" Susan said. "That would be embarrassing. As if you were photographing some rare animal." She hesitated. "Okay, this is enough about me. Darcy, what about you? How's your love life?" She sat back in her chair, very pleased with herself for wrenching the spotlight onto Darcy.

"The truth? I don't know. . . ." Could she talk honestly about her relationship with Nash in front of Willow?

"Well, *I* do!" Mimi spoke up. "She's got a hunk visiting her several nights a week. His truck is in her driveway until past midnight. Not that I spy on my neighbors," she added with a mischievous grin.

"I've seen the truck, too," Susan added.

"Okay, fine, I'm *seeing* a really good guy. Nash Forester. He's a carpenter."

"That explains the muscles," Mimi murmured.

"The problem is—I don't know if we're going anywhere. I mean, I only started dating him in the spring, but he doesn't seem to want to do anything but eat, watch the Red Sox, and, um, go to bed."

"And your problem is?" Mimi teased. She continued in a milder tone. "So you know you're both in lust, but you're not sure if you're both in love, is that it?"

"Precisely," Darcy answered. "I've been 'in love' before, married before, and divorced." She cast a quick glance at Willow before adding, "I don't want to rush into anything. I don't even know if I want to get married again."

"But you want him to be in love with you," Mimi said.

"Yeah," Willow echoed. "You want him to at least ask the question."

Susan frowned. "Willow, this conversation must gross you out a little."

Willow shrugged. "Wait, what? I know I'm naïve, but I grew up watching my parents divorce, and Mom dating a bunch of different guys, and finding Boyz, and marrying him. Not to mention that just about every friend I've had has stepparents."

"Your mother's very beautiful," Darcy remarked.

"Yeah, and she knows it," Willow shot back. "So she got to have a lot of fun, and she tries to make me live like a Victorian virgin."

"There are worse ways to live," Susan said. She lounged back into her chair and yawned widely. "I don't usually have alcohol so late in

266

the evening. I think it's suddenly hitting me."

"We should go," Darcy said. "I've got work tomorrow."

"But let's do this again," Mimi proposed. "It's fun to share experiences across generations."

Darcy shot an uneasy glance at Willow.

"Hey," Willow told her, "I'm not going to repeat anything to anybody. That would be too weird."

"My mother and I certainly never talked about anything approaching lust," Mimi mused. Smiling wickedly, she added, "Fortunately, I was a curious girl, and enjoyed many opportunities to further my education."

"Do tell!" Darcy pleaded.

"Next time," Mimi promised.

14

Sunday was gloriously hot, without even a lazy breeze to stir the leaves.

Nash picked Darcy up in his red truck and they drove out to Fat Ladies Beach to meet their friends. Umbrellas in a multitude of colors had been planted in the sand like a garden of enormous flowers. Everyone was either swimming or slathering themselves and their kids with sunblock.

"Ouch!" Darcy complained. "Hot sand!" She was barefoot, in a new peach-colored bikini, with a frothy cover-up that was as thin as a petal but still one more annoying layer in this heat. Tearing it off over her head, she tossed it down on her beach towel and raced for the water.

Waves dawdled toward the shore, where the water was low enough and warm enough for kiddies to play. Darcy swam out into the blissful cold. She enjoyed treading water, letting her toes drop down and down, each foot of water colder than the one on top.

On the shore, Nash set up camp, stabbing the umbrella's pole deep into the sand, spreading his towel next to hers, setting their coolers on the corners of the towels in case a breeze kicked up.

She lay on her back and floated, kicking idly,

eyes closed, hoping the sunblock she'd applied would keep her nose from burning. The ocean was rocking her so gently, it was like a cradle. Flipping over, she swam farther out. She floated again. Random thoughts drifted through her mind . . . that memorable evening with Mimi, Willow, and Susan, laughter and wisdom, too . . . the volunteer at the children's library who acted like a psychotic personal shopper for children, following them around, pulling books off the shelf and shoving them into the child's hand, saying, "Try *this* one! *This* one is crazy good!" She meant well, but several parents had complained. But she was a generous donor to the library . . . it wasn't Darcy's problem to solve. It belonged to the head of the children's library, Beverly Maison. Was she feeding Muffler too much? He was looking fat these days. Maybe—

"Hey." Nash's head emerged from the water. His hair was slicked against his head.

"Hey, yourself." Darcy let her legs fall as she faced Nash.

"Do you have any idea how far out you are?" Nash asked. He seemed angry.

"Actually, lifeguard guy, I don't," Darcy answered facetiously, trying to twine her legs with his.

"Stop." Nash wasn't smiling. "Come closer to shore."

Dread flashed through Darcy.

He read her mind. "No, no shark fins in sight, but you're still too far out."

She smiled as she swam back to shore, pleased that Nash cared enough to worry about her, to swim out to her, to frown like that.

"Gosh, my legs are wobbly," she told Nash. "You're right, I was too far out."

She staggered to her blanket and collapsed facedown, grateful for the umbrella's shade. Sounds drifted toward her—laughter, a baby crying, a seagull squawking as he scanned their group for food to swoop down and steal.

"It's too hot," a woman complained. Darcy thought it was pregnant Dee-Dee Folger.

"I agree," Angelica said. "Packer's getting cranky, and so am I."

Darcy opened one eye and looked. Packer, a toddler, was stuffing sand into his mouth with both hands. Angelica tried to distract him with sand toys, the sifter, the molds, the shovel and bucket, but he threw himself backward, wailing, when she took his hands away from his face.

"Come to our house," Jordan offered. "It's air-conditioned."

Someone said, "The three most beautiful words in the English language." It was a man's voice, of course it was. A woman would think the three most beautiful words were *I love you*.

By the time the group had lugged all their stuff back to their vehicles, everyone was grumpy.

Nash set the truck's air-conditioning to high. Darcy leaned her head back against the seat.

"I think I'm going to have a red nose," she said.

"Probably."

"I'm glad we're not staying there all day," Darcy continued. "It's muggy today as well as hot. It was like a sauna."

"Yup."

Darcy gave Nash a questioning look. "Is everything okay?"

"Everything's fine," Nash told her. "I'm just hot and tired."

They parked in front of the Morrises' house and carried their coolers around to the back door where they rinsed their feet in the outdoor shower before going into the kitchen. Jordan was there, holding Kiks's feet under the running water in the sink.

"One grain of sand," Jordan said. "Kiks can spot one grain of sand on a clean field of tile and put it in her mouth. Or her ear."

Laughing, Darcy helped the others set out the food, utensils, paper napkins. The gang wasted no time loading their paper plates with food and snagging beers. They all went into the den to watch the Red Sox game on TV. After a while, Jordan put Kiks down for a nap and Packer fell asleep on the carpet.

The women sat in the living room, looking at sleeping Packer.

"He looks like an angel," Missy said wistfully.

"Babies do that, when they're asleep," Jordan replied. "It's a trick to keep you adoring them even after they've been acting like little devils."

"Want to know something?" Dee-Dee asked. "I am having a seriously difficult time. There has been no decent celebrity gossip for weeks!"

Darcy laughed. "Right. Kate Middleton hasn't fought with the queen and Jennifer Aniston isn't pregnant with twins."

"I know!" Missy agreed. She shot an evil grin at Darcy. "You just wait, when you have toddlers, you won't have time or brain power to read a book. You'll live for the tabloids at the grocery store."

"I'm much more intellectual than that," Jordan joked. "I read *People*."

"Ice cream," Dee-Dee said. "We need ice cream."

"Yes!" Angelica rose. "Darcy, I'll dish out the ice cream if you'll take the plates of brownies and cookies in to the guys."

"Don't they get ice cream?"

"I don't know. Depends on how much we women eat." Laughing, Angelica led the way into the kitchen.

Darcy headed toward the den with plates of cookies and brownies. She paused in the doorway to keep one plate from tilting, and in that moment, she overheard Nash's voice.

"Yeah, the house is kind of crummy, but I'm tired of throwing my money away on rent. This way I'll have my own place and a kind of investment."

"Smart move, Nash," Lyle said. "Anything on this island is worth gold."

Darcy froze. *Nash was buying a house?*

Why did that make her feel so—*anxious?* Because he hadn't told her first? Because he was buying his own place?

Because he didn't foresee a future with Darcy, living in her gorgeous old home?

"What are you doing? Hurry up!" Dee-Dee appeared behind Darcy, carrying bowls of ice cream. "Let's give the guys their treats and go back to enjoy our own!" She nudged Darcy with her elbow.

Darcy forced a smile on her face and entered the den. Dee-Dee followed with the ice cream, and Jordan showed up with spoons and forks.

The rest of the afternoon passed in a fog for Darcy. She was curious and hurt and impatient. She wanted to be alone with Nash, to hear him talk about his plan for the future.

"What's up, Buttercup?" Jordan asked as people began to leave.

Darcy shook her head. No way would she tell Jordan how upset she was, not when the men were so near. "I'm just tired," she explained, shrugging. "I think it's the heat."

"I'll jack up the air-conditioning in my truck," Nash said, coming up behind Darcy.

Darcy hugged Jordan and walked with Nash to his truck. As they drove toward her house, he was unusually quiet. Darcy didn't want to ride in silence—that would seem as if she were pouting and, from his point of view, for no reason at all.

"How are the Red Sox doing?" she asked, for the sake of making conversation.

"Lost. I'll get the postgame report." Nash punched the radio on and spun the dial until he got to the broadcast.

Okay, Darcy thought. *The man doesn't want to talk to me.*

Fine.

When they arrived at her house, she opened the door before the truck came to a complete stop. "Thanks, Nash," she said, raising her voice to be heard over the sportscaster's.

Nash slammed his foot on the brake and gave her a questioning look.

"I've got so much to do," Darcy told him. She carefully shut the truck door, did an abrupt about-face, and strode to her front door. She didn't look back to see his reaction.

The moment she was inside, she reached into her pocket for her phone and hit Jordan's number. Then she canceled the call. Jordan would be dealing with Kiks now. She'd be carrying glasses, bottles, and plates into the kitchen, loading the dishwasher, savoring some quiet moments with Lyle. They might be trading news they'd heard that day, Jordan from the women, Lyle from his buddies.

Lyle might tell Jordan that Nash was buying a property, and Jordan might call Darcy. Or Lyle might not even think to mention Nash to Jordan. Nash wasn't the center of the world.

Another woman, braver, stronger in self-confidence, might call Nash right now. She might say, pleasantly, rationally, that she'd overheard Nash telling the men he was buying a house on the island.

He might say something sensible, even affectionate, about buying the house.

But Darcy was starting her period, and she felt crampy and bloated and irritable, and she knew she wouldn't be able to prevent her Most *Un*perfect Darcy from exploding into a whining, complaining, irrational geyser of accusations—*Why* did he tell the men first, before telling Darcy? Was Darcy so low on his list of friends—Was that all she was to him, a *friend?*

She paced the house, talking out loud, trying to offload her anger and hurt into the air, to use up her emotional craziness now, not on the phone with Nash. Muffler, who'd seen her in this state before, slunk away to hide behind the sofa.

Was Nash sleeping with her, just hanging with her, until he found a woman he wanted to spend his life with? Did *no one* under the age of eighty want to be with her? Her mother and father didn't want her, her relatives in Illinois were too busy with their own lives to do more than send a Christmas card. Boyz had loved her—she believed he truly had, at first, and never mind the reasons. If it had been simply infatuation, it had been sweet. But it had not lasted. He had chosen Autumn.

The tears were coming now, hot and fast, burning her face as she asked the empty kitchen if anyone would ever love her, really *love* her. She could not *stand* it if all she meant to Nash was an easy lay, because—

Oh, holy hell, because she was in love with Nash. Damn.

Her hurricane of tears and rage and need slowly calmed, like a storm over the ocean, leaving her sitting on a chair in the kitchen, wiping her nose with a paper napkin because she was too exhausted to get up and go to the box of tissues across the room. It was all she could do to drag herself into the bedroom. She dropped onto the bed like a fallen tree and blanked out into a generous oblivion.

When she saw herself Monday morning, she shook her head at her reflection in the mirror. She was less bad-tempered now, but still filled with the heavy ache of sadness. No way would she share this pathetic creature with anyone on the island. This was her day off, so she showered, dressed, and caught a plane to the Cape. She spent the day shopping and returned home that evening with bags of new clothes and costume jewelry. If she was doomed to a life alone, she'd look good while she lived it.

Tuesday, the library was crowded, partly because it was so hot and muggy outside, and air-conditioned inside. That night, Nash called.

"Good day?" he asked.

As if everything between them was normal. As if she hadn't rushed out of his truck on Sunday. As if buying a house on the island—buying a house! An *enormous* thing to do! Houses here, even shacks, were crazy expensive—as if buying a house was so insignificant he didn't think to mention it to Darcy.

Or he was trying to keep it a secret from Darcy.

"Good day," she said briefly. "You?"

"Miserable," he said.

Darcy swallowed. Was he miserable because she'd been abrupt with him?

"I've heard for years that Nantucket's summers were cooler than the mainland's, but today's heat and humidity were brutal. It saps all our energy, you know, this kind of muggy heat."

Ah. So he wasn't going to mention her mood. Maybe he hadn't even noticed—he was, after all, a man. But she was moved to sympathy at the thought of working out in the hot sun all day. She was kind of mad at him, but more than that, she cared that he'd had such a tough day.

"It doesn't usually last long," Darcy assured him.

"*I'm* not going to last long if it keeps up," Nash joked. "I'd like to see you, but I'm beat. I stood under the shower for about an hour just now. I got some pizza on the way home, I've got the air-conditioning jacked up, and the Red Sox are playing tonight. That's it for me."

"You are such a guy," Darcy teased.

She was tired, too, and happy enough to spend the evening with a book and a cold cranberry drink. Wednesday, more of the same.

Thursday evening the library was open late and Darcy was on the roster for that. It was quiet, because the heat had abated and people could enjoy being outside. After closing the library, Darcy strolled home, enjoying the rare clear summer night, replaying certain moments of her day at work. The story hours were her favorite time and that brought her smack-dab right into the rather frightening thought that she was beginning to want children of her own.

When she reached her house, she took a long cool shower, slipped into an airy, billowy caftan, and carried a glass of wine and her cellphone out to her yard. Stretching out in her lounger, she exhaled and relaxed, looking up at the summer sky. Even now, daylight lingered, and as she watched, the sky changed colors like a scarf pulled from a magician's sleeve, darkness slowly staining black into the blue. The stars came out.

Muffler rustled through the bushes, probably searching for the tiny velvet voles that crept through her garden at night. After a while, he jumped up on the table and began the elegant task of cleaning himself.

The bushes rustled again, more noisily this time. Darcy lifted her head.

"Darcy?" Willow whispered. "Can I come over?"

"Of course." Before Darcy finished speaking, her cellphone buzzed. She checked, found a number she didn't know, and answered.

"Darcy?" It was Susan. "I want to stop by a moment. I've got something to tell you."

"Of course," Darcy told her.

She set her wineglass on the table and walked to her back door. Just inside was a switch for the miniature sparkling white lights she had strung in a loose, scattered web along the hedges. She'd planned to wait until she had a party to use them, but she couldn't sit and talk to her friends in the total darkness that had fallen.

When the lights went on, pinpoints of brilliance twinkling around the yard, her mood lifted.

Susan and Willow came down through the

arbor and across her yard, both of them whispering and giggling.

"Hi, Darcy!" Willow cried, flinging her arms around Darcy and hugging her.

"What's going on?" Darcy asked.

Willow pulled Darcy by the hand to the patio. "Sit down. We have something to tell you." She glanced at Susan. "You first."

Illuminated by the gentle lights, Susan's face was soft, glowing. "I have a job in the yarn shop!"

Unable to wait for Darcy's response, Willow blurted, "And I'm babysitting her boys!"

"Wow!" Darcy had scarcely spoken when her cellphone buzzed again. Looking down, she saw it was Mimi's number.

"What are you all doing down there?" Mimi asked, without her usual polite greeting preamble.

"Come join us," Darcy replied. To Willow and Susan, she said, "Wait. Mimi's coming."

Willow jumped up. "I'll go help her."

"Where are your boys?" Darcy asked Susan.

"Asleep. I've enrolled them in a summer day camp. They love it, and they're put in different sections, separated for the day, which is good for them. They fall asleep the moment their heads hit their pillows. I wish I'd thought of this earlier in the summer."

"Hello!" Mimi called out. She came across the grass with her arm around Willow's shoulders for steadiness. In the radiance of the little lights, she looked amazing, like a woman stepping out of the past.

"What are you *wearing?*" Darcy asked, stunned by the older woman's plunging silk nightgown and magnificent silk wrapper thickly embroidered with a flamboyance of colorful birds.

Mimi chortled. "Fabulous, isn't it? It was my mother's. She was a clotheshorse, and I always coveted this, and now I have it. I don't often get a chance to wear it."

"Damn," Susan swore. "I sleep in an old stretched-out T-shirt of Otto's."

"Me, too," Darcy said. "Well, I don't mean I sleep in one of *Otto's* T-shirts. . . ."

Laughing, Mimi leveraged herself into a chair. "You young women can make a T-shirt look like a stripper's costume. At my age, I prefer silk and lots of it. Now. What were you gossiping about? I saw you from my bedroom window."

Willow and Susan rapidly repeated their news.

"But if the boys are in a day camp, when does Willow babysit?"

"In the late afternoon," Willow said.

Susan added, "For three hours. From four to seven. That's a quiet time for Merry Wicks— she's the owner—but people do come in from time to time, especially on cloudy days. I give her a chance to do errands and eat a proper meal. She returns and keeps the shop open until nine.

It's amazing, how people find the place, even though it's not in the center of town."

"And I'll bring the boys to my house," Willow added. "Because we've got the trampoline and the badminton set there. If it's raining, we'll play some of the games stored in our cupboards."

"But won't your mother mind?" Mimi asked. "Three rambunctious youngsters—so much noise?"

"I checked with Mom, and she's cool about it. Dad's up in Boston all week, so Mom said she'll go shopping, that will only take her a hundred hours, or drive out to some beach and have a long walk and enjoy the island."

"Of course, she won't always have the boys at her house," Susan cut in. "Otto can take his laptop to the library, so if Henry or George or Alfred want to play at home, Willow can watch them there and they won't be a bother to him."

"We can always walk down to Flock so the guys can say hi to their mom," Willow said.

"I'm guessing the shop will be boring to them and frankly, three boys in a yarn shop is not a mix made in heaven," Susan said.

"What does Otto think of you working?" Mimi asked.

"I thought he'd object. It's not like we need the money. But he understands—who better?—my desire to escape my darlings, and my need to do something adult."

Mimi set her eagle eye on Willow. "And what do your parents think of you spending all your time with old ladies and children? They must want you to make some acquaintances of your own age."

Willow rolled her eyes. "I met an 'acquaintance' my own age when I first got here, Mimi. That didn't work out so well. Ask Darcy about that sometime. But anyway, I'm happy at the library, and I enjoy the boys. I think they're the totally right age for me this summer."

"You've only had them for two afternoons," Susan reminded Willow. "Wait until you've spent a week with them."

"If they get bored, I'll walk them into town for ice cream, or we can go to Children's Beach," Willow added.

"If it rains," Mimi told her, "bring your tribe over to our house. There's a Ping-Pong table in the basement."

"Awesome!" Willow cried. "I love Ping-Pong!"

"Alfred is too young for Ping-Pong," Susan mused. "He isn't tall enough yet."

"I'll take them shopping," Willow said. "The Sunken Ship has cool toys. . . ."

"Alfred likes monster trucks," Susan told her.

"But, Mimi!" Willow suddenly looked distressed. "When will I be able to read to you? I forgot, we're right in the middle of *The Age of Innocence*!"

"I don't work on Mondays or on weekends," Susan quickly informed them, worried.

"There you are, then," Mimi said, soothing them with her easy voice. "You can read to me on Mondays and weekends—if you don't need the time for yourself."

Darcy settled back in her chair, letting the conversation fade into the background, enjoying the moment, the three other women of all ages leaning toward one another, sharing information, making plans, talking of yarn and toys. The pinpoints of light gave an air of mystery and drama to their faces, a kind of depth. It was as if this conversation could be taking place a hundred years ago, or fifty years from now. Women would always plot about childcare and knitting.

She especially enjoyed watching Willow. Her long auburn hair was twisted up in back and held with a clasp so that much of it stuck out in all directions from the top of her head, like a spout. She wore cutoffs, flip-flops, and a blue T-shirt with the joke logo *Nantucket University*. Willow was animated as she talked, completely at ease, laughing and waving her arms and shouting "No way!" or "Totally!" at something Mimi or Susan said. She was a sweet, funny girl, and Darcy was fond of her. More than that, she felt proud of her for making such an about-face in such a brief period of time from baby bombshell needing the attention and sexual lessons of Logan to this child/young woman, comfortable hanging around with old ladies. She felt connected to Willow—and just at that moment, as if the girl had intuited Darcy's thoughts, Willow flashed a grin full of affection at Darcy before returning to the conversation with Susan and Mimi.

But when Darcy looked at Susan, a little midge of worry buzzed in Darcy's thoughts. Boyz was gone five days of the week, working in Boston, leaving the bounteous Autumn free. If Susan was ensconced in the yarn shop, and her boys were with Willow, that meant that Otto was free to go anywhere to do anything with anyone.

To do anything.

But really, what business was it of hers? She liked Susan, and would hate to see her hurt, but Darcy had no real idea of Susan and Otto's relationship. Other people's marriages held private pacts and arrangements so intimate they were kept hidden from everyone else, even from the children. Maybe Susan would be relieved to have the tyrannical Otto release his energies on another woman. And would it surprise Darcy at all if Boyz, up in Boston for the week, had a mistress? Ha.

"Darcy?" Mimi's voice broke into her thoughts. "You look like you're fading."

"Oh, sorry, I guess I was thinking about work tomorrow . . ." Darcy looked around the table. "Would anyone like some lemonade?"

"Goodness, no," Mimi said. "As it is, I have to get up fifty times a night. . . ."

"Well, *I* should get some rest," Willow stated with dramatically fake self-importance, "because I have to do two story times tomorrow and babysit three wild boys for three hours."

The women wandered off, tossing kisses, saying good nights, walking beneath the arbor and home. Darcy switched off the lights and the magical glow vanished. Darkness fell on her backyard. She wasn't tired yet. She didn't want to watch television or read. She enjoyed her new friends immensely, but she always had needed a moment or two of solitude. She returned to her lounger and sank back, looking up at the starry sky.

"Good night," Willow called.

Three doors banged shut. Silence fell.

From beneath a large hydrangea, Muffler came slinking out. He jumped on Darcy's lap, claiming his rightful territory. Darcy ran her hand over his long silky fur and his low satisfying purr lulled her like a lullaby.

15

*H*ey, Darcy. Want to get together tomorrow
night? I'm going sports fishing with some
guys this weekend.

Darcy stood over her phone, glaring down at
the message from Nash. They'd spoken briefly
on Tuesday, both of them complaining about
the unusual heat and humidity, and she'd known
a casual conversation was the wrong time to
broach the subject of his prospective house.

*Sure. Come over for dinner tomorrow night.
We'll eat inside with the air conditioners on full
blast.*

She put together a pot roast with veggies in the
slow cooker and went off to the library, feeling
slightly cheerful, slightly anxious. On her way
home from work, she stopped to buy a bottle of
red wine and a six-pack of Whale's Tale Pale
Ale, Nash's favorite. At home she changed into
a sundress so loose she could wear it without a
bra, and pulled her hair up into a high ponytail,
away from her neck. Then, barefoot, she padded
downstairs and into the kitchen to put together a
salad.

When she opened the door to Nash, his face
lit up. He stepped inside, pulled her to him, and
kissed her vigorously.

"I've missed you," he said.

Darcy turned away, leading him into the house. His kiss had unsettled her and his words had surprised her. He had missed her?

She'd better drink a little wine before she said anything she'd regret.

"Want an ale?" she asked.

"Thanks." He leaned against the kitchen counter, looking at her quizzically as she took the bottle from the fridge. "Something smells good."

"Pot roast. Bless the man who invented slow cookers." She paid great attention to pouring herself a glass of wine. "How's work?" She led Nash back into the living room and settled into an overstuffed chair.

Nash sank onto the sofa. "Hot."

"Your nose is red, and look at your neck. Do you put on sunblock? Because you should or you might be sorry when you're older."

"Thanks, Mom," Nash teased. "How was your week?"

"Great. The children's story time is such a crush of children, and Willow is an enormous help. In the evenings, Willow's babysitting Susan Brueckner's children, three boys who seem to be the inspiration for the term 'attention deficit disorder.' Susan's working in a yarn shop in the evenings, and it's making her so happy—not just because she's escaping her noisy children, but because she feels good being around yarn and meeting people and being herself rather than Otto's wife and the boys' mother." Talking about her friends changed her mood, cheered her up, and made her feel less paranoid about Nash. "Do you construction men ever—I don't know—discuss your personal lives with each other?"

Nash laughed. "You should spend a day at our site. We can't hear ourselves over the noise of the chain saw and the hammers. When we break for lunch, we collapse in the shade and eat. The most intimate moment we've had was when Juan passed out from acrophobia."

"What about the guys we hang out with on Sundays? Lyle and the others?"

"You know what we talk about—the Red Sox. Maybe, occasionally, to break the monotony, the Patriots."

And the words spilled out of Darcy's mouth before she took a second to think.

"So you're not close to Lyle and the others, but you told them you're buying a house on the island and you didn't tell me?" She didn't intend to sound angry, but her voice shook.

Nash blinked, surprised. "You mean on Sunday? Okay, well, Paul is a real estate broker. I wanted to get his opinion. The owner is trying to sell it himself. I don't know the island property values that well. I've only been here since March. I needed some friendly advice."

Fists clenched, Darcy stood up. Then she sat

down. She would not, she *would not* allow herself to go into a pitiful, needy, clingy pit of begging. She would never say those terrible words: *Where do you think our relationship is headed?* She would not say *I think I love you.* She would not say *Do you think you love me?*

It took all her self-control, but she shook her head and held her hand up in a stop gesture. "Give me a moment." She forced a smile.

She would not even ask if they were a couple. This wasn't high school.

Finally she decided to attempt a kind of reasonable explanation. "I'm sorry, Nash. I guess I'm overreacting because I hate it when people keep secrets from me."

"I wasn't keeping a secret from you," Nash told her. "I just hadn't had a chance to tell you yet. I'm only beginning to think about this, about buying a place."

Okay, that was good, that was better. She aimed for a casual tone. "Housing is ridiculously expensive here."

"Tell me about it. You're lucky your grandmother left you this house."

"I know. I couldn't live on the island otherwise. And this house is special to me. I hope I never have to leave it. It's in a perfect location, and it's got the fabulous backyard, and"—she swallowed the words: *It's so big that if I ever marry and have children*—"there's lots of room."

She couldn't read the expression in his eyes. But they were talking, inching into intimate territory, and her anger, her sense of betrayal, evaporated, leaving hope in its place.

"Come have dinner," she said. "Let's dish it up and we can eat in here and watch the Red Sox."

"Ah, you seductive wench," Nash said, rising and pulling her to him.

She stepped back. "Stop that or you'll be eating dinner at midnight." A surge of power rushed through her when she spoke those words, when she backed away even though her body craved his like air and light.

The pot roast was delicious, and it was a luxury to eat a hot meal while sitting in a cool, dry house. The Red Sox won their game. Darcy led Nash upstairs, where they made easy, lazy love, and Nash went home and Darcy fell asleep with a smile on her face.

That Sunday Nash went sports fishing with friends, a strenuous sport that would have them rolling on the heaving Atlantic. They would return late in the evening with bluefin tuna and sunburns, and Monday morning most of them would be hung over.

Darcy decided to give herself a Self-centered day, which was the opposite of her Perfect Darcy day. She avoided her computer as if it had a contagious virus. She'd prepared for today the night before, when she bought ice cream and ready-made salads and microwavable lasagna, and she vowed to stay in her silk kimono all day. She'd taken a few enticing books from the library and began her day by curling up on the sofa, drinking coffee, eating not one but two chocolate croissants from the Nantucket Bake Shop, and reading.

When she was younger, she could read all day without stopping. Of course she could, because some adult, usually her grandmother, took care of everything—food, shelter, all her personal needs. Also, whomever she stayed with—Penny or one of Lala's daffy relatives—seemed to like Darcy most when she was quiet, tucked into a corner, asking for nothing, needing to go nowhere. She learned to go everywhere through books.

She'd finished her coffee and croissant and the first two chapters of the compelling mystery when someone knocked on her front door. *Susan's probably out of milk again,* Darcy thought with a smile. She strolled to the door and pulled it open. And stopped smiling.

Boyz stood there, all Ralph Lauren in his golf shirt and Bermuda shorts and loafers without socks. He'd gotten a beautiful tan, so even it looked painted on, and his hair gleamed in the sunlight.

"Boyz!"

"Hey, Darce. Could I come in? I'd like to talk to you about something."

"Um, okay. . . ." She led him into the living room. "Would you like some coffee?" She couldn't help it; she was relieved and a little smug because she was wearing the silk kimono when she could have easily been clad in an old T-shirt.

"Thanks, no. I've finished breakfast, had enough caffeine to blast me to Mars. Autumn and Willow are still sleeping. That's why I decided to come over now."

"Oh?" Darcy said, slightly wary. She motioned to a chair. "Sit down." She took the chair across from him.

Boyz set his elbows on his knees with his hands dangling down between his widely planted legs.

Oh, please, Darcy thought, *don't call my attention to your equipment. I'm so over you.*

Boyz got right to it. "I need to talk to you about Willow. No insult intended, just a friendly observation, from a man who knows you well, who understands what you lack and what you need."

Darcy wrinkled her nose in confused disgust. "Wait, what?" The moment the words left her mouth, she realized that was exactly the way Willow spoke.

"I know you're sore about me and Autumn. I know your pride's been mangled and you're unsure of your desirability. It's absolutely understandable. Anyone would feel that way.

But, Darcy, honey, it's kind of foul play to bring Willow into the mix. She's a young, impressionable girl. She might get the idea you like her for herself."

Had the man gone insane? Darcy's eyes widened. "But, Boyz, I *do* like her!"

"Come on, Darce, don't forget I was married to you for three years. I know you inside and out." Boyz treated her to one of his superalluring lascivious grins.

"Oh, for God's sake," Darcy said.

"If you want to get together with me, privately, I mean, I'd be all over that like white on rice, but it's not necessary for you to try to sneak in through the back door."

"Really, Boyz. I have no idea what you're going on about."

"Well, first of all, I need you to know I care about Willow. She's my stepdaughter. I don't like her used to get to me. Second, if you'd like to join me in bed for old time's sake, I'd be up for that." Another grin. "Really *up*."

Darcy was horrified. "Are you saying you think I'm friendly with Willow so that I can get you to notice me, to have sex with me? Boyz, that's over-the-top vain, even for you!"

Boyz continued to smile. He was almost leering at her.

"Darcy. Honey. Don't try to pretend. You and I had some pretty sweet times together. And I want you to know I still consider you a beautiful woman."

"Boyz. Listen to me. I have no interest in you at all. Really. Truly."

Boyz tilted his head and dimmed the wattage of his smile. "So why are you hanging out with Willow?"

"Because she's *wonderful!*" Darcy was so angry and insulted on Willow's behalf she wanted to punch her ex-husband. "And I'm not 'hanging out' with her! Willow helps at the library, she's great with the little kids during story hour. She reads to Mimi Rush who lives next door and is eighty-nine years old and has bad eyes. She's babysitting Susan Brueckner's three boys during the week—when you're in Boston. She's a sweet, intelligent girl and if I see more of her than you do, it's not my fault, it's yours!"

"Oh, Darcy," Boyz said softly. "If that's all true, why aren't you involving Autumn in these arrangements? Autumn is her mother, after all."

Darcy bit her lips. She could tell Boyz exactly what Autumn was up to with Otto Brueckner, but maybe she was wrong, and she didn't want to be vindictive and it wasn't relevant anyway. "I've discussed all this with Autumn. I phoned her several weeks ago to invite her to join us. Autumn declined. She wants Willow to have her own group, away from her mother. She told me I didn't need to contact her all the time. She trusts

Willow when she's with me, with us." Angry, Darcy demanded, "Don't you even talk to your wife?"

She'd taken one step too far. She'd embarrassed Boyz. His face went red. Gone was his seductive tone. Now he wanted to hurt. "Whatever. The point I'm trying to make here is that *Autumn* is Willow's mother. You are *not,* and you've got to stop pretending you are. I sincerely hope you'll have a child of your own someday, but until then, hands off Willow. Okay?"

"Boyz." Darcy was embarrassed to see her hands were trembling. She rose. "I think you'd better leave."

Like a chameleon, Boyz switched back into his charming self. He stood, walked close to Darcy, his pale blue eyes warm with affection. "Darcy. I'm sorry if I hurt your feelings. Come here. Let me make it all better."

Before she could react, Boyz had taken her in his arms and kissed her.

Her body hit her with a whirlwind of memory. The way he cupped her head in his left hand while pressing his right hand on her hip, moving toward him and his erection. The way his lips felt, even the scent of his breath—coffee and a tang of Listerine, because Boyz always kept small bottles of Listerine around so he'd have clean breath when he spoke to his clients. It amused her that he'd used it this morning before coming to see her, and she smiled at the thought, right in the middle of his passionate kiss, and then pulled away from her ex-husband's arms.

"Boyz, go home. I don't want this. Try to believe for once in your life that one woman in the world is not infatuated with you. That would be me."

Boyz dropped his arms. He stepped back. But he kept his eyes on Darcy. "You know, Darcy, if we do—enjoy ourselves together—I would keep it all secret from Autumn and Willow."

Darcy laughed. "Well, I have to say I'm well aware that you can keep your affairs secret."

"Ah," Boyz said softly, nodding his head and creasing his forehead in an expression of sympathy. "Of course, you're still hurt over catching me with Autumn."

Darcy began, "Honestly, Boyz, I'm not—"

"Then why aren't you married? It's been three years." Boyz couldn't keep back a look of satisfaction at a shot well placed.

"Look, Boyz, I have a lovely boyfriend. You don't need to know anything about me. Please, just go home." Darcy turned her back on him and walked away before he could speak again.

She opened the front door. She stood next to it, unsmiling, arms crossed over her chest, like a matron in a reform school.

Boyz took his time sauntering out of the living room, into the hall, and right to the threshold. He gave Darcy a smug look. "Remember, all you have to do is call."

Darcy shuddered. How could she have been attracted to this man? Was she really so easily seduced by good looks? He did have a kind of magnetism, she had to admit that, but she'd built up a powerful shield against him.

"Boyz, I only want to go back to my very good book." She stepped back and closed the door, practically pushing him out of her house.

But of course when she returned to her living room, she couldn't read. An enormous hurricane of energy and emotions whirled through her. She was still trembling. She couldn't sit down. She paced up and down her hallway, muttering to herself, wanting to strike something or pull out her hair.

It wasn't because Boyz had come on to her. Boyz would come on to a statue if it had big enough breasts. It wasn't his belief that she wasn't able to get pregnant, it wasn't his air of superiority and pity.

It was because he'd hit on a soft spot, because he did have one righteous point.

Willow wasn't her daughter. Willow belonged to Autumn. Even if Autumn ignored Willow, she was still Willow's mother. Even if she was a *mediocre* mother, she was still Willow's mother.

Was Darcy "hanging out" with Willow? Yes, kind of . . .

But so were Mimi and Susan. That was what made them such an unusual and fascinating group, their different ages and lives.

Still, if Darcy were honest with herself, she'd admit that she felt something more than friendship for Willow. She loved her.

Was it wrong to love someone who doesn't belong to you?

Memories flashed her back to the year she was nine. Darcy was living with Lala's parents, and then Lala's mother had a bad fall. She had an operation for a new knee and spent months in rehab, leaving Darcy with her grandfather, whose only cooking skill was stirring hot water into bowls of oatmeal from small packets. Darcy was shuffled off to live with an aunt and uncle, who made it clear she was an annoyance and a burden. Her only haven had been the school library, and it was there she developed an unexplainable fondness, a quiet adoration, for an older woman.

Bessie Bogan, the school librarian. She was African American, in her forties, happily, comfortably, bouncily fat, and endlessly kind. Bessie had taken an interest in Darcy when no one else seemed to give her a second thought. She noticed Darcy's passion for reading and introduced her to nonfiction, fiction, and biography that opened up worlds to her. When Darcy spent an hour after school in the library— because no one cared what time she got home—

Bessie was receptive to Darcy's questions, and often, she'd say to Darcy, "Pull up a chair, honey. Let's talk about this."

As they talked, Darcy studied Bessie, trying to decide what made her so wonderful. Bessie wore a fragrance like vanilla and cinnamon. She wore pretty dresses in flower colors, often with lace at the neck or the wrists. Her teeth were a brilliant white, and she wore her very curly hair pulled back and held with a variety of hair clasps that coordinated with her earrings and necklaces. But it wasn't Bessie's beauty that fascinated Darcy. It was how she listened to Darcy speak, focusing all her attention on her, often remaining silent for a minute or two while she contemplated Darcy's words.

"Um-hum," Bessie would hum. "Let me think on that."

The subject might be as enormous as the Holocaust—How could such a thing happen? Or as trivial as why women needed to possess so many pairs of shoes.

Often, Bessie would reply, "Child, I don't think that's a question anyone on this earth has the true answer for. The best advice I can give you is to keep reading."

Darcy was in fourth grade at the time, and she moved to Nantucket when she was in fifth grade, and Bessie herself was no longer in Darcy's life. But the lessons Bessie taught Darcy—not through words but through example—stayed with her forever. Bessie had a kind of patience with not having all the answers, with not being in control, and Darcy worked to achieve that in herself. Her mother lived a water-bug life, darting here and there, appreciating where she was or with whom only until something shiny gleamed, and she would zip away, never minding the turbulence she left behind.

Bessie Bogan never did anything with Darcy out of the library, although she had mentioned taking Darcy and three other interested fourth graders to the Chicago Art Institute. The trip never took place, and Darcy was sorry about that. She kept in touch with Bessie with Christmas cards for a few years, but the link between them gradually faded. Still, Darcy knew it was Bessie Bogan who had inspired Darcy to become a librarian.

Darcy returned to the living room, curled up on the sofa with her mystery, and opened the book. Her thoughts wouldn't settle. *Did* she care for Willow because she didn't have her own child? Did she care for Mimi because she had no grandmothers left? Okay, but why, then, did she care for Susan? True, Darcy didn't have a sister, but Susan wasn't sister material—she was a friend. A friend with a tempestuous life and, although she wasn't aware of it, an unfaithful husband. *Possibly* unfaithful. For all Darcy knew, Autumn and Otto were spending their time together discussing the stock market.

She couldn't explain it. Mimi, Willow, and Susan were simply delightful people, and Darcy enjoyed their company. It had absolutely nothing to do with the fact that she'd fallen so hard for Nash, and wanted a commitment with him *now* and he was so unhurried. It had nothing to do with that at all.

Her cell burbled. Darcy snatched it up.

Beth O'Malley said, "Darcy, a bunch of us from the women's chorus want to go for a walk at the beach and then spend a loooong evening at the Nautilus drinking te-quil-a mockingbirds and eating tapas and roasted Peking duck. Want to go with us?"

Darcy grinned. "I thought you'd never ask."

"Good. Dress sexy. Bring gossip."

Darcy laughed. "I'll do my best."

16

Thursday evening, Darcy was ironing a dress for the next day while she idly watched the evening news. When the phone rang, she answered it with her eyes on the television.

"Darcy, could you help me?" Willow pleaded in such a rush her words were jammed together. Before Darcy could speak, Willow continued, "Henry cut his finger with a knife, it's my fault, we were making watermelon slices, he's okay, he's not even crying now, but I can't find any Band-Aids in the house and he can't just stand holding a paper towel around it!"

"I'm not sure I have any Band-Aids, either," Darcy said, "but I can run out and buy some."

"No, that's okay, we have some in our house, I know right where they are, I just need you to come watch the boys while I run over to our house. I'd take them with me, but I promised they could watch the *Lego Movie* while they eat their watermelon. They're in front of the television now, but Henry has to stand in the kitchen because I don't want him dripping blood on the owner's furniture!"

And they're not dripping watermelon juice? Darcy thought, but she said, "Good thinking. I'll be right over." She wanted to check on Henry's cut, be sure he didn't need stitches.

She turned off her iron. She didn't bother to comb her hair or put on fresh lip balm, not for those three little rascals. It took her only a minute to go out her door and cross to the Brueckners' house, where she found Willow waiting.

"Thank you, thank you, thank you!" Willow cried, throwing her arms around Darcy. "I really need to get a Band-Aid, it's only a little cut, but I can't let Susan come home to find her son bleeding on the rug!"

Darcy smiled. "I'm sure it will all be fine."

"I'll just run over to our house, I won't be a minute, I'll be right back."

Darcy found Henry standing in the kitchen with his right arm up in the air.

"Hi, Henry," Darcy said, keeping her tone mild. "Willow says you cut yourself."

"She told me to hold my hand over my head so the blood wouldn't fall out as fast."

"Willow's awfully smart," Darcy assured him. "Could I see your cut?"

Proudly, Henry extended his hand.

Darcy gently unwrapped the paper towel and looked. The gash was across the top of his third finger, deep enough to pool blood up over the wound, where it then dripped down onto the kitchen floor. She didn't think a Band-Aid would be sufficient. When Willow returned, Darcy would drive them all to the hospital's ER to see if Henry needed stitches.

"I'm going to wrap your finger in an ice-cold paper towel," Darcy told the boy. "It won't hurt, it will just be cold, and it will make the bleeding slow down."

"Then can I go sit and watch the *Lego Movie*?"

"Let me wrap it, and I'll come with you and keep my hand on your finger. I want to press on it a little bit."

Henry seemed more upset about missing the video than by his bleeding finger.

Darcy walked into the living room with the child, holding his finger tightly. Henry plunked down on the sofa next to his brothers and Darcy sat on the arm of the sofa, amused that neither George nor Alfred seemed concerned about their brother. *Boys,* she thought.

On the coffee table sat two empty bowls and another bowl still full of watermelon chunks.

"I want to eat my watermelon," Henry cried.

"Shut up!" George yelled.

"Here, Henry, I'll hold the bowl. Can you use your left hand?" Darcy leaned over and held the bowl close to the boy, still managing to keep her other hand firmly around his wound.

The back door slammed and Willow charged into the room. Her eyes were so wide she looked like an enraged animal, and her complexion was paper white.

"We have to go." Willow said. *"Now."*

Darcy stood up, her hand still on Henry's finger. "Willow, are you all right?"

"It's so gross, they're so gross!" Willow burst into tears. "People are *disgusting!*" She clenched her fists and brought them in front of her, holding her body tight, as if to make herself smaller in the world.

"Okay," Darcy said calmly, "we're all going to the hospital now, because I think a doctor should see Henry's finger."

"No!" Henry yelled. "I don't want a shot!"

"Needle, needle, Henry's gonna get stuck with a needle!" George chanted, and Alfred chimed in.

Henry yelled *"no"* even louder, and wrenched himself away from Darcy, causing the cold, bloodstained towel to fall on the sofa.

"Willow, do you know where the car keys are? We need the boys' car seats."

Willow burst into tears.

"Oh, for heaven's sake," Darcy said. "This is like a carnival." She was fairly certain threats wouldn't get the boys in the car, so she went for treats. "Let's all get in my car. After we go to the hospital, I'll take you to the Hub and buy you any candy you want."

"Yay!" George and Alfred shouted, jumping up and down.

Darcy picked up the paper towel, seized Henry by the wrist, and stuck the paper towel back over his finger.

"Willow," she ordered, in a no-nonsense voice, "you need to hold this on his finger while I drive."

"Nothing matters anymore," Willow sobbed, but she obeyed.

"Willow! Calm down!" Darcy was stunned that the girl was overreacting so dramatically.

George did a transformer move, switching from crazed boy into his father. "You can't drive unless you have your driver's license with you."

"Right," Darcy agreed. "George, go in my front door and fetch my straw purse. It's sitting on the front hall table. You can't miss it."

George's chest puffed out with pride. He marched off.

Darcy guessed that the Brueckners would be organized, and they were. Susan's keys to her car were on a hook in the kitchen, with a labeled tag. With Willow's sobbing help, Darcy herded the boys out of the house and into the car. George came running to hand Darcy her purse and squeezed in with the others. Henry sat on Willow's lap so she could hold his hand.

"We need our seatbelts on!" George screamed.

"It's only a few blocks to the hospital," Darcy assured him, "and all the streets are one-way. I'll drive slowly. We can't get all your seatbelts on with Willow in the back, and Willow has to be in the back to hold Henry's finger and you children are too small to sit in the passenger seat in front."

To her delight, her logical explanation satisfied George. He nodded once sharply.

"Willow," Darcy said, "Get out your cellphone and call Susan. We need to tell her what's happened."

"No!" Willow cried. "I can't talk to her!"

Had everyone gone mad? It was impossible to think with the racket the boys were making. George and Alfred had begun to chant, "Henry's going to die-i, Henry's going to die-i!"

"What's going on with you, Willow?" Darcy yelled, looking at the girl in her rearview mirror.

Willow wailed and at last managed to say, "I saw my mother with—" She jerked her head at the boys.

"You saw your mother? What?"

"They were on the dining room table! I'll never eat again!"

"You're not making any sense, Willow," Darcy said.

But she had a pretty good idea what Willow meant. It seemed that Darcy's suspicions about Otto Brueckner and Autumn were true.

"We're here," she called to the menagerie in the backseat. She pulled into the ER parking lot. "Boys. Settle down. You have to be quiet in a hospital. George, hold Henry's hand. Willow, hold Alfred's hand."

The three boys and Willow untangled themselves. The boys pitched their frenetic bodies out onto the pavement. Darcy clicked Susan's cell number.

"Susan," was all she managed to say before Susan gasped, "Oh, no. What's happened to the boys?"

"Henry cut his finger when they were slicing watermelon. It's only a little cut but we're going into the ER to be sure he doesn't need stitches."

George jumped up and down, yelling, "Henry's dying, Mom, he's bleeding like ketchup on a hamburger!"

Susan snapped into Sergeant Mother mode. "I'll close the shop and be right there. It's only a few blocks. I'll run."

"Okay, kids, let's go into the hospital. Look, Henry, magic doors."

"Duh," George scoffed. "They're not magic, they're electric. We're not *idiots*."

"Then stop acting like ones," Darcy snapped.

The ER waiting room was full, of course it was. It was summer on Nantucket. Most of the chairs lining the perimeter of the room were taken. Darcy saw a mother holding a squalling baby, a carpenter with a handmade tourniquet wrapped around his arm, a couple of drunks passed out in the corner, and a family talking rapidly in Spanish. She registered at the counter. The exhausted nurse told her it would be ten minutes. *That means twenty,* Darcy thought.

Willow looked so dazed Darcy feared the

doctors would think she was in for a drug overdose.

"George," Darcy said. "Here's some money. Take your brothers over to the vending machine and buy some candy. Henry, keep the towel on your finger and you can go, too."

The boys raced off.

Darcy took Willow gently by the shoulders and faced her squarely. "Willow. What happened?"

Willow's tears rained down her face. "It was so awful! I can't even tell you."

"You have to tell me, Willow. Maybe I can help you."

"No one can help me," Willow sobbed.

"Did someone hurt you?"

Willow shook her head so ferociously her tears flew.

"Tell me, Willow. At least give me a hint. The boys will be back in a minute and we won't be able to talk."

Willow covered her hands with her face. "My mother," she whispered. "My mother and Mr. Brueckner." Her knees sagged and Darcy had to hold her up. "On the dining room table!"

Good grief, Darcy thought. *What a thing for a daughter to see.*

"Oh, sweetie." Darcy gathered the girl into her arms. "It's going to be okay," she said, patting Willow's back.

Willow stopped sobbing. She took a few deep

breaths. She pulled away from Darcy. "What am I going to do?"

"Did anyone see you?"

"Ha." She sniffed contemptuously. "No, they didn't see me, they were too busy. . . ." She couldn't go on.

"All right," Darcy said. "First, we have to decide whether or not to tell Susan. She'll be here any minute."

"Ick! No, Darcy, we can't! Mr. Brueckner is her *husband.*"

Darcy thought it wouldn't come as an enormous surprise to Susan that her husband was unfaithful, but at this moment in time, she agreed with Willow. "Okay. If Susan asks why you've been crying, you can tell her because you're sorry that Henry cut his finger."

Willow nodded. Darcy felt in her purse for a tissue and handed it to the girl.

"She was *naked,*" Willow moaned. "I hate her."

The boys ran back, packs of Skittles in their hands.

"I can't open mine," Henry complained. He had dropped the paper towel near the vending machine. A line of blood crept down his arm.

"Let's go in the bathroom and get you a fresh paper towel," Darcy said.

"Willow, you wait with the boys for Susan."

Automatically she washed her hands, pulled out a fresh paper towel, wet it, and wrapped it around

Henry's hand. The boy had managed to wedge his pack of candy into his pocket, and his hand went from this pocket to his mouth and back to his pocket as if he were automated.

She held the boy's hand, pressing on his finger, as they returned to the waiting room. Her mind was in a traffic jam of thoughts. Poor Willow, to have to see her mother like that! Poor Susan, whose husband was unfaithful in addition to being a creep. And, oh, right, poor *Boyz,* whose wife was unfaithful to him, to Boyz, that model of fidelity! She couldn't help smiling.

Her smile fell away when Susan rushed in through the automatic doors. Darcy flashed a look of caution to Willow, who was clutching her hands together like a Victorian heroine caught in a snowstorm. Susan threw herself around Henry.

"Your hand, let me see your hand!"

Henry held out his hand, unable to keep from looking proud.

"Oh, darling, that doesn't look so terribly bad," Susan told him. "You'll have such an adventure, getting stitches."

George butted in, needing his share of fame. "I got Darcy's purse for her!"

"Yes," Darcy agreed. "George was a big help. All the boys were good."

"Susan, Mrs. Brueckner, I'm so sorry about this," Willow cried. "I was cutting some water-melon for the boys, and Henry said he wanted to cut his own piece, and I had put the knife down on the cutting board and he picked it up and it happened so fast!"

Susan smiled. "Alfred, sweetie, scoot over one chair so Mommy can sit next to Henry." When Alfred had reluctantly obeyed, Susan took Willow's hand. "Sweet Willow, don't worry. These things happen all the time with boys, with my boys especially."

"Yeah!" Alfred piped up, wanting to be part of the drama. "I fell off my bike last year. Look at my scar!"

"Henry Brueckner?" A nurse with a clipboard beckoned them. "We don't need all of you," she added, seeing the entire group jump up.

"You take your son in," Darcy said. "We'll stay out here with Alfred and George."

As soon as Susan and Henry went off, Willow sat down next to Darcy. The two boys were now engaged in a contest to see who could name the color of the next Skittle they would take from the bag.

"Susan is so *nice*," Willow said mournfully. "Her husband is a pig, and my mother is . . ." Tears welled in her eyes.

"Willow, don't say things like that near the—" She jerked her head toward the two boys, who weren't within hearing distance but might wander over at any moment. "Besides, you're old enough to know that people are unfaithful sometimes."

313

Darcy knew she sounded like a schoolmarm, but this was a course she'd never navigated before. "You really can't judge people by one act. You don't know what else is going on in their lives."

"Yeah, well, I know my stepfather would never be unfaithful to my mom!" Willow crossed her arms over her chest and stuck out her chin defensively.

"Honey," Darcy softly reminded the girl, "your stepfather was unfaithful to me. You know that."

Willow frowned, perplexed. "Yeah, I know, but that was different. That was my *mother*." She picked at her lip. "I mean, my mom is so beautiful." Embarrassed, she hurriedly added, "Not that you're not beautiful, too, but in a different way. Plus my mom said Boyz never really loved you. That you two knew it was a mistake right away." She wrinkled her nose, doing that sinking into herself thing. "I should stop talking, right?"

Darcy put her arm around Willow's shoulders. "No worries, Willow. Your mom was right. Sometimes people make mistakes, and Boyz and I both made a mistake when we got married. I was sort of enchanted by his family, and Boyz was looking for someone he didn't find in me."

Willow shrugged. "But if he's found it in my mom, then it will make him so sad . . . and the dining room *table*. That's so gross."

"You need to talk this over with your mother. You need to tell her what you saw, and how sad that makes you. Everything. All of it."

Willow nodded again. In a little voice, she agreed, "Okay. I guess I will."

George and Alfred had finished their Skittles and were blowing into the bags, making fart noises.

"What about Susan?" Willow asked.

Trying to lighten the mood, Darcy said in a comedian's voice, "What am I, the oracle at Delphi?"

Willow pulled away from Darcy. "Huh?"

"Sorry, Willow. I was kind of making a joke. The oracle at Delphi was a wise woman who answered questions about what to do . . . this was in Greece, a long time ago. We don't have anyone that wise in this day and age except maybe Oprah and I don't have her number. For now, I think we shouldn't tell Susan. We don't know how her marriage works. Maybe she doesn't mind if her husband is unfaithful. Or maybe she has so much pressure in her life with the three boys that one more problem would cause her to melt down. Let's think about it, okay? And not say anything yet."

"Okay," Willow agreed.

Susan and her son came out from the ER.

Henry held up his hand for his brothers to inspect. "I got *two* stitches!"

"Here, Susan," Darcy said, handing Susan the

car keys. "You drive home with your boys. I'm going to walk home."

"Are you sure?" Susan asked.

"Absolutely. It's only a few blocks and the night is so beautiful."

"Oh, well, then, thank you," Susan said. "Willow, thanks for babysitting, and please don't worry. Things like this happen all the time with the boys."

Willow shrugged, nodded, smiled, and looked worried all at the same time. "I'll walk home with Darcy," she said.

Susan gathered up her brood and herded them out the door and into her car.

"Come on, kid," Darcy said to Willow. "The walk will do you good. Clear your head."

"I wish it really could. I wish it could clear my mind of the image of my mother—*naked!*— with Otto. He still had his shirt on and his pants were down around his knees. I saw his butt. So weird."

"Yes, well, sex can look pretty bizarre." They crossed South Prospect Street and walked along Atlantic Avenue. The sidewalk was so narrow they had to walk single file. Darcy was glad. She didn't want to answer all of Willow's questions about what she'd seen.

When they reached Pleasant Street and could walk side by side, Darcy asked a question of her own. "Did you have sex with Logan?"

Willow shook her head violently. "Yeah. No. Maybe."

"Well, which is it?"

"We didn't *do it*. But we messed around a lot. I touched his—him. He—I can't talk about it. It was fun, it was exciting, he's so hot, and he wanted to be with *me* and I don't know whether I let him touch me because I enjoyed *it* or because I was so impressed, kind of *honored* that someone so old would pay attention to me."

Darcy put her arm over Willow's shoulders. "You're pretty smart for someone your own age, Willow."

"Well, I know *this* much. Sex makes a mess of everything."

Darcy walked quietly, wondering how to respond. Finally, she said, "Sometimes it does. But sometimes, if there's love, it makes everything all right, at least for a while."

17

Darcy and Willow arrived at Darcy's house to find Susan's car parked in front of her house and Susan sitting on Darcy's doorstep. The front door was open to the Brueckners' house and sounds of the boys shouting carried out to the street. Darkness had fallen, and the lights of the houses up and down the street glowed, softening the edges of the houses, blurring the trees, erasing the lines on Susan's face so that she looked young again.

Susan rose. "Willow, let me pay you tomorrow, okay? I'm in too much of a flap and the boys are wild, and their father just got home." Before Willow could respond, she reached out and folded Willow into a hug. "You did such a perfect job, taking care of my sons. I can't thank you enough."

"Mrs. Brueckner—" Willow cried.

"It's not your fault Henry cut himself. My sons are walking disasters. I'm only surprised a hurricane didn't hit the house at the same time."

If you only knew, Darcy thought.

Willow had frozen, as if she were playing the old game statues.

Darcy reached out to take Willow's slender wrist. "Come with me, Willow. I'll make hot chocolate."

Willow allowed herself to be pulled away from Susan. The three kissed each other's cheeks and said good night. Susan went into her noisy house and shut the door.

"It's too hot for hot chocolate," Willow said as she trudged next to Darcy to her house.

"You don't have to drink it," Darcy responded calmly. *She* needed hot chocolate, preferably with a shot of rum in it. Making it would give her something to do while she thought about this mess, and it would allow Willow a chance to settle down. Sometimes sitting at a table, turning a spoon over and over, staring down at a cup of warm sweetness was exactly the thing that helped one's poor confused brain to mend.

Willow sank into a chair at the kitchen table. Darcy gathered the box of Hershey's cocoa powder, the sugar, the milk and carefully mixed them in a pan. She didn't speak. She focused all her attention on the easy concoction, as if she were a scientist creating the world's newest, most potent antibiotic.

It was quiet in the kitchen. As if she and Willow were serene.

But, Lord, this was a mess, and Darcy had no idea how to advise Willow.

She poured the hot chocolate into mugs, sprinkled the tops with miniature marshmallows, and sat down with her own mug.

Willow stirred her drink. Without lifting her

head, she mumbled, "I can't tell Boyz. That would be too gross. Besides, it would hurt his feelings."

Darcy sat back in her chair, surprised that Willow was worried about Boyz's reaction. Immediately, a sense of relief moved through her. So Willow cared about Boyz, and felt cared for by him, connected to him.

"Maybe," Darcy suggested, "you could talk to your mother about tonight. Let her be the one to tell Boyz. Or not."

Willow lifted her head. "Really?"

Darcy was quiet. This was such an odd situation. She wasn't sure she should even be counseling Willow, and she remembered Boyz's visit, his admonition to stay away from Willow, his belief that Darcy was befriending the girl for her own twisted reasons—to get his attention, to seduce Boyz. Plus, there had been that weird and unpleasant visit when he came to her house and suggested they *enjoy each other* and then forced a kiss on her. He was smug and offensive, but Darcy didn't care about him. She cared about what would be best for Willow.

"Well," Darcy said after a long silence, "whatever the reason for what you saw tonight, you need to talk to your mother."

Willow met Darcy's eyes. "Will you come with me?"

Darcy flinched. "Oh, honey, no."

"Please?" Willow put her hands together, as if she were praying or begging. "I can't do this by myself."

"Willow, I'm sure your mother would be angry if I were there. This is a private matter, a family matter." Darcy pushed back her chair and stood up. She walked to the sink and set her empty mug down. "I'll go with you to your door," she offered.

"No! *Please* come in with me!" Willow dissolved into tears, her shoulders shaking, her face turning scarlet. She pushed back her own chair and rose, her chest heaving as if she couldn't get her breath. She gasped out the words: "I need you to be there to help me!"

"Willow—" Darcy's sense of compassion streamed toward the girl.

"I can't do it. I *won't* do it! I'll run away, I won't go home, I'll disappear and you'll never see me again, and my mom will never see me again, and then *you'll* have to tell her about tonight! Don't think I won't run away, because I will, I'll go find Logan, I'll have sex with him, I'll do the heroin, because why not?—all the adults in my life don't give a shit about me!"

"Oh, Willow." Darcy moved toward the sobbing girl, meaning to wrap her in her arms, but Willow shoved her away.

"No!" Willow's face contorted with anger. "Don't think you can hug me like a kid and give me a Popsicle and send me away! I'm *not* a kid!"

"No, you're not a kid," Darcy softly agreed. Willow was not an adult, either, but tonight she'd been presented with some confusing adult behavior.

She stepped away from Willow and leaned against the kitchen counter, waiting for the girl to calm down. *This was horrible,* Darcy thought. Should she tell Willow that Boyz had warned her off hanging around with his stepdaughter? No. That would only confuse Willow more. And anyway, why should Darcy even give the smallest damn what Boyz thought or wanted? He was no longer her husband. He was a philanderer himself, and an idiot besides. If she tried to put herself in Willow's position—and she thought she almost could, because she'd read so many of the YA books in order to talk to the middle and high schools about them—if she tried, she could guess how Willow felt. Sex was such a bizarre topic to talk about, after all, no matter your age. Beautiful words and angelic songs translated what, from the outside, appeared to be an awkward and even violent act, into the powerful, blissful, transforming experience it could be. Pascal said, "The heart has its reasons, which reason does not know." Or something like that. The body definitely had its own unreasonable reasons, too.

Could she explain this to Willow? But no.

Willow didn't need Darcy to quote a seventeenth-century French philosopher to her.

She watched Willow, who was standing her ground, fists clenched at her side, her face as ugly as fury could make it while tears flew down her cheeks.

"All right," Darcy conceded. "I'll go with you, Willow."

"You will?"

"I will. But first you need to wash your face with cold water. It will make you feel better. Help to calm you down."

"I wasn't having a tantrum," Willow said defensively.

"Oh, I kind of think you were," Darcy told her. "And when you're through with it, we'll go over to talk to Autumn."

"What if Mr. Brueckner is still there?" Willow asked with horror.

"Susan told us he was home, remember? Come on, now, let's get it over with."

She ran a clean dish towel in cold water and handed it to Willow. The girl obediently patted it over her face, and as she did, her breathing slowed. She touched her neck with the cool cloth and stood there for a moment, eyes closed, calming down.

"Okay," Willow said. "I'm ready. Let's go."

They walked through the house, out the front door, and around to the narrow path between

Darcy's hedge and the Brueckners' until they came to the small grassy spot at the end of the Brueckners' house that bordered on the Szwedas' garage. They turned left, behind Darcy's back hedge—which towered like a tall thick green wall. Little wonder people had no idea Darcy was over on the other side.

Lights shone from several windows of the house. Willow's pace slowed. She reached for Darcy's hand. Darcy continued walking, almost pulling Willow, across the lawn, up the steps, and into the kitchen.

As they entered the house, Willow made a whimpering noise, like a lost kitten.

"Shake it off," Darcy said. "Where's your mom now?" She certainly wasn't going to have this little chat in Autumn's bedroom. Nor in the dining room!

"Mom?" Willow's voice shivered.

"In here."

Darcy and Willow engaged in an almost comic struggle to make the other one be first to walk into the room. In the end, Darcy entered first, pulling Willow along by the wrist.

The luscious Autumn was curled at one end of a beige sofa, watching a baking show on the large screen TV. She wore a brief and clingy fragment of peach-colored silk and lace, and her abundant hair flowed over her shoulders and down her back.

Darcy remembered how she had worn an old,

overwashed, faded, and shapeless Red Sox T-shirt to bed with Boyz. Autumn wore her peach concoction when no one was around.

Darcy made a mental note to invest in some lingerie from Victoria's Secret.

"God," Autumn said, seeing Darcy and Willow. "*Now* what have you done to upset your precious librarian?"

Darcy could see lace at the top of Autumn's thigh. She noticed Autumn's finger- and toenails were shellacked a pale peach. She made a mental note to have her own fingernails shellacked sometime. That was supposed to last longer than polish, and didn't ever chip . . . What was she thinking? How could she be thinking about shellac at a time like this?

Willow froze in the center of the room.

"Let's sit down, Willow," Darcy said quietly.

She tried to tug the girl toward the other end of the sofa, but Willow shuddered and cried, "Ugh! Not so close to *her!*"

Autumn's eyes narrowed. Darcy half shoved Willow into a club chair across from Autumn. She sat in the other one. The glass coffee table was between them and Autumn.

Autumn sat up, tugging at the skirt of her lacy lingerie so it covered the few inches at the top of her thighs. Her expression had grown wary.

Darcy prompted Willow, "Willow. You need to tell her."

Willow, staring steadily at her feet in her sandals, mumbled, "I saw you and Mr. Brueckner."

"What?" Autumn reared backward. "What did you say?"

Willow raised her head and glared at her mother. "I saw you and Mr. Brueckner."

Autumn stonewalled. "I have no idea what you're talking about."

"On the dining room table," Willow said, and this time she spoke almost too loudly, and her words were clearly an accusation.

Autumn flinched, but immediately recovered, firing back a defensive shot. "Willow, I think you should tell *your friend* to leave. This is personal business, between you and me. I can't imagine why you brought her here."

"Because I need her!" Willow burst out, her voice strong and angry. "Because when I was babysitting, I needed to get Band-Aids because Henry cut himself, and I phoned her to come watch the kids so I could come home to get some!"

"Why didn't you call me?" Autumn asked, and she seemed to be genuinely curious.

"Because you said you wouldn't be home!" Willow shouted. "Because you said you were going to walk on the beach and fucking *think!*"

"Watch your language, young lady," Autumn said.

"My language? I'm supposed to watch my language while I tell you about seeing you *naked* with Mr. Brueckner on the dining room *table?*" The words spilled from Willow's mouth. "Darcy was home, and *she* came to help me right away and we had to call Susan, and we had to take Henry to the *hospital* and he had to have stitches and Susan was so nice to me even though I was babysitting when Henry cut himself, and all I could think about was seeing you with Mr. Brueckner!"

"Oh, honey." At last Autumn softened as she absorbed Willow's words.

"And I had to make Darcy come with me because I was afraid of telling you because it is so *gross.*"

"I'm sure Darcy was delighted to hear about what a tramp I am," Autumn replied, a sullen note to her voice.

"Believe me," Darcy said keeping her tone neutral, "this brings me no pleasure. Not any of it. And it's none of my business. I know that. I know it's personal between you and Willow. I came here to support her, but I'm going to leave now." Darcy rose.

"No!" Willow cried.

"Stay if you want," Autumn said. She made a mocking sound. "It might be helpful to *me* if you stayed. Willow needs to learn that she's still a girl, not a woman. She's not old enough to judge what *women* do."

Darcy almost said, *Not all women do what you do,* but she bit her tongue. She sank back into the chair and waited.

Autumn took a moment to gather her thoughts. When she spoke, it was gentle, directed right to Willow.

"You know that photo I snapped of you eating a chocolate ice cream bar and reading a book? You were completely absorbed by that book. You didn't see me come into the room. You didn't even know you had dripped chocolate on your favorite shirt. You were really going after that chocolate ice cream like a starving child. You hadn't combed your hair for hours and you had chocolate smeared on the end of your nose."

"Oh, please," Willow said in her most sarcastic voice, "don't tell me you're going to compare reading with sex."

"That's exactly what I'm doing. Reading while eating chocolate ice cream, to be exact. You were caught up in a world of your own. You were indulging your mind *and* your senses. You sprawled in that chair with your legs hanging over the side and your head practically on the bottom cushion. I snapped a photo of you with my phone and you didn't say a thing. You were in a *zone.*"

"But that's different!" Willow protested.

"Maybe. I could pull up that photo I took of

you, the one that you wanted me to delete when you saw it the next day. You couldn't believe what a slob you were. Ice cream on your face, on your clothes? Sex is like that, only more intense. It's body *and* mind. It takes you into a world of your own."

Darcy turned her face away from Willow, unable to hide her smile. Autumn was amazing, really, coming up with this comparison.

"Okay, then," Willow persisted, "but don't you have that with Boyz? He is your husband! You're supposed to be faithful to him!"

"Boyz is my husband," Autumn agreed quietly. "And you have no idea about the kind of pacts and compromises we have created to make our marriage work."

"Ugh!" Willow moaned. "You mean like an 'open marriage'? That's so gross!"

"I'm not going into any details, Willow. Let me just say that Boyz and I are both attractive people who enjoy being attractive. The most important thing is that whatever we do as individuals, as a couple we are absolutely devoted to you. We will never stop loving you, we will never stop putting you first in our thoughts and in our hearts."

"Yeah, right," Willow muttered, but she flushed and her eyes filled with tears.

"Come over here, Willow," Autumn said, patting the cushion next to her.

Willow stuck her bottom lip out stubbornly.

"Come on, honey. Come on." Autumn's voice was so low and sweet, Darcy thought *she'd* sit next to Autumn if invited.

Willow gave Darcy a quick sideways glance.

Darcy read the message. It had been a long night for Willow, with lots of drama and the scare of Henry's cut and Willow's sense of failing to keep the boys safe, not to mention seeing her mother with another man. Willow needed her mother now. Whatever Autumn had looked like a few hours ago, right now, Autumn was Willow's mother, completely focused on her. And Willow needed Autumn.

"I've got to get home," Darcy said. "I'll let myself out."

Before anyone could say anything, Darcy rose and left the room, heading for the kitchen and the back steps. She caught a flicker of movement in her eye—Willow moving over to be embraced by her mother.

By the time she reached her own back door, tears were pouring down her face. She collapsed at the kitchen table, burying her face in her hands. She had no single memory of her own mother hugging her when Darcy was a teenager. Darcy had been living with Penny then, and Penny had been a fascinating and loving person, but not much of a toucher. Boyz seemed like an overtoucher, if that was such a thing, and maybe Autumn was, too, but her connection with Willow was clear and powerful.

Darcy wished she had someone to put his arms around her now.

18

Going with Mom to Boston for shopping. Sorry can't do story time. xo W

Darcy sat at her kitchen table Friday morning, reading Willow's brief text.

It surprised her, how her mood plummeted, like an elevator with its cables cut.

"Muffler," she said to the cat who sat in the middle of the table staring at her, "we've been dumped."

Muffler lifted one paw and industriously licked it, paying no attention to Darcy.

"Et tu Brute?" Now her coffee didn't even taste good, and her first cup of coffee in the morning was one of her favorite pleasures in life. "Everyone is ignoring me," she said pathetically. "But I do know," she added, saying it aloud, as if someone were listening, "that Willow is not my daughter. She'll return to Boston, and I'll never see her again. I've allowed myself to get too involved with a summer person."

As a practical matter, she needed to find someone else to help with story time.

They had plenty of volunteers, but she needed to check her list and call someone.

"Enough whining," she told herself, and rose from the table to begin the day.

She chose one of her favorite sundresses to wear to work, mostly white, with scarlet poppies on green stems growing up from the hem. She slipped on a red silk headband, kissed herself in the mirror, and set off for the library.

The day was full of minor crises—all the copies of *Shrek* had been checked out, and *Nanny McPhee* had been misshelved, so it showed up as in on the computer, but displeased mothers and frantic circ staffers had to search through the shelves to find it. A little girl locked herself in one of the restrooms and wouldn't come out because she didn't want to be with her stepmother, and Beverly Maison spilled a cup of iced coffee down her new shirt.

At the end of the day, Darcy was delighted to leave the library. A lecture on coastal erosion was taking place in the Great Hall that evening; Darcy had planned on attending but decided she wasn't in the mood. As she walked home, her mind flooded with concerns she'd shoved into a mental compartment for the day.

Nash. They didn't always get together on Friday nights. He was usually beat and they both worked on Saturdays. And when they did get together, would they talk more about the house he wanted to buy?

Susan Brueckner. Should Darcy tell Susan about what Willow saw? Did she need Willow, the eyewitness, with her when she spoke with Susan? But, no, Willow had been nearly traumatized, seeing her mother naked on the dining room table with Susan's husband. The girl didn't need any more shocks from the grown-up world.

Maybe Darcy should simply let it go. After all, she hardly knew Susan and Otto. They would be leaving after Labor Day. Darcy might never see them again. Maybe Susan already knew about Otto's escapades, and Darcy would only bring unwanted attention to a situation the Brueckners had already worked out for themselves.

Mimi. Darcy should talk to Mimi about this. Mimi was wise. She'd seen everything twice, it seemed, and Mimi viewed life with more than a pinch of good humor and goodwill.

Impulsively, when Darcy came to Mimi's house, she stopped and knocked on the door. She'd invite Mimi over for a drink in the garden, or maybe Mimi would invite her in for a drink in her own back garden. Mimi would break Darcy's spell of gloominess. She'd make Darcy laugh, and without Willow there, Mimi and Darcy could talk without inhibitions.

The moment Darcy knocked, she wished she'd texted or phoned instead. If Clive wasn't home, Mimi would have to struggle down the hall to open the door. But she couldn't unknock the door, and while she stood dithering about, the door opened.

Clive was there, and he looked worried. His brown hair was rumpled and he had dark circles under his eyes. Several small stains marked his shirt, a handsome but wrinkled blue button-down hanging out over his jeans.

"Oh, I'm sorry, Clive, it looks like I've come at a bad time."

"Mimi's ill." He kept his hand on the door, as if it were holding him up.

He spoke so quietly, Darcy wasn't sure she understood. "Excuse me?"

He cleared his throat. "Mimi's not well."

Darcy heard him this time. The words struck like a blow to her abdomen. Mimi was worse than "not well" if Clive looked like this.

"Oh. I—I'm sorry to hear that, Clive. Is there anything I can do?"

"I don't know." He ran his hand through his hair, making it stick up all over. "She—I—Why don't you come in a moment."

"I don't want to intrude."

"Please. Intrude." He held the door wide.

Darcy entered, setting her book bag on the floor and following Clive into the living room. He collapsed on a sofa. She took a chair across from him. A pile of books had toppled off a side table, some lying splayed open, their pages bent, and Darcy had to hold back the urge to pick them up, smooth the pages, close them, and place them with care on the table.

Several glasses and mugs were scattered on the coffee table, the rug, and the hearth. Some had coffee. Some sent the sharp scent of alcohol into the air.

"How long has Mimi been sick?" Darcy asked. "Has she seen a doctor?"

"I shouldn't alarm you, Darcy. I'm sorry if I did. It's a cold, only a summer cold, but it's knocked the stuffing out of her. No, she hasn't seen a doctor here, but I've phoned her doctor at home to get advice. She's on several medications, you know, and I didn't want to give her decongestants or antihistamines in case they would react badly with her medications." He leaned back against the sofa and took a moment to close his eyes before continuing. "She's been in bed for several days. She's got a bad cough, and her chest is congested, and her breathing is labored."

Darcy was worried. "Clive, that sounds serious. Shouldn't she see a doctor here?"

Clive smiled ruefully. "Mimi says not. Says I'm making a mountain out of a molehill."

"Is she getting any sleep? Are *you?*"

"I've been making her drink beef broth from a cup."

"That's good," Darcy told him. "That seems like the right thing to do."

"And she has Scotch every afternoon," Clive added, smiling. "She says it's medicinal."

Darcy was relieved to see him smile. "It probably is."

Her sympathy went out to the man, so sophisticated, so talented, and so devoted to his grandmother. She really did know how he felt.

"Are you eating?"

Clive scanned the room, as if searching for evidence. He shrugged. "Probably."

"Clive, may I see her?"

He frowned. "She's in bed, and her hair looks messy, and the room smells like cough syrup. . . ."

"Clive, I lived with my grandmother most of my life. I was with her when she was elderly. I think I've pretty much seen it all when it comes to an older person's sickroom. You are such a dedicated person, but I would like to help. I think at a time like this, it would be right for someone to help."

"She'll be furious if I let you into her bedroom."

Darcy smiled. "I hope she is furious. That will be a sign she's still got plenty of energy."

"All right, then. . . ."

Like many old Nantucket houses, this house had two parlors, and when they moved in for the summer, Clive had turned one of them into a bedroom for Mimi so she wouldn't have the trouble of climbing the stairs. It was a pretty room, with a marble fireplace and a chandelier and good oil seascapes on the walls. Clive had closed the curtains to help Mimi rest, but the first thing Darcy noticed when she entered was how the room smelled.

Mimi lay on the twin bed Clive had brought down for her. She was propped on several pillows. Next to her was a table littered with books, tissues, a carafe of water, and a glass. Her eyes were closed, and as Darcy entered, a wracking cough shook the older woman's body.

Darcy turned to Clive. "Do you have a thermometer?"

He shook his head. "I don't know. I'll check the bathrooms." He left the room.

Darcy moved close to Mimi's bed. She took Mimi's hand. "Hi, Mimi," she said softly. "It's Darcy."

To Darcy's infinite relief, Mimi opened her eyes and croaked, "What? You think I don't recognize your voice?"

"Clive tells me you've got a summer cold."

"Yes, my darling, and you should go away right now. It might be contagious."

"After spending all day with children, I think I'm immune," Darcy told her. As she spoke, she evaluated Mimi and her sickbed. "When did you last use the bathroom?"

Mimi managed a feeble snort. "Darcy, you're not a nurse or a relative. I don't think that matter is your concern."

"Well, I do," Darcy insisted. "And if all you

have is a summer cold, you ought to get up and move a bit. That will break up the stuff in your lungs. I'm going to help you into the bathroom—"

"Don't embarrass me, Darcy," Mimi pleaded in a whisper. "I use Depends."

"Yes, well, you need a fresh one," Darcy told her in a matter-of-fact tone. "I doubt if you want your grandson changing your underwear. Come on, let's toddle off to the bathroom."

"You librarians think you know everything," Mimi moaned. But she allowed Darcy to help her sit up.

Darcy moved Mimi's legs so they hung over the side of the bed. She let Mimi have time to adjust to this new position, but even so, the move sent her into a fresh coughing fit.

Clive entered the room. "No thermometer."

"Never mind. Help me get Mimi to the toilet."

"Oh, misery and humiliation," Mimi moaned as Clive and Darcy each took a side and half walked, half carried Mimi down the hall. "Don't come in with me!" Mimi commanded once they were in the small downstairs half bath. "I can do the rest all by myself!"

"Fine," Darcy said. "I'm going to fetch you a fresh nightgown. I'll knock on the door and hand it in to you in a few moments." She turned to Clive. "Come help me."

In Mimi's room, she threw back the curtains

and opened the windows, allowing fresh air to sweep in.

"Clive, could you find some clean sheets for the bed?" she asked. She gathered Mimi's soiled linens from the mattress and shook out the light cotton quilt, hanging it over a chair to air out. She searched the dresser that Clive had brought down for Mimi, and when she'd found a nightgown—a violet silk sleeveless one that must have cost a bomb—she took it down the hall to the bathroom.

She knocked. "How are you doing, Mimi?"

Mimi's response was garbled. Fear stabbed Darcy. Then Mimi said more clearly, "I'm brushing my teeth. I never thought brushing my teeth would be such a pleasure. Just toss the gown in, dear."

Oh, Mimi sounded stronger, almost like herself! Darcy obeyed and returned to the bedroom to put clean sheets on the bed. Already the air smelled fresher, and she could hear the birds sing.

This time when Darcy and Clive assisted Mimi back to her room and her bed, Darcy noticed that Mimi felt lighter. She'd clearly lost weight.

"Mimi, I'm going to make you a little something to eat. You need food to keep your strength up."

"Thank you, dear, but I'm not really hungry."

"You still need to eat."

Before Mimi could object, Darcy left the room. In the kitchen, she quickly evaluated the situation—two eggs, a hunk of cheddar cheese, no milk.

She stuck her head into Mimi's room. Clive had turned on the television and they were both watching the screen.

"I'm going next door. I'll be right back."

She carried her book bag back to her house, went to her own kitchen, dumped her book bag on the table, and foraged in her cupboards and fridge for supplies. Eggs, oatmeal bread, milk, butter. She put the food in another book bag—she had plenty of book bags hanging on the hall hooks—and returned to Mimi's. She took a moment to stick her head in and wave at Mimi and Clive before heading to the kitchen.

As she moved around the room, putting bread in the toaster, cracking and whipping the eggs, melting butter in the skillet, a memory flashed in her mind of a day when she was a child in the house next door to this one, and she was recovering from a flu, and as she lay weak and exhausted in bed, her grandmother carried in her bed tray, arranged it over Darcy, and said, "Eat that. You'll feel better."

It had been *milk toast,* a concoction made of warm buttered toast torn into pieces floating in a bowl of lightly salted, perfectly warm milk. Darcy could still remember the comforting taste.

Did anyone eat milk toast these days? Darcy spooned the perfectly cooked, lightly salted and peppered scrambled eggs onto a plate, added toast buttered and spread with the strawberry jam she found in Mimi's fridge, along with a glass of water for Mimi, and carried it all into the sickroom.

Clive had cunningly constructed a bed tray from a jigsaw puzzle box resting on piles of books he'd placed on either side of Mimi's legs.

"Oh, how clever of you." Darcy laughed, putting Mimi's dish and fork on the flat puzzle box. "Does anyone use bed trays anymore?"

"Yes," Clive told her, "only now they're called folding lap desks for your computer." He moved to sit on the bed next to Mimi. "Can I help you, Mimi?"

Darcy pulled another chair near Mimi's bed. She smiled encouragingly at Mimi, who picked up a fork and attempted to lift the food to her mouth. Her hand was trembling, as if the weight of the fork was more than she could bear, and the sunny clump of eggs fell down the bodice of her violet silk gown.

"Rats," Mimi cursed. The effort seemed to have drained her of energy. She leaned back into her pillows and shut her eyes.

Darcy gently removed the clump of eggs.

"Hey, Mimi, let's try this." Clive brought a forkful of eggs to her mouth. "Come on, open up. Remember when you did this to me when I was a child? After I'd had one of my tantrums and sat at the table with my arms folded, vowing never to eat again, you were always the one who could coax me to eat."

Mimi's eyes opened. She looked at Clive with such adoration it brought tears to Darcy's eyes.

"I remember." Her voice was thin, but she opened her mouth and allowed Clive to gently feed her the eggs.

Darcy thought it might be difficult for Mimi to eat with Darcy sitting there gawking. She rose. "I'll just go tidy the kitchen."

The kitchen was clearly the room of someone who was preoccupied. It was littered with coffee cups, plates of uneaten sandwiches, glasses still half-full of Scotch, and an opened but untouched box of chocolates from Sweet Inspirations. It felt good to move around restoring order, and as Darcy stacked the dishwasher and put away dishes, an enormous affection for Clive filled her. She saw so many small signs of his care for his grandmother.

Clive came into the kitchen as Darcy was scrubbing the skillet.

"She ate a few bites," he said, showing Darcy her plate. "She's asleep now."

"Have you eaten?" Darcy asked.

A puzzled expression crossed his face. "Oh, I guess I haven't."

"Would you like me to make you some eggs? A nice hot scramble, with cheese in them?"

Clive looked dazed, as if she were speaking a foreign language. "Oh, thanks, but you've already washed the skillet."

"Yes, and, guess what, I can always wash it again." She dried the skillet and set it back on the stove. "Sit down, Clive. Rest a moment. I think Mimi will be okay."

Clive nodded and sat down. He rested his elbows on the table and sank his head in his hands.

Darcy melted more butter in the skillet and broke more eggs into a bowl. She felt oddly maternal and nurturing and very fond of this man who was so loving to his grandmother.

"You're wonderful with Mimi," she said over her shoulder.

Clive shrugged. "Thank you. I'm glad to do it, although I'm missing some good summer time with my daughters."

Darcy grated cheese into the eggs as she listened. "Oh? I thought you wanted to be here to write a book about jazz."

"That's what I told Mimi. And I am. The truth is this visit to the island matters a lot to her. I didn't want her to think I had anything on my schedule for the summer that I would have to give up to bring her here."

"Does she get to see her great-granddaughters?" Darcy said as she whisked the eggs.

"When we're back in Boston, she does. My

ex-wife has remarried, and she's got a baby, and the girls are enchanted with him. They love me, they love Mimi, but this year they haven't wanted to spend as much time with either of us." Clive leaned back in his chair, rubbed his neck with one hand, and sighed. "When Mimi sees you, Darcy, she rallies. She summons up all her charm and wit. With you, she seems like a younger woman, a stronger woman, a—a less-frail woman. Until this year, she was a firecracker of a grandmother. She took Alyssa and Zoe everywhere—she went on a roller coaster with them when they were five. I was afraid she'd die of a heart attack, but she had a grand time."

Darcy lowered the burner, slowly pouring the egg mixture into the skillet. "I can imagine Mimi on a roller coaster."

"But in the last year . . . Mimi had a stroke. We were lucky. It wasn't a bad one. But it slowed her down. Since then, she's been gradually becoming . . . slower. She's still *there* mentally, still has her sense of humor, but we can't leave the girls alone with her. It would be too awful if Mimi fell or had another stroke when they were there. Mimi knows this—she suggested it, that the girls not be left alone with her. And when I take them to visit her, sometimes she's in good shape, but often she's so tired. Alyssa and Zoe are too young to understand. I mean, they're sweet with her, they kiss her and talk to her, but they get restless.

She's not the great-grandmother they knew. And then Helen—my ex—has her own parents living nearby, and Ed and Janice are really fun grandparents."

"Where are your parents?" Darcy asked, taking toast from the toaster and buttering it lavishly.

"My mother died a few years ago. My father has remarried and moved to France. He's not really interested in the girls."

Darcy put the plate of hot cheesy eggs and toast in front of Clive. "Eat up," she told him. "You need your strength."

"God, this smells good." Clive picked up his fork and dug in like a starving man.

Darcy made herself a cup of coffee and set the skillet to soak. "I understand how you feel, Clive. I'm living in *my* grandmother's house. Penny. Penelope to many people, including my mother. I lived with my grandmother here on the island from the time I was ten."

"Are your parents—"

"No, not dead. Just not interested. My father's with his new wife in Florida and my mother is anywhere she can have a good time. If I hadn't had my grandmother to give me a stable life, I don't know what I'd have done."

"Tell me more," Clive asked as he spread jam on his toast.

Darcy sat down at the table and talked. About her beautiful butterfly mother, about her cold, emotionless father. About her gaggle of well-intentioned but irresponsible relatives in Chicago, about her years on the island with Penny. It was comforting, talking like this in a warm kitchen. It was ordinary, domestic, peaceful.

When Clive finished eating, he heaved a deep sigh. "That was manna from heaven, Darcy, thank you."

"You're welcome. Consider me your surrogate grandmother of the day." She meant only to imply that Mimi would be up and around as soon as tomorrow, that she was doing what their grandmothers did, listening, caring, helping.

"I don't think of you as a grandmother in any way," Clive said. And he fixed her with a steady stare that took Darcy's breath away.

"Well." She couldn't think of any other single intelligent word.

His look was full of need and desire, heat and lust. Embarrassed and completely unsure of herself, Darcy pushed back her chair and rose.

"I'll put your dish in the dishwasher—" she said.

She reached for the plate. Clive caught her wrist with his hand. He stood up, and keeping her caught by one hand, he pulled her to him with the other. He cupped her head in his hand and kissed her, a long, hard, ferocious kiss that swept over Darcy like a tidal wave. *This was wrong,* Darcy thought—*wasn't it?* She'd made no commitment to Nash. If he could plan to buy a house without mentioning it to her, she could certainly kiss another man.

Except she realized this was not going to be a simple kiss. Clive wanted her *now*. She understood that urgency, it wasn't wrong, it was natural, it was right, it was celebrating life in the midst of old age and illness and so many kinds of defeat. It was like finding a bubble of lifesaving air when you're helplessly sinking into the dark, fathomless ocean of death. It was the triumph of lust over loss. For a few moments, Darcy could help Clive forget the shadow of death hanging over his grandmother. For a few moments, they could both take their pleasure in being young and alive.

And yet . . .

Darcy pulled away from his kiss. "Clive, I'm sorry. I can't."

He frowned. "Because of that carpenter guy?"

She started to protest that Nash wasn't a simple *carpenter guy,* he was a lawyer, or had been. At the same time, she realized that it was *Nash* she loved, whatever his profession. It was Nash's gentleness and his humor, his lack of snobbery, his love of reading, the dark memories that made him who he was, and his unspoken determination to turn toward the light.

"Yes, actually, it's because of that carpenter guy."

Moving briskly, she headed down the hall to the front door. Clive followed.

"If there's any change in Mimi, call me, okay?" She picked up her book bag and opened the door.

"I want to walk you home," Clive said, catching her by the wrist.

She laughed again, trying to lighten the situation. "Clive, I live next door."

His grip tightened on her wrist. "I'm well aware of that. Still, it's what I want to do. Indulge me." He reached for her book bag and shouldered it.

"Fine." She allowed her hand to lie clasped in his and stepped out onto the small porch that led six steps down to the brick sidewalk.

"Ahh." Clive sighed, breathing in the fresh air. "I'm glad you stopped by today, Darcy. I mean, for Mimi. And the open windows, the fresh air, the clean sheets and nightgown. I didn't have a clue about all that."

They stopped at Darcy's doorstep, still holding hands. "She should see a doctor. Or, maybe, you could hire a private nurse. A professional caregiver."

"I'll talk to Mimi about it." In one silky move, Clive gave Darcy her book bag and brought his hands up to frame Darcy's face. He tilted her head toward his. "Darcy, thank you. For everything. And don't think that I'm confusing gratitude with honest personal desire. I'd like a chance to prove my point."

"You're welcome, Clive," Darcy replied, ignoring his words about desire. She remembered how she'd felt when Penny was ill, how confused, how much she'd needed someone to help her realize she had her own future ahead of her. She tried to turn from him.

Clive pulled her against him and kissed her again, hotly, possessively. Her hands were caught against his chest and she tried to push him away but his kiss continued. He was not a man who liked to take no for an answer. Finally she wrenched herself from his embrace.

"Clive, you shouldn't leave Mimi alone."

"You're right. I'm going." He gave her a deep look. "But I'll be back."

A vehicle shrieked, laying rubber right in front of her house. She turned.

She saw Nash's red pickup truck tearing away from her house as if Nash had slammed the gas pedal to the floor.

"Nash!" she called.

She didn't know how long he'd been parked there. Not long, she was sure, she hadn't seen his truck when they walked over from Clive's.

But long enough to see their kiss.

"Clive, I've got to go in now." She unlocked her front door and hurried inside, reaching for her cellphone as she went.

19

Darcy punched Nash's button on her direct dial. It went to voicemail.

"Nash, I need to talk to you. Please come back. I'll be here all evening. Nash, I—*please* call me."

Muffler strolled into the room, waving his beautiful tail.

Darcy paced the floor. "Damn! This is crazy!" Snatching up her phone, she hit Jordan's number. The moment Jordan answered, Darcy cried, "Jordan! Nash saw Clive kissing me at my front door!"

"Clive kissed you?" Jordan repeated.

"It was only a kind of thank-you kiss because I'd just helped Mimi, who has a cold, and then he walked me home—"

"You live next door and he walked you home?" Before Darcy could respond, Jordan said, "Hold her. Play with her. Watch TV with her. I've got to talk to Darcy." Shuffling noises and a few baby squawks reached Darcy's ears, then Jordan added, "Sorry, Darcy. Had to give Kiks to her daddy."

Darcy heard Jordan's breath change and she knew Jordan was climbing the stairs to the privacy of her bedroom. This was calming, unambiguous. Jordan was there for her. Darcy sank into a corner of her sofa.

A door slammed. "Now. Start over," Jordan demanded.

"I stopped by to see Mimi, because I wanted her advice about . . ." Good grief, was it only this afternoon she'd been worrying about Willow knowing about her mother and Otto? What was happening to this neighborhood? Had she been beamed up to an alien triangle of triangles? "Wait. Let me start over." Darcy tried to regain her composure. "I stopped by to see Mimi. She's quite ill with a summer cold. Clive was doing his best, but I helped her clean up a little, I changed the sheets, and I made her scrambled eggs—"

"Enough about Mimi! What do you mean about kissing Clive?"

"I'm trying to tell you. Mimi fell asleep and I was in the kitchen washing up and Clive came in, and I made him eggs and we talked about Mimi, and I told him about Penny, and we're both so worried about Mimi, but of course Clive is more worried, he's so close to her, like I was with Penny. It was a nice moment, friendly, warm. I'm not surprised he tried to kiss me. He's in an emotional tsunami with his grandmother's health. She could die, and naturally that's frightening to him. So he kissed me. But I pulled away. Okay, I didn't pull away for a moment, but then I did. I told him no, I told him I was with Nash, and I started to leave the house. He said he wanted to walk me home—he wanted to be a gentleman."

"Okay," Jordan said slowly. "So when did Nash see you?"

"At my front door. Clive was thanking me, and then he kissed me goodbye. It was a long kiss, it was complicated . . . Clive wanted more, and I was pushing him away but I guess it could have looked sexual. Anyway, right then, Nash drove up in front of my house, saw Clive kissing me, and roared off like an angry gorilla!"

"Wow. This is a lot to process, Darcy. Let me think." Jordan was silent for a few moments. "Okay, now back up. The kiss with Clive—was it nice?"

Darcy closed her eyes. "No, not nice. Passionate, but in a bad way. Clive is handsome and sexy, but this almost wasn't about sex."

"Right," Jordan snorted.

"No, really. I think it was about power. He was surprised, I think, and confused, that I wasn't all over him. I mean, he is handsome. He is sexy. But honestly, in my heart of hearts, Clive might as well have been a piece of macaroni. It *kills* me that Nash saw us kissing on my doorstep."

"Sounds like it didn't make Nash very happy, either."

"I know. And he won't answer his phone!"

"Are you in love with Nash?"

Darcy sighed. "I am. I haven't told him that yet. He's still so reserved. And now this."

"Okay, look, it's only natural for him to take

off when he sees you kissing another man. What would you expect him to do, get out of the truck and shake Clive's hand?"

"I know. I know. . . ."

"Let's go back to Clive again," Jordan suggested. "Obviously you felt something for him. You've talked about him, how he's an interesting, cultured, sophisticated guy."

"That's true. And he's charismatic. But I can't forget the Mimi element in all this."

"The Mimi element?"

"Jordan, have you ever been around an older person you care for who's really sick? I mean, Mimi is really sick. She's so weak we had to help her to the bathroom. *She couldn't feed herself.*"

"Feel free to kill me if I ever get to that point," Jordan joked.

"Not funny! Oh, Jordan, I'm terribly worried about Mimi, my stomach's all in a knot, and I don't know what to do! I want to *do* something. It's a terrible feeling to see someone you care for becoming helpless and weak, and to stand there knowing you can't change it, you have no power, I don't know, it fills you with such a furious kind of energy, you have to *do* something!"

"I get that, Darcy. But, honey, Mimi isn't your relative. You haven't even known her that long. Just a few summer weeks. I don't know, it seems your emotions are set on red alert when they shouldn't be."

Darcy sank onto the sofa. "Okay. That makes sense. I'm going to have to mull that over, but I think you're right. It's been such an odd summer. Thanks for all the listening, Jordan. I've got to go. I've got to . . . I'll call you tomorrow."

When she'd clicked off from Jordan, Darcy sat silently, trying to let her thoughts settle, but the sense of urgency remained. She needed to talk to Nash. She tried his number again. Again she was sent to voicemail.

"Nash, I really want to talk to you. I need to talk to you. Call me? Please?"

It was almost eight o'clock. She probably should eat something, but she had no appetite. Muffler did, however, and after he'd mewed piteously, she filled his food bowl and gave him fresh water. And then she stood in the kitchen, just staring.

She had reached that place in her spirits where her emotions were all jumbled up. She had what she thought of as a *dark heart*. She wanted to sit down and cry, but, no—What she wanted was to *change things*. *Now*. She wanted Nash to hear what she had to say!

She threw herself into her car and tore off, with much less noise and drama than Nash had in his truck. She headed toward Nash's apartment.

His red truck was in the drive. Lights were on in the apartment above the garage. Good, he was home.

She ran up the steps and knocked on his door.

When Nash opened the door, he looked really pissed off. Not a good sign.

Or—maybe it was! Maybe he was jealous, maybe he was angry that she'd kissed another man!

Nash wore clean board shorts and a T-shirt. He was barefoot and his sandy hair was wet.

She was strong. "Nash, I need to talk to you."

He said, "Okay." He didn't move.

"Could I come in? Please?"

He shrugged, turned his back on her, and walked away from the door.

Darcy stepped inside, shut the door, and followed him. He leaned his weight against the kitchen counter. His arms were folded over his chest in a classic defense pose.

She was shaking, but she had to do this. "Nash, I think you're angry with me because you saw Clive kissing me. I don't blame you. Lots of stuff has been going on in my neighborhood. It's been a completely crazy summer. So that doesn't excuse me for kissing Clive, but it explains it, I hope. I mean, his grandmother Mimi is sick. And Willow—but never mind that. Nash, you're angry with me, but is that fair? I'm confused. We've been seeing each other for about three months. I know that's not long enough to make a serious, um, commitment, and I know we haven't said anything important about us, you and me, where we might be headed, but Nash . . . Nash, it kills me to have you look at me like that. Nash, I came here to tell you—" Fear choked her. She reached out and put her hands on his arm. The warm skin, the electricity—it gave her strength, it gave her determination. "I love you."

Nash was made of stone. He didn't respond to her touch. "That looked like more than a friendly kiss."

"I can explain that. Could we sit down? You're so cold, and it's not easy, saying all this to you and you standing there like Mount Rushmore. It's *complicated*. This summer has been such a tangle. I know way too many secrets, and I had gone to Mimi's house to ask her advice, and she's sick, she's *really* sick, and Clive was beside himself, and I helped Mimi get cleaned up. I made her some scrambled eggs."

Darcy paused. Nash didn't move from the counter but continued to stare at her emotionlessly. Anger kindled in her chest at Nash's unyielding face, at his lack of sympathy. And she had told him she loved him! Didn't he *hear?* Didn't he *care?*

She pressed on. "It's excruciating to see your grandmother fading. I know how Clive feels, because I went through it. I've told you about that."

Nash took a deep breath. "So that kiss was his way of thanking you?"

"No, of course not." Darcy spoke with an honesty and a quiet passion that she *knew* would bring Nash around. "It was about desperation, about needing to be reminded of the simple joys of walking unaided, of seeing with clear eyes the faces of people you love, of breathing, of laughing and singing and walking and hearing, of having an appetite, of being hungry and then being fed."

"So you *fed* him."

"What? Oh, come on, Nash! Don't twist my words around."

Nash walked past her to the door. He opened it and stood next to it. "You should go."

"Nash, don't do this. You're breaking my heart."

"Call the guy next door. Maybe he can *comfort* you again."

"You're being horrible—and really damned *stupid!*" With as much dignity as she could muster, Darcy stormed past him, out the door, down the stairs, around the house to her car. She was angry, she was hurt, she was inconsolable.

And in the midst of her rage and confusion, she knew one thing for sure. She was not going to tell Susan about Autumn and Otto. Who knew what their marriage was like? How could Darcy judge when she'd known the Brueckners for only a few weeks? Maybe Susan was frigid, maybe Susan had a lover of her own back in

Boston, maybe Susan was grateful to have someone else bear the burden of Otto's arrogance and self-absorption.

When she reached her house, she switched off the ignition but sat as if captured in her car while her mind raced with thoughts.

How did anyone ever stayed married? Why was Nash so pigheaded? If he was this angry because of a simple kiss, didn't that mean he loved her, that he wanted her to belong to him; didn't it mean that when she said she loved him it moved him, it mattered to him? How could he hear her say she loved him and not respond?

She hit her head against the back of her seat as if she could knock some sense into it. Slowly she became aware of her surroundings. It was dark now. Lights were on in the Brueckners' house and in the Rushes'. She hadn't left lights on in her own house. Poor Muffler must be confused and worried.

Empty of emotion, exhausted by her thoughts, Darcy left her car and walked up the steps and let herself into the house. She needed a shower. She needed to be washed clean.

20

On summer Saturdays, the children's library was always crowded with families returning a week's worth of books and DVDs, and searching for and checking out new ones. The small area arranged for toddlers, surrounded by low shelves of books, became an unofficial preschool as mothers traded gossip while their little ones sat triumphantly in the jumbo-size stuffed fuzzy bear chair or stood clutching the chair and shrieking to be lifted into it. Older children were left to choose their books while their parents slipped over to the adult section; and when the older children were collected and herded off to other places, the books they'd scanned and rejected were left in towers on the round reading tables and the floor.

This Saturday, Darcy worked up in the children's library, helping keep some semblance of order. She returned books and DVDs to their shelves, sat at the circ desk to check books in and out, and reshelved books in their proper alphabetical order. It was impossible to spend a moment in her own private thoughts, and Darcy was glad for the relief.

By afternoon, the crowds had dispersed. Darcy and Beverly took separate breaks for lunch and tidied the room. Sunday the library was closed, and usually Darcy was glad, but this weekend loomed emptily before her. She couldn't join the gang on their regular Sunday beach picnics, not if Nash was going to be there, cold-shouldering her. She couldn't summon up the energy to be around other people, anyway.

The August day was hot and muggy. After she closed the library, she walked down to Jetties Beach for a swim. For a long time, she floated on her back, feeling the sun beating down on her face, trying to relax, to empty her mind. Instead, flashes of yesterday flickered behind her closed eyes. Mimi, so weak, so dependent. Nash, so cold, so enraged—so *hurt*. Tears seeped out of her eyes and trailed down her face into the salty water, and this seemed so frankly pitiful Darcy had to laugh at herself. Flipping over, she submerged her face and forced herself to swim as fast as she could, up along the beach and back.

She bent over her bag, pulled a towel out, and dried her face, then pulled on the loose sundress she carried and slid her feet into her sandals. As she headed up the boardwalk, her cell rang. She snatched it up, praying it would be Nash.

"Darcy, where are you? You've got to come over!" Willow's voice was half whisper, half scream.

"Willow? Are you okay?"

"Mom told Boyz. They're yelling at each other!"

"Oh, Willow. Oh, honey, I know that's terrible. I'm sorry. But *I* can't do anything about it. It's between your mother and Boyz."

Even as she said she couldn't do anything, Darcy picked up her pace, walking so fast she was nearly running.

"You *have* to do something! They won't listen to me. They won't pay any attention to me, no matter what I say. What about poor Susan?"

Welcome to the messes adults make, Darcy thought. Willow had scarcely entered the tempestuous teenage years with all its misery, elation, drama, and hormonal rampages and here she was, caught up in the adult world of jealousy. But what could Darcy do? What *should* she do?

"Willow," Darcy said, impressed by the authority in her tone, "I want you to leave the house and walk down to Main Street and meet me. We'll walk home together and try to figure something out."

"But Mother and Boyz—"

"You just said they won't pay attention to you."

"But—" Willow began to protest.

"If you leave, it might surprise them enough to calm down."

"Oh. Okay . . . okay, I'll meet you on Main Street."

"Good girl." Darcy clicked her phone off,

thinking *I have no idea what I'm talking about.* She couldn't stop the quarrel between Boyz and Autumn, but she was removing Willow from the scene of her parents' argument. That was something.

And when she arrived at her house, what then? Should Darcy charge to the rescue—but how, and who would she be rescuing? She didn't give a fig about Otto Brueckner or about Boyz's wounded pride. But she did care about Susan and her sons. But how could Darcy believe she could help Susan when she'd made such a mess of her own life? And *Mimi.* Willow needed to know about Mimi.

Not far away, a figure turned off Pine and raced down the sidewalk toward Darcy. Willow. Darcy hoped the girl wouldn't catch her foot on one of the many broken bricks and fall. She very well might, Darcy thought, it was turning out to be that kind of summer.

"Darcy!" Willow raced up to Darcy and grasped her arm, tugging her to move faster. She wore jean shorts and a T-shirt and her hair was a mess.

"Slow down and catch your breath," Darcy said. "Forget about your mother and Boyz for a moment. Have you spoken to Mimi today?"

"Mimi? No. Oh, gosh, I forgot. I think I'm supposed to read to her this afternoon."

"Willow, Mimi's sick. Not something frightening, just a bad summer cold. I went over there yesterday to visit her. Clive is taking care of her, but he doesn't think to do some basic stuff like bringing her a fresh nightgown."

Willow's face crinkled with worry. "How is she today?"

"I don't know. I haven't talked to Clive. Why don't we stop in and see Mimi now?" As she spoke the words, Darcy's conscience pinched her; Darcy hadn't planned to have Willow go with her to see Mimi so that Willow would be a buffer person between Darcy and Clive. But that's how it would work, and Darcy was glad.

"Why don't we call Susan and ask her to visit Mimi with us," Willow suggested.

"Willow, you're a genius."

Willow was already punching Susan's number in her phone.

"Hi, Susan, it's Willow. Oh, no, everything's okay, well, not everything— What? Oh, that's because I'm walking fast. I'm with Darcy. We're coming home from the library. I'm supposed to read to Mimi, but Darcy saw Mimi yesterday. She's sick. Not Darcy, Mimi. Just a summer cold. Right. Right. Anyway, Darcy and I are going to stop in at Mimi's and we thought it would be nice if you could, too. Sort of cheer her up? Darcy said Mimi might still be in bed, but— Really? That would be a brilliant idea. See you in a minute."

Darcy asked, "What did she say?"

"She's just finished making chocolate chip

cookies. She said she'll make a pitcher of lemonade and bring that over with some cookies."

"What about her boys?"

"She said they're watching television, and her husband is there—she can leave them for a while."

"Well done, Willow."

"I feel like Nancy Drew." Willow laughed happily and took Darcy's hand as they turned off Main onto Pine Street.

Willow's hand. Darcy wished she had a daughter of her own. No, she wished Willow were *her* daughter, but that was a ridiculous thought. Willow wasn't even her ex-husband's daughter, she was Darcy's ex-husband's stepdaughter. If Willow *were* Darcy's daughter, that would mean that Darcy had gotten pregnant with her fifteen years ago. When Darcy was fifteen.

Oh, what a troublemaker love was! And there were so many kinds of love. Darcy had loved her grandmother. She had thought she loved Boyz, but her divorce had been an astonishing relief. She loved Jordan like crazy; Jordan was her very best friend. She had been afraid to admit how she felt about Nash because it might cause pain, but she had admitted it, and it *had* caused pain—she completely, furiously, helplessly, *loved* Nash. Although right now she wanted to throw a pot at him for being so obstinate about one ridiculous kiss.

And she loved Mimi. Why was that? Why did

love happen like that, so fast, at first sight, so powerful it came as a *recognition: This person is mine.*

Darcy had met scores of older women, sweet grandmothers; kind older women; chic, witty older women here on the island, at the library, or in the women's chorus. She liked them, she enjoyed knowing them, but she hadn't felt that instinctive rapport when she first saw them. She liked Susan Brueckner and felt sympathetic toward her. She even liked Autumn and kind of admired her.

She was so fond of Willow. She felt connected to Willow.

And as if a flower were opening its petals, the knowledge unfolded in Darcy's heart that the love she felt for Nash had opened her to the possibility of caring for—really *connecting* with—other people, even those who were in her life for only a short while.

And sometimes that would hurt. And sometimes it would be wonderful.

"Come on!" Willow tugged on Darcy's hand. "There's Susan." She dropped Darcy's hand and raced to the front door of Mimi's house.

"Hi," Darcy called, joining Willow and Susan. "Go ahead and knock, Willow."

Willow knocked. They heard footsteps. Clive opened the door. Darcy was glad to have Willow and Susan standing between her and him.

"Hello," Darcy said. "We're the committee for the rehabilitation of grandmothers with summer colds."

Clive smiled. "What a coincidence. I happen to have one of those."

He held the door wide and they filed in, past the front parlor, and down the hall to Mimi's bedroom.

Mimi seemed better today. She was sitting up in bed, propped by dozens of pillows, with her glasses on and a book in her hands.

"Thank God!" she cried when she saw them. "I am bored silly!"

"I brought cookies," Susan told her. "And lemonade."

"Darling," Mimi said to Clive, "would you be kind enough to bring us some glasses, and also that handsome bottle of Grey Goose vodka?"

Clive crossed his arms over his chest. "Mimi. You're ill. Vodka is not on the list of drinks for elderly invalids."

"I'll just pour a soupçon in my lemonade," Mimi told him. "Besides, the others might want some. Not you, of course, Willow. Come closer, darlings, I can't see you when you're so far away. I'm not contagious anymore. This damned cold is almost done with me."

Susan pushed the armchair closer to Mimi's bed. Darcy crossed the hall and brought in a chair from the dining room. Willow perched on the end of Mimi's bed.

"Tell me everything!" Mimi requested. "What's been going on?"

Darcy couldn't restrain herself from exchanging a glance with Willow. For a moment, she regretted inviting Susan over. With Susan there, Darcy and Willow couldn't tell Mimi about Autumn's dining room table escapade with Susan's husband, and Darcy couldn't ask Mimi for advice about telling Susan.

Darcy also couldn't ask Mimi for advice about Nash.

As she passed the cookies, Susan said, "I'm working at the yarn store three evenings a week, Mimi, and Otto's been a champion about it. Well, that's because we've got Willow to babysit the boys. So I've learned a lot about myself this summer. And when we go home, after I get the boys settled in school, I'm going to find myself a job in a shop in my neighborhood."

"When are you going home?" Mimi asked.

"In about a week." Susan prattled on about the trials of packing for five people, and using up everything in the cupboards and fridges.

"Yeah," Willow said. "Boyz said we're going home soon, too."

It was as if the floor dropped right out from under Darcy.

Susan was *going home*.

Willow was *going home*.

"Oh, it makes me so sad to think of everyone

going their separate ways," Mimi said. "Summer always goes too fast."

Clive entered, carrying a tray of glasses and ice and a bottle of vodka. Darcy jumped up to help him prepare the drinks and hand them out. Once she accidentally touched Clive's hand with hers. She experienced not even the slightest physical response. Clive hardly looked at Darcy. *Thank heaven,* Darcy thought.

"We're not going until the end of next week," Susan assured Mimi.

"Susan," Mimi said, "you said your husband was fine with you working here. What do you think he'll say about you working when you're back home?"

Susan lowered her eyes. "That's a good question, Mimi. He makes some enormous amount of money—I don't know how much because he won't tell me."

Mimi bridled. "Well, that's ridiculous! You should at least have an idea of his income."

Susan fidgeted with the rings on her fingers. Still looking down, she said, "Mimi, not every marriage is the same. . . ."

"Yes, yes, you're right. Forgive me for interrupting."

"As I said, Otto supports us almost lavishly, although of course some of that—our house, our cars—are important for his reputation."

"And for his ego," Mimi murmured.

Susan acted as if she hadn't heard. "So he might balk at allowing me to work outside the home when we're back in Boston. He might think it would look as if we need the money."

"What will you do if he doesn't want you to work?" Willow asked.

Susan heaved a sigh. "I guess I'll cross that bridge when I come to it."

"Susan." Suddenly, Mimi's tone was serious. "Look at me. Does Otto hit you?"

Susan laughed. "Good grief, of course not. How can you ask such a thing?"

"Because you act as if he hits you," Mimi said.

Susan blinked. "I do?"

"You do," Darcy agreed. "Sometimes you have the saddest expression on your face. It worries me."

"You guys are wrong!" Willow jumped into the conversation. "When I babysit the boys, sometimes I see Susan and Otto together, and he's nice to her. I mean, like, when I see him not with Susan, he's a robot, but he's okay with Susan and the boys." The girl flicked a conspiratorial smile at Darcy, as if to say: *See, I'm being helpful.*

Susan tilted her head. "Darcy, Mimi, here's what I think. If you see me looking sad, I think I'm really looking *tired.* It's an exhausting business, raising three boys. And I worry about them, especially about Henry, although I won't go into that here, it's only typical growing-up stuff.

The truth is, I don't think I'm naturally inclined to raising boys. I mean, look at me, you can tell I've never played baseball or even tennis. It's *hard* work. Okay, I have help, I have a company that cleans my house once a week, and at home we have a couple of darling babysitters—" Quickly she smiled at Willow. "They're not half as good as you, Willow. But, anyway, it's not just the physical exhaustion of, oh, I don't know, just for example let's pick keeping them in shoes! Three growing boys, I swear their feet grow an inch every time they fall asleep. And, no, don't suggest I pass them down. Of course their feet aren't similar. I mean Henry has extremely wide feet and the other two don't. Alfred has fallen arches—already, at his age! Who ever thought that could happen? So he has to wear special shoes with arch supports. Other kids make fun of him, and I get so sad for him." Susan looked around the room. "That's why yarn is a lifesaver!"

Mimi nodded sagely. "My dear, I see exactly what you mean."

Willow frowned. "I don't. I thought we were talking about Susan and Otto and sadness."

"We are, in a way," Darcy told her.

"When you fall in love, when you have children, you'll know." Mimi reached over to take Willow's hand. "It doesn't have to be yarn. It could be reading books or sailing or clog dancing."

"Clog dancing?" Willow wrinkled her nose. "What's that?"

"You'll find out yourself someday," Mimi said. "The point is that we all need something in life that we enjoy that doesn't *need* us." She glanced at the other two women. "Am I right?"

"Well said," Darcy agreed.

Susan nodded. "Absolutely."

"Think of loving a pet," Mimi continued. "No, think of loving a celebrity. Um, let me see. Willow, think of loving Justin Timberlake."

"Wait, what?" Willow interrupted. "I don't love Justin Timberlake."

"Meghan Trainor," Darcy quickly suggested.

"Fine, then," Mimi said. "Think of loving Meghan Trainor. When you think of *her,* or of what's his name, that muscular man that starred in *In the Heart of the Sea*—"

"Chris Hemsworth!" Willow almost shouted.

"Good. When you think of Meghan and Chris, you're happy. You're filled with such joy at their existence, it makes life almost magical. But if you had to be responsible for their health and safety, for what they eat every day and when their dentist appointments are and if you read in a newspaper or online that someone thinks Meghan or Chris is stupid or ugly or *lame*"—Mimi's eyebrows rose in triumph as she thought to use the word *lame*—"you'd be sad and angry that someone said something mean, and you'd be exhausted from buying their food and cooking their meals and driving them to dentist appointments. But you're not responsible. You can love without protecting. If you ignore a skein of yarn or drop it on the floor or even step on it, it's not going to get its feelings hurt."

Willow pulled on her lower lip. "So you mean you can't love anyone without getting hurt."

"Not quite that," Mimi corrected. "More like you can't love anyone without the *possibility* of getting hurt, and not by the person you love but by, let's call it, *circumstance*."

"But what if you get in a terrible fight? What if you've done something wrong?" Willow asked.

"All parents fight," Susan said. "And no one's perfect. No one. When you love someone, you have to accept their faults."

"Not completely true," Darcy argued. "You can walk away from some of their faults, especially if that includes dealing heroin."

"Well, that's a little extreme," Susan said. "I mean, to bring it right back to the personal level, I'm not unaware of what a prick Otto can seem like. Excuse my language, Willow. I know he doesn't know how to play with his sons. But I know how his parents brought him up, and I know a lot of intimate stuff about him that other people don't know. So I love him, as they say, warts and all."

"Thank heaven!" Mimi clapped her hands

together. "I'm so glad to know that, Susan. Still," she continued, setting her piercing gaze on Susan, "people can change. Not by, let's say, a mile or even a yard. But by an inch."

"How—" Willow began.

Mimi interrupted her. "My dears, I do believe the vodka has mellowed me right into a mind slump. I need to close my eyes and take a nap." A cough shook her frail body. She put her hand to her mouth. "Excuse me."

Willow, Susan, and Darcy stood.

"I'm sorry if we tired you," Susan said. She leaned over and kissed Mimi's forehead.

"Me, too," Willow echoed, also kissing Mimi's forehead.

"You're wonderful," Darcy told Mimi. She kissed Mimi's forehead.

Mimi sank back, her eyes closed, and her body sagged into the embrace of her pillows. The three guests quietly saw themselves out, into the sunny late afternoon.

Darcy hugged Willow and whispered, "Feel better about your parents now?"

"Yeah, I guess I kind of do," Willow replied. "I've got a lot to think about."

"Call me if you need a referee," Darcy joked.

Willow snorted. "See you later," she called, heading down the narrow path next to Darcy's hedge.

Darcy and Susan waved.

"She's a nice girl," Susan said. "She's got a good head on her shoulders."

Darcy nodded. "She'll need it."

"True. You don't think of having *that* kind of conversation on a beach day," Susan said. Leaning over, she kissed Darcy's cheek. "We're all going to be fine, Darcy."

Darcy nodded, but she wasn't sure that Susan was right.

21

Sunday, Darcy didn't go to the beach. Jordan pleaded with Darcy to come, even if Nash was there, even if Nash wouldn't speak to Darcy. The beach wasn't *only* Nash's, Jordan insisted, and the group were Darcy's friends as much as Nash's. But Darcy was in an introspective, sulky kind of mood. She wanted to be alone. She wanted to let her feelings about all her neighbors sort of stew in the back of her mind, because, really, that was all she could do. She couldn't expect Mimi and Willow and Susan never to leave the island. She couldn't solve everyone's problems—she couldn't even solve her own problems! She had made an effort with Nash, and he had rebuffed her. She wasn't going to embarrass herself, if he didn't want to forgive her, at least to hear her out. . . .

What a mess of a summer!

She knew from experience to force herself to do some kind of mindless household task when she was wallowing in self-pity, so she put a bandana around her head and worked in the garden, weeding and deadheading and watering. The day was hot, but her huge old trees cast shade on part of her yard, and she didn't mind the heat, really, it felt cleansing somehow. At first she worried that something would happen in one of the adjoining gardens—Mimi would fall or Willow would meet Logan near the hedges or Otto would storm at his sons. But all she heard from her neighbors were a few voices and then slamming of car doors as the Brueckner family set off for the beach.

In the late afternoon, Darcy surveyed her kingdom with her hands on her hips and patted herself metaphorically on the back for a job well done. She put away her tools, stepped out of her gardening clogs, and took a long, blissful shower. It was always such an emotional lift, working hard physically all day and then bathing, massaging body lotion into her tanned limbs, slipping into her silk kimono, and feeling the healthy ache of well-used muscles. She poured herself a glass of wine and prepared a platter of treats—cheese, crackers, olives, sliced peppers, carrots, bluefish pâté, and smoked salmon—to munch while she curled on the sofa and read. Muffler sat on the back of the sofa, patting her face with one gentle paw, claws neatly tucked in, reminding her he also liked bluefish and salmon.

"What a pest you are," Darcy said. She got up, put some salmon and bluefish pâté in his bowl, then went back to her book.

The book was a mystery, engaging and suspenseful, and she passed the lonely evening without trying to call Nash, without phoning

Jordan to see if Nash had been at the beach, without crying. She was proud of herself, in a miserable sort of way.

PBS's *Masterpiece Theatre* was about to begin when a knock came at her front door.

Nash! It had to be Nash. He'd missed her too much, he wanted to talk with her—

She almost tripped on her own feet to get to the front hall.

She yanked the door opened. Boyz stood there.

He wore shorts and a blue-checked shirt, untucked, sleeves rolled up, the pale blue of the shirt setting off his pale blue eyes.

"Darcy, could I come in? I need to talk to you."

Darcy hesitated.

"Please?" He seemed earnest, not in game-playing mode. "It's about Willow."

"Willow? Is she okay?"

"Yes, but . . ." Now Boyz hesitated.

Darcy pulled the door wide. "Come in."

She led him into the living room where the signs of her single life were laid out before him—the glass of wine with only an inch left to drink, the plate of munchies for one, the book lying on the sofa, its bookmark protruding like a small sign of someone's overorganized, tidy, and lonely life.

Boyz chose a chair across from the book. Darcy returned to her place on the sofa. She waited, not speaking.

"You look good, Darcy," Boyz began.

Darcy cut him off with a quick shake of her head. "No. Stop. You came here to talk about Willow. Right? What about Willow?"

Boyz smiled charmingly and nodded in agreement. "Of course. Willow. The thing is, she's gotten very attached to you over the summer. You must be aware of that."

Darcy nodded, and her posture softened. "I'm fond of her. She's a special girl."

"Autumn and I are grateful to you for all you've done, taking her under your wing, getting her involved with the library, with story time, with your friends. You have been incredibly kind."

"It hasn't been kindness, Boyz. Willow is a wonderful young woman. She's bright and funny and generous. You and Autumn should be proud."

The Nantucket newspaper, the *Inquirer and Mirror*, lay on the coffee table, neatly folded. Boyz gestured to it. "We saw Logan Smith's name in the recent court report. He was caught dealing drugs."

"Yes. I saw that."

"This is such a worrisome time in our lives. I mean, Willow is a teenager, and although you have so marvelously averted what could have been a tragedy with Logan Smith and his heroin, well, we're aware that similar situations are waiting for her everywhere back in Boston."

"All parents of teenagers face that possibility,"

Darcy told him. "I'm sure there are many support groups in Boston. I know there are—"

Boyz chuckled, looking satisfied, as if he'd caught Darcy in a familiar embarrassing act. "*Books,* right? You were going to advise me to read some books."

He'd pushed her buttons—the same ones he had manipulated when they were married, subtly disparaging her work and her passion for reading. For one quick moment, Darcy felt anger shoot up in her chest, and she almost let it take her over. But she breathed deeply, sat back on the sofa, and let her anger evaporate.

"That wouldn't be the worst thing you could do," she replied gently, as if she were wise and he was a bit of an idiot.

Boyz patted his chest, smoothing a nonexistent tie, always a sign he'd been rattled. His voice was almost angry when he spoke. "I didn't come here to argue."

Darcy shrugged and said nothing. She was a librarian after all, and she had learned the power of silence. And it was a *lovely* feeling, that moment when at last she kept silent and didn't rise to his bait, didn't blurt automatically, *I wasn't arguing!,* which *would* be arguing.

Finally, Boyz conceded gracefully. "Yes. Sorry. I'm getting off topic."

This was fun, Darcy thought, *not speaking. This was having a bit of control.* So she said nothing.

"You're making this hard for me, Darcy," Boyz said.

Darcy laughed out loud. "Boyz, why are you here?"

"Because we—Autumn and I—were hoping you could continue to be part of Willow's life after we leave the island."

Darcy blinked. She was truly shocked by his words. "Boyz, I would like that very much. But what can I do? I suppose I could invite her down here on weekends, especially the long weekends like Columbus Day, for the Cranberry Festival. . . ." She cocked her head, envisioning the coming months.

Boyz leaned forward, his face alight. "Yes, of course, but we were thinking of *more* than that. We'd like to offer you an apartment in Boston, right in Back Bay. You could use it whenever you wanted, and you could take Willow to plays and galleries and for tea at the Ritz, whatever."

Something was wrong here. It brought a sour taste to her mouth, as if she'd eaten something rotten. Darcy was suspicious. "Boyz, all that isn't for *me* to do. That's what Autumn and you should do, or Willow could go with her friends. Especially Willow could go with her girlfriends."

Darcy was only slightly surprised when Boyz rose from his chair, came around the coffee table, and lowered himself so close to Darcy, their legs touched.

She drew her legs away, to the side.

Boyz turned toward Darcy. Reaching out, he took both her hands in his. "Darcy—"

Darcy pulled away. "Come on, Boyz, don't do this. It's not worthy of you."

"But just *think*," Boyz implored. "Think of what you and I could do. We could have a little love nest—"

"You've got to be kidding!" Darcy tried to rise, but Boyz held her hands tightly.

"Tell me you don't still feel attracted to me."

"I don't feel the slightest bit attracted to you." Darcy shot off the words like bullets.

Boyz smiled patronizingly. He nodded his head toward the coffee table. "Wine for one? All those clever little bites for one? Very brave of you, Darcy, not to give into the sadness of being single and simply eat takeout or a container of ice cream."

Darcy jerked her hands away. "Boyz, you're giving me whiplash here. I thought you were concerned about Willow—"

"I am! Of course I am. But, gorgeous girl, when I see you, I can't help wanting to hold you in my arms again—"

Boyz lunged forward to embrace Darcy, to pull her to him. He lowered his mouth in a clumsy attempt to kiss her. Darcy squirmed, put both hands on his chest, and pushed him away. Her blood heated, and she knew her face was flushed.

How had she ever loved this shallow excuse for a person? And what in the world had she done this summer to make him believe she wanted to have sex with him? She struggled free. She stood up.

"Boyz, you need to go. Now." She moved toward the door.

Boyz cast a desperate look at Darcy. Then he folded over, his arms tight against his stomach, as if he'd been stabbed.

Darcy made a face. "Oh, for God's sake, Boyz, this is over the top."

Boyz dramatically lowered his head, catching his breath. He stood. "Just let me . . . I won't. . . ." He walked toward Darcy. He put his hands on her shoulders and positioned himself to look her directly in the eye. "Darcy. Autumn is pregnant."

"Oh, that's wonderful, Boyz! Congratulations!" Darcy attempted to step away, but Boyz held on tight. Like a drowning man holding to a lifesaver.

"She just found out." The light went out of Boyz's eyes. "I mean, *just* today. They can do that now, you know. They've invented kits so you can find out if you're pregnant when you're only barely pregnant. I mean, Autumn's missed one period. That's all, *one.* She is absolutely like clockwork with her period, twenty-eight days almost to the hour, boom, here's her period. She missed her period, and she bought a test at the pharmacy and she took it."

"Okay," Darcy said slowly.

"She's pregnant."

"Okay," Darcy said again. "I don't see the problem, Boyz. You always wanted children. You're the heir, the future patriarch of the Szweda family."

Boyz released Darcy. He turned away. With his back to her, Boyz muttered, "The child can't be mine." He sounded as if he were about to cry.

The name popped right into her mind. *Otto Brueckner.*

"Oh, Boyz," she said, restraining herself from going to him. "What a ridiculous thought."

"No. Not ridiculous at all. I had myself tested this spring. I have something called *idiopathic oligospermia.* It means I don't have a huge concentration of sperm in my semen. I mean, I've got some, but not the million like I should have."

"Oh, Boyz, I'm so sorry," Darcy said, and she truly was. "Is there a cure?"

He shook his gorgeous silver-blond head. "I'm taking vitamin C and zinc and eating a high-protein diet. I was planning to try some serious drugs, but Autumn's already pregnant and the chances are low that I'm the father . . ." He was on the point of tears. "And Darcy, you never got pregnant when we were married."

He didn't need to say it: *Autumn was probably pregnant with another man's baby.* Boyz turned to face her. Tears shimmered in his eyes.

Darcy's thoughts raced. What responsibility did she have here?

Maybe her responsibility was simple: She could tell the truth.

"Boyz, I have a confession to make. It's important."

"Tell me."

"When we were married, *all* the time we were married, I was on the birth control pill."

Boyz stared at her, blank faced.

"I mean, I never stopped taking the pill. *I* didn't get pregnant because I took that pill every day."

Boyz lifted his head. His face cleared. "So if you didn't get pregnant because you were on the pill, then maybe I do have enough sperm to make Autumn's baby." He rubbed his forehead, looking thoughtful. "The doctor said I have some sperm . . . so this baby could be mine?"

"I don't know that. I can't say that. All I can do is tell you the truth about why *I* didn't get pregnant."

"Why didn't you stop taking the pill?" Boyz asked, but he didn't speak with anger or pain. What Darcy had done in their marriage wasn't compelling; what mattered was his marriage to Autumn, the possibility of Autumn carrying his own child.

Darcy was glad for that, glad she'd revealed her secret. "I'm not sure, Boyz. At first, I suppose, in the early months, I didn't want to get pregnant until I sort of got my sea legs in your family. I wanted to be part of your family, but you are all so powerful, so convinced of your own importance, and so tangled together. I couldn't find a way to get in. As time went on, I realized I didn't love you, not really, and you didn't really love me. We were young, we had dreams, but we were so different, you and I. We wanted such different things."

"Okay. I guess I can understand. Although people do have babies when they aren't prepared for them. Babies can come at inconvenient times."

Darcy smiled at Boyz. "That's true. They can also come at convenient times."

"So you're saying since I want a child, I should stay with Autumn and let her go through the pregnancy. There's a chance the child is mine."

"I'm not saying anything," Darcy insisted. "Whatever you decide is for you and Autumn to discuss, and by the way, I believe it's Autumn's decision about going through with this pregnancy, not yours. Or not yours alone."

"I know, feminist blah-blah-blah," Boyz muttered.

Darcy watched her ex-husband struggling to come to terms with it all. "I suppose another option you have is to divorce Autumn. After all, she's been unfaithful to you."

Boyz's face cleared. "I couldn't do that, Darcy.

I *love* Autumn." All of a sudden, he looked strong and sure. "Darcy, thank you for telling me about your, um, secret. It helps me a lot to know that."

"And no hard feelings?" Darcy asked.

He grinned. "I could have some very hard feelings if you'll give me a minute."

Darcy laughed. "Oh, for heaven sake. You're ridiculous." She couldn't help but wonder what Boyz would do if she took him up on his offer. If she wrapped herself around him and kissed him . . . how would he respond if truly put to the test?

She'd never know, she decided, because truly, she didn't care.

But she did care about someone else.

"Boyz, sometime before you go, I'd like to speak with you and Autumn about Willow. I *would* like to keep in touch with her. I'd love to have her come visit me, here on the island. Fall is gorgeous, and we've got the Cranberry Festival. And Willow is such a smart, wonderful girl. . . ."

"Sure, fine," Boyz said. "But no apartment in Boston, right?"

They smiled in shared understanding.

"Absolutely no apartment in Boston."

Darcy walked him to the door.

At the threshold, he turned. "Goodbye, Darcy, and thanks."

"Goodbye, Boyz." She considered kissing his cheek. Decided against it.

After she'd closed the door and returned to her sofa and her one inch of wine, Darcy stared into space, trying to juggle her ideas into a sensible line. It was true, she had come to care about Willow and would enjoy having the girl visit now and then. But it was also true that if that happened, Darcy would have to be in touch with Boyz and Autumn, *connected* to them in a way she hadn't foreseen. She wasn't certain she wanted to be connected to them.

Boyz hadn't mentioned the real estate business at all this summer. Darcy hoped that meant that whatever he'd found on Nantucket had deterred him from opening a branch of his family's company on the island. She did not want Boyz or Autumn on this, *her,* island. They could have all the rest of the entire world, but this isolated territory out in the sea was hers.

And what else, what else did she claim as hers? The Nantucket Atheneum, because it was where she worked and where she felt at home. She felt sheltered by the library but also responsible for its well-being. This house of her grandmother's, absolutely she claimed as hers. And what else? Well, Muffler.

But maybe other people, too. Definitely Jordan was hers, her best friend. She wished she could claim Nash, but she couldn't, and she couldn't think of him now. It hurt too much. As for Willow, Susan, and Mimi, they weren't really hers at all. They would all leave soon. Darcy felt a pang of guilt. She had ignored her island friends, Beverly Maison and Beth and the women in the chorus . . . but of course they'd ignored her as well, overwhelmed with summer responsibilities. Labor Day was late this year, giving vacationers an extra week on the island. Once that week was over, those who remained on the island could take a deep breath and relax. They could find time to chat as they walked into town, they could run into people they knew in the grocery store, they could swim in the ocean and lie on the beach without braving the summer crowds.

Of course, as the season turned toward fall, a new set of tourists would still come to the island, and Darcy enjoyed this bunch, whom the islanders jokingly called "the newlyweds and the nearly deads." These visitors would come without children, and they would leisurely stroll the streets and the beaches, taking time to appreciate the sun on the water, the glitter of the sea. Summer people in general cared much more about the fundraisers and galas where they could *be* the glitter themselves and schmooze with other, even more wealthy and high-profile people than themselves.

Two more weeks. Two more weeks, and summer would be over for this year.

22

For a few days after Boyz's visit, Darcy remained hopeful. If Boyz could forgive Autumn her affair, surely Nash could forgive Darcy for one stupid little kiss with Clive. Nash would call. She was sure of it. Or he would come by her house. She had told him she loved him. Those words had to mean more to him than the sight of a brief kiss with another man.

She worked tirelessly at the library, as cheerful and helpful as Mary Poppins. By Thursday, though, her optimism sagged. But Melody was throwing a birthday party for her husband, Rick, Sunday night, a huge crazy bash at their enormous old house near Surfside Beach. Nash would be there, for sure, and if he hadn't forgiven Darcy by then, she would maneuver him into a quiet corner and convince him to stop being so stubborn.

Sunday evening, Darcy was in the process of getting dressed, which meant trying on clothes, deciding they looked awful, tossing them on the bed, and trying on something else, when her cellphone rang.

"Darcy," Jordan said, "have you left the house yet?"

"I'm almost ready," Darcy stalled.

"What's the holdup? I had to get Kiks fed and rocked to sleep, and I'm almost to Melody's house. All you have to do is dress yourself."

"Yes, well, that's the problem," Darcy said. "Nothing I have looks right."

Jordan snorted. "*Everything* you have looks right! You're only nervous about seeing Nash again. You want to look irresistibly sexy so he'll fall at your feet and beg you to take him back."

"You're absolutely right. The problem is, I've got nothing sexy to wear."

"Oh for heaven's sake. Put on one of your sundresses, the one with the halter top. That looks fabulous on you—"

"I've worn it so often this summer—"

"You don't seriously think that man keeps track of how many times you wear something, do you? Anyway, stop procrastinating, throw something on, and get to the party."

"I'm not sure . . . it's hard to come into a party alone, Jordan."

"You can do it. Put on your big girl panties and sashay in. I'll wait for you on the deck."

"Thanks, Jordan. I'll be there in five."

She had already put on her makeup. In the summer she seldom wore much except lipstick and mascara, but for the party—for seeing Nash again—she'd gone full force with eyeliner and blush and perfume. She was wearing the halter dress Jordan had suggested. It was crimson crepe, formfitting at the top, with a flowy skirt. It set off her tan and made her figure look its sexiest. She wore dangling silver earrings that floated against her dark hair, and a thin silver bracelet on her upper arm. She knew she looked as good as she could, but she was on the verge of hyperventilating.

She wanted to be with Nash so badly. After all they'd shared this summer, after he had told her about his brother's death, after all their intimate conversations, he couldn't just walk away.

Her phone rang. She saw the caller ID and answered.

"Clive, is Mimi okay?"

Clive laughed. "Yes, and I'm fine, too."

"Sorry, I—"

"No, no, I appreciate how you worry about Mimi. She isn't her normal self yet, but I think she's gaining strength. She's sleeping right now."

"Oh, good. Clive, I can't talk. Sorry, but I'm just leaving for a birthday party."

"How late will you be out?" Clive asked, a certain warmth to his voice.

What does that matter? Darcy almost said— and then she understood what he meant. It gave her a twinge right in her stomach. Was he phoning in hopes of getting a few minutes of quick "consolation"?

"Because," Clive continued, "the Perseid meteor showers are still going on. They're supposed to be an astonishing sight. I was hoping I could drive you out to a dark beach and we could lie on a blanket and look up at the sky. A weathercaster said it will be like watching shooting stars."

Impatiently, Darcy said, "Sorry, Clive, I'm not sure how late the party will go, so I'd better decline, although that really is a marvelous idea."

"The meteor showers continue tomorrow," Clive told her. "Maybe that would work for you."

"Oh, well, let me see what my schedule is. Sorry, but I've got to leave now. Let's talk tomorrow."

Darcy hurriedly gathered her purse and car keys, dropped some treats in Muffler's bowl, and went out to her car. Because she'd told Clive she was leaving for a party, she felt obligated to leave at once, since he could watch from his window to see if she was true to her word. Not that she thought he would check up on her—that would be ridiculous. Even so, she drove away from her house, and once she'd turned the corner, she pulled over to the side of the street, put the car in park, pulled down the mirror on the visor, and took a moment to double check her reflection. Yes, she'd put her eyeliner on evenly and her lipstick was perfect . . .

. . . and her heart was cantering away beneath her red halter-top dress like a racehorse at the finish line.

She took a few minutes to do deep-breathing exercises. She didn't want to come on to Nash carelessly, as if this were some kind of game. No, she'd spent a lot of time thinking about Nash, thinking about how she felt not only about him but about her life, her entire life.

Years ago, she'd hoped to become the director of the Boston Public Library. Not that she believed she could achieve such a goal when she was young, no, but she'd daydreamed about how it would go as she climbed the professional ladder. Her plans had not included being the assistant children's librarian at a small but distinguished library on an isolated island. Her plans had also not included being enchanted by Nantucket and her way of life here, but Fate had sideswiped her, spinning her around so that she understood she was meant to live here, in this small community, walking to work, gossiping with Tita and Vilma and Robin at the post office, strolling to the docks to view the grand yachts flying flags of other countries, helicopters and Jet Skis riding on their upper decks, or stomping through snowbanks in the winter to watch Bill Blount's famous old fishing vessel come in to harbor from the storm.

Darcy had had a long serious talk with herself, and she had to admit, when it came right down to it, she wanted to live on this island with its eccentric population and quirky calendar for the rest of her life. Well, probably for the rest of her life. She was only thirty; she couldn't predict how she'd feel in twenty years. Much of her desire to remain here was because she was living in her grandmother's house. She made herself face that fact and all it said about her personality, her deepest needs. She admitted to herself that it was hard for her to feel safe, at home, tethered, because for the first ten years of her life she'd had to shuffle from house to house according to the whims of her delightful mother, the Queen of the Whiplash Life. So Darcy was wounded, so she was off-kilter—so what? Who wasn't, one way or another?

The thing was—and her soul swelled as she thought of him—she now understood that Nash was the love of her life. With him, she felt safe, more than safe: She felt strong, new, capable, ready for whatever life threw their way. She needed to tell him this. She was going to speak to Nash tonight—she wouldn't flirt or grovel or beg—she was going to speak to him calmly. She wouldn't attempt to talk all this through with him; she didn't even know what she was proposing, except getting back together, maybe living together to see how that went—she knew exactly the space for Nash's books in her grandmother's library.

She had to move now, into reality! She couldn't sit here nervously planning this evening and the next and the next. She had to, as everyone said, *be here now.* So she put her car into drive and headed for Melody's house.

Rick and Melody's house, just off a bumpy dirt road off Surfside Road, was the opposite of Darcy's. Modern, sleek, boxy, it was an upside-down house, with the bedrooms on the ground floor and the living rooms on the second floor. Second-floor decks of silky smooth pine boards extended across the ocean side of the house, providing fantastic views. Outdoor furniture and huge pots of flowers turned the deck into another room, and as Darcy parked her car and walked up to the house, Jordan and Melody waved at her from the deck.

Jordan called something down to Darcy—it sounded like "I have to talk to you!" but that couldn't be right. Darcy would be in the house in a minute and she'd talk to Jordan right away. She always did. Well, she always had, before she was with Nash.

It had taken some courage to enter a party by herself. Jordan had always been her go-to person, the face Darcy would look for in a crowd, a momentary anchor. Now that Darcy knew the gang, she didn't have to make a beeline for Jordan, but she planned to do that anyway. While she and Jordan were chatting, Darcy could casually search out Nash.

His red pickup was parked down the road. So she knew he was here.

The Holdgates were arriving now, so Darcy entered the house and went up the wide spiral stairs chatting to Tina Holdgate about how fast the summer had gone.

"You must have had a fab summer," Tina told Darcy. "Girl, you look awesome!"

"Thanks," Darcy said. The compliment was exactly what she needed. She knew it made her cheeks glow. She'd never felt prettier than now, and she knew she was turning a few heads as she made her way through the crowd toward the deck and Jordan.

"Martini? Cosmo?" A waitress held a tray of drinks for Darcy to choose from.

"For now, just sparkling water," Darcy said, lifting a tumbler of ice and water. She wanted to be sober when she approached Nash. She was already high on nerves and hope.

"Hi, Jordan," she called, waving as she did a sideways squeeze between a cluster of guys replaying the recent Red Sox game.

Jordan returned a wave that seemed more like a stop sign. Jordan was frowning, no—not *frowning* as such, more like her face was squeezing up like she'd just sucked a lemon. Darcy hoped Kiks was all right as she slid past a woman resting against the door jamb, a tall man leaning down to speak to her. . . .

She couldn't breathe. Her knees buckled.

The woman in a formfitting slip of black silk,

her blond hair shimmying against her shoulders, her pretty young face radiant, was Kate Ferguson. She'd been in the women's chorus with Darcy. She was a nurse. She was nice.

She was beaming up at Nash, who had his hand resting on the doorjamb as he talked to her, leaning toward her, clearly taking possession, marking his territory.

Darcy stumbled. A man—she couldn't think of his name, she knew him, he was somebody's husband—caught her arm and kept her from falling.

"No more gin for you," he joked.

"Right," Darcy agreed, not bothering to hold up her glass of water. She was nauseous. She was cold. Her fingertips and lips felt icy. She was filled with an enormous scream that pushed against her throat, her lungs, her belly. . . .

She wanted to collapse on the deck and die.

She continued to walk, robot-like, toward Jordan.

"Oh, honey," Jordan said, putting an arm around Darcy and swiveling her so they both faced the ocean as she talked. "I was trying to warn you."

Darcy choked out a few words. "Have you—has Nash?"

"I haven't seen Nash with her anywhere before now. I don't think he's been seeing her or I'd know through the grapevine. I don't think they're a *thing* yet, Darcy." Jordan squeezed Darcy's arm. "Come on. Buck up. Don't let him see you looking all sad and desperate."

"I can't stay here."

"Yes, you can. Stick with me. Slap a smile on your face. They're bringing out the cake any minute now. It's early, I know, for the cake, but everyone here has to work tomorrow, so it's not going to be one of our normal drunken orgies."

"I'll leave when they bring the cake out."

"Okay, fine, but until then you've got to fake having fun. At least look as if you're glad you're alive."

"I'm not sure I am."

"Suck it up. It's not the end of the world."

Feeling was returning to her fingers, and the shock was draining away from her mind, replaced by a dark, rational, and overwhelming grief. "I think I really messed up, Jordan."

"That's not for you to decide right at this moment in time, Darcy. What will people think if you go all pathetic and wretched at a party?"

"You know what, Jordan? I don't care what people think. Here, please take this."

Darcy handed her untouched glass of water to her friend. Without another word, because she had no strength to speak another word, Darcy walked across the deck to the far end and went down the outside steps to the lawn. She heard Jordan hiss "Darcy!" but didn't turn back. She had been hit by lightning. A tree had fallen on her life. A tsunami raced toward her, its towering waves threatening to crash down on her, and all she could think of was getting away.

She took off her stilettos and carried them as she ran to her car. Once inside the relative privacy of her Jeep, she tossed her shoes and small party purse on the seat, stabbed the key in the ignition, and drove away from the house, the party, the doorway where Nash leaned possessively over beautiful little young Kate. She turned onto the Surfside Road and drove to the parking lot overlooking the Atlantic. The beach was still crowded with swimmers, bodysurfers, and groups of friends sharing seaside cocktails and munchies. She wanted to be on the beach, but if she went down to the ocean and screamed like she felt like screaming, she'd frighten everyone and probably get hauled off in a police car.

So she drove to the far end of the rutted dirt road and parked in front of a house with no lights on and no sign of life. She kept her windows rolled up as she buried her face in her hands and wept.

Darkness fell. Darcy watched the beachcombers walk up the sandy hill, carrying coolers, beach umbrellas and chairs, sleepy children. She gazed numbly at these fortunate people tucking kids into car seats, reminding each other to fasten their seatbelts, and finally hitting the headlights that flashed over Darcy's Jeep as they turned in the lot and drove back toward town.

She had cried herself out. She had thought this all through. Nash wouldn't date a sweet young woman like Kate on any kind of a whim. He wasn't a frivolous man. Nash was done with Darcy. He had moved on.

Still, she could not rid herself of the hope that she was being overdramatic. She had dated Nash for barely three months. Much too brief a time for her to consider him the man she'd spend her life with, right? After all, she'd married Boyz after knowing him for only five months, and look how that had turned out. Jordan, on the other hand, had known Lyle all her life, had been his girlfriend in high school, and then hadn't seen him for years when he was in the military. They certainly had not rushed to the altar, and now their marriage was solid.

Was it possible, Darcy wondered, that she'd inherited some of her mother's tendency to rush into romance? It was a special thrill, falling in love—it was exciting, turning all one's senses to high. That first spark, that first sidelong glance, the first phone call, the first kiss . . . the first time making love. All engraved in the memory and illuminated by the neon lights of infatuation.

But *staying* in love with one person for a

lifetime? Maybe Darcy simply wasn't capable of that. After all, she had kissed Clive. And if it had been out of sympathy and kindness, it had also been from desire. From the moment she set eyes on Clive, she'd wanted him to want her. And if that was purely a selfish egotistical urge, it came from her own body, without any thought or decision. She looked at him; she was . . . *interested* in him. She admired him, and she desired him. Was there ever any wisdom in desire?

How did people manage to stay faithful to one person all their lives? Closing her eyes, she rested her head against the seat and contemplated the lives of her summer neighbors. Mimi was widowed. Clive was divorced, and happily divorced, it seemed. Boyz was divorced and married to Autumn who had been divorced. Willow was not Boyz's daughter. Autumn clearly enjoyed flirting with and having sex with other men, yet even after Boyz found out, even after he knew there was a chance Autumn was pregnant with another man's child, Boyz loved Autumn. He stayed with her. Well, Boyz had also propositioned Darcy. Only those two knew the rules of their relationship. Otto was clearly unfaithful to Susan; and if Susan knew, she seemed too overwhelmed to care. Was that the cure for giving a damn about your mate's infidelities—simple exhaustion?

Well, Darcy was simply exhausted now, exhausted and despairing. She put the key in the ignition and drove back to her home. Her home, where she lived alone, with a cat.

23

When her alarm clock chirped on Tuesday morning, Darcy automatically shut it off and forced herself from her bed. She was exhausted, listless, even after having a day off. But she wasn't going to call in sick and lie around all day in a puddle of self-pity. She would put on a bright summer dress and go to her second home and be around books and people who loved books.

She almost changed her mind when she saw her reflection in the mirror. She looked like a one-hundred-year-old woman. Make that a one-hundred-year-old troll. She hadn't really slept for the past two nights. She'd spent yesterday watching romantic movies while she ate Cheetos and ice cream. She hadn't combed her hair or brushed her teeth yesterday and Sunday night's mascara and eyeliner had migrated to different sections of her face, most of it ending up in bizarre patterns just below her eyes. Her hair was limp.

"Gawd," she said to herself in the mirror. "Aren't you a treat for the eyes."

She trudged around the house, feeling slightly hungover, but she hadn't drunk alcohol, so this was an emotional hangover, not easily cured with aspirin and ginger ale. Darcy made herself a cup of strong coffee and carried it back to the bathroom. She took a long shower. After that, she was almost her normal self, except for the sadness that had lodged itself in her center like a heavy stone.

Nash.

So quickly he had moved on. As if it had been only lust and fun between him and Darcy. As if she were so replaceable.

"Stop it!" she ordered herself.

Muffler meowed stridently in return.

"You're right," she told the cat. "It's you and me, babe."

She stepped into her prettiest, pinkest, girly-girlest dress and brushed her hair thoroughly and tied it back with a pink grosgrain ribbon. At work, she forced herself to hum show tunes as she tapped away at the computer, and when one of the librarians impulsively invited her to go to Fog Island for lunch, she agreed. The sunny, windless day was perfect for the beach, which meant Darcy and Monica got a table without waiting in line. Monica was a second-generation native, meaning her parents had been born on the island, so she knew all sorts of hometown gossip, and, more than that, she knew who was voting for what on the special town warrant coming out in October. Darcy listened, laughing, for Monica had a salty way of expressing herself. As they walked back to the library, Darcy emotionally recharged and reconnected to the island. Her island.

After work, she pulled on her Speedo and walked down to the Jetties for a long, lazy swim. Floating idly, she heard the ferries' horns as they entered and exited the harbor. She heard children laughing and smelled hot dogs and hamburgers from the concession stand. Wading back in the shallows of the beach, she saw three brightly colored beach umbrellas, like a painting of a summer paradise. Painted in watercolor, of course, she joked to herself.

By the time she walked home, she was nicely tired out, ready for a drink and a shower and later a book and maybe a long talk with Jordan. Jordan might have wonderful news, like news that Kate was a traveling nurse just transferred to Seattle. Darcy smiled at herself, but all day long she had been covering her sadness with a gloss of pretend happiness, and she was drained by the effort.

She entered her house, kicked off her shoes, and walked barefoot into the kitchen. On the counter, the answering machine for her landline blinked. She couldn't hold it back—her heart leaped with hope.

She hit the play button. "You have one message. Message one."

"Darcy. Could I stop by after work? Around eight?"

Darcy froze. *Nash's voice.* She replayed the message, staring down at her small electronic messenger with her hands clasped at her breast like a silly Victorian maiden gazing at a valentine.

She took out her cellphone and tapped his number. He answered. Not a machine, the real man. For a moment she choked with excitement.

"Nash? It's Darcy. Yes, please come by, whenever."

"Around eight." Nash spoke without emotion and clicked off immediately.

"Wow!" Darcy cried. She couldn't help speaking aloud. "Nash is coming over. Is that good? Or is it bad?"

She glanced at her watch even though she was too excited to take in the time. She flew around the house, dusting, washing, tidying, and singing all the nonsense children's songs she knew because she wouldn't allow herself to sing anything happy or hopeful because that might jinx what Nash was going to say.

Because what if he were coming over to formally break things off with her? Because that *could* be why he was coming over. She shouldn't assume that because he called, he wanted to be with her. It could be the exact opposite.

She felt as if her life were balancing on the edge of a spinning coin. One side, heads, the other tails, and she had no control over how it would land.

She decided to change out of her sundress. It was too pretty, too *hopeful*.

She took the world's longest shower, sudsing herself up with perfumed soap. She slathered moisturizing lotion all over her body and pulled on a T-shirt and shorts, nothing fancy, nothing seductive. She decided not to wear any makeup. He'd seen her waking up with morning breath and without makeup, he'd seen her curled up on the sofa with a blanket and a carton of Ben & Jerry's while enduring menstrual cramps. If Nash wanted her, he could take her as she was, warts and all.

If he didn't want her, she wouldn't get mascara all over her face when she cried.

24

Nash. Hi. Come in." She stepped back for Nash to enter.

"Thanks." Nash went into the living room and sat on one of the overstuffed chairs.

He went into the living room, not the kitchen where he often went. Did that mean anything? And why did he choose to sit in a chair, not the sofa where Darcy could sit next to him?

"Would you like a drink?"

"In a minute. Let's talk first." Nash had obviously showered. He wore a white button-down shirt with the sleeves rolled up and khakis. Definitely not casual. Not here to watch the Red Sox and drink beer.

"Okay." Darcy settled at the end of the sofa, facing Nash. She was grateful for the fat arm of the sofa next to her left arm. It gave her a sense of security.

"Darcy." Nash cleared his throat. "We should get some things straight."

Damn. That sounded ominous. Darcy bit her lip to hold back a whimper.

"Okay."

"Darcy, I'm in love with you—"

"Oh, *Nash!*" His words almost launched her off the sofa.

He remained stern. "Wait. Listen. I'm in love with you, but you're making it hard for me. And, no, not like that, stop grinning. This is serious. You say you love me, but you say you never want to leave your grandmother's house, this house. Then you kiss another man."

"Nash." Darcy leaned toward him, as earnest, as truthful, as she could be. "It didn't mean anything. Truly."

"And it didn't mean anything when I flirted with Kate Ferguson. Darcy, I don't know what to think. I had thought you and I were—headed toward a serious relationship. Maybe more. I was happy with you."

"I was happy with *you,* Nash. I wanted—I *want*—to be in a serious relationship with you, but I don't know, we never spoke about being exclusive, anything like that—"

"Have you been sleeping with anyone else?"

"No, Nash! God!"

"I haven't, either. So I thought we were a couple, even if we hadn't made it official somehow. Even if we hadn't said so in words."

"I guess I need to hear the words," Darcy told him.

"Are you ready to say the words?"

"What? Oh, Nash, I love you! You know that." Darcy strained toward him, wanting to kiss him, to touch him. "I didn't know you loved me, so . . ."

"Darcy, I told you something I haven't told anyone else. About my brother. About his death, all that."

"I haven't spoken of that to anyone. I would never—"

"I thought you'd understand how I feel about you when I told you about Edsel. But, Darcy, come on, settle down, we need to talk this out. You say you love me. I love you. What does that mean? In my world, it means we're pretty much on our way to being together permanently."

Darcy's eyes went wide. She half choked, half whispered, *"Marriage?"*

"Well, that's what normal people do when they fall in love, when they're as compatible as I thought you and I were. But I can't get a clear reading from you, Darcy. I wanted to talk to you about the future, but only a few weeks ago you said you hoped you never had to leave this house."

Darcy frowned. "You don't like this house?"

"That's not the point. If you're never going to leave it, that means you never want to get married or live with anyone, or it means you expect whoever you marry to move in here."

Darcy gazed around the room, this familiar, beloved room that had held her grandmother's life and her own childhood.

"I guess you're right. I mean, about what I said. I never really thought about it that way, Nash.

I guess when I daydreamed about living with a man, having children, having grandchildren, it was always in this house." She straightened her back; she met Nash's gaze. "Could we just pause for a moment to be like *fireworks happy* that you and I love each other?"

Nash smiled, but his eyes were sad. "I'm glad if all this makes you happy. It makes me miserable."

"Nash, no. If we love each other, we can work things out, right?"

"Can we? Can we really 'work things out'? If I give you a couple of days or a couple of months, do you think you'll be able to decide to sell this house? All this furniture"—his arm swept the room—"your grandmother's garden?"

"But, Nash, why should I have to? Isn't it a great house? Isn't it wonderful to be in town, walking distance to the library, the post office, the shops?"

"What if I want to get a dog, a big dog that needs lots of room to run? What if I get an Irish setter or even a Lab? What if I want to live in a modern house with a large yard out of town, bordering the moors, where I could let the dog run?"

Darcy took a deep breath. "I think this is when I get myself a drink. Would you like one?"

"Please."

"Wine?"

"A beer, if you've got it."

Darcy rose and walked toward the kitchen.

Her head was spinning, and her heart had gone into some kind of gymnastic performance that sent tremors through her hands. She poured herself a glass of wine. She took a Heineken from the fridge, popped off the cap, and carried the drinks out to the living room.

She handed Nash the beer. "Would you come sit next to me on the sofa?"

"Thanks for the beer. No, I'm not moving. We can't solve this problem physically. We'd only delay it."

Darcy returned to the sofa. "But being physical is part of the solution, isn't it?"

"Is it?" Nash asked. "If we make love, will you be a fraction more likely to sell this house and choose a house with me?"

"You're making me feel so *pressured,*" Darcy said. She took a sip of wine. "Nash, when *you* think of the future, where do your dreams take you? I mean, do you think you could live on Nantucket for the rest of your life?"

"I've given this a lot of thought, Darcy. Yes, I could live here all my life. I've traveled a lot. I'm tired of traveling. I like my work here, I like the guys I hang with. I like eating fish I've caught right out of the ocean. I like seeing the stars without light pollution, and I like that I can admit that and it doesn't make other people think

I'm odd or weak. I've been part of the world of lawyers and judges and writs and summonses and that's not for me. It's not who I am. I've been discovering who I am and what I want since I've been here. And I want to live here, on the island, with you."

Darcy nodded. "But not in this house."

"I don't know. Maybe. Maybe not. But I don't want this house to be what you choose over me."

"So we're kind of talking about deal breakers," Darcy said.

"If you want to put it that way, yes."

"It seems clinical. Cold."

Nash shrugged. "You've often said you thought you got married to Boyz too quickly. You rushed it, you didn't get to know each other, you were all about what you dreamed would happen and you never took time to understand the reality."

"I did say that, didn't I?" Darcy nodded, her mind working fast now. "So here's another, I guess you could call it, deal breaker. I've come to care for Boyz's stepdaughter, Willow. She loves books, like I do, like you do. She's smart and funny and working hard to make sense of life, as if anyone can make sense of life. What I'm trying to get at is, Willow might be part of *my* life. Maybe not, I don't know, but I'd like her to be part of my life. I'd like to have her visit here, by herself, without her family, but it means I'll have to be in touch with Boyz and Autumn. Would that bother you?"

"I don't think so. We both know we have complicated pasts. It *would* bother me if having Willow in your life changed whether you'd want to have children. Your own children. Do you want that?" Nash asked.

"Gosh, *yes,* Nash. I really want children. I want *your* children."

For the first time that evening, Nash broke out in a spontaneous smile. "So do I."

"Oh, wow, that's great!" Darcy set her glass on the coffee table. "Please, could I come kiss you now? This is driving me crazy, all this questioning, it's like taking some kind of bizarre quiz."

"Not yet, Darcy. I'm not comfortable about us yet. I want to answer your question about Willow. No, I wouldn't have a problem if Willow became part of our lives. I'm not thrilled about contact with Boyz, but it doesn't worry me. Willow's swept up by the whirlwind of adolescence and she should have as many people caring for her, guiding her, as she can."

"Oh, good, Nash. I don't know what will happen with Willow, but I want to be there for her if she needs me. Boyz told me that Autumn is pregnant, so a new baby in the house might make Willow ecstatic, or she might feel pushed away, replaced. So that's good then! So *now* can I kiss you?"

"We need to settle the matter of the house. This house."

"Oh, Nash, that's so complicated!"

"I think it's simple, actually. I'd like to know whether or not you love me enough to live somewhere else. If you could sell this house and live in a house that you and I would choose together."

"Nash, please. This house has been my home, my security, ever since I was ten years old. Even when I was married to Boyz, I knew the house was here, waiting for me. It would be painful to have to give it up. And I can imagine us living here. Even with children, even with a big dog. You know, the garden can be changed. If I remove all the flowers and low bushes, and seeded it with grass, it would have much more room for a dog, for croquet, even for badminton." She bit her thumbnail, envisioning the changes. "Maybe not for badminton."

"You still haven't answered my question. Could you sell this house and live in a house that you and I would choose together? Yes or no."

Darcy met Nash's eyes and held his gaze. "The honest truth, Nash, is that I don't know the answer to that question. I'm going to have to think about it, but can't we be together while I'm thinking? I don't mean only tonight, I mean for a few days? Or maybe even a few weeks? I don't think I can

416

come to a decision if I have to worry about you leaving me."

Nash nodded. "That you'll even think of leaving this house is more than I thought you could do, Darcy. Why don't we agree to giving you a year. One full year."

"Okay. That's good. And during the year, we'll be—together, right?"

"Yes. Together. Exclusively. No more coming on to any other men."

"Or women," Darcy added. She needed so badly to touch Nash, to trace his cheekbones and feel the bristles along his jaw, to be touched by him, anywhere, everywhere, and it wasn't sex that she needed, or not only sex. Her soul yearned to connect to him, to be whole with him. She wanted to cook with him; to walk the moors with him; to slob out with him in front of the television, eating ice cream from the same carton; to arrive at parties with him at her side; to sit in silence in the living room with a fire burning in the grate while a blizzard rattled the windows, the soft glow of the reading lamps illuminating them as they each lost themselves in books. To go to sleep with his body warm and sturdy next to hers. And, yes, to have sex with him.

"One thing," Darcy said. "Whatever decision I make while you and I are making love is to be considered automatically null and void on the grounds that I'm not completely rational."

Nash grinned. "The same goes for me."

"Should we put it to the test?" Darcy asked.

Nash stood up. In two steps, Darcy was in his arms. Nash held her, and she knew she was coming home.

25

Summer was gently slipping away. Along the beach paths and walkways, orange rose hips glowed like small round lanterns. The rose of Sharon bushes were dropping their white and pink flowers slowly, while no one was watching. Shadows fell longer and slanted differently as the sun moved lower in the sky. The days were hot and humid, the beaches still crowded, the library still in full spate, but in the evenings the air grew cool quickly and the trees that had blossomed with pastel flowers in the spring were now dotted with red berries.

The Brueckners left three days after Labor Da. One morning there was a knock on Darcy's front door. When she opened it, she found the three boys and Susan standing there, all of them laden with bags of groceries.

"I've packed as much as I can into the cooler," Susan told Darcy. "But I don't want to let all this go to waste."

"Thanks for thinking of me," Darcy said. "I'm sure I'll use it all up. Come right back to the kitchen."

Susan marshaled her troops and they filed to the back of the house and deposited their donations on the table.

"Now what do we do?" Susan asked her boys.

Shyly, each boy held out his hand to Darcy, and as they shook hands, each boy said, "Thank you for helping us this summer, Miss Cotterill."

"You're very welcome," Darcy told them.

"Thank you for story time!" Alfred impulsively chirped, turning red with embarrassment.

Darcy wanted to hug him, but was afraid he'd go into shock. "Thank *you* for using the library."

"You may go home now," Susan said, and her boys thundered down the hall and out the door. Susan turned to Darcy. "I want to thank you, too, for all you've done. I don't think I could have made it through this summer without you."

"It's been wonderful having you as a neighbor," Darcy said honestly. "Do you think you'll come back next year?"

Susan hesitated. "I'm not sure. Otto wants to try a place in Maine . . . but we'll keep in touch, won't we, Darcy?"

"Of course," Darcy said, although she knew from experience that summer people often forgot island people when they returned to their "real" lives.

Susan hugged Darcy tightly. Darcy kissed Susan's cheek.

"Goodbye, have a good fall," Susan said.

"Goodbye, have a safe trip home," Darcy said.

Susan went down the hall, stopped at the front door to turn and wave. And then she was gone.

That night, when Darcy looked, there were no lights on in the house next door.

Willow, Boyz, and Autumn were the next to go. It happened all in a rush. Willow knocked on Darcy's door in the late afternoon.

Willow was breathless. "Darcy, Boyz said our car is number one on standby on the car ferry. We have to leave now and hope we can get on. He's pretty sure we'll be able to get on. We have tickets for the ferry tomorrow afternoon, but Boyz wants to get home as soon as we can."

Darcy felt a little stab in her chest. Somehow she couldn't take it all in. She knew Willow was leaving, but now that the moment was here, Darcy felt off guard. This was too important; she'd left something unfinished. She stuttered, "Oh, oh, so soon, I—"

Willow was in too much of a hurry to wait for Darcy to make sense. "Thank you so much for everything this summer, Darcy, and I'll text you *all* the time, and I hope I can visit you this October for the Cranberry Festival." She threw her arms around Darcy, squeezed her so hard it hurt, then took a few steps in place, like a jogger waiting at a traffic light. "Thanks, thanks, thanks!"

Willow was gone. It was like a light being switched off. That fast, that conclusively. Darcy stood at her doorway like a coma patient, and not until Muffler rubbed up against her ankles did she close the door.

Her mind flooded with questions. Did Willow know Autumn was pregnant? How would Willow feel about that—probably thrilled to have a baby sister or brother. Willow was starting high school next week, always a turbulent period of life. She would seem more grown-up. Well, Willow *was* more grown-up, and a great many events had happened in her brief time on Nantucket to blast her out of the world of innocence and, in a way, out of the Garden of Eden. Willow had seen her mother with another man. Willow had been seduced by a handsome older boy into sex play and invited to try drugs. Willow had learned that the deliciously painful emotions of attraction and desire could lead her into all kinds of trouble. That was good. Willow needed to know that, and she'd come through it all stronger and more optimistic. Willow had chosen to spend the summer in safety, with pleasant older women and with children. She was about to be plunged back into the world of adolescence. Darcy wished the girl well. And she doubted that Willow would return for the Cranberry Festival. Maybe Darcy could go up to Boston someday and take Willow out to lunch. . . .

"Stop it!" Darcy said aloud. She had to wrench her mind off Willow. She had to return to *her* world and her own challenges. Would she give up this house, her house that held all her memories and hopes, and was also a fabulous house in a wonderful location . . . would she give it up in order to live in another house with Nash?

It was much easier to wonder about Willow.

Finally, Mimi and Clive left. Clive and Mimi enjoyed a goodbye dinner at Darcy's the night before, and Mimi and Darcy had promised to email and text and phone. Mimi still had a bit of a cold but promised she had tucked nasal spray and throat lozenges into her purse. Leaving was an emotional time for Mimi, who might never see the island again, so Darcy promised to drive out to the airport to wave goodbye.

It was always hard to see someone off on a plane. The passengers had to mill around in a small holding area like cattle, waiting for their release to the plane.

"I bought this paperback to read, but I'm not sure it will hold my interest," Mimi murmured to Darcy, fishing around in her enormous bag for the book.

"Mimi," Clive said, "you've got your e-reader with you. You can order another book or you can work a crossword puzzle on it."

Mimi brightened. "Oh, yes, of course, what was I thinking?"

Darcy and Mimi had said their goodbyes and hugged each other several times, and still they were left to wait restlessly in a kind of limbo.

Then suddenly the flight was called and the mob morphed into an orderly line, and the passengers went out through the gates, waving and calling goodbye, goodbye.

And Darcy was left standing alone. She gave herself a moment to recover from the sadness that had settled on her. Then she walked out the door and called Jordan and told her she was taking Jordan and Kiks out to lunch.

September was always an orphan month, not still summer, not yet fall. When Labor Day passed, people thronged to the ferries and planes, going back to school, back to work, back to reality. Many of the beautiful houses on Darcy's street were empty, their windows dark. Landscaping crews came around to keep the grass cut, to water and prune and fertilize, and to empty the window boxes or fill them with orange gourds and purple mums, which were unsettling, still unseasonal.

At the library, Darcy and her colleagues did the professional version of cleaning up a house after a wild party. Books were reshelved properly, emails were caught up, and the staff had a chance to linger and reevaluate the summer and discuss plans for the fall.

On a rainy Tuesday morning, Beverly Maison came into the office carrying her umbrella and a floppy foul-weather hat.

"You're here early," Beverly said.

"It's the perfect time to clean up this desk and go through all the papers I've been avoiding," Darcy told her.

Beverly shut the office door. She took off her raincoat and hung it on the stand and leaned her umbrella in the corner. She smoothed her hair down and settled in at her desk. She swiveled her chair around so she could face Darcy.

"Let's talk a moment," Beverly said.

"Okay." Darcy picked up her coffee cup and drank. The coffee was still nicely hot.

"You know I'm not so young anymore," Beverly began.

Well, this was odd. "You seem young to me," Darcy said.

Beverly laughed. "You're a good friend, Darcy. And a good librarian. You did a sterling job keeping the children's library on track this summer."

"Oh, well, thank you, Beverly."

"I had a meeting yesterday afternoon with Edith and Grace."

Darcy swallowed and her thoughts flashed a red alert. Edith Simon was the director of the library, Beverly's boss, and therefore Darcy's superboss. Grace was the president of the board of trustees, and therefore everyone's boss.

"We talked about the future," Beverly continued. "I told them I'd like to retire in about three years—"

"Oh, no, Beverly!" Darcy's cry was genuine. What would they all do without Beverly?

"And we all agreed that you should become head of the children's library then."

Darcy said, "Oh."

"With a view in mind of eventually, in ten years or so, making you director of the library."

Darcy couldn't help it. She grinned like a child at Christmas.

"It's not a done deal, of course," Beverly continued. "We agreed that you'll need sprucing up in several areas and responsibilities. We'd like you to take some courses in administration, fiscal management, and fundraising. Not all at once, of course. One or two a year, and done via the Internet. You would continue your duties here and have half a day off for course work." Beverly smiled. "What do you think?"

"There are no words," Darcy said. "It's beyond my wildest dreams."

"If I recall correctly, I don't think it is," Beverly said. "When I first met you, you told me your goal was to be director of the Boston Public Library."

"That's true," Darcy said. "But, believe me, if I became director of the Nantucket Atheneum, I'd be over the moon. I never want to leave this island. Gosh, Beverly, this is amazing."

"Well, it's not carved in stone. But it's our plan. Keep it to yourself, please. I'm not retiring for two or three years."

"Can I hug you?" Darcy asked.

"No. Nothing has happened yet. Hug me in three years. For now, we've got work to do." Beverly swiveled to face her computer.

Darcy faced her computer, too, but for a long while she sat smiling, unable to stop smiling, unable to think a single practical thought

That Sunday, Darcy and Nash joined Jordan and the gang at the beach. More and more they had free run of the beaches as the summer people left. Nash was patient, never mentioning the choice Darcy had to make, and, thank heaven, for Darcy found herself incapable of thinking of moving out of her house and just as incapable of imagining not being with Nash.

The second Sunday of September, a tropical storm near the Outer Banks of North Carolina blew north, flooding the eastern coastline. Gale force winds screamed across Nantucket Sound and joined the high tides to send the seas thrashing through the harbor. In spite of the Weather Channel's dire warnings, quite a few of the islanders delighted in these storms. Nash took off work and drove Darcy out to Cisco Beach, where they stood facing the surging waves, watching them tower and plunge as the wind, as if personally insulted, slammed against their bodies, trying to make them back off; and, of course, when they were both drenched and shivering, they slogged their way back to the truck and drove home.

First they took hot showers together, which led to spending a luxurious day in bed, making love and napping. By early afternoon the sky was dark with storm clouds, and inside the house it was cold and damp enough for a fire. Nash built one in the living room fireplace while Darcy brought out wine and crackers and cheese. She'd started a beef stew in her slow cooker that morning, and its mouthwatering aroma mingled with the scent of the crackling wood.

They sat together on the sofa, their feet propped on the table, gazing at the fire. Darcy wore yoga pants and an old flannel shirt. Nash wore sweatpants and a sweatshirt.

Darcy wondered if there was a movie they'd both enjoy watching when Nash spoke.

"I have an idea," Nash said.

"Oh?"

"What if I moved in with you for the winter? We could see how we muddle around together in the house—"

"Oh, Nash!"

"I'm not finished talking. And while we're living in this house, we'll work with a real estate agent to see if there are any other houses on this island that would be as good, or better, for us."

"I think that's an excellent idea." Darcy forced herself to speak mildly, as if this wasn't the most exciting news she'd heard in months.

"And maybe we'll clean out this house, clear it of a lot of the stuff that isn't essential to you, and figure out how it would work if I lived here."

"Oh, yes, absolutely. I've been intending to do that for months."

They began working on the house on Sunday. The storm was still raging. None of the group of friends wanted to leave their cozy houses. Perfect weather for decluttering. With Nash at her side, Darcy went through her house, determined to get rid of books or end tables or mementos she didn't really need or want.

She was astonished at how many cardboard boxes they filled to take to the Seconds Shop. Some of the books had been Penny's—and she'd probably gotten them from the Seconds Shop to last her through the long winter nights. Also, there was the glass unicorn a friend had brought back from a trip to Venice, and the wooden bison bookends another friend had brought from a trip to Wyoming. Several pitchers and vases for all the flowers Penny used to grow, more than Darcy would ever need. Into the Seconds Shop box. Penny had collected small, intricately constructed boxes not large enough to hold a paper clip, made from wood or porcelain or cleverly folded paper. Seconds Shop. Old rubber boots. Ripped raincoats.

And upstairs! During the week, Darcy and Nash continued their task every evening after work. First, they tackled Penny's room. Darcy was still sleeping in her childhood bedroom, which was too small for two people. Finally, Darcy thought, she'd outgrown that sweet room with its bookcase full of Nancy Drew mysteries. Penny's bedroom was spacious, with large windows welcoming in light. With Nash's help, she plunged into Penny's room. She was surprised at how little she wanted to keep. The ancient mattress had a trough down the side where Penny had slept. Most of the furniture was antique but oddly impractical, and everything was slightly warped, cracked, or missing a leg and propped on hardback books piled to attain the right height. Boxes of costume jewelry, clip-on earrings, a seventies assortment of chains with Buddhas, astrological signs, peace signs, and one odd brass cylinder that might have held rolling papers. More books. Framed photos of relatives and old friends whom Darcy had never met. Brocade drapes thick with dust and a chest at the end of the bed filled with heavy, scratchy wool blankets that Penny had put away when she discovered the warm, light pleasure of down comforters.

When they finished, they'd cleared the room of almost everything in it. They carried it all down to put into Nash's truck to go to the dump.

As the days passed, the storm moved away. True autumn arrived, with its crisp air and pumpkins. Nash worked on the construction crew every day, returning home to Darcy and dinner and television or sometimes dinner out. Often, they simply sat talking about everything, sharing anecdotes of school days and family foibles. They took long walks on Sundays, crunching through the forest at Squam Swamp or viewing the darkening ocean from the Bluff Walk in 'Sconset. During the winter, when blizzards kept them indoors, they went around the house more carefully, deciding if there was anything they'd really like to have. Gradually, Darcy and Nash freshened up Penny's room. They swept it clean and washed the floor and windows. They painted the walls a pale cream with marshmallow-white woodwork. They leaned shoulder to shoulder in front of the computer, discussing and comparing furniture, and one day a beautiful, sleek, king-size bed arrived. For weeks they slept in the bed, with nothing else in the room. The bed was quite enough.

All this time, they spent most Sundays touring houses with Marlene deCosta. They saw houses in the quaint small village of 'Sconset and on the other end of the island in Madaket. They saw historic houses that "needed work" and newer houses in pristine condition. They saw houses with small yards and houses that bordered the moors and seemed to have yards going on forever. They ran spreadsheets on mortgage rates and real estate taxes. They discussed the advantages and disadvantages of Penny's in-town house for the children they just might have in the future.

One gray Sunday in November when the rain fell steadily and the temperature dropped to the low forties, they lay together in bed, drinking the coffee Nash had brewed and brought up. It was almost noon. They'd spent much of the morning making love and napping. Now it really was time to get up.

"Let's talk," Nash said.

"Mmm." Darcy murmured, but her pulse began to race. "I know. I know we should talk. I've been dithering about, but I've made a decision. About the house." If she could do this now, while they were sitting here in what was practically heaven for them both, she knew she loved Nash more than anyone or anything she had ever loved.

"Okay," he said quietly, waiting.

"I'll sell the house. It's okay. I want to be with you anywhere. It will be hard, but I can do it. This house is my past. You are my future."

Nash took her mug from her hand and set it on

the bedside table. He pulled Darcy against him and held her to his chest. She could feel his heart beating. His breath came faster than usual. She could sense how he was struggling to contain his emotions. Men did not cry, but she wanted to cry not only for the loss of the house but for the enormity of her feelings for Nash, her love for him that had opened her heart to all kinds of love.

He ran his hand over her hair, nuzzled his chin against her, and when he spoke, she felt his breath on her skin.

"Darcy."

She nodded, swallowing back her tears. The way he said her name said everything. This was a moment they would never forget. This was the moment of their marriage.

Nash pulled away. He cleared this throat. He said, "I suppose my main objection to living here is that it's not my house. It's your house."

"True, but—"

"Hang on. Let me finish. I don't think we've found anything special when we looked at other houses. Nothing that makes us say, 'Hey, this is it! We've really got to live *here!*'"

"True . . ."

"What if I made this house half mine?" Before Darcy could question him, he hurried on. "By giving you exactly one half of the value of the house."

"You mean, money?" Darcy asked.

"I mean, money. We'll have the house appraised and I'll give you half its worth. We'll have the deed changed to reflect our joint ownership."

"That's a lot of money. . . ."

"I've got a lot of money. At least enough to buy half the house."

"Oh, I like this plan." Darcy's pulse sped up. Hope shot through her like a lightning bolt. "And we could do something symbolic, like planting a tree in the backyard."

"Or," Nash said, "we could do something practical, like having the fireplace chimney in this bedroom repaired so we can have fires here in the winter."

"Oooh. *Brilliant*." Darcy closed her eyes, envisioning how Penny's old bedroom/Darcy-and-Nash's new bedroom would look with amber flames flickering, the only light in the room at night when they made love and when they slept.

"We'll have to get smoke detectors," she said.

"We'll have to get smoke detectors," Nash said, at exactly the same time.

Nash's parents came to visit for Thanksgiving. Darcy and Nash invited them to stay in their house, but they opted for a B&B. Their decision worried Darcy, who was jittery about meeting Peggy and Allen Forester until they walked off

434

the fast ferry. Nash's father was a tall, stern, quiet man who didn't approve of Nash giving up the law to be a carpenter on a small island. But Peggy was warm and kind, obviously the peacemaker in the family. They hadn't been to Nantucket before, so Nash and Darcy gave them a tour, which helped ease them all into conversation.

The Thanksgiving dinner, prepared by Darcy and Nash together, went off smoothly. Nash's mother was chatty and affectionate even though Nash's father was formal and slightly distant. By the time the pumpkin and pecan pies were served, they began to discuss books, movies, and television shows, especially *Downton Abbey*. Darcy thought she'd send a check to their PBS station for providing subjects they could all agree on.

The next day, Nash and Darcy drove his parents around the island again. His parents took them to a gourmet lunch at the Brant Point Grill, and that evening they had a dinner of leftovers at Darcy's. Nash's father was impressed by the beauty of the island and by his son's knowledge of the island's history. That night when they sat around the dining room table to eat, Nash told them he'd been asked to join the Nantucket Conservation Commission. His father perked up at that, and conversation flowed more easily.

After dinner, Peggy insisted on helping Darcy clear the table. Nash took his father outside to see Darcy's garden. As soon as they were outside, Peggy took Darcy's arm.

"Quickly, dear, while we have a chance . . . I need to ask you. . . . Nash told you about his brother, didn't he?"

Darcy put her hand on Peggy's. "Yes. I'm so sorry."

Peggy patted Darcy's hand. "I'm glad he told you. Nash took it hard. It changed his life. I was afraid he'd become insular and odd, living out here where you're all so disconnected, but Nash seems fine. He seems happy. I think that's because of you."

Tears came to Darcy's eyes. "Oh, thank you." Impulsively, she hugged Peggy and for a moment the two women clung to each other, thinking of Nash and his brother and the past and the future.

Peggy and Allen left for Amherst the next morning. They were a busy couple, sitting on several important boards, belonging to a bridge group and book clubs, and taking luxurious cruises in the winter. Darcy and Nash discussed their visit and concluded it had been a success. A few days later, a packet arrived for Nash, wrapped in yards of tape and heavily insured and requiring Nash's signature. Inside, Nash found his grandmother's engagement ring, a large, clear diamond surrounded by eight smaller diamonds.

I thought you might like to have this, Peggy Forester had written.

"Let's try it on you," Nash suggested, taking Darcy's hand.

"Wait. Not so fast. You have to ask me a question first," Darcy told him, smiling but not quite joking.

"What?" Nash frowned, then understood. He dropped to one knee, holding Darcy's hand in his. "Darcy, will you marry me?"

"I will." She surprised herself as she suddenly burst into tears. "Sorry," she told him, "I didn't know I'd get so emotional."

He slipped the ring on her finger. They kissed, a light, friendly kiss. They settled on the sofa together, discussing details, while Darcy admired her ring. Darcy wanted a church wedding with a reception and all the trimmings, partly because when she'd married Boyz, it had taken place in a nursing home with very few guests. This time, she wanted something more celebratory, more of a fabulous occasion.

"We'll have a proper wedding," Nash said. "And a proper wild reception."

"Shall we pick a date?"

"May eighth," he answered without hesitation.

"May eighth? Why?"

"That's the day we stopped eyeing each other and actually talked."

"Oh, gosh, you remember the date? How romantic!"

Nash arched an eyebrow. "Don't *you* remember the date?"

"I remember the day, the place—we were at the beach with the gang, and *I* approached *you*. I remember I asked you over for some lasagna."

"And I said I'd come over if you offered me a bowl of cereal."

Darcy melted. "Gosh. You remembered that."

"How could I forget?" Nash pulled Darcy into his arms and kissed her soundly.

"But is that too soon? Nantucket's such a wedding destination, everything gets booked months in advance."

"No one gets married here in May. The weather's too iffy. Besides, you and I know a few people. That's got to be one of the advantages of living here."

And, yes, amazingly, May eighth was available at St. Paul's Episcopal Church. With Christina Hall's help, they booked their reception at the White Elephant ballroom with the Brant Point Grill to cater. When the amazing Gypsy band Coq au Vin signed on, they knew things were headed toward fabulous.

After that, life became one perpetual party. They gave a party at their house to announce their engagement, although Darcy had phoned Jordan about two seconds after Nash proposed. Then it was Christmas with Stroll parties and Christmas Eve parties and New Year's Eve, and Darcy was glad when January arrived. This month the island lived up to its nickname, "the Gray Lady." Wind, snow, and cold blasted the island. The heavy seas made traveling difficult and sometimes impossible. Usually this was Darcy's favorite time of year. It gave her lots of long dark evenings for reading. But somehow this year was different.

This year it was *wonderful,* because Nash was there, reading by her side in front of the fire. Muffler had adopted him and frequently sat on his lap.

She and Willow had been texting about once a week. In January, Willow announced that she had a boyfriend. She told Darcy about Justin in her texts, and when her parents took her to a posh ski resort in February, Justin was invited along, staying, Willow told Darcy, in a separate room. Willow promised Darcy she'd come for a week in the summer and bring Justin, but Darcy doubted if that would happen. In April, Willow phoned Darcy to announce that Autumn had given birth to a beautiful baby boy who looked just like Boyz. Darcy asked Willow to congratulate her parents and smiled at Autumn's good luck. After that, Willow's texts came less frequently. Clearly the girl, now fifteen, had a baby brother and a gang of friends and a full schedule. Still, Darcy invited Willow to their wedding, both informally via email and formally with a handsome invitation.

For a few weeks, Willow didn't respond. Darcy was secretly sad. But she had always known that Willow was going to blossom into full adolescence, and she told herself to be glad the girl was happy, so she sniffed back her tears.

In late April, Darcy checked her cell and found a new text.

I am SO going to be there! Can I bring Justin? You have got to see him! Can we stay with you? We can sleep on the living room floor. Do I have to wear a hat? We'll take the ferry and just walk to your house. Will you let us have champagne at the reception? Just kidding. Not. What do you want for a present? It can't cost more than twenty dollars. Just kidding. Not. Can't wait!

Darcy laughed out loud and quickly texted back.

SO glad! Bring Justin. You sleep in our guest room, Justin on the sofa, no hat required, no champagne allowed—you are fifteen! No present required—your presence is the present! ☺

Susan Brueckner sent Darcy a gorgeous snail mail Christmas card trimmed with red velvet and covered in sparkles, framing a photo of the Brueckner family on Nantucket. The entire family, all dressed in white, stood together on the beach, a calm blue ocean in the background, Otto's arm around Susan and the three boys clustered in front of them, smiling their gap-

440

toothed smiles. Darcy sent a holiday card to the Brueckners, and she and Susan each scribbled on their card that they would write soon with all the news, but somehow that never happened. When Darcy ran into a real estate agent while she was in Nantucket Pharmacy eating one of their delicious grilled cheese sandwiches, Elton, the agent, told Darcy that she hadn't heard from the Brueckners. Another family had rented the house for the summer.

Still, Darcy sent Mr. and Mrs. Otto Brueckner an invitation to the wedding. Unfortunately, they couldn't attend.

Mimi and Darcy kept in touch over the winter via emails and once or twice, Skype. In early January, Mimi phoned Darcy to explain why she wasn't coming to Nantucket for the summer. Clive couldn't come; he was busy with other matters, and Mimi, almost ninety, couldn't come by herself. When Darcy told Mimi about the wedding, Mimi said, "Oh, child, I'm so happy for you!"

But Mimi sadly told Darcy she wouldn't be able to come to the wedding either. It was her legs, her stability, her balance. After their phone conversation, Darcy sat at her desk with her head in her hands, not thinking, and trying not to feel. It was Mimi's rejection that hurt her most of all. She had really *loved* Mimi, and she'd thought Mimi had loved her.

A few days later, an insured box arrived for Darcy from Mimi. Inside was an antique tiara made of silver-plated brass with one small diamond—Darcy had gasped when she realized it was a real diamond—set in the flower that rose above the other small silver flowers in the middle.

I wore this to my wedding, Mimi wrote on the enclosed card. *I hope it brings you as much joy as I had in my married life.*

Darcy cried so hard her shoulders shook.

She was more cautious and less optimistic when she called her mother and her relatives in Chicago to tell them about Nash. They all congratulated her and wished her well, but regretted that they wouldn't be able to attend the wedding. Her mother texted Darcy a message: *Better luck this time.*

She cheered up when Jordan and Beverly told her they'd appointed themselves in charge of the Dress. This required a three-day trip to New York, where Edith Simon, the library's director, had friends who ran a posh wedding boutique. Jordan and Beverly had a dog in the race, as the men liked to put it, because they were going to be matron of honor and bridesmaid and wante to find something sexy and not magenta. Darcy was overwhelmed by the range of bridal costumes, as if this was the day the bride got to dress like her fantasy. She tried on ruffled, sashed dresses in the Scarlett O'Hara mode and dropped-waist Art Deco beaded flapper dresses in the *Great Gatsby* style. Little Bo Peep. Vegas showgirl. Seventies' flower child. Finally, she found the perfect dress. Because this was her second marriage, she didn't want to wear white. Instead, she chose a very simple silk gown of creamy, glossy ivory, with long sleeves, a plunging neckline and back, and a small train. No beads, no embroidery. The price was exorbitant, because the cut of the gown was so elegant. It had to fit perfectly, and it did.

"It's a bit King Edward and Wallis Simpson," Jordan said.

"Good," Darcy replied, "because I want Nash to remain as gaga over me as Edward was over Wallis."

"Also," Beverly said, "I think anything embroidered or beaded would be over-the-top if you're going to wear the tiara."

Time blurred. Darcy and Nash, with Jordan's calming assistance, took care of the five thousand details necessary for a simple wedding and a brilliant reception. Jordan threw a bridal shower for Darcy, complete with silly hats and ridiculous games. Lyle hosted a bachelor party for Nash, with whiskey and steaks and, Darcy was happy to learn, without strippers. Willow and Justin arrived, holding hands constantly and exchanging meaningful looks. Justin was a tall, skinny, silent boy. Willow had the same bounteous body her mother had and wore long loose shirts to camouflage her figure as she fluttered around the house. Justin hardly spoke and Willow talked incessantly. Willow glowed and danced, and Justin seemed like the string steadying the bright, flippy kite that was Willow.

Suddenly Darcy and Nash were in the church, and a moment later, it seemed, they were married and standing in a receiving line at the reception. Darcy laughed through the toasts before the sit-down dinner of scallops and filet mignon, and drank a glass of water for every glass of champagne, and floated on air when Nash pulled her into his arms for the first dance of the evening.

Later, as Darcy was leaning over the table to pick up a glass of water, she looked out at the dance floor, and everything seemed to freeze, as if, for a moment, time stood still.

She saw Nash dancing with his mother. Jordan danced with Lyle, the two of them giving each other such intimate looks Darcy bet there would be another baby conceived that night. Beth O'Malley, who had conducted the women's chorus, was in what looked like a deep and serious conversation with Juan, the Dominican carpenter on Nash's crew. It was likely that Beth had found a new member of the church choir. Beverly Maison laughed at something Nash's father was saying. Edith Simon, the director of the library, was dancing with her eight-year-old daughter, both of them wearing frilly lavender dresses. Karl Ledbetter, the contractor who headed up the crew Nash worked for, was in the corner of the room, chatting up beautiful Dee-Dee Folger, obviously not aware of Dee-Dee's husband sitting at a table giving their new daughter a bottle. Dee-Dee looked mischievous; Darcy knew Dee-Dee was having fun flirting after so many months of pregnancy. Several of the local mothers who faithfully and with gratitude brought their children to story time were at one table with their husbands, laughing and looking ravishing in silk and stilettos. Eileen McFee, who had helped Penny in the garden until her death, sat next to her husband, completely focused on the wedding cake on her plate. Marlene deCosta, the real estate agent who had so gamely shown Darcy and Nash the houses they never bought, was chatting up Grace Pindell, the head of the library's board of trustees. Katherine Gibson, the town clerk, was whispering something to Ward Sullivan, the head of the board of selectmen, and Sarah Stover, Darcy's lawyer and the town's counsel. Willow and Justin were sneaking sips of champagne from Darcy and Nash's glasses and Amy Tyrer was walking toward them with a determined frown. She spoke to the teenagers, who quickly put down the glasses and returned to the dance floor.

So many people, Darcy thought. They had seventy guests, so many clever, bright, funny, adorable people. She allowed herself a brief moment to miss those not here—her parents, the Chicago relatives, and Susan Brueckner and Mimi. Yet deep in her soul she knew they were part of it all. The love she was given as a baby and child still sustained her as a grown, married woman. The lessons she'd learned from last summer's summer neighbors were with her still, twining like climbing roses around her heart. She might never see Susan, Willow, and Mimi again, but they had changed her life, and in that way they remained with her always. She smiled when she thought of them.

How fortunate she was.

Tonight she and her husband would leave for their honeymoon in London. In two weeks they would return to their jobs on Nantucket.

That summer Nash would begin building a swing set in their backyard, complete with a swing for the baby.

Books are produced
in the United States
using U.S.-based
materials

Books are printed
using a revolutionary
new process called
THINKtech™ that
lowers energy usage
by 70% and increases
overall quality

Books are durable
and flexible because
of smythe-sewing

Paper is sourced
using environmentally
responsible foresting
methods and the
paper is acid-free